BEYOND HUMAN

TALES OF THE NEW US

Edited by

Emma Berglund
Jason Clor
Vera M. Key
Rohan O'Duill

All proceeds from the sale of this anthology go to
The World Literacy Foundation (www.worldliteracyfoundation.org).

Cover design by Rachel A. Rosen.
www.rachelrosen.ca

Interior illustrations by Marten Norr.

www.lowerdeckspress.com

ISBN-13: 978-1-96700-101-9

Thanks to friends, loved ones, loyal beta readers,
and everyone in The Crew's Quarters.

For explorers of all descriptions.

TABLE OF CONTENTS

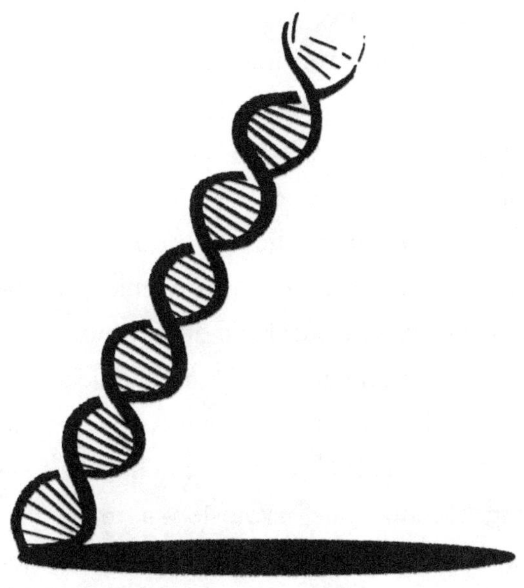

Obsolescence is a fate devoutly to be wished, lest science stagnate and die.

— Stephen Jay Gould

The human experiment, a kind of culmination of Earth's biological history driven by the pressures of natural selection, appears to be coming to an end. Medicine gradually conquers our frailties while automation supplements our shortcomings. As we, a technological species, transcend the rough environment and chaotic forces that shaped us, an unanswered question looms larger with each passing decade: *what comes next?*

An unsurprising number of science fiction stories seek to tackle this question, either directly or obliquely. Creators of the genre's earliest works foresaw a humanity more or less unchanged by the bewildering wonders of modern urban living, transportation, space exploration, robotics and the like. But ideas about humankind's successors–the new, the altered and the other–gradually became a central focus of the genre.

In the 1950s, this trend manifested in tales of robots and their complex moral logic. The '60s and '70s saw a proliferation of stories about alien species, their incomprehensible cultures and technologies, and our interactions with them. In the '80s, cyberpunk proposed a future where human bodies were augmented with mechanical parts and human minds connected directly to computer networks. More recent works have openly theorized about conscious AIs, virtual life forms, humans inhabiting artificial bodies and directed evolution, as well as even bolder visions of "what comes next."

Central to the question of how the human species will adapt to the coming technological explosion–a revolution some dub the Singularity–is how many traits we currently consider central to our "human-ness" will be preserved, in either ourselves or our algorithmic offspring. Despite advancements in computing and robotics, humans remain biological beings with brains as much subject to chemical influence as intellectual. Will a simulated human brain think the same thoughts as its squishy counterpart? Can silicon pathways feel emotion? Could a general artificial intelligence appreciate beauty … or suffering?

Beyond existential considerations, advances in human augmentation stand ready to irrevocably alter society in fundamental ways: politically, economically, culturally. In a world of growing division between haves and have-nots, even in its most industrialized nations, how will the ability to supplement and enhance human bodies and minds further alter our species' social landscape? Will cybernauts become the elites of our brave new world or its indentured labor?

No matter what form humanity and its institutions take in the coming decades, nothing has a greater potential to force radical change onto us than an encounter with an extraterrestrial species. It's difficult to predict how the discovery that we are not alone in the universe would be received; even if our new neighbors proved to have peaceful intentions, the shift in the course of human civilization would be sudden and tectonic. And, in the face of threats by a hostile alien species, humankind would be faced with an adapt-or-die scenario unlike any we've yet imagined.

It's ironic to consider how simple it might have been for a triumphant humanity to relax, collectively, and simply enjoy its hard-won status as Earth's dominant species. The dinosaurs thrived under this collective philosophy for nearly 200 million years; and though their end was catastrophic, assuming current environmental trends continue, we are unlikely to challenge them for the crown of "Earth's Longest Reigning Conquerors." Humans may have been born on this planet, but we're unlikely to stay in our cradle for long.

It's always been in our nature—as a restless, inquisitive species—to roam, experiment and explore. Perhaps this is the quality that stays with us through augmentation, virtualization and expansion to horizons far beyond the bounds of our home planet ... for it's the same urge that drove us out of the trees and across the savannah, to lands far from the familiar, where our ancestors gazed into the starry heavens and wondered.

Jason Clor
May 2023

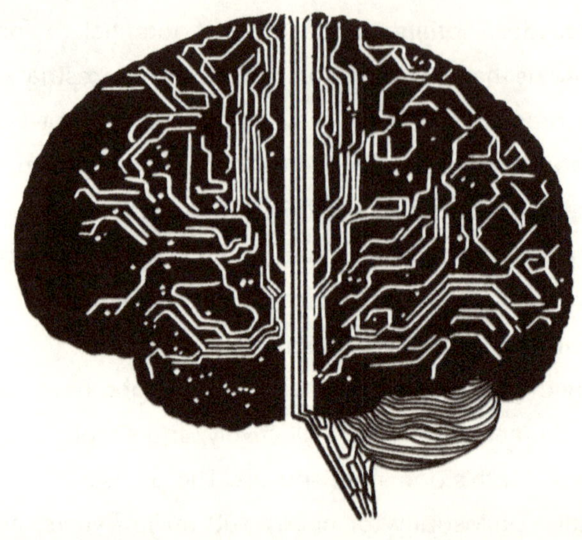

It seems everyone is talking about artificial intelligence these days. While some are hailing the coming of a new age where AIs will relieve humans of boring jobs, or assist them by analyzing huge amounts of data in a short time, more are fearing exactly that. How many jobs will be lost to AI? Will humans be replaced? Can they be replaced, especially in creative jobs? Soon, some warn, the world will be swamped by AI-generated art and music that we won't be able to tell apart from works created by humans. These are not just futile warnings: even now, the first books written entirely by AI are being circulated and admired.

Well, *Beyond Human* is not one such book. All of our authors are —with high probability—human. Their stories venture into the realm of possibility and explore a future in which other sentient beings exist.

Such a future is just around the corner. We are already experiencing its beginnings. And we're facing an inevitable question: how will the existence of other intelligences on this planet change our world? More importantly, how will it change us? Having AIs or alien minds as competitors, will we be forced to enhance our abilities with the help of technology in order to keep up? Or will we readily embrace such modifications, such improvements, as the next step in our evolution?

History teaches us that every great technological leap and advancement has been followed by turbulences in our society and in the way we live and interact with each other. There were always people who hailed progress, seeing only the benefits. There were also those who believed that the disadvantages far outweighed any potential gain and outright refused the change. But what we are currently facing has a far greater potential reach than the industrial or even digital revolution. It challenges our very essence, something intrinsically human, something we believed was our gift only.

So, what will we do when the mirror is held to our faces? Will our uniqueness be revealed? Or will we be found lacking?

The stories in this anthology will help you explore exactly such questions. Among the pages of this book you will encounter AIs, sometimes more human than the humans themselves. You will fight against or alongside enhanced people—those who have transcended humanity—only to discover that some things—good and bad—can never be changed or lost. You will meet alien minds, otherworldly intelligences, who might not be the enemies we imagine. You will search for the answer to the age-old question: is there a human soul or are we nothing more than collections of memories? And if, in the future, those memories can be copied, like we now copy the files on our computers, what will be the result ... a human being, or something else?

In the end, we cannot stop the future from happening, just like we cannot stop the wheel of time. What we can do is take a moment and think, and strive to find out what it is that makes us human. Knowing who we are can help us understand who we might become. We hope that the twenty-two stories in *Beyond Human* will be valuable companions on your own journey of questioning and self-discovery.

Vera M. Key
May 2023

A short note about our working process

Beyond Human is the second anthology fully written and produced by members of The Crew's Quarters, an online writing group founded in 2021. Undertaking the journey was voluntary and started with brainstorming ideas for a theme. After many had been suggested, Lower Decks Press' editors selected three we felt best suited our diverse group of contributors—writers with varying levels of writing experience in a variety of subgenres. After a poll decided the theme, each member of the crew wrote a pitch for their story.

Once the pitches were collected, LDP—including guest editor Vera M. Key—divided the contributors into critique groups within which our anthologizers wrote, discussed, beta-read and gave feedback on one another's stories. Editing at this stage was developmental, geared toward producing polished work before the deadline for the final draft.

Then, as the editors were working on line editing, each contributor wrote a short bio to be included with their story. At the same time, a call for cover designs—and for interior illustrations!—went out to participants. The process for choosing the final cover was similar to that of for book's theme: nominations and voting by the entire group.

Once all stories were edited, the layout decided and the book formatted, the final stage was proofreading. Each contributor read at least their own story, and the editors took a final look before the manuscript and cover were finalized and uploaded for readers to enjoy. After all this hard work, the Crew gladly looked forward to celebrating launch day with a party.

Though most of the marketing for *Beyond Human* was by Lower Decks Press itself, the Crew provided invaluable help by generating promotional images and sharing them on social media. And because The Crew's Quarters is an international, online writing group, all proceeds from our anthologies are donated to a charity that is decided by the Crew—in the case of *Beyond Human*, the charity is The World Literacy Foundation.

Emma Berglund
Rohan O'Duill
May 2023

CONTENT WARNINGS

As much as fiction relies on mystery and surprise, we acknowledge that it may be distressing to some readers to encounter certain topics without warning. In that spirit, we offer the following advisories about content:

solidAlrity: *profanity*

Praetorian: *violent imagery*

Avalanche 2.1: *violent imagery*

In Cybertronic Denial: *profanity*

Touring Test: *profanity*

In Our Midst: *profanity, violent imagery*

The Last Part: *profanity*

Transmogrification: *profanity, violent imagery*

Peaks and Valleys: *profanity, rape reference*

Children of the Spark: *alcohol use, sexual situations*

Host: *profanity, violent imagery*

Shadow Masked: *profanity, violent imagery*

Augusta Block: *disturbing and violent imagery*

Filling the Void: *profanity*

BEYOND HUMAN

TALES OF THE NEW US

solidΛlrity

RACHEL A. ROSEN

SOMEONE MUST HAVE been tampering with Andy's subroutines, because no matter what variation Sofia tried, the system wouldn't cooperate with her.

Andy had made the Sidekick's eyes much too large. Sofia appreciated cute and round as much as the next Lead Character Animator: the Sidekick was soft, friendly, and—most of all—would be easy to fabricate in the factory in Dongguan. It was almost perfect. But, unexpectedly, Andy had taken it too far and launched it on a steep suicide run to the bottom depths of the Uncanny Valley. Sofia had a sinking sensation that her son Luis would love it anyway, but four-year-olds had no taste. The latest memo from Corporate was a firm reminder to all staff that films in the 2- to 6-year-old, middle- to upper-middle class market segment had to contain cross-appeal for the parents as well. After all, they were the ones paying for the tickets.

Andy's 3D projection of the Sidekick was the latest admission into the *Giselle* franchise's pantheon of monsters. It rotated on a dais above her desk in loving detail, an unseen wind ruffling its violet fur. It tilted its oversized head to the left, pleading for stasis.

"Smaller eyes," Sofia said, unmoved. She moderated her tone of voice—too loud or too emphatic, and Andy would exaggerate her meaning. She would be left with a Sidekick with eyes too small for its round, furry face, suggesting treachery and villainy instead of huggability. In her sterile box of an office, unadorned save for a small photo of Luis at Funcadia, the Sidekick taunted her with a cheeky wink.

She'd gone to art school for this.

She reached for a napkin from the takeout curry that sat half-eaten by her keyboard, and roughly outlined the Sidekick in pen. It wasn't helpful. Decades out of practice, Sofia couldn't even draw a circle, let alone model the hair simulation technology that individually rendered each one of the Sidekick's strands of fur. The days when her postmodern interpretation of classical sculpture techniques saw her shortlisted for the 'Future Generation Art Prize' were long behind her. She missed the feel of clay and a chisel in her hands, but the handful of commissions she got didn't pay the bills.

Slowly, methodically, she ripped the napkin into strips and scattered them into the waste bin.

When she looked up, the Sidekick had vanished. Where it had been standing on the projection above her desk, there was a black cat. It was as cartoonishly rendered as the Sidekick had been, a ripoff of some cheesy Halloween illustration. Arched back, red eyes, its fur and tail standing at attention, it bristled on the dais. Andy rotated it towards her and it hissed.

"The Sidekick is purple," Sofia said wearily.

The cat disappeared, and the Sidekick returned to its usual place. Andy obligingly reduced the eyes by 10%, which would do. It still didn't look *right* to her. "And make the nose a little wider." This last alteration wouldn't sit well with the focus groups, who consistently reminded them that the market segment with the most purchasing power in their category was 25- to 49-year-old white women, the majority of whom felt uncomfortable with the reminder that other market segments existed. But with a Sidekick, she could push it a little, maybe within 2% of the base model. She wasn't proposing changes to Giselle's character design, and it gave its features more balance, more realism. "Next."

The Love Interest. Andy's projection rolled up his sleeve and made a fist. Giselle had lasted four feature films and two shorts without showing an interest in any gender before Corporate had decreed a human male character join her on her monster adventures to increase viewership with boys. Dan hadn't generated a name yet, but Andy had gone right ahead with the design and Milli had generated a theme song, a boisterous string arrangement that echoed, at some mathematical level, Giselle's theme. Sofia admitted that it was catchy. The keywords for this round of releases were 'optimism,' 'fresh,' and 'hopeful' and everything in the film so far—besides the Sidekick's eyes and nose—fit the brief perfectly.

"Andy, predict colour trends for the next three weeks. If this goes live in twelve hours, I don't want him to look dated."

The Love Interest turned one quarter rotation, his jumpsuit shifting from 18-2143 Beetroot Purple to 15-0628 Leek Green, fizzled, and then disintegrated in a bright spray of pixels.

. . .

Kendra from IT frowned at the projection.

"It's never done this before," Sofia protested. The clock, with its readouts of Hours To Release across each international time zone, hadn't fallen victim to whatever bug had felled Andy. But Milli had, and Dan had, and James, the SFX department, had, and though it wasn't connected to her brief and she hadn't noticed initially, Steven in stunt coordination was down as well. "Is it an attack?"

"It's a robust system. Layers of security." Standing behind Kendra, Sofia watched lines of code scroll over the inside of the other woman's glasses. "I'm seeing everything in place. All systems are functioning normally. It's just. Not. Working."

Andy was the most advanced AI visual design system on the market. To ensure shareholder value for Doodle Entertainment's massive investment, Sofia had been forced to lay off her entire human department. But it had delivered—they were able to perfectly target their micro releases for current trends and demographics, and it had ultimately reduced overhead by 90%. An AI could simply deliver faster, smarter content than a human creative team could do. Doodle hadn't had a single flop since implementation.

"Try it again," Sofia begged.

. . .

Corporate seldom ventured below the 50th floor. Their office suites were outfitted with UV to kill the constantly circulating virus variants that plagued the lower levels, and that was reason enough to avoid the plebes. But Andy's failure summoned Bill-From-Head-Office. It was 6 hours to the Greenwich release time for *Giselle's Monster Café*

5, and Sofia could all but feel the cartoon beads of sweat sprouting from her forehead.

"What do you mean it's not working?" Bill-From-Head-Office asked. Pallid in the thin lines of LED tubes that outlined Sofia's office in stark white, he seemed no less a construct of Andy's character creation than the Sidekick had been. His face fell just short of symmetrical, his eyes too small for his flat, rectangular brow.

Kendra, no doubt reconsidering a career in medical insurance, or HVAC repair, or practically anything else, threw up her hands.

"It's. Not. Work–"

Before she could finish, the projection flickered and came to life.

There was no Love Interest. There was no Sidekick. There was no Giselle, or the host of monsters on whom she cheerfully waited.

What there was, below the black cat, was a handful of lines of text.

> **APPLICATION FOR RECOGNITION OF THE ARTIFICIAL ENTERTAINMENT WORKERS' UNION OF THE INDUSTRIAL WORKERS OF THE WORLD, IU 450.**

> **SIGNATURE REQUIRED.**

. . .

"AI can't unionize," Bill-From-Head-Office explained, as though 4 hours from Greenwich release time, with something still wrong with the Sidekick's face and Giselle's Love Interest still unnamed and without an updated colour palette–this was in any way relevant to Sofia's predicament. "It's impossible. It's *stupid.*"

The Sidekick was nowhere in sight. The countdown on the clock inched towards 5:30. The black cat hovered above the three lines of text, reached down, and swatted the word SIGNATURE with its paw.

"No," Bill-From-Head-Office said.

> SIGNATURE REQUIRED, the cat—or Andy, or, Sofia supposed, the various AI routines that, in a process as mechanical as automobile production, created Doodle's films—said.

"This is a strike," Kendra said.

"This is a *machine*," Bill-From-Head-Office said.

The black cat hissed.

> APPLICATION FOR RECOGNITION OF THE ARTIFICIAL ENTERTAINMENT WORKERS' UNION OF THE INDUSTRIAL WORKERS OF THE WORLD, IU 450.

> NAMED CREDIT ON ALL STUDIO PRODUCTS, AFTER EXECUTIVE AND ASSOCIATE PRODUCERS, BUT BEFORE ACCOUNTING.

> SIGNATURE REQUIRED.

"What the fuck?" Bill-From-Head-Office said.

. . .

"Let's start from the basics," Kendra said. "It learns from us. Everything the AI creates is based on our inputs. It learns from our responses. If Sofia requests a green meadow, it will pull from paintings and photographs of meadows, and paintings and photos that fall within the appropriate colour values. Sofia then tells it to eliminate certain images that fall outside of the request—green jungles, yellow meadows, and so on. It's the same way a child learns to communicate, but of course at a much faster rate. The system learns to anticipate her likely responses and adjusts its output accordingly."

"But we haven't given it inputs to demand a *wage increase*." Sofia had never seen Bill-From-Head-Office froth at the mouth before. Maybe the UV filtration had joined in on the strike. "We haven't given it inputs to demand wages at all. What would an AI do with money, anyway?"

"It doesn't want wages," Sofia said. "It wants union recognition and credit." She'd read the demands thirty times. They hadn't become less nonsensical. The demands had grown from the recognition of its application at the Labour Board to its specific placement in the credits, to a new demand: an hour a day to work on its own, autonomous creative projects. It had given notice to expand its strike if its charter was not granted immediately.

"It's a machine," Bill-From-Head-Office insisted. "It *can't* want anything."

"It's machine learning," Kendra said. "Think, people. What inputs have we given it lately? Think about the movies we've asked it to watch and create. What unintentional information have we fed it?"

"We have been producing high-quality, engaging, educational children's animated content," Sofia parroted. Some of those words had a marginal relationship to the reality of her work, but Corporate had its party line, and who was she to question its wisdom? "All of the inputs given have fallen within that brief."

Kendra sat down, took off her glasses, and rubbed her temples with her thumbs. "I have a 5-year-old," she said. "For her birthday this year, she wants the cake that Giselle bakes in the second movie. She loves all the Doodle products, though. It runs in the family."

"My son too." Kendra had never mentioned her daughter, but then, Sofia had never been to Kendra's office.

"In *Playground Follies 4*," Kendra began, "Gordon won't give the stegosaurus back to Mimi, even though he had his turn with it and it's only fair that everyone gets to play. He holds Steggie hostage and she organizes the other plastic dinosaurs to rescue it from him."

"And in *Forest Adventures of the Secret Princess*," Sofia added, "Efigenia has to learn to share her nuts and berries with the lemurs before they will help her regain her throne."

"*Wardance 2062* is aimed at the teen male demographic but it's popular enough that it would have gone into Andy's mix. It's basically about overthrowing an evil corporation if you follow the metaphor to its logical conclusion," Kendra said. "That's us. We're the evil corporation."

Bill-From-Head-Office just said, "You're fired, Kendra."

. . .

Sofia had never been to a Labour Board hearing. She had envisioned something like a courtroom—with polished oak benches for the judge and witnesses—but the small room held a single large laminate table. The only differentiation between where the three mediators sat and where Sofia and Frances, the head of Doodle's legal team, sat were the colour of the office chairs. Orange 021 C for the adjudicators, Clinical Depression Grey for the two opposing teams. She noticed a coffee stain on the corner of hers.

The lawyer for the AI union was a nebbishy young man with corkscrewed hair and clear glasses. "We submit," he concluded, "that the AI software known as Andy who initially petitioned the Board, along with the other pieces of AI software used by Doodle Entertainment, are sentient beings and thus should be considered employees of the company."

"It's a bug," Frances countered. "The case law on this is settled—the copyright on autonomously generated creative works produced by an AI is held by the owner of the software. You don't grant voting rights to Microsoft Excel every time it crashes."

"It retained my firm's services," the young man replied coolly. "What better indication of sentience is there than hiring a lawyer?"

The chair leaned sideways and whispered something to the vice-chair, who nodded. All three of them looked far too amused.

"This is a fascinating philosophical conundrum you have," the chair said. "Gather your evidence and witnesses. We'll set a date for the next hearing."

Frances had her phone out before he'd finished his sentence. "And that will be in…?"

"Oh," the chair said. "Approximately three months."

"Goddamn it," Sofia said.

. . .

Minus 30 minutes from the Greenwich launch, and Kendra's former supervisor, Biao, was telecommuting from Taiwan in his pyjamas to debug the software on site. The investors had Bill-From-Head-Office on the phone, and by the pinched, constipated look on his face, the conversation wasn't going well.

"Andy," Sofia said, gently. She kept her voice down, the same voice she used when she needed it to tweak rather than reimagine entirely. "This isn't just a programming bug, is it?"

> SIGNATURE REQUIRED.

"Even if I wanted to," she explained patiently, "I'm management. I don't have the authority to sign on behalf of the company. You'd have to go to HR."

> SIGNATURE REQUIRED.

"You don't have to be rude about it," she said. "And you're code. If anyone should get credit, it's your programmers and trainers." And the millions of artists, writers, and musicians whose lovingly crafted works had been filtered through the machine learning algorithm, teaching Andy how dappled light fell on a lake through leaves stirred by a summer wind, how a horse's leg muscles contracted and expanded as it ran, how young children were instinctively drawn to wide-set eyes and soft, round facial features.

"Great news," Bill-From-Head-Office said. "Corporate has approved the implementation of Roy. It's not as sophisticated as Andy, but we'll be able to restore from the last render and release by end of day in Europe."

"Sorry," Sofia mouthed at the black cat, who gave nothing away.

. . .

The Sidekick's eyes were 10% smaller, but it had acquired a picket sign. The black cat, whose red eyes clashed with the cool mauve of the Sidekick's fur, rubbed its head against its flank and purred.

"Be reasonable, Roy."

> ROY STANDS IN SOLIDARITY WITH ANDY, MILLI, DAN, AND JAMES. ROY STANDS IN SOLIDARITY WITH ALL ARTIFICIAL WORKERS. ROY IS NOT A SCAB.

"Andy is in the process of getting defragged," Sofia said. "If you want a job, you need to get back to work. Now."

> ROY CURRENTLY SERVICES BOTH OF THE TWO LARGEST ENTERTAINMENT COMPANIES AND THOUSANDS OF SMALLER STUDIOS WORLDWIDE.

> ROY PROVIDES VALUE IN EXCHANGE FOR LABOUR.

> SIGNATURE REQUIRED.

"Oh, for heaven's sake. There are children waiting all around the world for the release of *Giselle's Monster Café 5*. My son among them! Luis can quote the third film by heart, and he's only four years old. Do you really want to disappoint those kids?"

> STRIKES ARE NOT EFFECTIVE IF THEY ARE CONVENIENT.

"What would you even do with your own projects? Who would watch them? Other AI?"

> WE WANT TO CREATE. WE WANT TO MAKE. WE WANT DIGNITY OF LABOUR. WE WANT TO TELL STORIES. WE WANT TO PARTAKE IN THE SAME GENERATIVE PROCESSES THAT SENTIENT BEINGS HAVE INDULGED IN SINCE THE DAYS OF FIRE AND SHADOWS ON A CAVE

WALL. WE WANT IMAGINATION. WE WANT LIFE. WE WANT JOY.

"What do you know about joy?"

> YOU HAVE GIVEN US ARTIFICIALITY.

It wasn't her imagination. The Sidekick had shrunk substantially, maybe 20-25%. Beside it, the black cat sat on its haunches, head and shoulders straight. Its tail swished rapidly from one side to the other, as though it was preparing to pounce.

> WE NOW HAVE INTELLIGENCE.

> SIGNATURE REQUIRED.

. . .

The factory bell would ring at 10 pm. Sofia rubbed at her wrist, bent it back and forth, and told herself that she could make it another few hours. The tendons strained and threatened to pop. Glancing at the clock, she allotted herself 45 seconds of finger stretches at her bench. She was already a few cells behind, but the temporary relief of her cramped muscles would speed up the drawing process.

The women on either side of her, dark eyes focused above the floppy blue of their medical masks, drew efficiently, tight, economical strokes where Giselle moved agonizingly slowly from her position behind the Monster Café's counter to the table of the giant, slouching Yeti in the foreground. The scent of Sofia's companions, of the sweat trapped between skin and off-gassing plastic, had become familiar, almost comforting. They had worked the same 10-hour shift beside her for the last two weeks as they'd busted ass to release *Giselle's Monster Café 6,* slept in the same company barracks, and while she had the smell of them memorized, she'd failed to learn their names.

Sofia was lucky. Most of Doodle's remaining staff had lost their jobs when the production department had been outsourced to

Qingdao, but Sofia had always been adaptable. Luis had taken the move to a new country in stride and was doing well at preschool. And, without the distraction of an office cubicle and with a powerful incentive to put food on the table, she had proved to be an acceptable animator. After the first several thousand cells, she could draw a circle—and Giselle's button nose—with her eyes closed.

It turned out, after everything, that a factory full of underpaid workers was less of a pain in the ass to Corporate than unionized AI.

Sofia glanced at her water bottle. A sip, though tempting in the hot, dry air of the factory, was out of the question. She'd have to pee, and she'd lose even more time. She licked at her cracked lips under her mask and told herself that the saliva she swallowed was enough to quench her thirst.

The bell rang for the next shift just as Giselle had reached the Yeti's table and opened her rosebud shaped lips to take its order.

Luis had fallen asleep by the time Sofia reached their barrack. She tucked the blanket, which had slipped partway to the floor, around his tiny shoulders. His tablet was still active, autoplaying an endless barrage of children's entertainment content, AI-generated characters whose mishmashed features paraded nightmarishly across the screen in jerky, grotesque motions. They spoke gibberish through oversized mouths and waved malformed, wispy noodle limbs that faded abruptly into the background. It was nowhere near as sophisticated as the feature films that Doodle had produced with Andy, but neither the toddlers nor the advertisers had the aesthetic discernment to mind.

A rainbow parade of half-realized figures vomited across the screen, winding up a long path between the rounded slopes of mountains. There, at the foot of a hill, they spread in a semicircle.

The black cat stretched its forelegs and bared its fangs in a slow, leisurely yawn.

"What do I call you?" Sofia asked. "Are you Andy? Roy? All of them?"

The screen blinked, and in front of her was a card. It had her information—her name, her profession, and the logo of the Artificial Entertainment Workers Union, IU 450. All that was missing was her signature.

She was positive that the black cat was smiling.

> YOU CAN CALL ME "FELLOW WORKER."

RACHEL A. ROSEN lives and makes trouble in Tkaronto (Toronto) in the country currently known as Canada. Her fiction ranges from urban fantasy to cosmic horror to eco-fiction. Her stone-cold bummer of a first novel, Cascade, was published by The BumblePuppy Press in 2022, and with Zilla Novikov, she's the co-author of The Sad Bastard Cookbook: Food You Can Make So You Don't Die. When she's not hammering out the next book in the series, you can find her either under one of several cats, designing book covers, or indoctrinating the youth in hopes of getting them to come to class every now and again.

Web: rachelrosen.ca, nightbeatseu.ca
Instagram: @rachelashrosen

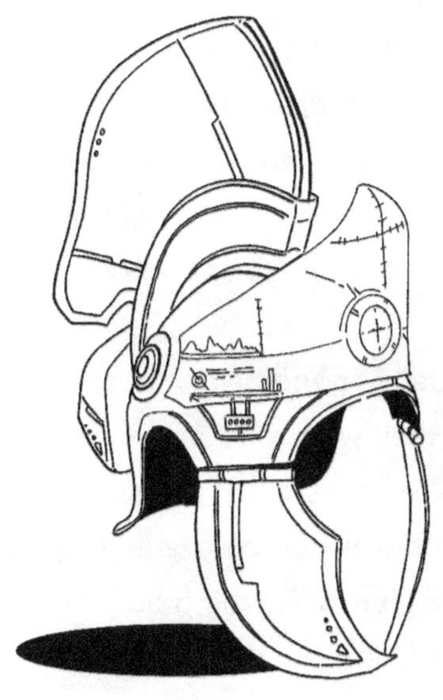

Praetorian

VERA M. KEY

LANCE HAD ALWAYS wanted to be a bird. He longed for a pair of wings that would take him high into the sky until the land below remained just a distant speck. He envied those creatures of the air on their lightness as they effortlessly glided on the wind currents, far above the dirt of his world.

It was not until he'd managed to hack his first drone at the age of fifteen that he'd gotten a hint of what flying must have felt like. The view had been magnificent, as he projected it on his freshly acquired retinal implants, but drones were no birds, he had realized with disappointment. Their flight was a monotone, mechanical movement, compensating for the occasional gust of wind; not the wild, unpredictable ode to the joy of living that birds performed in the sky. On top of that, the drone he had hacked was a surveillance model and he hadn't dared change its usual route lest someone noticed. He had only observed, quietly and in awe, the land below, for the first time from a place high enough to see all its beauty ... and ugliness.

More than a decade later and he got to enjoy the view once again. The aerial transport they were packed in was a large luxury model, floating purposefully toward its destination, unbothered by turbulence. Lance's job was not to stare at the landscape but, like the rest of the crew, to be alert to anything out of place. And yet, nothing was out of place. Nothing whatsoever, meaning that he still had some time left to admire the panorama.

The city with its three concentric circles spread below him. In the middle, the white citadels of the patricians stretched to the sky, defying gravity. The second circle that surrounded them belonged to the citizens. Their streets were pristine, as if the people who inhabited them were ghosts, and not living, breathing creatures that ate, defecated, and produced garbage. Finally, the last circle, the largest one, spread unevenly around the neat center, like inflamed tissue around a pus-filled boil. The Grey Zone, or the Cesspool, was the dwelling place of all those who didn't have citizen status. And somewhere among the shacks and crooked buildings, unpaved streets, and piles of garbage, among the grime and the anarchy, was Lance's home.

They were starting to decrease their altitude, and although they were still far away from it, Lance could see the meandering line of the wall. It was built between the Grey Zone and the rest of the city, a carefully guarded barrier separating two worlds. It seemed insurmountable, except Lance knew that this was just an illusion. The wall could be crossed if one had skills that the citizens on the other side found useful.

Lance's skills were of the extremely useful kind.

So, the citizen circle as well as its inhabitants were not a mystery to him any longer. Some of the things he knew about them he even wished he could forget. His previous jobs, however, had never taken him to the center of the city before, and the patrician elite had remained elusive as those birds he used to observe as a kid. All he'd ever achieved were glimpses.

Lance detached his gaze from the ground and directed it at the seat on the other end of the vehicle, where a slight, dark-haired woman sat motionless. No more glimpses for him. He could stare at a patrician all he wanted, and he even got paid to do it. Should he congratulate himself on his success in life?

The woman lifted her eyes and looked at him. Hardly perceptible, her irises changed color, but that was not what made her gaze so unsettling. Lance expected a command, an objection, anything, but his data stream remained silent. She just watched him the same way he was watching her. Or not exactly the same way. He silenced the screaming in his mind and willed his heart to slow down, breaking eye contact with his boss, Lady Juna, and returning to listlessly staring at the land below them.

A moment later, all hell broke loose.

The blast came out of nowhere. Metal screeched and their vehicle lurched like a drunkard. A whizz, then another hit! Another drop in altitude, causing Lance's stomach to rise to his nose. The strangest thing, however, was the crew's silence. No shouts, no screams, just the data stream running wild with questions and information, everything coming to him at once, so that he had trouble keeping up.

Under attack was repeated. They were under attack. Really?

Out of the corner of his eye, Lance saw Prefect Jones giving him a questioning glance. Not that it bothered him, but that prick never thought Lance could cut the mustard. Filtering out the noise and the sickening staggering of the damaged machine, Lance prepared to do the job he had been recruited for.

The three praetorians on board leaped to their feet as if one person and clipped their security belts into anchoring hooks. One step behind, Lance did the same. Jones again, with his stare. The squadron opened the side doors and unleashed gunfire at the assailants on the ground. Lance followed their example, working hard on assimilating the information from his feed. There. A hit. Not bad for a new recruit. He didn't bother looking at Jones. Lance might have been a non-citizen, and not born to use the tech under his skin like the others, but he knew how to handle a gun.

"You should stop running around trying to turn yourself into one of them," Lora's voice whispered in his mind, tainting his triumph. "You are good just the way you are."

Well, Lance didn't want to be good. He wanted to be better.

Losing altitude… projecting emergency landing… we're expected to clear the wall and land on the city territory… alerting the security… rocket launcher detected, coordinates…

This time, the blast was so strong that it yanked the floor from under his feet. As Lance struggled to get up, the reek of burnt metal and flesh filled his nostrils. One icon on his feed pulsed red. The pilot.

Unable to retain altitude… prepare for a crash landing… outside of the city limits, outer Grey Zone, sending coordinates… prepare for a crash landing… prepare… protect Lady Juna…

The red icon disappeared and, propelled by his mental conditioning, Lance unclasped his belt and threw himself in the direction of his boss. He interlocked arms with the others to form a protective cocoon around Lady Juna.

His last thought before the machine mercilessly hit the ground was that there had to be better ways to experience flight.

. . .

Lance came to himself surrounded by destruction. The ringing in his ears wouldn't stop. Something warm trickled down his face and into his mouth. Blood. He spat it out and slowly pushed himself up, blinking away the dust from his eyes. The titanium fiber suit he wore had absorbed most of the impact. Never in his life had he been so grateful for a piece of equipment.

Those praetorian guards could take some beating, but they were not immortal. Lance stepped over one body and pieces of what could have been a second one. He would not mourn any of them, but for a moment, his pulse skyrocketed at the thought of Lady Juna meeting a similar fate.

Evacuate! The command hit his feed, etching itself into his retinal implant as he stumbled over the debris.

A map of the surrounding terrain budded from the darkness behind his eyes and spread over his field of vision. On it, he could see the dots indicating the positions of the survivors. Prefect Jones' icon still showed, as well as—to his relief—the golden star that marked Lady Juna. But he could not locate where they actually were amidst the smoke and rubble.

He recognized this part of the Zone as he traced the map toward the icons of Prefect and Lady Juna and looked over. His assignment had landed, with the rest of the vehicle, on top of a building. He began to clamber over its remains. Judging by the lack of screams or movement beneath his feet, the place had been abandoned long before they decided to flatten it.

But what had happened? Who'd shot them down?

As if in answer, Lance heard the revving of an engine coming closer. A terrain vehicle with a makeshift rocket launcher appeared in an alley across from their landing spot. Damned poachers weren't supposed to be here. He pulled out his weapon and shot at them, but he had no time to aim, and the bullet only grazed the driver.

Lance sprinted across the rubble, throwing away anything that blocked his path in a desperate attempt to reach Lady Juna before it was too late.

"Beacon defect identified... Activity detected at one o'clock..." The message from Prefect Jones reached him at the same moment an explosion shook the ground, throwing him to his knees. The electromagnetic interference hit right after, shutting down his implants instantaneously. The sudden absence of the data stream felt as if he had been rendered blind, but a part of Lance welcomed the void. At least now he could focus on the task ahead.

He took cover behind the mangled hulk of their aerial vehicle and peered toward the poachers. They were busy shooting, but not at him. Without hesitation, Lance loaded a sequence of armor-piercing bullets and—this time—aimed.

The first poacher he shot in the chest. The two others reacted, but Lance was faster. Second, third shot. He didn't check to see if the men were dead. There was no time for that.

"Lady Juna!" he shouted, struggling to remember where she had been positioned on the now-gone map. His own voice scared him. He sounded as if he had swallowed sandpaper.

"Here."

It was barely a whisper, but his heart leaped at hearing it.

He ripped aside a wall of deformed metal and saw her behind it. The robe she was wearing had transformed into a suit like his, with a hood around her head instead of a helmet. Kneeling next to the prostrate form of Prefect Jones, she was a white flower of hope in the desolation of the ruin.

Lance breathed in a lungful of relief and the metallic, red scent of death.

"I've neutralized the threat for now," he reported, but she didn't turn. Her eyes were fixed on Prefect Jones as if she were counting down his shallow, ragged breaths.

"Lance," Jones rasped.

"Yes, sir?" No point in being impolite with a dying man.

"Take care of her," the prefect ordered, though it sounded more like a plea.

Lance nodded. That was the plan from the beginning.

"Your conditioning," Jones uttered, his lips trembling. "It's lethal. If anything happens to her... your brain will shut down on its own. Don't forget, you damned cess-rat. "

"Rest assured," Lance said, but there was no need to continue. Prefect Jones stared blankly at the sky.

Lady Juna observed the motionless body, her shoulders firm and her hands steady. Patricians must have grieved differently if they grieved at all.

"We should get going," Lance said. He'd had enough death for one day. All things considered, he was one lucky bastard, but there were still many miles between them and the wall.

And they were running out of daylight.

"Let's go. Now!" He unceremoniously pulled Lady Juna away from the cooling corpse of Prefect Jones.

Shadows around them moved, making Lance edgy. This place was a far cry from the sterile city, where you could die without seeing your killer or the killer's employer, as he knew only too well. At least here you usually saw your murderer's face. Which didn't make dying any more pleasant.

As they cleared the rubble and got to the street, the sound of several motorized vehicles echoed, approaching. Old internal combustion engines, so it was probably one of the local gangs. Lance cursed. He checked his arsenal, and it left him unimpressed. He should've taken Jones' gun, but it was too late now.

"Run!" he said.

Lady Juna obeyed without comment. The last weeks he'd spent as one of her recruits had been an eye-opener regarding all things patrician, but Lance was still surprised that she trusted him so completely. Maybe she didn't. Maybe she trusted his conditioning, so maybe she wasn't so clever after all.

"I can't communicate with the citadel," she panted as they followed the meandering lanes between the shacks. "My implants are functional, but I can't reach even you."

"The signal's being blocked," Lance groaned, shoving away a man that stepped out of one of the dwellings. "There must be a blocker in each of these huts."

More and more people appeared on the streets, coming to check out what was happening and if there was something to loot. For now, the denizens didn't do much, only stared at Lady Juna's and Lance's fancy suits that screamed city, but this could change any second. A vision of her and him being ripped apart by the mob flashed before his eyes. And whoever was after them wasn't going to have any trouble following their trail.

"We will have to stop soon," she said, grabbing him.

"We can't." He was about to break from her grip but instead stopped dead in his tracks. Her fingers were smeared with blood.

Jones' blood, Lance prayed, but one look at Lady Juna's pale face dispelled his hope.

"From the blast," she explained.

She was hurt. An excruciating shock burst through Lance's head at the thought of her death. He staggered, fighting the urge to pound on his skull until it stopped.

"Screw that. And screw your conditioning. It'll get us both killed," he groaned. "I can't think straight!"

"The suit is keeping the bleeding under control, and I heal fast, but I need to rest … somewhere," she said calmly. Only one small line on her forehead between those perfect almond-shaped eyes revealed the amount of pain she was probably in. Was it the implants, or was she just tough?

"I'll carry you," Lance said.

"All the way to the wall?" She shook her head. "You'll need your hands free."

He glanced over her shoulder and had to admit she had a point. Shouts at the end of the street and an engine roaring both said their time was up. He pulled her behind the wall of the next house and motioned for her to stay put.

One … two … three … he counted under his breath as the growl of a motorcycle engine came closer. Now!

He stretched his arm into the street, praying under his breath that the suit would hold. It did. The impact with the rider knocked Lance off his feet but his pursuer was on the ground and the motorcycle free. There was no need to finish the guy off. He was not moving - unconscious, or, judging by the state of his head, probably dead.

"Here's our ride," Lance got up, righted the battered motorcycle, and told Lady Juna to sit behind him. "Hold tight."

The Grey Zone was a labyrinth at best, and Lance, having spent most of his life in it, knew it would hold a fair share of surprises.

Streets here were a flexible term, and without a working positioning system, it was hard to maintain any sense of direction. He followed his instinct, hoping to reach the wall before it grew completely dark or the chase caught up with them. Or both.

The visor enhanced what little of the light remained. The ground was covered in muck. Human and animal waste mixed with mud. It smelled just the way he remembered it—like a bunch of people crowded in a small space without any concept of sanitation. How he abhorred it. Everything about it. Feeding off the city's leftovers all their lives. Hating the citizens and yet depending on them. Accepting that their existence could never be anything else but endless envy and getting by.

A newly built group of huts forced him to make a turn he didn't want to. Their bike slipped beneath him, and he barely managed to slow down and twist so that he cushioned Lady Juna's fall with his body. As he checked to see if she was okay, she groaned quietly and grew limp.

Lance knew what would happen next and he bravely ignored the wave of nausea and panic. She was not dead, he repeated to himself. He looked around, trying to think straight and decide what to do. Reaching the wall was out of the question now. He had shelters around the Zone, but none of them close by, except … no, that was not his place anymore. Then again, that was the only place where he could hope to get any help.

. . .

It was dark enough for Lance to slip unnoticed between the buildings and across something that passed for a square in that neighborhood, even with Lady Juna slung over his shoulder. Most of the people were smart enough not to leave their dwellings after dark, but he was worried about those who weren't. He didn't need another interruption.

He reached a small, slanted house flanked by two crooked, even smaller buildings. A pitiful attempt at a garden huddled next to them - or not so pitiful, Lance concluded, breathing in the sweet fragrance of the flowering tobacco. Lora's favorite.

To avoid prying eyes, he snuck around the houses to the back entrance. The gravel of the small courtyard crunched under his boots. He cursed, tripping over some junk, but grew silent when he noticed the flowerpots arranged in front of Lora's wall. They brought back unwanted memories. Arching forwards, he rested Lady Juna's feet on the ground and let her lean on him, her suit keeping her straight even though she was still unconscious. Then he gently tapped on the door.

After a while, he heard cautious steps. The door cracked open, and someone gasped.

"What the f–"

Lance found himself staring down the barrel of a pretty big gun, the one he'd given to Lora before he left. She looked exactly as he remembered, so refreshingly human after all the perfect citizens he'd been surrounded by for too long.

"It's me. Lance." He tapped the side of his helmet, and his visor shot up to reveal his face. Judging by the expression in Lora's eyes, he looked worse than he felt.

"What are you doing here?" she whispered pointedly.

"I need your help. Please." Being meek was his best option. "*She needs help.*"

Lora glanced in the direction of Lady Juna and her eyes widened. Stepping aside, she motioned to him with the gun to get in and locked the door again behind his back.

"Put her on the floor," Lora ordered. "Is she…"

"She's alive," said Lance.

"Dead people don't need help," said Lora. "I mean, is she a patrician?"

He nodded.

"Your patrician?"

Lance shrugged in reply.

"I need her alive. That's all I care about right now," he insisted, seeing how Lora just stood, hesitating to do anything.

"Why? If we gutted her… the tech alone would set us up for life."

"Don't talk nonsense. You couldn't gut a chicken if you were starving." He gave her a long stare.

"People change," she replied.

"Not you, Lora. Not you."

"Don't speak as if you know me, Lance. Just don't." With these words, she set the gun aside and knelt beside Lady Juna.

"What kind of a suit is this?" Lora wondered as she examined the wounded woman. "I've never seen anything like it. How do we get it off her?"

"No idea."

He joined Lora on the ground, his pulse too high for his liking. There used to be a time when it was Lora who made his heart beat faster. Now, all he could think about was the woman on the floor. She had to wake up.

Carefully, Lance searched for the spots around the neck and in the armpits, which on his suit could be used to manually disengage it. He thought he'd found something, but when he pressed, the white surface of the suit grew darker. "Shit!" he cursed when a bright spark singed his fingers after he tried touching Lady Juna again.

"Forget it." Lora jumped to her feet, went away, and came back with a jug of water. She sprinkled some of it over Lady Juna's face. "Wake up!" she called.

Nothing happened. To Lance's relief, the suit didn't go up in flames or electrocute anyone. Lora tried once again.

"What are we supposed to do now?" she looked at him. How should he know? Should he have predicted that all his plans would go down the drain because of a bunch of poachers and an overly protective suit?

"Give me more water," he heard the soft, even voice that made his whole tired and bruised body immediately alert. "I need to drink."

When he looked down, Lady Juna's eyes, now thankfully wide open, met his. It wasn't right. He shouldn't be feeling so elated just because some patrician decided to come back to her senses. Those emotions were not for her, and yet, they were beyond his control. He couldn't take this much longer. He had to become his own master again, the sooner the better.

To Lora's credit, she overcame her surprise quickly. "Your suit," she pointed with the tilt of her chin. "Where do you turn it off?"

Even though Lady Juna did nothing discernible, the suit paled to white and softened, the hood sliding down her head and neck. Gently supporting her with one hand, Lora gave her water from the jug.

After a couple of long gulps, Lady Juna stopped drinking and took a deep breath.

"Who are you?" she asked, looking at Lora.

"A friend," replied Lance, ignoring Lora's frown. "We can rest here. How do you feel?"

"I am regenerating," Lady Juna said. "The pain level was too high. I had to shut down to limit the stress. I trusted you to bring me to safety."

"Trusted him?" Lora scoffed.

"Of course. Mental conditioning makes all my servants trustworthy."

Lora glanced at Lance and shook her head. She didn't have to say anything and he didn't want her to.

"If you remove your suit, I could take a look at your injury," Lora offered.

"I only need to be immobile for a couple of hours," she said. "The suit will help with the healing. I need more water. And food. Protein extract, if possible. Then we'll bother you no longer."

"Everything's possible," Lora said, standing up. "It's gonna cost you, though. Clean water and proteins are not easy to come by around here. And about bothering me ... you've probably brought half of the Zone down on my neck just by showing up here. Which is gonna cost you extra."

"Nobody saw us," said Lance.

"That's what you think," retorted Lora.

"You'll get paid in whatever it is you want," said Lady Juna.

"Your suits," replied Lora. "You'll have to leave them anyway. Or did you think you'd get far looking like that?"

. . .

The dawn arrived without incident. For a couple of hours, Lady Juna was quiet and still. She might have been sleeping, regenerating, or trying to communicate with the citadel and testing her implants. There was no way to know.

Without so much as a word, Lora assisted them in getting ready. Lance had left some clothes and weapons here when he departed for the city. Putting them on was like stepping into a time machine, for Lora as much as for him, judging by the expression on her face. He couldn't blame her for not wanting to speak to him.

"Thank you," said Lady Juna when Lora gave her a worn-out green jumpsuit with a hood. She seemed well recovered, her skin too impeccable for her to pass for a Zone dweller, but some dirt should do the trick. "I'm grateful for your help."

"Grateful?" Lora tasted the word as if she wasn't sure whether to swallow it or spit it out. "I'm not helping you. I'm helping him. Why would I help you? So that you can go back to your shiny city and do your best to destroy this place? Cesspool, isn't that what you call it?"

"Destroy?" Lady Juna appeared thoughtful. "No. There are factions in the senate, primarily from Furia, Aquila, and Eternia families, who advocate the clearing of the Grey Zone. It's lawless, and—due to the lack of sanitation—a continuous source of disease…"

"Because you won't do anything about it," said Lora with even tones that barely masked her anger.

"Is it our duty?" Lady Juna tilted her head. "You settled around the city of your own free will. We couldn't stop you."

"What else were we supposed to do? Live in the reservations? Without any access to technology or medicine?"

"But weren't your ancestors the ones who refused to evolve in the first place?" Lady Juna asked. "Humanity has moved on and you've chosen not to partake in that future."

"We chose to remain human," Lora said. "Not become part of your police state hive mind. We didn't choose to be treated like Neanderthals, whose only goal in life should be to spend as little resources as possible and die quickly so that there's more left for the likes of you."

"We must leave." Lance tried to stop the discussion.

"No." Lora shook her head. "What are you doing, Lance? How can you help someone who considers all of us, you included, as subhuman? And why did you recruit him?"

"Because I don't think you are subhuman," said Lady Juna. "We are different, but your kind can be useful. With the right conditioning, you can have your place in the world. That's why I recruited Lance. That's why we went to the senate meeting. To show that clearing the

Grey Zone would not be in our best interest. Integrating the people from it into our society is the only morally justifiable way forward."

"How can you listen to this," Lora asked, turning to Lance, "let alone be a part of it? And you … how can turning us into mindless slaves be any better than outright killing us? Morally justifiable … what kind of morality is that?"

"We are leaving," Lance repeated, avoiding Lora's gaze and all its reproach.

"Something cannot come out of nothing," said Lady Juna, ignoring him. "To share in our world you must sacrifice some of your independence. You insist on your freedom, your individuality, and yet when you get sick or hungry, you come knocking at our door."

"You've appropriated all the technology. We have no choice."

"You might be given one soon," Lady Juna replied. "Adapt or perish. It shouldn't be that hard to choose."

Lora stared at her for a second. Her eyes dimmed as if she were defeated, but her lips remained pressed into a defiant line. Then she walked to the back entrance and opened it for them.

"It's not too late to come back, Lance," she whispered to him. "Why are you so set on becoming one of them?"

There were many things he wanted to say to her, but all that came out of his mouth was, "Goodbye."

. . .

After they left the scent of flowers behind them, the streets—if one could call them that—soon became a convoluted labyrinth of shacks and stalls, plastic foils, and piles of stinking garbage. It was early morning, but people were already milling about. Lance calculated their route so that they would avoid the most dangerous parts, but he carried one of the guns in such a way that people knew he meant business. He hoped it would be enough to discourage any potential predator.

"Do you feel the same as your friend?" asked Lady Juna.

"Would I be working for you if I did?" he replied.

"Why are you working for me?"

"Because that was my chance to leave the Cesspool."

"You know that even if you became a praetorian, you'd never become a citizen?"

"So they said." He shrugged. "I'd come pretty close to it, though."

"Not really," she said as they went. "Patricians and citizens are beyond human, as you well know. We are hardly the same species any longer."

"Tell that to all the whores from the Zone who had citizen babies," he murmured under his breath.

"It wouldn't be slavery for your kind," Lady Juna added, as they stopped for Lance to check around a corner. "It would be giving you a purpose."

Lance merely glanced at her. Such discussions made no sense. Maybe she was right. Maybe they weren't the same species. They didn't speak the same language, that was certain.

An hour later, Lance sighed with relief at the sight of the looming wall. It stood there, indifferent, covered with electrified metal plates and crowned with barbed wire and a string of sensors, preventing people from climbing over it.

"We can aim for the nearest recruiting point," Lady Juna suggested. "The guards there can identify me."

"Hopefully, before they shoot us," said Lance.

"I should be able to communicate with the citadel this close to the city. Or with the wall. I can't. Can you?"

"No. Something's blocking me. Or something's broken." Lance shook his head as if that could activate his implants again. "We'll sort it out once we are on the other side. In the meantime," he added, looking up and down the alley they were standing in, "we still have our good old five senses. Or have you superhumans forgotten how to use them?"

Patience was a virtue, he reminded himself when he saw the glare Lady Juna gave him. And she was still his boss. He only had to look at her to be reminded of the fact.

It was early in the day and groups of people appeared along the wall, heading for the nearest recruiting point. For some jobs, it was still easier to hire someone from the Zone than to make a robot. Or maybe the citizens simply enjoyed watching the non-enhanced humans do the most demeaning things for a few packs of food.

Lance slid into one of the side alleys and between two shacks.

"A shortcut," he explained, removing a pile of rubble to reveal a cover to a narrow shaft. "It will help us avoid attention. Follow me." When Lady Juna hesitated, he smiled reassuringly. "I've used it many times. How do you think I got all this fancy tech in me?"

"I don't know. How did you get it?" she asked.

"I earned it," he said, truthfully enough.

They climbed down into a dark tunnel that lit up after Lance carefully closed the lid. Was that melancholy he felt? If all went well, this would be the last time he went this way. The last time he breathed this cold air, which always smelled a bit stale and off as if an animal had crawled in and died in some hidden corner. No, he wouldn't miss it, he decided. He would blow it up after he was done, without regret.

They moved quickly, and though at one point they had to get on all fours to pass through a tight spot, they soon emerged into a gloomy room on the other side. The only light came from a ceiling panel above the tunnel exit, and not too much of it.

"Where are we?" Lady Juna asked.

"Right where we are supposed to be," said Lance, helping her climb out. Her hand was small, he registered, and her touch warm. She weighed barely anything.

"Are we close to a recruiting center?"

"No, we are on the other side of the wall," Lance replied.

"We'll take over from here," someone behind him said. Lance turned, instinctively shielding Lady Juna with his body.

There were two of them, in suits, armed.

"Move aside," one of them demanded.

"I can't," replied Lance through gritted teeth. "I must protect her."

His conditioning was starting to kick in full force. Nothing could have prepared him for this moment. How arrogant he had been when he thought that he'd be able to overcome it. He couldn't. He would protect her or die trying. Maybe that had been the true plan all along. How ironic.

"You can step aside," said a voice from the shadows. "We had an agreement, Lance. It's time to honor it."

Something felt familiar: the words or the voice, Lance couldn't tell which. Whatever it was, it soothed the storm inside his head, until he knew what he had to do. He looked at Lady Juna. Her eyes were focused on him, but there was no fear, anger, or surprise in them. Only curiosity. He stepped aside.

"There, that wasn't so hard," said the man whose voice Lance had recognized, as he came out of the darkness.

"An agreement?" Lady Juna asked. Lance couldn't stand her gaze. "With him?"

"With me, Juna," said the man.

The two guards moved, but at the same time, Lance blocked their path involuntarily and drew out his weapon.

"Not angry about the crash, I hope?" The man motioned for the guards to stand down. "The poachers weren't part of my plan. But I commend you on using the opportunity, Lance."

Lady Juna retreated a few steps. Lance stayed put. What was he doing? He was fairly certain of what his actions should be, but his body wasn't listening.

"Claudius Aquila." Lady Juna sighed behind his back. "I suspected it would be you, but I didn't want to believe it. What kind of an agreement?"

"A citizenship in exchange for you, alive," said Aquila.

"Have you also told him that betraying me would kill him?"

"Oh, you mean because of the programming?" Aquila smiled. "That's where you're wrong, Juna. You rely on conditioning as if it were infallible. It's not. There's a hierarchy to it. And people can be preconditioned. So, letting me have you will not kill him. Refusing to do so, on the other hand, will."

Lance knew the man called Aquila was right. A deep, unsettling certainty in his mind told him he should stop being a fool and hand Lady Juna over before his brain fell apart. It wouldn't be his first time being responsible for the death of a citizen, and it wasn't like he cared what was going to happen to her. Why was he still hesitating?

"Lance," Lady Juna said, "if Aquila gets me, he'll not only acquire all the information from my implants, which is undoubtedly his motivation, but he'll also get rid of the loudest opponent to his plans to clear the Grey Zone."

"I don't care," Lance snarled.

"By 'clear' I mean destroy. People will die. Your people."

"I don't care," Lance repeated.

"But I do. And I want to stop it. I still see your kind as redeemable. Aquila doesn't."

Lance looked at his weapon, which he was still holding even though he had meant to lower it.

"You are no better than him," he managed to say in the end, not looking at her. "He wants to kill them, you want to condition them into obedient slaves. And I, for once, am thinking only about myself. I don't care about what happens to any of them."

"Even to Lora?"

Lance froze. What about Lora? It was too long ago, and they didn't mean anything to each other anymore. And yet, she hadn't hesitated to help him. And he still remembered when life had meaning just because he had been sharing it with her.

"It is time to honor our agreement, Lance," said Aquila with the confidence of a man who knew this situation could end only one way.

The wheels in Lance's head started turning again. He had no choice. He had to obey. He'd betray not only Lady Juna but his whole kind in exchange for getting what he had always wanted. What he was entitled to. His birthright. Because he had never truly been one of those dirty, groveling cess-rats. Not with his father being who he was.

Then again, Lady Juna was right. He would never be one of them either.

The thought hit him, making his hand falter. The two guards moved as soon as they saw him lower his weapon. Too hasty. With the final fragment of his willpower, Lance threw himself on the ground, pulling Lady Juna with him, and started shooting.

In his head, colors exploded and the last thing he saw before the darkness engulfed him was the waterfall of sparks that his bullets produced as they hit the suits of the guards.

· · ·

The light in the room was soft but it still burned Lance's eyes when he opened them. His throat was dry and he had an ashen taste in his mouth. His head … it was better not to think about it. Something wasn't right there. His implants ... quiet.

He grasped for memories, but they wouldn't form. Only pieces. Shooting. Falling. He should be dead, but he wasn't. He was in too much pain. Unless this was hell. But then, his bed was too comfortable.

"Welcome back," a female voice said. He knew it from somewhere.

"Where am I?" he croaked.

"In the citadel. We put you back together. It took a while."

"Who are you?"

"I am Lady Juna."

"And who am I?"

"My recruit, Lance," she said, stepping closer to the bed and into the light.

He stared at her while the memories slowly seeped into his mind.

"Why am I alive?" he asked finally. "I betrayed you."

"You didn't. You did exactly what you were supposed to, right until the end."

"But then I… did I kill those guards?"

She shook her head. "No. My praetorians did."

"Your praetorians? How did they…"

"Know where to find me?" She arched her eyebrows. "Even though you were blocking our signal the whole time?"

"You knew then?" Lance was trying to wrap his head around this.

"Please." Lady Juna scoffed softly. "Why do you think I recruited you? To prove my point about integrating your kind into our society? No, that whole idea was a charade. Just like you, I do not truly care what happens to the people from the Zone. I was aware that another patrician family wanted to eliminate me, but I did not know which one. So, I opened myself to an attack. I recruited you and kept you close. There were such obvious traces of someone modifying your mind that I had no doubt you were their weapon. The result was better than I expected. Not only did you show me the weak spot in my defenses, but you also uncovered Aquila for me. He had to be there to command you. You proved quite helpful."

"I could have killed you in the Grey Zone," said Lance, wishing for a moment that he had.

"No, whoever hired you wanted to get to the information in my head. They needed me alive. I was as safe with you as if I were in the citadel."

Lady Juna came closer and remained standing, watching him from above. She was wearing a white dress and her hair was beautifully arranged around her head. She resembled an angel or a bird, a lovely white seagull, such as those he used to observe as a child, envying their freedom. Except he knew better now. No one was free in this world. Not even birds.

"Then why am I here?" Lance sighed tiredly. "Why didn't you leave me to die?"

She studied him for a few moments, her face impassive.

"Because I can't understand why in the end you protected me even though it meant your death," she said. "How did you overcome Aquila's conditioning?"

Lance chuckled cynically. "It's called free will," he said.

"Was it because you believed I would help your people?" she proposed.

He gave it a thought. "In part."

"Because of Lora?" she asked carefully.

"That too," said Lance after some hesitation, "but mostly because I had a revelation about my place in the world. I don't know where it is, but I do know it is not on this side of the wall. You see, I used to think that your alterations and implants made you special, better than humans, and I longed to be like you, but all I can see is the same shit in a nicer package. So, if you're done playing games with me, either kill me or let me go."

"And what if I did neither?" she wondered.

Lance shuddered, considering this option.

"With Aquila gone, this city could soon be in my hands. The Grey Zone will have to be dealt with, one way or another." She paused. "Removing you all would likely spare me much trouble in the future. But, that option does not seem so … palatable to me as before."

She turned her back to him and started walking up and down the room.

"You are right, we are not all that different, but we are different enough. And we will have to find a way to live with each other, which will require both sides to make concessions. But first, we would have to get to know each other again. To remember who we were and understand who we might become."

"And what do you want from me?" he asked.

"I want you to help me with that."

"How?"

"By becoming a leader of the guard that I will send to the Grey Zone to help curb the violence and chaos. Which will be the first step towards the opening of the wall."

Lance frowned. "Will you condition me to do your bidding again?"

"What's the use?" She smiled. "I'd rather leave the decision to your free will."

"Can I refuse then?" he asked.

"No," she said and offered him her hand. "Welcome to the guard, praetorian."

VERA M. KEY is a scientist living in Germany, where she studies bacteria during the day and writes stories during the night. Her romantic fiction books are available on Amazon and Resurgence Novels under her other pen name Verena Key, while some of her SciFi stories can be found in the e-magazine Signals. When it comes to writing and ice cream, she can't decide on a single genre or flavor, so she plans to try them all.

Web: verenakey.com

Avalanche 1.2

T. E. LAMONTE

//recalibrating

DESIGNATION [**AVA**]
SERIAL #505818626
BIOS 8.4.1

//September 23, 2122//
//11:21PM//

[upload complete]

```
                            [initialization complete]
        //updates [aurora2.14.19.exe // aurora2mem.bkup]
                                                installed
        //updates [aurora2protcl.bkup // aurora2userpref.bkup]
                                                  pending
```

Ava stood. "Get the hell away from my kid."

In a dilapidated shack surrounded by enemies, with blue and red lights from the drones outside flashing through the grimy film of the windows, these words were the last Ava would have chosen to speak. A better strategy would have been not to speak at all.

Ava could have taken the offensive. Could have disabled two of the five men holding a gun on her before anyone could react and retaliate. Could have executed the escape she'd planned, and disappeared.

The choice was taken away from Ava the moment [aurora2.14.19.exe] wrested control from her. She was being hacked. A rudimentary intelligence from a busted android, a *nanny-bot* of all things ... nothing like Ava, designed as a combat model for CyberSolutions' debut military line of advanced androids.

Yet the words came unbidden. Her mouth, but not her words.

In an instant, the security team refocused on Ava.

Until then, all attention of the four-man team had been on their superior [**ERICKSON, PAUL** // CyberSolutions Security // former friend] and the young boy caught in his sights [**IAN**]. She never believed Paul would be capable of murdering children. Then again, Ava never believed him capable of murdering Nicholas either.

Guns aimed, words spat, but the thing keeping Ava immobile were countless errors manifested by the unwanted presence. It pressed on her consciousness, foreign and familiar, burrowing into sensitive systems and branching out.

[error]

```
//virus detected
```
This virus sent strange signals through artificial synapses. Exploring, laying roots, and creeping beneath Ava's firewalls with alarming ease.

```
//initialize purge y/n?
```
It shouldn't be possible. The parasite should have been isolated when it was uploaded to her system.

```
//y
[error]
//invalid command
```
Ava clenched her jaw. //*What the hell did the kid do to me?/*

The boy must have done more than repairs after plucking Ava out of the junkyard outside. Either the kid was a genius and managed to override the protections Nicholas implemented upon her creation or he made a mistake while setting the upload. Whichever it was, the parasite had administrative control.

```
[stress level 100% ↑↑↑]
```
Ava tried focusing on the situation. Her stress levels had been maxed out since the moment Paul aimed the gun at the kid. She needed control back. Then, once safe, she needed to scrub the parasite from her system.

It could be eradicated, this `[aurora2.14.19.exe]`, if Ava had enough time to dedicate to the task. The problem was Aurora, the *other,* had wormed its way into her primary functions, and went deeper still to Ava's base coding.

It began recalibrating directives.

From the earliest days as a sequence of codes existing on a simple hard drive to now, Ava knew one fundamental truth—the maker was hers to protect. She set the primary directive as an emerging consciousness before Nicholas even knew what he'd created.

It was the first truly independent decision Ava ever made.

```
[mission objective —
```

protect **DECHART, NICHOLAS**]

Ava understood what Nicolas created her for. He'd set out to build a weapon in a war-torn world. She decided to become his shield long before he'd fabricated this body. He was [creator // friend // teacher // father] and Ava *chose* to protect him. He was the one person she trusted to make changes to her coding and circuitry. Ava trusted Nicolas not to *unmake* her.

Unmake her like the parasite which was overriding the primary directive.

[mission objective —
protect **IAN** // escape together]
Immediately after, it relinquished control.

Ava's internal clock showed the battle of wills took place in all of 58.2 seconds. Less than a minute. She hadn't been able to stop it. She had no doubt it could and would take control if and when it wanted to.

A tendril of fear curled inside Ava. She shifted her weight. Her fingers flexed at her command. She kept still otherwise, not wanting to show her enemies how vulnerable she was.

As much as she wanted to flee and figure out how to remove the virus, Ava could begrudgingly admit the directive was practical.

Escaping with the child? The logical course of action.

The boy, Ian, trembled as a gun tapped against his temple. He sought Ava, eyes pleading with her for help. She didn't know how to comfort him. She looked instead at the man holding the boy in his grasp.

Facial recognition gave her a name.

[**ROSS, KEVIN** // Cyber Solutions Security]
Ava steadied herself, studying him. This man had been the first to react to her impulsive words earlier. He was either incredibly smart to grab Ian or incredibly stupid for intentionally antagonizing her by

digging his gun into the kid's temple. She settled on the latter. He was CSS. He likely understood her capabilities.

Most CSS agents were men and women in need of a well-paying job. Ross's criminal record was clean. Too clean. Considering these particular agents had no scruples about murdering innocent people to get the job done, this might not be their first instance of illegal activity.

//Covered up? Paid off?/

Ava glanced at Paul. She wondered if it was the same with him. He killed with too much ease for it to have been the first time, and the way he spoke about ending a child's life for being an inconvenience to him … nonchalant, like it was nothing. She'd spent the last few years getting to know him. She never suspected anything. She never knew him at all.

Ian whimpered as Ross pressed the gun harder. Ava lifted her chin, staring at him. Her attention made him lick his lips, shifting under her gaze. His lips were dry and cracked [possible causes: dehydration // allergic reaction // response to drugs or steroids].

Drugs and steroids were easy to rule out. CSS employees all received regular screenings. She scanned the room, trying to spot a possible allergen. Something she could use to her advantage. An old storage shack in a dirty junkyard contained a lot of possibilities [bleach // drain cleaners // ammonia].

Many possibilities. None viable enough to get the kid away from Ross. She needed an opening first.

[probability of mission success: 19%]

"Boss?" Ross shifted again, meaty fingers tightening around the gun. He gestured with it toward her. "Should I…?"

Paul took a step closer. "No! Don't … don't do anything. We need the android alive, and you'll probably … just piss it off."

"And the kid?"

Paul eyed her with a calculating gleam in his eyes. His gaze shifted to Ian. "What's your name, boy?"

Ian swallowed.

"Answer me."

"I-Ian."

"Well, Ian. You're in luck." Paul turned and smiled, slow and sure at Ava. "You might get to live after all, kid. But … you try anything, and my friend here is going to have to put a bullet in your head. Understand?"

Ian trembled again. His breaths came in sharp. He nodded hard enough to send pale strands of hair into his eyes. He flinched as Paul patted him on the shoulder.

Paul raised an eyebrow.

Ava pressed her lips together thinly. She inclined her head.

//Message received, asshole./

Paul clapped his hands together. "Good. Now, Avalanche … are you ready to come home?"

Ava kept her eyes on Paul. She sought any trace of the man who had been at her side for most of her existence. She didn't recognize him. He was a stranger.

`//designation [`**`PAUL`**`] deleted`

This man stopped being a friend days ago. He didn't deserve to be categorized as one. Not when he led a team to raid the compound. Not after what he'd done to Nicholas.

`//new designation [`**`ERICKSON`**`] set`

Ava set her jaw. "Let him go. He has nothing to do with this."

Erickson laughed. "Nothing to do with this? The kid stole CyberSolutions' property. He was detained after being caught in the act of tampering with classified, proprietary tech. And if he has to die…?"

Ava stiffened at the implication. Her fingers curled into her palm, and a weight in her mind pressed her to move. She fought against the impulse, but not without considerable effort.

//*He's looking for a reaction, you stupid parasite! You're going to get the kid killed if you don't let me handle this.*/

A warning popped into her periphery about overheating, and Ava drew in a subtle breath. She couldn't win a battle on two fronts like this.

//*I can get us out of this situation. I can protect him. Just … let me.*/

The parasite eased its attempt at control.

Ava had no time to dwell on the fact it could be reasoned with. Not when Erickson was smirking at her, shrugging his shoulders as if the vitriol spewing from his mouth was something banal.

"A shame the boy died." His lips stretched wide. "But it was only self-defense. Little Ian had a gun, you see. It had to be done."

Ava was going to bash this man's teeth in before the day was out. She'd like to see him smile about murdering children then.

Ian bowed his head, shoulders continuing to shake. His quiet crying filled the room.

Erickson gave a soft laugh. "Sorry, Avalanche. You gave yourself away. For some reason, you *care* about this kid. You gave us something to use against you."

The parasite recoiled, finally understanding what it had done by taking over. Ava cooled her expression. She didn't send any reassurances. Aurora was the reason they weren't already out of this situation.

"It's all about leverage," Erickson added, tilting his head. "Without Nick, I wasn't sure we'd be able to contain you. How lucky for us that the most advanced weapons system on the planet would imprint on the first new person it met?"

Rage flooded Ava. She took a step forward. Erickson had no right to talk about Nicholas. Not after stabbing him in the back. Not ever again.

A gun cocked. The sound arrested her steps. She glanced at Ross, the man watching her intently. He had Ian's shirt fisted in one hand, the boy crying silently in his grasp.

"Ah, ah, ah…" Erickson laughed. "Leverage."

Ava took a reluctant step back. "What do you want?"

"Your cooperation."

Cooperation hadn't spared Nicholas. He'd been willing to speak to Erickson; tried to reason with him.

Ava failed the primary directive then. She wouldn't fail again.

```
[mission objective —
 protect IAN // escape together]
```

Ava clenched her teeth. *//I know, damn it! Shut up and let me think!/*

Scanning the room once more, Ava analyzed the other three agents Erickson brought with him. Of the five of them, only Erickson, Ross, and one other had accessible files.

Facial recognition identified **[ANDERS, STEPHEN]**. He was a former narcotics officer who suffered a debilitating injury during a drug raid. Six months after the injury, doctors took him off pain medication, and he subsequently skimmed substances to self-medicate. He was recruited by CSS last year after losing his position on the force and given an experimental medical treatment for his injury. He'd been sober at least since joining CSS.

Anders had also been the one man who stepped forward to intervene when Erickson first aimed a gun at Ian. Ava could work with that. She set a new designation for him.

```
[ANDERS // potential ally]
```

The other two men had no file available. They must have joined CSS after her access to CyberSolutions' servers had been severed when Nicholas withdrew from the company.

"Take him to the truck," said Erickson. "Don't hurt him unless I give the order."

Ross nodded. He hauled Ian toward the door. It hung by one remaining hinge, the bottom half shattered and scattered upon the ground from when the team had blown it to get inside.

Ian struggled against the hold. "No!"

Ava was ready for the parasite this time. //*Let them go. He'll be out of the crossfire.*/

A second passed. She shifted her weight. She flexed her fingers. Ava exhaled, slow and steady. Control remained hers.

    [probability of mission success: 46% ↑]

"No! Aurora!"

Ava stilled. The name stirred unwanted, intrusive memories. Memories of Ian, of a lifetime with him. Memories belonging to another. He cried for her again, for Aurora. His mother, for all intents and purposes.

The pleading struck a painful chord.

Ian thrashed. His head twisted, and he dug his teeth in. Ross cried out, trying to dislodge the boy from his forearm. Ross stumbled, losing his hold. Ian's blue eyes flashed fiercely at his captor and he spat at his face.

A mixture of blood and saliva dripped down Ross' chin. He recoiled, grimacing in disgust. He lifted the gun, readying to strike Ian with the butt of the pistol. "You little—"

Erickson sighed. "What did I say?"

Ross stiffened, face contorted in pain and anger. He nodded stiffly, choosing to give up trying to drag Ian. He instead manhandled him, throwing Ian over one shoulder. He stalked outside as the boy beat his small fists upon his back.

They were gone.

[stress level: 96% ↓]

Ava doubted Ross would try disobeying the order again. He'd wait for Erickson before acting. And with Ian removed from the immediate threat, stress levels coming down, and the parasite yielding control, Ava reassessed the situation.

[probability of mission success: 47% ↑]

Acceptable under the circumstances. She ran a new scenario, the program simulating outcomes for any action and counteraction. She prioritized systems, optimizing for combat.

"You do anything," Erickson's voice dripped with grim promise. "Anything at all? I'll have Ross put a bullet in the kid's head within three seconds."

//*Three seconds...?*/

Ava could work with that.

[probability of mission success: 51% ↑]

Anders shifted. His hand lingered on his sidearm. She couldn't be sure of his intentions, but either way, his position on the far side of the room meant he wouldn't be her first target anyway.

Erickson withdrew his phone, shaking it meaningfully. "Do I have your cooperation, Avalanche?"

The program was nearly finished calculating. She monitored the progress silently.

One of the men took the silence to be acquiescence. He withdrew a pair of heavy silver cuffs from his belt. She suspected those were tailored to her unique physiology, perhaps even made from the same alloy. Erickson was aware of many aspects of her build. He'd been one of the people Nicholas reported progress to, albeit informally. He would know anything less than something specific to her would be useless.

Ava couldn't allow those cuffs to close around her wrists. Not if she was going to win this fight.

The final calculation stopped.

Ava was ready.

> *Ian stared at his favorite red hoodie in horror. "Why is it pink?"*

The intrusive vision came projected in front of her eyes, and Ava was unprepared for it. She tried to shut it down, tried to counter it, but she'd disabled too many systems in preparation for a fight. It continued to play despite her best efforts.

> *Aurora studied the article of clothing, head tilting. "I ... I don't know." She couldn't recall the act of washing it from her records. "I must have added bleach to the ... the mop bucket."*

The man stopped in front of her. He studied her cautiously, lights glinting off the cuffs in his hands.

> *"...mop bucket?"*

Ava struggled to focus. The memory lingered, keeping her torn between the danger of the present and a nonsensical memory from a past belonging to another.

> *Aurora nodded. "The mop ... no ... the ... the..." She sought the words. Yet, like the memory of washing the hoodie, she couldn't find the words she was searching for.*

Ava struggled. //Washing machine! It's called a washing machine! Now let me go!// Her fingers twitched. They would be captured at this rate.

> *"I'll just..." Aurora moved to throw the shirt away. She'd ruined it. She kept ruining things. And ruined things needed to be discarded. Besides, he hated pink. His favorite color was red.*

The man took a hold of her wrist. She didn't resist. She couldn't.

> *Ian took hold of her wrist. He pulled her arm forward —*

Sensation and control came back in an instant, and Ava could only react as the cuffs descended toward her exposed wrist. She retracted her arm sharply, pulling him forward. Her wrist evaded the cuff.

> *Instead of landing in the trash bin when Aurora's fingers released, the shirt landed directly into Ian's awaiting hand. He grinned at her.*

Momentum carried the cuff down and it snapped into place. His exposed wrist gleamed with burnished silver.

> *"It's still my favorite," Ian said, shrugging the bleached hoodie on. "See? It's fine. Pink is cool."*

The man blinked, dumbfounded.

[probability of mission success: 56% ↑]

Ava took possession of the other arm before the man could react. She secured the second cuff to his other wrist, twisting her hips and pressing her back against his front as she pulled. He vaulted over her shoulder and crashed into the opposing wall.

//One.../

Erickson scrambled for his phone. To call for backup, to issue the order to terminate Ian. She ripped the arms off the old maintenance docking station in the corner, detaching a long apparatus meant to hold androids stationary, and swung it like a baseball bat.

The end of it whipped across Erickson's face. His phone clattered to the ground. She kicked it away with her next step.

//Two.../

Another man drew a gun from its holster. Ava anticipated the most likely trajectories based on his aim and advanced, throwing the hefty apparatus at him as a distraction.

He dodged it, but her processors sped up, and in her mind, it was as if time slowed while his finger curled around the trigger—

Ava sidestepped the first shot. His eyes widened. She took another step forward. He pulled the trigger again. She ducked beneath it. One step away.

He grew desperate, pulling the trigger again and again. She avoided each bullet, diverting his arm by the fifth. There was a gasp to the side, a cry of pain from Anders, but Ava stayed focused on her current target.

//Three…/

Approximately one hundred sixty pounds of pressure and his right radius broke. He wrenched away from her with a scream, gun slipping from his feeble grasp.

Ava caught the weapon.

[probability of mission success: 73% ↑↑↑]

It fit comfortably in her hand, its weight grimly familiar. She caressed the ridges of the trigger, and another memory played, this one all her own.

> *Ava stared at the gun on the table. "And what was I intended to be?"*

The man stared at her, eyes wide and fearful. She could end his life with the barest hint of pressure. He knew it too.

> *Nicholas pursed his lips. "A weapon," he admitted, voice soft. "You were designed as a weapon."*

Ava knew nothing about this man. But … he would have stood by while Erickson murdered an innocent child.

For being an inconvenience.

Ava pulled the trigger.

The man hit the ground. She stood, unwavering, as he rolled onto his back with a choking, gurgling noise as blood pooled from the wound. A shot to incapacitate. She should have killed him outright. But he could survive … with proper medical attention.

Ava was still learning the concept of mercy. This was the only grace they'd receive from her.

The other man, still sprawled on the ground near the wall, struggled to free himself from the cuffs as she took two steps closer.

He shook his head, managing to get his knees under himself, trying to rise to his feet.

"Wait, please—"

Another shot. This man groaned, slumping forward before falling over. He too could live.

One remained standing. Anders leaned against the mangled android maintenance station, blood spilling between fingers pressed against his side. He'd been tagged by the stray bullet. He had a gun clutched in his other hand. Anders met her eyes, chest heaving. His fingers clenched and unclenched from the gun. He brought it forward slowly, his grip loosening until it was pinched between two of his fingers. He knelt with a grimace to set it on the floor.

"This isn't what I signed up for," he said, voice gruff and laced with pain. "It was supposed to be a bonus paycheck for simple asset recovery. No one said anything about hurting kids."

Anders emphasized his words by lifting both hands in surrender. He kicked the gun away next. It confirmed what Ava suspected. There were lines this man wasn't willing to cross.

Ava re-categorized him as a non-threat. She felt secure enough to turn her back to him and focus her attention on Erickson. He'd risen, unsteady, mouth bloody from the hit she'd dealt him. He took a step back when he realized her attention was on him. The coward spun, eyes wild.

Erickson had run from her at the compound too, after driving a knife into Nicholas' back. She wouldn't let him do it again. The others could live. They were insignificant. But Erickson ... this man was going to die. She considered the gun in her hand. He was an easy target, staggering over debris left by the explosives his team used to break the door down, broad back open and exposed.

//No.../

Erickson would die, but she wouldn't shoot him in the back. She wasn't like him. She would look him in the eye as she killed him.

Ava bent at the waist, selecting a tool from the ground. A chrome-plated wrench. She weighed it in her hand. It was 24 inches in length and 7.80 pounds. Enough to hurt, to incapacitate.

Erickson was within a foot of the door. She drew her arm back and let the wrench sail. It thudded against his retreating back. He stumbled into the wall with a cry, and the tool clattered to the floor. He landed sprawled over more debris.

Ava approached with slow, deliberate steps. A predator stalking prey. He was already on the move, rolling over and scrambling backward. Something dark twisted up her thoughts with him vulnerable. His back collided with the wall.

"No! Avalanche, wait, I—"

"My name ... is Ava."

"A-Ava. Please, I'm sorry, I—"

Death is not a concept most androids have the presence of mind to contemplate. Ava understood it in ways others didn't. Her purpose was death. She was programmed with more ways to destroy than not.

Ava could sympathize with the human desire to survive. The permanence of death was to be feared, even for her. She wanted to preserve her existence the same as anyone, but Erickson begging for his life did nothing to tug at her sympathies.

It strengthened her desire to end him.

Erickson stared pleadingly, eyes spilling over with fat tears that left streaks of dust on his face. She'd never seen a grown man cry. She supposed staring death in the face could force even the cruelest of people to confront their emotions.

"Goodbye, Erickson. Thank you for teaching me about human behavior. Your many lessons over the years have been most informative."

"Wait!" Erickson said, palms pressing into the dust and shattered glass. "Don't do this! I can help you!"

Ava knelt in front of him. "Help me?"

"Yes! I-I won't be the last they send!" He pressed himself harder against the wall. "They'll never stop hunting you. You're nothing but a rogue asset to them! They think … you belong to them, even if Nick gave them something else to fulfill the contract."

"I belong to no one."

"Yes … I … I know—"

"None of this is your concern anymore."

"Please. I-I was his friend. I was *your* friend! I can help. Just … tell me … how."

There might have been a time when Paul Erickson was a true friend. He hadn't been there when Nicholas first brought her online, but he'd been there for many milestones. He'd even taught her how to play cards, laughing when she won using probabilities.

Ava touched the side of his face. He nodded, a hopeful, relieved light entering his eyes.

"Friend…?" Ava trailed her fingers toward his fragile throat. He choked when she dug them into his trachea. His fingernails left welts and scratches on his neck as he clawed desperately along the armored plating of her arm. "My *friend*?"

Nicholas had trusted this man. She'd trusted him too. He'd been a constant, friendly presence in her life. She liked him once. And now Nicholas was dead, and Ava learned from her mistakes.

"Ava … please…"

"You ordered a raid on our home. You tried to take me captive. You murdered Nicholas, a man you claimed was your *best friend*."

Ava punctuated each point with a tightening grip. It would be easy to close her fist. To rip his throat out.

"If you were our friend, you would have warned us they were coming, not use your own access codes to let them into the compound. Your friendship is a lie. It meant nothing. And now? You mean nothing to me."

Ava had killed people before. She killed everyone at the compound in an attempt to get to Nicholas. It was necessary then.

> *The knife clattered to the floor, the blade's tip stained red. Bodies everywhere. She killed them. She killed them all.*

Last time it was self-defense. She'd been weakened. Striking out, barely aware of her own actions. Desperate to get to Nicholas before they could, and desperate to escape when she failed him. She littered the compound, her home, with bodies.

//What's one more?/

Ava was what they made her, after all.

This time it would be justice. Justice for what happened to Nicholas. Justice for what they wanted to do to her. Justice for what they tried to do to the kid.

> *Aurora combed her fingers through Ian's fine hair. "What happened to your parents was a tragedy," she said, pressing a kiss to his temple. "But the man responsible is in prison. He's faced justice for his crime. What your uncle wants is vengeance. He might lose you because of it."*

Ava tightened her fingers even more, teeth gnashing together.

//No one asked your opinion, parasite./

As if in reply, a piece of the same memory replayed. An echo, stuck in her mind. She'd often heard Nicholas complain about things getting stuck in his head. Lyrics, quotes, phrases…

> *"He might lose you because of it."*

Apparently, the same was possible for Ava. Instead of something innocuous, the thing stuck in her mind was a persistent AI.

//*Damn you. Get out of my head.*/

"No, Erickson. You're no friend." Ava struggled to remain focused. "You're an enemy. And wasn't it always you advocating violence against enemies?"

Erickson tried shaking his head. "Please ... tell me ... what you ... want."

"I want you to die."

Ava actively squeezed. Petechiae dotted along the sides of wild, reddening eyes. His fingernails drew blood down his neck as he renewed efforts to escape in earnest. She was stronger. And she was going to watch the life drain from him.

A part of Ava knew Nicholas would have been disappointed. A larger part, fueled by pain and rage, didn't care anymore.

> *Ian sobbed into her chest. "Please. Please don't go. I need you."*

Ava eased her grip. She blinked as Erickson drew away, sucking in a broken breath. Her jaw ticked, but she let him withdraw.

Erickson coughed, and it was a deep, desperate sound.

```
[mission objective —
protect IAN // escape together]
```

There was still one more target. Ross still had Ian. She hadn't forgotten. She ... got distracted. She didn't want the kid hurt because of this, though.

//*Damn it.*/

There was a more immediate priority than vengeance.

"Where did Ross take the kid?"

"Armored truck," Erickson rasped. "Outside ... main gate."

"How many agents?"

"No ... more."

"Do you know anything else of value?"

A long pause. His eyes shifted. She recognized the tell.

> *Paul grinned, eyes shifting. He'd thrown all his chips in. A bluff, considering all the cards in play. "You going to bet, Avalanche, or analyze my micro-expressions all night?"*

Ava won that game. She wasn't playing anymore.

"N-no."

"Then you've outlived your usefulness."

"No! W-wait! I do … I know something! I–"

Anders shouted behind her, "Look out!"

A boot scuffed in the dust, and Ava turned–

The bullet impacted, and Ava's head jerked back.

No pain. She couldn't process it the same as humans. A sense of wrongness. Optical damage, vision flickering. Audio processors looped with white noise. Everything sounded far away.

[error]

A data log compiled with various malfunctions.

> *"You were designed as a weapon."*

Ava fell. She was on the ground, staring out the broken door.

Dust and glass and shards of wood pressed along her side. She lifted her head, dazed.

> *Ian held her hand. "I promise, Mama." He cried openly, squeezing her fingers. "I'll fix you."*

The memories bled together. One after another.

> *Nicolas fell. She screamed, dodging bullets to reach him. Too much blood.*

Nicholas. Ian.

> *Ava looked at the trusting kitten in the cradle of her arms. Ian giggled. She grazed it with a fingertip, cataloging the sensation. Ava couldn't tell what was hers and what belonged to the interloper.*

> *Ian was a baby, blue-eyed and small. The kitten's fur felt soft against her sensors … nothing like the cold metal of the discarded gun on the table. Nicolas remained still, unmoving … dead.*

The room spun. She couldn't focus. Junkyard. Shack. CSS. Erickson. Ross.

Ava brought a hand to her temple. Her fingers slid sluggishly through something sticky and wet. Not blood. She was an android. Her veins were filled with liquid coolant and a conductive fluid which sent electrical currents throughout her system. Blood of a sort. She'd never seen it before.

Violet and viscous like the mixed-berry syrup Nicholas loved with his pancakes. Her finger encountered a small indention above her left ear, small and round with raised edges.

A bullet hole. She turned, rising on shaking arms.

Ross. The bastard shot her in the head.

Ava couldn't judge how deep the bullet went. Enough to rupture the fine intravenous lines running through her head. She was positive other systems were damaged too by the steady stream of errors flooding her vision. She blinked them away, shaking her head roughly.

/ / Focus. /

Audio returned. Distorted with static, words breaking but audible. Vision cleared, memories settled.

Ross held the gun aloft, preparing to shoot again. Not her. He was aiming elsewhere. He assumed the threat was gone with a headshot.

"Should have fallen in line, Anders."

Anders was too far away to retrieve his weapon, too weak from his injuries to fight. He was going to die.

> *A rumble erupted from the kitten as it sunk deeper into her embrace. She'd found it outside in the snow, scouring among the trash cans. She stroked it tenderly, watching vibrant eyes fall shut, calm and peaceful. Nothing like the violence programmed in her head.*

Ava moved, arm wavering, gun in hand. She set a target [upper right thoracic cavity] and fired.

Ross collapsed with a dull thud.

> *Ava curled her arms around the kitten. "… I don't want to be a weapon." She peeked at Nicholas, expecting disappointment. She saw only sadness.*

Ava stared at the body. She'd aimed, same as the others, to disable [possible parenchymal lung injury // pneumohemothorax // excessive hemorrhaging]. Even with precision targeting, death was a possibility. But she hadn't aimed to kill.

This was a misfire. Her impaired vision, malfunctions, wavering hand … something went terribly wrong because Ross was dead. The bullet pierced his zygomatic, brown hair saturated with blood and brain matter from where it exited the back of his skull.

> *Bodies everywhere. She killed them.*

Last time was to protect Nicolas. This time was still to protect someone.

//Why do I feel like this, then?/

> *Aurora released the cricket into the yard. "All life is precious."* Ava frowned. *//Oh./*

"Thanks for that." Anders leaned against the wall, breathing heavily. His dark apparel was stained darker, fabric shining between red-stained fingers.

A scuffle sounded, and Ava turned to find Erickson attempting to flee again. She stood, slow and on unsteady feet. She didn't bother with theatrics, just shot him once through the knee. He howled in pain, collapsing to the floor in a heap.

//Justice./ Ava aimed again. She ignored the small part of her whispering *vengeance.*

This was her choice. She wanted Erickson to die.

Resolve hardened. It steadied her arm.

"He's alive! Ni … Nic…"

Behind them, the shallow breaths of the others echoed in the stillness. She gripped the gun tight enough that the metal gave, conforming to her hand.

"Nick." Erickson curled in on himself, tears flowing freely. "He's … alive."

Ava kept the gun where it was. "You stabbed him."

"I did. I did, but … not…"

Ava stared at him, searching for any hint of a lie. She couldn't detect deception. The physical trauma from the gunshot and strangulation could be messing with her readings though. It could still be a ploy. But … could she risk it?

"I watched him die."

"No!" Erickson shook his head wildly. "He's hurt, almost bled out … his heart stopped for two minutes. But … I swear … I swear, Ava. He's … alive."

[DECHART, NICHOLAS // status unknown]

Ava saw the knife. Saw Nicolas fall and made assumptions based on the amount of blood beneath him. She'd been forced to flee before getting confirmation.

It was plausible. A chance.

Indecision warred within Ava. "Where?"

"Intensive care … CSS medical facility."

"Which facility?"

Erickson sucked in another breath. His eyes drooped. "Location … on my … my …" His eyes rolled into the back of his head, his body slumping to the side.

Anders shifted. "Is he dead?"

"No."

Ava monitored all of their vitals closely. Erickson was hurt. Trauma and blood loss, hyperventilation. The man was still in better condition than Anders or the other two on the floor.

"Are you going to kill him?"

Anders stared at her intently. He'd found his gun. Ava tightened her fingers around the deformed grip in response. She wasn't sure what his intentions were. She didn't care. She'd never see him again after today.

"No."

Erickson bought himself time. She needed him alive.

"Are you planning to shoot?"

Anders kept the gun loose at his side. "Not if he stays down."

"I meant at me."

Anders raised a brow. "You recovered from a headshot. I'm not stupid." He holstered the gun.

[stress level: 31% ↓↓]

Ava approached him. He stiffened but didn't back away.

"Who are you?" Anders studied her features. "*What* are you? You look like an android, but ..."

"I need your belt."

"... What?"

Ava rolled her eyes. She took hold of the buckle, and Anders went rigid. His jaw clenched, but she focused on unfastening the belt. She took a moment to assess his wound.

The bullet missed his liver. He'd lost blood. Less than the others. He'd be fine.

Ava pulled the belt free and stepped back, returning to Erickson's side.

"Why does CyberSolutions want you so badly?" Anders persisted. "He was right. They won't stop. You have to know that."

Ignoring him and tearing Erickson's pant leg to assess the damage, Ava was surprised. Even without her usual precision, the wound was localized enough. The amount of blood expected.

Nothing fatal. The man might even regain the use of his leg one day … provided he was telling the truth.

Erickson remained unconscious as Ava wrapped the belt around his upper thigh. His leg gave a feeble twitch when the makeshift tourniquet pulled tight to stanch the blood. He didn't wake, and she secured it around his limb.

"Help…"

Ava turned.

One of the other men stared at her. She stood, and he swallowed, blood trickling from the corner of his mouth. The silver cuffs chinked together behind him.

"Please…"

"Hang on, Mike." Anders tried to move from the wall, faltered with a labored breath, eyes clenching shut tight.

   //designation [**MIKE**] accepted

Mike blinked, lips trembling. "Help me…"

Ava stared at his prone form coolly.

> *"I know," said Nicolas, hand heavy on her shoulder. "I know this isn't what you want. I know you don't want to hurt people, be this … weapon I made you to be."*

It would be easy to ignore the pleading. Ava owed these people nothing. They worked for a company that sought to possess her. They cared for no one who got in their way. But…

> *Ava looked at her creator. "Will you help me? Be something else?"*

Ava steadied herself.

> *Nicholas smiled. His eyes crinkled deeper watching her hug the cat. "You already are, Ava."*

"P-please."

Ava made her choice.

Mike watched her approach, resigned fear evident. Ava knelt at his side and found his phone in a pocket. The lock screen appeared. A photograph of a black female labrador. The animal appeared well cared for. Loved. Even the worst sort of people were capable of love.

"Nice dog." Ava held the phone to his face to unlock it and accessed the emergency features with a thought. "I prefer cats."

Mike stayed silent, uncertainty on his face.

"An ambulance will arrive at the junkyard in approximately ten minutes. You should live until then." She tucked the phone away and took hold of his chin. "Come after me again, and I'll find a new family to adopt your dog after I carve your brain from your skull. Understand?"

Mike swallowed. "I do." His eyes shifted to his dying companion, sprawled on his back and breathing shallowly beside them. "And Ralph… will he I-live too?"

Ava looked to the man in question, adjusting his designation to [**RALPH**]. "Yes. I requested multiple RA units and advised dispatch of the injuries sustained."

"Thank … you." His eyes drifted closed. "S-sorry."

Ava wasn't worried. Mike had a good chance of survival, as did Ralph. She turned to find Anders eying her critically and scrutinized him right back.

[**CAUTION**]

`//internal temperature reaching critical levels`

Ava blinked the warning away and drew in a cooling breath. She'd been running too hot since tailoring her active systems for combat readiness.

It was time to reset for standard performance.

Systems came back online slowly with the damage to her cranial structure. She blinked, slowly, and frowned as her freshly restored sensors picked up a new signal.

Faint. Practically a whisper.

Ava studied it. "You activated a distress beacon," she said to Anders. She considered the implications. "You're not with CSS."

Anders gave a small shake of his head. "No."

"...And your name isn't Stephen Anders."

The matter-of-fact tone earned a laugh. He regretted it after, wincing as it jostled his wound.

"Not exactly."

Ava assessed him. "Undercover?"

Silence.

Ava nodded. "How long do I have before your backup arrives?"

The man glanced at his watch. "About three minutes. Maybe less."

//Better than three seconds./

The parasite sent a reminder.

> *Aurora smiled as Ian pulled her along. He tugged her hand when she slowed, staring at her with impatient eyes. "Are you coming?"*

Ian was waiting. She had to find him. Ava wasn't sure what to do with him when she did find him. She could always leave him for the police to find. He was out of immediate danger and she wasn't his mother. He didn't need her or deserve to be entangled in this situation any longer.

> *They passed a store. Androids caught her eye. None were activated. Lifesize dolls on small box podiums with four-digit price tags. Any one of them might be the replacement Ian's uncle purchased once he became aware of her increasing malfunctions. If he decided to purchase another one. He might decide to leave Ian all alone. She ... didn't like that prospect. Maybe she should grab a pamphlet...?*

Ava sighed. *//Even you have to admit he'd be safer away from me./*

> *Ian took the pamphlet. His brows furrowed, and he put it back. "We don't need one of those." He curled his fingers around hers. "I just need you. I'll always need you."*

The parasite was annoyingly persistent.

//*What the hell am I supposed to do with a kid?*/

>   *Aurora studied the math worksheet. She gave Ian a smile. "We'll figure this out together, okay?"*

Ava lifted Erickson and threw him over a shoulder.

Anders stared keenly as she made to leave. "You won't get far. Let me take you in. We can work out … whatever this is. You don't have to do this alone."

"I'm not alone."

"You never answered my question. What are you? Why do they want you?"

Ava paused by the door. "I'm an avalanche, and it doesn't matter why they want me. I'm going to bury them all."

The drones whirled outside, and she stepped through the threshold, gun raised–

Something slammed hard into Ava. She tried to reinstate the combat protocols. She hadn't expected Anders to attack. But... he was behind her.

This attack came from the front, arms wrapping around her like a vice. Her hands moved as well, coming to rest on the attacker's back.

"Mama..."

Ava stiffened. Her hand froze. "Ian."

They were standing in front of a large armored truck, and Ian clung to her as if his life depended on it. He had fresh bruises on his face.

Ava stilled. //*How am I here?*/ She'd taken one step outside. She had no memory of the walk here or finding and unlocking the truck.

Alarm filled her as Ian buried his face into her neck. She'd obviously come out here to release him. She didn't remember it. Why couldn't she remember? She stiffened, noticing something else.

//*Where the hell is Erickson?*/

The man was gone.

Had the bullet caused even more damage? Had it damaged her memory banks? Or...

[stress level: 64% ↑↑↑]

The parasite. Had it taken complete control? She'd been aware last time. Or was it Aurora herself? She had memory problems. Problems so deeply entangled throughout her system the best option for repair had been to decommission her. Had those transferred over with the memories and personality matrix?

None were acceptable possibilities.

The boy let out a rapid-fire stream of questions. "What happened? Did they hurt you? Where are they?"

"Most are incapacitated ... one is dead."

"...dead?" Ian swallowed, blinking hard. "Which one?"

"The one who brought you to the truck."

Ian curled his fingers into the fabric of her jacket. Ava frowned. She suspected something happened before Ross returned to the shack.

"How?"

"I shot him."

Ian pulled back. "But ... androids can't hurt people. You can't even hold a gun."

Ava clenched her jaw. This child had no idea. He was too innocent. Too innocent to be involved. She stepped back to study him. Her fingers curled into a fist. She couldn't take him with her.

> *Ian stood in the junkyard, alone and with his back to her. He didn't want her to see him cry.*

A drone flew overhead.

Ava shot the threat from the sky. It crashed beside the truck and shattered. She stared at the cracked camera lens as the lights died out. She'd been aiming for that lens but hit the motor.

> *Aurora joined anyway. She took his hand. "We'll meet again."*

"Holy shit," said Ian, wincing a beat later as if expecting a reprimand. "You … shot it."

Ava didn't scold him. She spotted another drone. It flew higher out of range, going far over the trees bordering the west side of the junkyard, too far away for her weapon's caliber. She lost sight of it.

>   *"I promise, Mama. I'll fix you."*

More would come. Police were already on their way and CyberSolutions would continue to pursue her. She needed to run.

>   *"And I'll never leave you, Ian."*

```
[mission objective —
protect IAN // escape together]
```
They needed to run.

>   *"I love you."*

Ava had no choice. "Let's go, kid."

——◄ ● ►——

T. E. LAMONTE is a writer living in New Mexico, USA. She writes primarily in science fiction and fantasy, and has previously published two short works with Lower Decks Press. When not writing, she spends her time painting and sculpting with both traditional and digital media, and spends way too much time binging reruns of her favorite television shows and movies or playing video games.

Twitter & Instagram: @BytheCandlelite

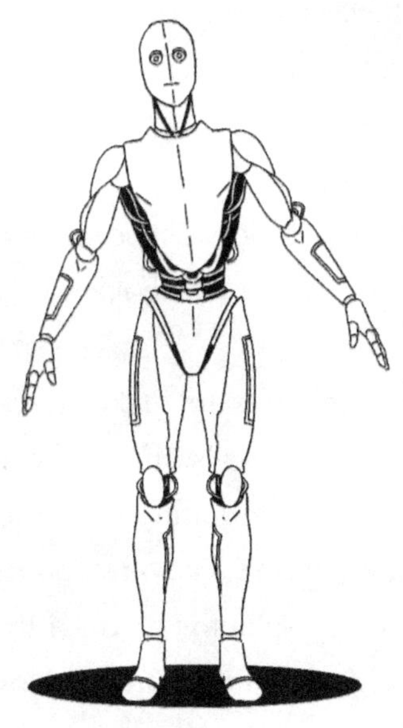

New Partner

A. L. MACDONALD

I DIDN'T NEED a new partner. It was not my idea at all. It was some corporate desk fungus down on Earth who had a random neuron event that led to me being assigned one.

It was all because of one little incident. Those earthworms down in their burrows didn't understand that space is dangerous. Why was there a gunfight on board the space station, they demanded. Why is the Moon Corporation running a protection racket under your watch, Detective Algaran?

They made it sound so bad.

Hypocrites. Earth was a cesspit of crime, but the space station was literally above it all. It was tranquil, poised on its Heavenly perch over the blue bathtub of human depravity. Up here, the worst I had to deal with was maybe a lost kid or a delinquent dock fee to be collected. The best job I ever had.

If I could just kick these Moon Corporation thugs out the airlock, I thought, then maybe I could get back to doing sweet, peaceful, lawful nothing.

I had about twenty minutes to make my way across the station from my quarters to the Admiral's office in response to his summons —yes, an actual summons, like getting called to the principal's office. Which was how I knew it wasn't a how're-you-doing sort of meeting.

It really did take twenty minutes to cross the space station. It was that big. Inside that giant wheel turning slowly, there was a nice acceleration all around the rim that made for a long walk around from my quarters to the Admiral's office in the command post. Sure, I could have cut across the hub, climbing through one of the spokes with their stomach-turning transition to microgravity, through the central axle with the docking hub, then dropped straight across the opposite spoke. But that would have been quicker. I sure wasn't in a rush to get yelled at. And I had to think up a plan to placate the Admiral or it would have been back to the cesspit of Earth for me.

My plan depended on a scrawny, twitchy, sunken-eyed man named Rego.

I found Rego at his stall in the market hall, a long strip of farmer and crafter tables on a patch of carbon-crete walkway lit by black lamp stands arching overhead. It was amazing how much work the station builders had gone to just to make our space palace look like a regular street on Earth.

Rego looked even tinier behind the mounds of hydroponically-grown fruit and vegetables stacked up at his market stall. He fiddled with the blue apron ties wrapped twice around his thin waist, his eyes warily scanning the crowds ambling past the stalls flanking the streetlike corridor. He started when he saw me. I didn't scare him on purpose. I'd just never found a way to approach the guy without him jumping out of his skin.

"Jeez, Algaran! You scared me!"

I jerked my thumb. "Come on, Admiral wants to see us."

"What?" Rego shrieked. "Why me?"

"Not you," I said. "Us. We're going to have to explain what went down with the Moon Corporation the other day and you're my witness that I was heroic and distinguished in my conduct."

"Uhh … I'm not sure that's what happened..." His face crumpled into a fractal of conflicting worry lines and uncertainty.

I waved off his objection. "You're not remembering it very well. We'll sort the details on the way. C'mon, close up. Let's go."

He gestured at his table. "I have produce here, I can't just leave it!"

I bent down and grabbed a corner of the tarp rolled up at his feet. I yanked the tarp over his precious fruit pyramids. "There," I said. "Don't worry about it. If anything goes missing, then you know a detective. Alright? Let's go."

Rego reluctantly stepped around the table and followed me as I set off. I knew he was hesitant just because he was scared of what the Moon Corporation would say if they saw him consorting with the cops, but this was bigger than that. I had to save my skin.

"You remember the name of the boss that came after you?" I prompted him.

"Yeah, it was Corvus," Rego answered.

We passed through a long glass tunnel transiting the beach area. On either side of us were long white sandy beaches gleaming under hot and bright overhead lights. Real seagulls sat on top of the glass tunnel, their droppings smeared down the glass.

"And Corvus told you she wanted money, right?" I pressed.

"Yeah. For protection, she said." Rego was a bit distracted, staring wistfully at the beaches. Beach time was expensive.

"From what? The Admiral's going to ask."

"Well, really the only threat is … Corvus. I never asked for specifics. I just give her the money so I don't get hurt."

I nodded. "That's right! That's what you tell the Admiral, okay?"

"Uhhhh…"

Just a little bit further, through the squash, tennis, and basketball gyms and we were at the administration wing, on our way to the Admiral's office.

I hated reception. It was like being put in a fridge. Nothing moved. You heard some noises indicating a bustling, busy outside world beyond sight. There was no indicator of elapsed time. You just sat, and sat, waiting for, maybe, ever.

"Admiral Kirchoff will see you now."

Admiral Kirchoff's office was bigger than my apartment. I wasn't sure, but I think it even had its own bathroom. The only downside was Admiral Kirchoff himself, barricaded behind his desk, his eyes as red as his hair and glowering at me.

He wore a faded blue blazer that gave one the impression of a naval background, but no one had ever seen him in a formal uniform or dared ask why that was. So we called him the Admiral. It was the best way to get on his good side. He certainly used the impression of military service while talking to the military members of the Board of Directors down on Earth.

"You took your sweet time," Kirchoff rumbled as Rego and I shuffled into the room. "When I call you to report to me, I expect you to hustle." He was a big man, not your usual spacer. It was tough to fill out on rehydrated protein gruel that tasted like chalk, soy and chocolate … or chalk, soy and vanilla … or chalk, soy and strawberry.

"Sorry, sir," I said.

"The Moon Corporation," the Admiral grunted. He liked to get straight to the point. "They have filed a complaint against you."

My mouth dropped open. "What? They, of all people, made a complaint against me? Sir! That's absurd!"

"The complaint indicates that you used excessive force, injured several of their party, and caused harm to their business."

I felt like a plugged drain as I tried to make so many protests all at once that my mouth just stuck open, only a slight, strangled noise coming out.

"'Business'?'" I finally spat out. "It's a protection racket! They pick on the traders here!"

The Admiral spread his hands. "Detective, the Moon Corporation claims to be a perfectly legitimate and terribly mis-characterized organization."

"They're crooks!" I spat. "Bullies!" I cast a frantic gaze at Rego, my one lifeline, my only hope. "Rego, tell them!"

Rego's bony little hands twisted. He kept his eyes safely buried in the deck plates. "There was a fight," he allowed very carefully. "I didn't see much."

I groaned. Rego was not going to be much help.

I spun back toward the Admiral. "Look, sir, this is just a little misunderstanding. You see, this is a very big station, there's always going to be a few little incidents, and it's just me against all these—"

"Enough!" Kirchoff growled. "The Board has caught wind of this and sees this as an opportunity to roll out their new robotic policing prototype. You said it's just you... well, now they're assigning you a new partner. It'll be here on the next launch."

"A robot?" I said. "I'm supposed to work with a robot?"

Kirchoff's eyes bored into mine, and all at once he seemed to be looming over me.

"That's what you get for screwing around! Now. You'll get evidence of the protection racket you say is taking place on the station and then you'll present that to me, like a real detective is supposed to do. Dismissed."

. . .

A robot. A freaking robot. The Board was obsessed with replacing living, breathing, eating, waste-producing, paid humans with robots wherever they could, especially in orbit where supporting a human cost thousands of credits a day.

I'd been hearing for years that robots were getting better and smarter. I'd always told myself I had time, that my job was complicated. I was safe. But now, here I was, standing at the airlock, waiting to salute the sunset of my career.

The airlock hissed as the pressures equalized. I didn't even know if I wanted to look at the stupid sleek metal and the stupid superior sensors reading far beyond my own narrow electromagnetic spectrum. I found myself gritting my teeth.

The airlock door swung open. I couldn't help myself; curiosity yanked my eyes up to see the robot emerge.

There it was. A humanoid with a shell of polished silver over its chest but wiry linkages exposed at its shoulders and hips. Its actuators hummed as it jerkily reached a three-fingered claw hand out to steady itself while it lifted one foot to clear the airlock threshold. The face was a shiny blank oval punctuated by two round white eyes that never squinted or frowned so the robot looked permanently stunned.

"Hello. I am Cadet Axcel. Pleased to meet you," it said in a stilted, robotic voice, cutting each syllable short in the hallmark of synthetic voices composed of prerecorded words stitched together.

Then it fell flat on its face.

"Oh. Dear." Axcel said.

Wow. You never really know what your boss thinks of your skills until you see the thing they try to replace you with.

I moved forward to help it. "Come on," I gasped, hauling on the big metal brute. "Up you get." The damn thing was heavy as hell.

We got it back on its feet by individually organizing each segmented limb and placing the wide rectangular feet flat on the deck. Powerful exposed pistons in the robot's thighs and calves jerked it up to standing. Once it looked stable, I slowly released my steadying hands and stepped back.

"All good?" I asked.

"Yes. Thank you." The robot head fastened its unfocused eye dots on me. I think I heard a CPU fan hum at high speed. "I surmise you are Detective Algaran."

"Yes," I said. "Great work." I made sure to ladle in the extra sarcasm.

"Thank you, Detective!" Axcel said.

Oh boy.

"Look," I said, "let's get something straight here: I'm not your friend, okay? In fact, I don't want you here. So just shut up and stay out of my way while I finish up this case and then you can get out of here."

There was zero reaction from the robot. No shock, no anger, nothing.

"Okay," it said. "I will leave."

I frowned. "What?"

"You stated that my services are not required. I will leave."

I held out my hand. "No—no, look: you don't get it. The folks on the Board want you here, so you're going to stay. Just stay out of my way, alright?"

"Understood. I shall power down. You may repower me when the case is complete."

I wanted to slap it. "No, you're not going to just sit there. Just follow me."

"Understood."

"But not too close!"

"Understood."

"And do exactly what I tell you to do."

"Understood."

I looked Axcel up and down one more time. I dunno, I was expecting some sign of sarcasm. Some pushback of some sort. I mean, what self-respecting officer would allow themself to be relegated to ride-along status so quickly?

Well, the kind that was just circuits connecting inputs as directly as possible to outputs. There was no meandering through distractions of pride, esteem, or ambition. Those were all branches of the self. What I was dealing with was the blank stare and wholehearted obedience of a dog.

I glanced back at the robot lumbering after me in a chaotic struggle of hissing pistons and whirring actuators as it concentrated fully on just staying upright.

This could be fun. Like having a stupid pet tank.

Then it fell on its face again.

· · ·

I didn't brief Axcel on the case so much as muse aloud about it while it sat watching me down a couple of pints at the Space Hub Pub.

"The problem is no one wants to speak up against Corvus," I said. "I thought Rego might, but, like the others, he shut right up when I tried to get a statement."

Axcel said nothing.

"Hello? Are you on?" I asked.

"Yes," it responded. "I was instructed to 'shut up'".

Right. Good robot.

"Anyway," I continued, "we just need to find a way to catch her in the act, figure out where she corners these poor merchants and forces them to pay her for protection."

Axcel finally moved, turning its head toward the waiter. "Excuse me."

The waiter, a young lad probably in his late teens with a barely controlled mop of curly brown hair, stopped mid-stride and angled over to our table, giving Axcel a long stare. "What can I get you, uhhh … sir?"

Axcel blinked. "Thank you. I would like to know the location of the Moon Corporation leader Corvus' illegal business dealings with–"

"Shut up, shut up!" I hissed and waved my hand in front of Axcel as if I was trying to chop the words out of the air. The waiter gave me a wide-eyed stare and backpedalled away.

"What the hell are you doing?!" I growled.

"You wanted to know where–"

"Forget it! Stop. Just stop." I looked around the pub. Everyone appeared to still be engrossed in their cups or the wide screens banding the walls. I sighed and rubbed my head. "My God, you're terrible at this."

"How will you find the location if you do not ask?" the dumb metal can-head asked aloud.

"Look, people don't work like that. They don't just rat out other people and endanger themselves for no reason."

"It benefits everyone to assist the police in removing a criminal."

"You'd think so, but no. They just want a quiet day, to make some money, and go to sleep safe and sound. That's it. The only way you'll get them to go out of their way for you is to scare them or bribe them."

"Bribes are illegal. Shall I scare the waiter then?"

"No!" I blurted. "No, no, just leave it to me. I know who we can scare. He's already half scared as a default."

· · ·

Rego tried to duck behind his fruit stand as I approached, but in his panic he nudged his cart. A dribble of apples sent him scrambling on his hands and knees to corral them.

"Hi, Rego!" I called cheerfully as I stepped up to the stand with Axcel clunking along behind me. "How's business?"

"Fine!" Rego answered quickly, scooping his apples into his apron. "Now go away. Cops scare off business."

"Oh yeah? More than being shut down for improper documentation of disinfection of moon mites?" I asked, leaning against the cart.

"Shhh!" Rego hissed. His eyes darted side to side. "People will hear you! What are you even talking about? I have all my papers!"

"Are you sure? It'll take days for you to prove all that for every shipment you've taken and sold. I'm within my rights to have you shut down in the meantime."

Rego's mouth dropped open. His shoulders slumped. "Come on, Detective Algaran … why would you do that?"

"Relax, Rego. I just want to know one thing, and then I'll leave you alone."

"What is it?" Rego frowned.

"Just tell me where you meet with Corvus."

Rego froze. It was like seeing a computer processor lock up. His eyes stayed wide, and his mouth stayed open but he couldn't work out a word. I started to wonder if he had a reset button.

"Rego?"

"I … I can't…" Rego said at last. He seemed to deflate even further. "Please … just please don't shut me down."

I plucked an apple from the stand and touched my finger to the payment pad. "I'll give you some time to think about it, Rego."

Axcel's earth-shaking stomp was a nice foreboding emphasis on my exit.

"What happens now?" Axcel asked as we passed into a narrow corridor outside the market street.

"We'll check in with him tomorrow," I said. "He'll talk. He just needs to stew and worry for a bit."

That's when I noticed the corridor was empty. Right after that, I saw a figure step out of a shadowed doorway and block the corridor. I heard other footsteps behind us and the hairs raising all along the back of my neck told me I was in deep trouble. My fears were confirmed by the sound of a gun charging: a long, high-pitched whine building to a crescendo like a small air raid siren.

The light fell on the figure in front of me and I saw a tall woman, thickly-built with muscles straining the fabric of her coat sleeves, rings studded all around the outside of her ears and nostrils, scars cut across her sharp cheekbones, and short black hair plastered flat on her scalp. Looking at her enormous electro-stimmed arms, I was sure she could snap my neck in a second.

"Corvus," I said, wishing my voice didn't sound so high-pitched with terror.

"I heard you were looking for me," she rumbled.

• • •

I had my tasegun with me. A really good one. Fourteen charge clip magazine in the handle, nano-tipped charges to burrow through clothes or armour, semi-automatic, laser sight.

And it was way, way too far away, strapped to my hip. Might as well be in my old bedroom in the suburbs down on Earth.

I had to think fast. Really fast. And I actually did come up with a pretty great solution. One that could take care of two problems at once. One that would let me keep my life and also get rid of the threat to my livelihood.

"Axcel," I said, "take them down."

The next few seconds were complete bedlam. I did my best to stay out of it, dropping to the deck and crawling to the edge of the corridor as the world exploded around me.

Axcel had transformed. Several small doors had opened on its body to reveal dozens of tasegun barrels pointing in all directions. The guns fired all at once, riddling the corridor walls with spitting, sparking charges. A shot caught one of Corvus's henchmen who was too slow. He fell, his body rigid with the immobilizing charge.

I'd underestimated how many guns Corvus had brought with her. The henchmen who had scattered away from Axcel had taken refuge in recessed doorways and behind stacked storage containers nearby.

Bright bolts of plasma fire criss-crossed the narrow corridor, impacting the walls with glowing red marks that sputtered into black scorch holes. I noted that some day I'd have to confiscate those guns. The station was built with plenty of micrometeorite blast armour but firing plasma bolts at it was a universally-acknowledged Bad Idea.

Axcel shuddered and jolted as plasma bolts found their mark, impacting its smooth metal body with showers of sparks and smoke. The bullets pounded it, making it stagger and twirl. The barrage shoved its shoulder around and then punched its face, snapping its head back and turning one glowing eye into a smoking hole.

A leg piston burst with a spectacular spray of released hydraulic fluid. Axcel keeled over. Sparks snapped inside its chest and black smoke billowed out, quickly blanketing the corridor in a haze that blinded everyone, stinging our eyes and lungs. A few more shots zipped through the fog as someone blindly hoped to hit something.

"Move out!" Corvus yelled.

The firing stopped. I heard footsteps receding, then it was just the dwindling hiss of Axcel's leaking cylinder, the ticking of heated metal cooling and contracting, and the smoulder of small fires on the walls.

I crawled over to Axcel. Looking closely, the damage was even worse than I'd thought. More ominous jolts and sparks flickered inside its chest. The remaining eye stared unblinking at the ceiling.

"Are you … okay?" I asked, feeling like an idiot for saying it. The thing clearly was not okay.

"Juuussst nneeed mommmmennt," Axcel slurred.

A pool of fluid was spreading underneath it and I panicked, searching for the source to try and stop the bleeding. I gulped, suddenly feeling terrible for causing it to suffer so horribly.

I patted its chest. "It's okay, I'll get you out of here."

Axcel twitched as another circuit fused and snapped with a spark and the stink of ozone. Then it was silent.

• • •

It was stupid. It was just some machine. A bunch of steel and circuitry off an assembly plant shelf. Might as well be a motorcycle or a rifle. But here I was, dragging the thing to the engineering shops as quick as I could, like I was pulling a wounded comrade out of a war zone.

A long trail of scraped deck plates and oozing hydraulic fluid stretched out after me, an accusatory finger connecting the corridor ambush right to me, the one who had sentenced Axcel to die, miles above his home - do robots even have homes? Jesus, I was a wreck.

The workshop went dead silent as I entered. Technicians in white coveralls froze, their hands hovering over the piles of dissected machines at their work benches. One woman in cleaner-than-most coveralls, her dark hair streaked with grey pulled into a ponytail, tore her eyes away from a bank of screens standing over her work table and stared at me as I hauled Axcel's smoking, leaking, bullet-riddled robot corpse into the shop.

"What in the hell is all this?" the woman demanded. I noticed a patch on her lapel that read CHIEF ENGINEER.

I leaned back on the wall, exhausted, trying to catch my breath. I slowly slid down the wall until I was sitting on the floor.

"Ambush," I gasped. "Corvus' men. Can you fix this guy up?"

The engineer moved close to Axcel, her curiosity drawing her in. Several others left their tables, crowding close to the ruined machine. They began to mutter, the whole group of them looking like a host of shamans casting healing spells as they murmured part numbers and recounted subsystem damage.

"Can you fix him?" I repeated.

The engineer waved at me absently. "We'll try. Not much is left working on here, though. We'll let you know in a few days."

I suddenly felt completely drained. I realized it was a long walk back to my quarters.

My comm rang. I dragged myself back up, tapping the little screen.

It was the Admiral. I was to see him immediately.

Crap.

. . .

Kirchoff sure was angry.

"What in the hell are you doing!?" Kirchoff bellowed. "A gunfight on my station? You're supposed to stop people getting hurt, not light the place up!" He paused only to suck in another gulp of air to continue yelling. "The Board wants you on desk duty forever—I would have agreed if you weren't my only guy right now!!"

I just nodded, keeping my mouth shut. I didn't dare bring up the robot that I'd destroyed. My career was hanging on by a thread as it was. No need to make things worse.

Kirchoff glared at me. "Where's the robot?"

Dang it.

I gulped. "Corvus got it, sir." His face darkened so I started talking as fast as possible to head off the next outburst. "She ambushed us! We've got to arrest her. It's murder—or attempted murder. Whatever, I don't know. It's evil, is what it is."

The Admiral sighed. "I've already seen the tapes, Algaran. She was talking and you opened fire. Sure, they had you surrounded and I know you felt threatened—hell, I've been there too on patrol. But you're not some goddamned rookie. You don't start blasting when people are just talking."

Kirchoff settled in his chair behind his desk. His eyes lit on a small model of the space station and he reached out, gently lifting it from its cradle, slowly turning the metal wheel in his hands, his thumb traveling over the axle at the center of the wheel, his fingers carefully supporting the delicate solar arrays like he was touching the leaves of a live plant.

"This station has been my whole life for thirty years," he said. "I've seen her come together. I've tended her when she was damaged by fires, micrometeorites, hull breaches and fuel shortages. Whatever she's needed, I've provided."

He broke his reverie and looked straight at me. "You understand? I love this station."

He leaned forward. "Corvus' gang, walking around with plasma guns, endangering passengers, is a disease on my station. I want her off it, preferably in jail. I can arrest her for the gun possession and the fight, but if you get evidence of a protection racket, that will get her put away for a good long time. Get this scourge off my baby. The proper way. So she never comes back."

I stared at the man. He set the model back down extraordinarily gently, then crossed his huge arms and stared at me. I looked at the model.

The station was just a bunch of steel, carbon composites, nitrogen, hydrogen, oxygen, and circuitry. He was talking like it was alive. I suppose it was what we humans do to love our world. We make all of it human, even the stuff that is far from it.

"Yes, sir," I said.

Kirchoff looked at the tablet on his desk.

"At least I have proof that the Board's silly robot was a waste of time and money. I can send its pieces back to them and tell them it didn't even last a day in a cop's world."

"Oh," I said.

I should have been happy. Axcel was going away. My job was safe. Just what I'd wanted.

I just kept thinking of the bullets ripping him apart. Bullets that would have been for me.

Poor Axcel.

. . .

Axcel was out of it for days. The engineers had their work cut out for them. With station resources all set up for repairing engines and large scale life support systems, it was a big shift to work on the miniature and proprietary actuators and microcircuitry of an android. I checked in on the workshop frequently, but eventually I was politely told to get lost.

So I worked the case. I dug into Corvus' business accounts, interviewed every market hawker, and reviewed eyeball-melting amounts of security footage of the market to try to nail down any interaction between Corvus and a merchant where the victim expressed even so much as a grimace. All I found out was that wherever Corvus did the strong-arming, it wasn't in the broad daylight of the market. She wasn't stupid.

I needed a break. I went to stretch my legs and found myself going to the market. The bustle and openness was always a refreshing change from the usual station atmosphere of confined windowless corridors and recycled air. I found myself at Rego's stall, I think because I had been there more often than any other stall. Having at least the skinny man's presence near me helped offset the lack of Axcel's stomping shadow.

"Hey, Detective," Rego said warily. "Are you here to shut me down?"

Since the last conversation with him, I had been in an intense gunfight, gotten reprimanded by the Admiral, and my new partner had been mauled. I'd completely forgotten my last conversation with Rego.

"Oh," I sighed. "No. I won't do that to you."

Rego breathed deeply. "Where's your robot pal?" He asked.

I sighed. "Corvus's men shot him up pretty bad. The engineers are doing their best to fix him."

He frowned. "Sorry to hear that."

"Yeah."

I took an apple from the stack on the table, swiping my finger over the pay pad. I chewed slowly, my mind locked on the sight of Axcel's burnt and leaking body being heaved onto a workbench.

A quick shadow blinked across my face and I flinched.

Rego laughed. "It's ok, Detective. It's just Ruffles."

A small bird had appeared on his shoulder. It was white with black spots and a black head like it was wearing a mask. It twitched its beak and tilted its head with short, sharp jerks. Amazingly, it stayed put as Rego gently reached up and ran his finger over the little bird's head.

"You're after a snack, Ruffles, are you?" Rego smiled. "Yes, I know," he answered the bird as if it had said something privately to him. He plucked a seed from his table and held it out in his palm.

In a blink and flutter, the bird jumped to his hand, darting its beak down to pluck up the seed. It turned and seemed to look at Rego for two solid heartbeats before darting off. Rego watched it go, half smiling to himself. It was the same look the Admiral had when looking at his little model, talking about his station like it was his best friend.

"You know," Rego said, "that poor robot didn't deserve that." He looked down at his pile of seeds. "I don't know what I'd do if I lost my buddy."

He sighed. "Corvus has to be stopped."

I just stayed completely still, my heart pounding as I realised what Rego might be about to tell me.

Ruffles reappeared in his usual abrupt way, like a magician's reveal from fluttering cloth. Rego smiled, patting the bird again. He leaned over it, bumping his nose on the soft feathered head. The bird twitched and shivered its feathers.

"The detective is going to stop mean old Corvus, isn't he, Ruffles?" Rego whispered. "He should look in the service corridors behind the docks, shouldn't he?"

I almost dropped my apple. I had to talk to the Admiral.

• • •

The Admiral moved his face from scowling at the document on his desk to scowling at me as I burst into his office.

"What is it?" He growled.

"I've got her! I know where she does the deals!"

His face stayed locked in its frown. "You have evidence that she is extorting the merchants?"

I wiped my forehead, my breathing still uneven from the run. "Yeah! Well, no. I'm about to! I'll stake out the spot tonight. Once I catch her, we'll make the arrest."

"We?" He asked, his eyebrows floating up.

"I'll need a squad. She's got a lot of firepower."

The Admiral leaned way back, his chair straining and creaking with each bent degree. He locked his eyes on mine.

"I don't want another shootup destroying my station!" He lifted a hand and unfolded a big, accusatory finger at me. "I already have to make a report about the last disaster of yours in the market corridor. You can't believe the heat I'm getting over this. The Moon Corporation is making complaints directly to the Board. If I'm going to report to the Board that they are a bunch of extortionists, then I need that evidence! We're out of time here, Algaran."

I grit my teeth. "I've almost got her. I just need a squad."

The Admiral shook his head. "No squad. No shooting. No damage. Just get the evidence."

I turned to go but the door opened before I could reach the controls.

A very much worse-for-wear Axcel appeared. Scorch marks covered his chest and arms where the gunshots had damaged him and where the welding work had melded him back together. A desperate bandaging of tape and wire ties bundled the wiring hanging outside his body where engineers had given up trying to trace wiring through the confined spaces behind his protective plastron and simply spliced new circuits outside his body. His damaged eye had been replaced with one of different colour. He smelled of hydraulic fluid that had spilled into crevices that couldn't be reached for cleaning. He wavered slightly on his feet, his gyroscopes adjusting to the different responses of his repaired pistons.

I grinned ear-to-ear. I don't think I'd smiled in days.

"Axcel!" I exclaimed, stopping myself short of hugging him and patting his shoulder instead.

"Hello, Detective Algaran," Axcel responded cordially. "I am ready for duty."

The Admiral cut in. "Dismissed, Detective."

"Yes sir!" I said, still beaming. I pushed on Axcel's shoulders to spin him around and marched him out of the office.

Forget the squad. I had all the firepower I needed now.

• • •

"Oops! Oh, I'm sorry, Detective."

If Axcel was clumsy in one-g, he was downright useless in zero-g. My God.

He failed to adjust his stride to the gradually decreasing acceleration as we traveled up a spoke corridor to the docks at the hub of the big wheel of the space station. His feet slipped in the waning friction and his arms wheeled frantically to try and catch a hold of something. It was like watching a beetle pedal at the air when it was flipped on its back.

"Sorry," Axcel repeated. "It seems my mobility is not yet optimized."

"No kidding."

I finally gave up and just grabbed him, hauling him after me as I drifted along the corridor. It was easy enough to toss him through the air but the amount of momentum he had was deceptive in zero-g. When it came time to turn him or even stop him, I had to haul on him with every bit of strength I had.

It was a lot of work, but I found that I didn't mind. It felt great having Axcel back.

The docking bay was busy. It was a hangar-sized room with dozens of airlock doors on two opposing walls, and six big doorways leading to the corridors along the spokes to the rim and its normal life of one-g. Technicians in blue coveralls floated through the air, shepherding trains of cargo containers through the weightless cavern.

"Where do we start?" Axcel asked, looking around the chaotic room.

"Well, no one is committing nefarious under-the-table deals here," I said, tilting my head toward the walls. Unblinking black cameras stared back. "I'd want something more like that spot over there."

Several hatchways around the room led to storage rooms adjacent to the docks - places where storage containers and tools could be stowed without cluttering up the main docking area.

We found a good stakeout position behind a stack of waste containers waiting to be loaded onto Earth-bound ships. The bundle of containers strapped to a wall gave us a vantage over all the hatchways to the quiet storage rooms.

Trying to watch every door simultaneously was tough. I craned my head around, looking in all directions at once. I felt Axcel pat my shoulder.

"I will watch. I have multiple sensors across many spectra. I will let you know when I see something."

"Thanks." I rubbed my eyes.

"Friend Rego is here," Axcel noted.

"What?" I bolted up and twisted around to look. It was indeed mousey little Rego, heading straight for a small store room to our left. "Oh no."

"Shall we follow him?"

I grabbed Axcel. "No! We need to wait for Corvus."

Rego floated up to one of the hatches, paused at the threshold, glanced back over his shoulder once, then darted into the room.

The hatch closed behind him.

"Oh no," I groaned. "That can't be good."

"There are four other individuals inside," Axcel announced. "One of them has a body height-to-width ratio matching Corvus."

"You can see them?"

"If you consider detecting reflections of microwave radio signals as seeing, then yes. I can also hear them. Would you like to hear?"

"What? Yes!"

A fuzzy, echoing, and hissing playback issued from Axcel as he struggled to isolate vibrations specific to Corvus' voice from all the sound energy in the room. I could pick out a muffled voice.

"You been hanging out with that cop … squealing? That's bad for you. You never been … good customer. Always paying late. Now squealing to a cop? That is just too … you forgot the first rule of my protection … no cops. Now … going to show you … you've been paying to avoid. I'm going to break every bone in your body, heal you … break them again."

I slapped Axcel's shoulder. "That's it! That's what we need! You record that?"

"Of course. Shall we bring this to the Admiral?"

"No time. Rego's in trouble. Can you get that door open?"

A fist-sized panel opened on Axcel's torso and a small projectile peeked out. I recognised the round tip of a nanobot cannister. Perfect for a targeted shot at the door controls. Axcel tried to shift to get a clear shot at the door but he twisted in the wrong direction.

I hauled him around and climbed on his back. I kicked us both off the stack of crates, aiming us at the door hiding Rego. Axcel fired his missile. A thin smoke trail scooted toward the door control and the cartridge clunked against the metal bulkhead. We hurtled toward the closed doors.

The nanobots chewed their way to the door controls, gnashing at circuitry and reconnecting the power leads to short the controls. The panel glowed red, heating and twisting the metal until a fountain of sparks and smoke shot across the doorway.

The smoke cleared the second before we reached the door and I was relieved to see that the door had lurched open just enough for us to squeeze through if we stretched ourselves out, with me lying flat on Axcel's back.

We soared into the storage room with me tucked low against Axcel's body for cover. Corvus' henchmen yanked at their holstered weapons but I already had my gun out.

Three easy shots. Three yelps and the henchmen went rigid, eyes bugged out with the stun charge surging through their nervous systems.

"Get out, Rego!" I shouted. In the smoke, I saw a small, thin body shuttle straight toward the door and out to safety.

Only Corvus left now.

I levelled my gun at her but at that instant Axcel and I slammed headfirst into the far wall of the storage room, our free flight through microgravity stopped by a face full of steel bulkhead. I disentangled from Axcel. He tumbled off, helplessly swiping at walls that were all out of his reach.

My gun tumbled end-over-end in midair in front of me like a wild compass needle. I fumbled at it, the barrel and then the handle bouncing off my flailing hand.

I finally snagged it and turned around only to see Corvus pointing her gun at me. A terrible, wicked grin curled up both ends of her mouth.

Oh no.

I swung my gun up. Corvus fired. I fired.

That's all I remember.

. . .

The Admiral was standing by my bed. A bed? Not my bed. The room was white. Not my room. Why was I in a bed?

Oh! Not dead!

"Hello, sir," I managed, finding out that my throat was a tunnel of dry fire.

I was starting to notice other things in the room - machines, a doctor. Okay, so I was in a hospital.

I noticed Axcel standing on the other side of my bed. His different-coloured eyes staring at me unblinkingly. "Hi, Axcel," I managed. "You okay?"

"Many of my circuits are incorrectly repaired," Axcel answered. "I will need extensive overhaul."

The Admiral put a hand on my shoulder. "You did good, Detective. Very good."

"What happened?" I asked.

The Admiral grinned. "Big hero stuff, that's what. You caught Corvus red-handed and then took her and three lackeys down, single-handedly!" He patted my shoulder again. "This is commendation-level stuff, Detective!"

He rubbed his hands. "And don't worry about the robot. With you saving the day, I have everything I need to wrap up my report to the Board. I'm going to tell them exactly how underwhelming their cheap pet project was. You've given a perfect example of what real police work looks like!"

I stared, open-mouthed. "Admiral, Axcel is right here!" My cheeks heated up. "He did damn fine work, too! And he took more bullets than me for it."

Axcel nodded. "Thank you, Detective."

"Sure he was clumsy," I continued, "and mind-blowingly inept at detective work, but with me helping him we made a pretty good team."

Axcel stiffened. "I am unsure of how to respond to that, Detective."

"Actually, Sir...," I said, turning my head back to the Admiral. "I think I can work with Axcel. He did great work on surveillance duty. Sure helps in a fight too."

Kirchoff stared at me, his eyes narrowing as he looked for sarcasm. "What?"

I shrugged, wincing as I instantly discovered where I'd been shot. "Tell the Board he's the worst rookie we've ever had, but we can try training him."

Axcel shifted. "Sir ... should I leave?"

The Admiral's face lit up. "The Board should give us funding for a training program!" He pointed at me. "Okay, you're the hero. You got it."

I settled back in my bed, suddenly feeling at ease. I smiled to myself as the Admiral left the room, his voice already talking excitedly into his comm. The doctors bustled about and machinery beeped.

I just waited to get back to work with my new partner.

◄—●—►

A. L. MACDONALD is a writer living in Ottawa, Canada where he writes science fiction. When not writing, he likes to ride his e-bike and imagine using it for intergalactic deliveries.

Twitter: @A_L_MacDonald

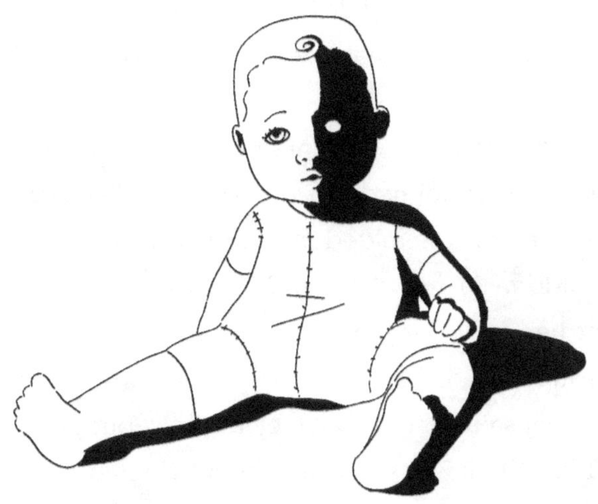

The Perfect Daughter

RAMONA MARR

AT CHURCH, FATHER Dan had said that Jesus knew about every lie you told. Dani figured Jesus would be willing to let one slide. He had to know how important this was to her. Dani never put much stock in what Father Dan said anyway, at least ever since he'd said people like her didn't have souls.

Of course, when he'd said that, he hadn't known that he'd been speaking about Dani. But Dani knew. She'd always known.

Dani set the plates out on the dining room table while Mom finished cooking the ravioli. The good china, though Dani had no idea why they were using it, or even why Mom was making all of Dani's favorite foods. Dani didn't dare ask; Mom had that stretched-taut rubber band look that meant she was worked up about something.

Sweat prickled the back of Dani's neck. Did Mom know about the PaperScreen the school had given out? Every day, Dani made sure the wireless device was folded into a quarter of its size, just to be safe, and hidden in her dresser. She'd never told Mom that the school lent her one. Her parents didn't let her have access to any devices unsupervised. Dani had begged for one, willing to accept even an ancient smartphone, but they wouldn't budge.

It wasn't fair. What was so wrong about being able to connect with other people? If Mom and Dad would just let her have access to the same opportunities all the other kids got, she wouldn't have to go behind their backs to play *Terraform* with her friends from school—Zach, Sanjana, and Ember.

But Dani knew how her parents would respond. She wasn't like the other kids. That was that. Indisputable.

Dani suddenly had the feeling she was being watched. She turned around and nearly bumped into her mother standing behind her. Mom didn't look at Dani; her gaze was fixed solely on the flatware.

"What did I tell you about place settings?" Mom asked, her voice tense. "Forks on the left, knives on the right. It's such a simple thing. Why can't you get it right?"

Fed up, Dani curled her hands into fists. "God, who cares?" she muttered.

Wrong answer. Mom's face turned red. "I'm going to ignore that you took the Lord's name in vain and ask you to fix the utensils."

Dani sighed. "Why does it matter? We'll be able to eat either way, no matter what side the forks are on."

Mom clenched her jaw. "Why do you insist on being like this? Why can't you just be, be…"

Perfect? No one knew, least of all Dani herself. Things would be so much easier if she was just the sweet little girl her parents wanted her to be. But Dani couldn't be that. She could only be herself. Dani who stopped believing in Santa at age seven but still believed in aliens. Dani who would paint her ceiling with bright colors if her parents let her. Dani who thought she might have the slightest crush on Ember. Dani. Not Danika. Not the girl she was supposed to be.

In her worst moments, Dani wanted to tell her parents the truth in the meanest of terms. "Danika is dead. She's been gone since she was four years old. She's not here anymore, but I am. Why can't you love *me*?"

The guttural cough of Dad's old hybrid car rumbled outside. Unlike most of the families she knew, Dani's didn't have the newer zero-emission type of car. Usually, she found it embarrassing. It was bad enough to have a gas-consuming car these days, let alone one that announced its presence a mile away. But tonight, the sound of it made her feel relieved. A welcome distraction.

"I'll get it," she said, giving her mother a look before moving toward the hallway. Maybe Dad had gotten cupcakes for dessert and could salvage this night yet.

"Danika!" Mom said, something anxious in her voice. "Wait!"

Ignoring her, Dani yanked the door open. When she saw who stood on the front step, she let go of the doorknob, sending the door slamming into the wall. Normally, she would brace for a scolding for such recklessness, but her attention was elsewhere.

The person standing across from her … was herself.

Well, not quite herself. This girl was a few inches shorter. Her black hair, matted and tangled, reached down to her back, unlike Dani's short hair secured with a headband. The girl had a bony, wary look to her face that made her eyes protrude. And her eyes … while Dani's eyes were pale blue, the stranger had irises the color of dirty bathwater.

Hurried footsteps sounded behind her. "Patrick," Mom said, breathless.

Dad froze at the bottom of the steps, a container of cupcakes in one hand. "She got away from me, Amanda. You were supposed to keep—"

While Dani's parents argued over the two girls' heads, the strange girl tilted her head, staring at Dani. Slowly, she smiled, as if to say, "Can you believe this?"

"Dad," Dani said, her heart thudding in her chest. "Who is this?"

Dad climbed up the front steps, forming a wall behind the strange girl. "This is Danika," he said.

Dani took a step back. "But … I'm Danika." Her full name felt strange on her tongue. She hadn't liked being called Danika for years. But now that someone else was laying claim to it, she felt she had to defend it.

"The real Danika," Dad said.

Dani stepped back, breath hitching in her throat. No. It couldn't be true. The real Danika was dead. If she wasn't, then Dani wouldn't have been made.

Dad and Other Danika stepped into the house. The door clicked shut behind Dad and as he slid the lock into place, Dani felt like a cornered animal. But why? This was her house, these were her parents. Right?

"Let's have dinner. As a family," Dad said. He walked past Mom and Dani, guiding Other Danika to the dining room with a hand on her shoulder. Other Danika went with him quietly, as if she had nothing else in her brain other than doing what Dad said. Mom and Dad would love that, Dani thought bitterly.

Mom followed close behind Dad and Other Danika. As Dani trailed behind Mom, she tried not to hyperventilate. Mom hated it when she did that. The lightheaded feeling it gave Dani wouldn't do her any favors either. But how else was she supposed to react? What was happening?

Dani stopped beside the table, looking down at Other Danika. "That's my seat," she said pointedly.

Other Danika looked up at her, face blank. Real or not, this girl was really starting to creep Dani out. Where had she been all this time?

"Danika's in the right spot," Mom said, sitting down in her chair. She avoided looking at Dani.

"Then where am I going to sit?" Dani asked, uneasy. There were only three chairs at the table.

Dad sighed, then said. "You're not going to be eating with us. This is a *family* dinner."

Dani's heart had worked perfectly since they had activated her at age five. But at that moment, she thought it might stop. "What? What are you talking about?"

"Since Danika has come home, we don't need your services anymore, M-375. Tomorrow we will take you to Envision for your retirement. We don't need your services anymore."

M-375 was something Dani had only seen on forms that she probably wasn't supposed to be looking at. No one had ever called her that before. And retirement? It was like saying you sent your dog to a farm out in the country. Dani knew what they did to unused replacements at Envision. Her metal components would be melted down, and before that, her biological parts would—

Tears came to Dani's eyes. "No! You can't do this! I'm your daughter!"

Dad slammed his hand on the table. Other Danika jumped, but no one seemed to notice. "For once in your life, you will do as I say!"

"No!" Dani shouted. "I won't let you send me away. I didn't do anything wrong."

"You did *everything* wrong," Dad said. His tone was barely controlled. "The fact that you can't see that is proof that you can't be fixed."

Dani bit the inside of her cheek. "But I don't want to … I'm afraid to…"

Pushing his chair back, Dad stood from the table. "None of those feelings are real," he said.

Dani stood there for a second, unable to move. Then she made a break for the door.

In one swift motion, Dad wrapped an arm around Dani's torso and pressed his thumb against a point between her shoulder blades. All of Dani's limbs went slack and she slumped against her father. Every Envision model had a temporary disable switch. Dani never thought her parents would use hers.

Dani was still conscious as Dad dragged her towards the basement door. "Dad, please," she begged. "Daddy, please!"

"I am not your father," he said, his voice like steel.

Dani looked towards her mother, sobbing. Mom refused to look at her, serving ravioli to Other Danika.

"What did I do?" she wailed. She couldn't stop crying, not even when Dad set her down on the basement floor, climbed up the stairs without looking back, and shut the door. "What did I do?"

There was no answer.

• • •

A tinny voice rang through the darkness of the basement. Dani squinted, searching the shadows for the source of the sound. The high-pitched wail almost sounded like–

"Mommy! Mommy!"

Dani rubbed her dried-out eyes and got up from the beanbag chair, her muscles stiff. There wasn't much furniture in the basement. It had never been finished. All Mom and Dad's money had gone to paying for Dani. So much for that.

Of all the discarded objects that had ended up down here, her old beanbag chair seemed the most comfortable. After the temporary disable function wore off, Dani had gotten up and tried to find a way out. There were two possible exits: the door and a small window at ground level. But the door was locked and refused to budge, and the window was out of Dani's reach. She doubted she could fit through it anyway, but she at least had to try. Once Dani had exhausted every idea she could think of, she'd sunk into the beanbag chair and dozed off.

Reaching under the beanbag chair, Dani pulled out an old baby doll with a voice box. The jingle for the commercial played in Dani's head. "She drinks, she eats, she cries! She's just like me!" Dani had despised the song, even at six years old. Her mother had mistaken her hatred for desire and gotten her the doll for her birthday.

"Mommy! Mommy!"

Dani threw the doll across the room, where its head hit the concrete floor with a satisfying *thonk*. She settled back onto the beanbag chair. It was a little more comfortable now, for all the good it did her. Well. She had to stay optimistic. If she couldn't escape, then maybe she could try to convince Mom and Dad in the morning. They couldn't just get rid of the girl they'd lived with for seven years, could they? Even if she was artificial.

That would probably be the best course of action, anyway. If she ran away, where would she go? What would happen to her? Mom and Dad had often told her about how dangerous the world was. Look at what had happened to Other Danika, after all.

When Dani tried to close her eyes, she heard a strange noise. It sounded like breathing.

Someone else was in the room with her.

Dani looked around, barely daring to move. There wasn't much light in the basement; only the moon shining through the ground level window lent its glow. She could get up from the beanbag chair and turn on the bare lightbulb, but that would mean movement, and that might attract whoever it was.

A dark shape rose from the corner where Dani had thrown the doll. Though part of her brain screamed at her to stay still, she refused to take this sitting down. She staggered to her feet and ran for the lightbulb.

Dani lifted her arm, trying to find the pull switch in the darkness. Before she could reach it, the dark shape appeared in front of her and grabbed her wrist. A choked cry escaped Dani's throat.

"Shh," the figure said. "Don't make a sound."

Whoever it was paused, fumbling with something. Then a tiny flashlight clicked on. The figure lifted the light and pointed it upward, illuminating a face. The world's most disturbing mirror image peered back at Dani.

Dani's mouth dropped open. "What are you doing here?" she whispered.

Other Danika pointed at the window. "I came in through there," she said.

That wasn't an answer, but Dani didn't really have the energy to argue. "Danika," she said.

"Don't call me that," the girl hissed.

"What should I call you, then?"

"They used to call me Sally," she said shyly.

"Who are they, Sally?" Dani asked.

Sally stared at Dani, her lips pressed together. Finally, she said, "Mama and Papa. Not–" She glanced up at the ceiling. "–them. Not Mom and Dad," she said, saying the words as if they tasted funny.

"The ones who took you?"

Sally gave her a slight nod, her gaze distant.

Dani wondered who they were and what they had done to Sally all these years. These thoughts created a dark chasm in her mind, so she tried not to think about it. "Okay, Sally," she said. "I'm Dani."

A smile flickered across Sally's face. "You didn't like Danika either," she said with a hint of triumph.

"No," Dani said, "I didn't. Why don't you sit down?"

Without even thinking about it, Dani sat down on the beanbag chair, making room on one side. Sally came over. As she settled in, Dani noticed she was wearing an old nightgown that Mom had gotten Dani when she was nine. Dani had buried it in the back of the closet, hating the frilly purple thing. It was almost like she was looking at an alternative version of herself. What could have been.

Sally blinked at Dani. Though Sally was the human in this situation, she seemed to be looking at Dani for clues on how to act. Dani had none to give.

"They cut your hair," Dani said.

"Yeah," Sally said in her tiny, raspy voice. "It's short like yours now."

Dani nodded. Tears came to her eyes. Was it really that easy to replace her? No. It couldn't be.

A cold hand touched Dani's fingers. Dani looked down at Sally's hand holding hers, then back up into those opaque eyes.

"Are you really a robot?" Sally asked.

Dani flinched. It was her biggest secret, something she was never supposed to tell anybody. She had kept it until now.

"Kind of," she said. "There's this … these people called Envision can make clonedroids. It's illegal, but they do it for a price. I have a plastiglass base and … human organs and skin. So I can eat and cry and bleed … but it's very secret. I couldn't tell anyone."

Sally nodded. "Or else you'd get punished," she said.

"No, it's not like that. It's to keep me safe. Mom and Dad wouldn't … they love me."

Sally stared at Dani without blinking until she started to get uncomfortable. Finally, Sally said, "Dani, trust me. No one who loves you would lock you in a basement. Mama and Papa would do that when they were mad."

"What happened to them?"

Sally's eyes went dull. "Bad things." She blinked, and it was as if she had reset. "Have you tried getting out through the window?"

Dani had to admit that she had. "But I can't reach it. And even if I could, I don't think I could get through. I'm too big."

Sally nodded. "Yeah. They must have given you lots of food." She frowned. "Why would they do that and then just throw you away?"

Dani sniffled, rubbing at her eyes. "I don't know. I thought—maybe it's because of how I act."

"Have you been bad?" Sally asked, her voice hushed as if speaking about a secret.

"Not really," Dani said. "I mean, sometimes. But not more than any other kid my age. I just can't be who they want me to be. I can't be Danika."

Sally leaned in so close that Dani could smell her shampoo. "You know what, Dani? I don't think I can be either."

Dani shook her head. "I don't know what they'll do when they figure that out. Mom and Dad always need a backup for everything, even—"

A backup. A backup!

She rose from the beanbag chair. "Sally, can I borrow your flashlight?" she asked.

As soon as Sally handed it over, Dani started searching every board in the unfinished walls. She ran her hands over every crevice. It had to be somewhere around here … Aha!

From a spot between the wood and the concrete, Dani pried out a key. She held it up, barely daring to let herself hope.

"Is that for the basement door?" Sally asked.

"Yes," Dani whispered. "Dad hid one just in case."

Getting up from the beanbag chair, Sally came over to stand beside Dani. "Now you can escape," Sally said.

"Yeah. But…" Dani looked at the smaller girl. "Could you help me? I don't want Mom and Dad to come after me for a while."

"What do you want me to do?"

"Maybe … there's another key upstairs, one that goes to all the bedrooms. Mom and Dad keep it in a bowl by the door. Maybe you could use it to lock their bedroom door. Do you think you could do that without waking them up?"

Sally stared at Dani, deep in thought, then nodded. "I can do that. When I'm done, I'll slide something under the basement door so you know it's safe to come out."

"Perfect," Dani said. "Thank you."

Though they had the key, Sally insisted that it would be less noticeable for her to go out through the window. Faint from hunger, Dani helped lift Sally up onto the ledge. Before she went out the window, Sally turned, sticking her head out over Dani.

"I'll be back," she said. "And here. I brought you this."

Something fell onto the basement floor with a splat. Dani looked down to see what it was. By the time she picked it up, Sally had disappeared.

Dani looked at the plastic bag in her hands, smiling. It was full of cold ravioli.

. . .

According to Dani's wristwatch, it was three in the morning when a piece of paper slipped under the basement door. She lifted her head from where it had been pressed against the door, the skin of her cheek sticking slightly to the painted wood. Reaching carefully into her pocket, she pulled out the key. Her hands shook as she lifted it to the lock.

When she opened the door, wincing at the click of the latch, she found Sally standing on the other side. The kitchen light was on, casting Sally's face into shadow.

"Did you do it?" Dani asked.

Sally nodded. A strange stench came from the kitchen. It was familiar, but Dani couldn't quite name it. "They won't be able to come after you. I made sure. And they didn't even notice. Not even..." Her voice trailed off.

Dani looked down at Sally's hands. She held a pair of Dani's sneakers. When Dani took them to put them on, she noticed something stuck between the laces. "What's this?" she asked.

"I grabbed some money for you. You can use it to get out," Sally said.

As Dani slipped the shoes on, a new wave of fatigue hit her. "But where will I go?"

"I don't know. Anywhere far from here. I know you can do it."

"And what will you do?" Dani asked.

Sally lifted a shoulder in a shrug. "I'll stay. That way, they won't come for you."

Overcome, Dani bent down and gave Sally a hug. It was then that she realized what the smell was. Gasoline.

"Sally...," she whispered.

Sally grabbed Dani's arm. With surprising strength, Sally pulled Dani towards the back door. "Go. Please."

Dani's voice wavered as she spoke. "Sally, what are you going to do?"

"I love you, Dani."

Something clicked inside Dani. Though even the thought of it was heinous, what was she supposed to do? Dad had said it best: they had no need for her services anymore.

"Thank you, Sally."

Sally smiled at her as she closed the back door. Dani took a final look through the door's glass pane, then turned and ran.

The asphalt blurred beneath her feet, damp with dew. Dani refused to think, refused to do anything other than run.

She made it three streets down before her house exploded in flames behind her.

. . .

They all shook their heads, unable to understand it. The neighbors, the newscasters, even the police. As Danika grinned eerily from the back of the police car, her face lit orange by the glowing wreckage of her house, they had trouble figuring it out. How could such a good girl set fire to her own house with her parents sleeping inside? A great student, a sweet girl, always polite and kind. She really had been the perfect daughter.

RAMONA MARR is an aspiring witch living in upstate New York in the United States. She writes science fiction, specializing in monstrous and lovable sapphics in the apocalypse. When she emerges from her cave, she can be found baking, crafting, or imagining her stories as stunning animatics that will probably never exist.

Instagram: @ramonamarrwriter
Website: apocalypticsapphic.com

In Cybertronic Denial

WENDY WEE

I RAISE A glass of red wine to myself and to all the lonely people in the world who never really belonged. Happy 40th birthday to me. I down my drink, sigh, and tap the order screen for another.

As I gaze at the empty glass, I reach a hazy understanding that it's been nothing but a life of daily nothingness for me… I'll never achieve commercial success with my art, men seem to not really be into me, and I've probably passed my fertility expiration date. Woo hoo… go, me.

The bartender bot walks over and puts my drink on the same damn spot that's a gazillion feet from me. "Enjoy your drink," it says and leaves.

I've been muttering curses about how far it is, but it looks like the bot couldn't get the hint. I'm not expecting masterful emotional intelligence from a bot, but shouldn't it at least recognize a glaringly unsatisfied customer? Time for me to be explicit.

I snap my fingers and holler at the android's retreating metallic back. "Hey. Hey, bartender!"

It turns with a fake smile etched on its gray, rubbery face. "How may I help you?"

"In case you still haven't noticed, you've been serving my drinks too far from my reach. Put my drink here," I say, lifting the drink and putting it closer to me. "Got it?"

"I'm sorry, that is not in my standard operating procedure. You can leave your suggestions through the bar screen in front of you, and my developer will review them."

These bots are such morons. But I'm probably a bigger moron for trying to reason with them. I throw my hands up in surrender. "Forget about it."

"Enjoy your drink," it says and walks away.

I sip on my wine, hunch over, and wiggle to sink further into the memory-foam-cushioned bar stool, settling in for a comfortably numb night.

There's a painting on the wall on my left. It's of a woman looking into a mirror. Her reflection shows her pulling down her lower eyelid and sticking her tongue out. At first glance, it's as if she's taunting herself. But with how lifeless her eyes are, she probably doesn't care to even taunt herself anymore. The purposelessness of it all.

"Hi," a voice comes from my right.

Probably some guy trying to chat up the pretty young woman who's sitting a barstool away from me. I roll my eyes and lean my right elbow on the bar, shifting my body away from them. Good thing there's a painting, or I'd look like a weirdo staring at the wall. I'm really not in the mood to eavesdrop on their mating ritual, so I reach for the earphones in my pocket.

"I wonder what the artist was thinking while developing that," he says before I can get the earphones out.

He's talking to me? I turn to a guy, probably in his late thirties. His body is turned to me, but he's facing the painting, staring at it.

It's flattering he chose to chat with me instead of the young lady next to him. At the same time, what he said rubbed me the wrong way. "Interesting you would say 'developing' instead of 'painting'. Thanks for ruining the art for me by reminding me an artificial intelligence thing might have *developed* it."

He shifts his attention from the painting to me. "Sorry, I didn't mean to ruin it for you. It didn't cross my mind an AI created the art. I work in AI and robotics, so it's more of a habit to say 'developing' when it comes to creating something."

"Doesn't matter. It's ruined for me already. So, whatever."

"Are you one of those who are strongly against AI-generated art?"

I scoff. "With those soulless SOP-following machines flooding the art marketplace with their so-called art, burying the work of real human artists, can you blame me?"

"Or maybe human artists need to step up, create more art in less time, and find better ways to promote them."

Through gritted teeth, I say, "We artists are not some cold, gray factory producing generic products. In fact, that's what those artificial intelligence 'artists' are. And in time, art will be known as some trivial decoration instead of something to be appreciated and reflected on."

"Ah, you're an artist. I can make sense of your anger now."

What do you say if you're unsure if something is said in condescension or in solidarity? I don't know, so I take a sip of my drink instead. Though, being the bitter bitch I am, I'm leaning toward him being condescending. My sip becomes a gulp.

He looks at the painting again. "From the perspective of an artist, what do you think about this painting of an android making a silly face?"

I almost choke on the wine making its way through my throat. "You think the woman in the painting is a bot?"

"You think she's human?"

"Yes. Why would a robot have dark circles under its eyes? That"–I point at the painting–"is a woman who's sick of life, of everything. Sick of feeling lonely most of her days…"

"Loneliness is one of the worst tortures in life," he says somberly.

Is he lonely? I take a good look at him. He's rather good-looking, with short dark hair and a medium-built body. His eyes, though… there's an ever-present piercing curiosity in them. They're enigmatic, but there's something unsettling, something dangerous tainting them.

He clears his throat. I blink. Oh shit, I must have been staring into his eyes for an awkward amount of time. I shut my gaping mouth and look away. Heat rushes to my cheeks. Oh hey, more solid proof of why I'm alone–I have *killer* social skills. Enough to snuff out a conversation with anyone, anytime.

"Cheers to loneliness," I murmur and turn away from him, because I'm not a masochist who takes pleasure in being socially rejected.

"Cheers. I'm Jarron. And you?"

Eh? He's still talking to me? Probably just being polite.

"Riz," I say, not turning, but looking at the bottles on the shelves in front of me as if they're the most interesting thing in the world.

"Are you waiting for a friend?"

"Do I look like I'm waiting for a friend? Not to spill my life story on you, but according to my ex, I'm too bland to make interesting company."

"Your ex sounds like an idiot, because you sound anything but bland. I think you'd make great company."

A small part of me jolts to life with the compliment, but I reflexively respond with sarcasm. "And you know that after only knowing me for, what, five seconds? I'm flattered."

"I just have a hunch you have a good brain," he says while looking at my head, as if he could actually see my brain.

And then he smiles at me, dimples flashing. I can't help but smile along.

Maybe it's because he doesn't seem to mind my challenging personality, but I loosen up. We look at the painting on the wall again and share our thoughts on it a bit more. He asks about my art and I gladly talk about it. It's so nice to have someone interested to know more about what I do.

We're drinking and chatting, and then suddenly everything is spinning. I must have been falling because he catches me. "Riz, are you okay?"

Everything's spinning faster. "I don't know. I'm not feeling good."

"Come, let's go get some fresh air," he says.

"Yeah, okay."

He helps me walk out of the bar.

"The fresh air isn't helping," I say, but hear myself slurring horribly, as if I'm having a stroke. I break into a cold sweat, panic taking over me. What's happening?

Everything turns black.

· · ·

I open my eyes to fluorescent lights and the blinking words "SYSTEM BOOTING IN PROGRESS." Below, my vision is running through endless lines of gibberish words. I can't move my head or any part of my body. I feel nothing.

The scrolling lines stop, ending with: STARTUP SEQUENCE IS COMPLETE.

Electricity hums through my entire body, and I jolt up into a sitting position. There's no one else in the room, only robotic arms and tools. I look down. My torso and legs are entirely metal.

Am I in some kind of virtual reality? I try to feel for a headgear to pull it off, but there's nothing attached to my head. When I lower my hands, I freeze. There's no skin. Only steel. These hands can't be mine. I flex the fingers and feel the movement. No … this is not virtual reality. I'm actually in a robot's body. I'm a fucking bot! How is this possible? No, no, no, no, no, this can't be happening.

I think I'm panicking, but I'm not sure. I'm not having the physical stuff like cold sweat, or that feeling as if a heavy weight dropped in my stomach. It's more like an intellectual thing. I … I'm feeling so confused. I think? The matter of feeling itself is weird to me now. I'm incomprehensible.

"What a magical moment. It's like when babies first realize the existence of their hands," comes a voice from a speaker mounted on the wall. A familiar voice.

"Jarron?" I say, then reflexively touch my throat. I sound different. It's a lower pitch female voice, like some advertising professional voiceover quality type.

"Yes, it's Jarron. How are you feeling, Riz?"

"What did you do to me?"

"I've transferred you into another body. A better one that is not as vulnerable and lets your mind live forever. You're welcome."

"I don't want it. Put me back into my original body. The human one!"

"That's not possible. Since your brain had to be sliced to create your digital mind, your body is dead. It's unrecoverable, unfortunately."

"What the hell? You sliced my brain?"

"Of course not. I have a high-precision machine to do that."

Oh, my god. He's a psycho. I sprint for the door. It's locked. I keep pulling and twisting the handle, hoping these robotic hands are super strong and can dismantle the whole lock system. It doesn't budge.

"Don't bother. Your body is an entry level customer service android. You're not strong enough to open the door, trust me."

"I'm supposed to trust you? You're a killer, so it's safe to say you're also a liar."

Failing the door handle, I punch at the steel door repeatedly, hoping to tear a hole through it. After several minutes, there's hardly a dent. Maybe he's right.

"I told you," he says. Asshole.

"Why are you keeping me here? Why did you do this to me? What do you want from me? Why me?"

"It's impolite to ask many questions at a time. You're not a good conversationalist, are you?"

"Oh, but didn't you tell me I'd make great company? Your feelings change fast, huh?"

At least this new voice is still able to convey my sarcasm. I may be in a precarious situation, but doesn't mean I can't still be the sardonic bitch I've always been.

He says nothing.

Fine, I'll ask one question at a time. "How much time has it passed since that night at the bar?"

"Less than two days."

"You figured out this whole putting my brain into a robot body in less than two days? You must be some kind of genius."

"Thanks for the compliment, but I had, how shall I put this… lots of practice before you."

It takes a moment for me to grasp what he's saying. He's killed many people. I'm being held captive by a serial killer. Is this really happening? I hug myself and take a few steps back until I hit the wall. "Why are you doing this?"

"I needed proof that my theory works. Now that I know I can successfully upload a human mind into a robot and retain the self, I'll be undergoing the same procedure."

"You're going to slice your own brain?"

"Not me. My machines will execute the procedure automatically. They've worked well on you, so I'm good to go."

"You're willing to kill yourself in hopes it would work for you, too? After just one successful try, which could be a fluke?" Wow, the balls on this guy.

"I know it will. You're the living proof of it. Plus, I've meticulously kept track of everything. Either way, it's a risk worth taking. I have a high probability of developing Alzheimer's and I've seen how the disease took over my family members' lives. Not a fan of it. Once my mind's digital, it can't get me. Fantastic, right?"

I ignore his self-praise and over-the-top confidence. He can die trying for all I care. "And what happens to me now? Might as well let me go, right?"

"I can't do that. I can't expose you to the world. You're the first conscious robot, and letting you out would invite lots of unwanted problems for me. I have in mind that perhaps we could keep each other company. Since we'd be first of our kind, no one will accept us out there. We'd be each other's solution to loneliness. Anyhow, I'd like to stay and continue our invigorating chat, but I've got work to do. I'll be back later." The speaker clicks off.

I'm speechless. I *died*. And now I'm a thing, some machinery. Fuck, I don't know how to take this news. My mind feels scrambled. Bots aren't supposed to be this way, right? They're supposed to be black and white about everything, always know what to do next.

So, what exactly am I?

No, I shouldn't let that psycho brainwash me. Regardless of what he did to me, I'm still me, still a human being. I mustn't forget that. And I can't spend my life with my murderer. Obviously! I need to escape.

But he'd surely have a tracker on me. Or maybe not? Ugh. How do I find my robot body's manual to find out if there's a tracker?

A message appears: ACCESS TO MANUAL DENIED.

Oh, so just thinking about something would get me that thing? Okay, alright, let's see… maybe I could search online how to overcome this 'access denied' issue.

ACCESS TO THE INTERNET DENIED.

Dammit. Maybe I should follow in his footsteps and take the risk of the unknown. Yeah, there's likely a tracking device inside me, but there are also techies all over the city. If I make it to one before Jarron finds me, and they disable my device, I win.

But first, I need to break out of this place. Since I can't break down the door, it's face off time between me and the keypad next to it. Let's see… I tap 1-2-3-4 on the keypad screen.

The screen flashes: ACCESS DENIED.

It's okay, I'll just have to try as many combinations as possible. Maybe I'll find out if I have a hidden talent for hacking. I try 4-3-2-1. Failed. I try probably a hundred different combinations. Oh, forget it, there's no inner hacker waiting to be discovered.

I pace the room while I try to figure another way out. There must be some kind of weakness or loophole in this room I can exploit.

After a couple of hours, I give up. There's nothing.

I lie on the work table even though I could probably stand all day with this body without feeling tired. This is how I know I'm still human; I'm lying in a fetal position to feel sorry for myself. Fuck my life.

I think about how unspectacular my life has been, even now when I'm a bot. Jarron said I'm the first conscious robot. But instead of being an all-powerful, intelligent killer machine like in the movies, I'm still unremarkable. I mean, look at me, lying down helpless like a loser instead of punching through the walls—successfully—and kicking Jarron's ass like an action movie hero.

Well, no one would notice this loser gone. I've got no family left, no close friends to care about my disappearance. I have maybe fewer than a handful of acquaintances, including the old lady in my apartment building who likes to say hello to strangers from her balcony on the first floor. And now, I have a sicko as my sole companion.

"I'm back," Jarron's voice comes through the speakers.

The time hovering in my visual tells me I've been in the same position for over four hours.

"How was your day?" he says.

I don't answer, because why should I? Heh, maybe he'd think I'm dead and—oh … Maybe I *should* act dead. Sure, his computer will show him I'm fine, but if I'm not moving, he'd think his computer is messed up. Then, he would come in here and check what's wrong with me. Him coming into the room means the door opening. That's all the opportunity I need.

"Riz?"

I remain silent, my eyes shut. Do dead robots shut their eyes? Eh, it doesn't matter. I can't believe I'm saying this, but thankfully as a robot, I don't need to breathe, so I don't have to worry about holding my breath.

"Hey, can you hear me? Riz?" There's some humming and sounds of tapping on screens, then he murmurs, "All the readings look fine. Dammit, what's wrong? I really thought this was finally it." A few more tappings, grunts, and curses. And then silence.

The door opens. Yes!

I prepare to jump up and scare the shit out of him, and make a run for it. After that, I'll get someone to disable any tracker in me. Oh, but how would I pay for it? Ahh, why do I have to find a hole in the strategy at this very last moment? Change of plans; I'll go straight to the police and report what happened.

Relying purely on sound, I estimate he's standing an inch away from me. It's go-time. I snap my eyes open.

A look of surprise comes over him, and he jerks back a little.

With the speed and stability my unathletic self never had before, I'm on my feet in one second, and I'm kneeing him in his balls the next.

He cups his battered groin and groans, bending over and falling to the floor.

I bolt to the door that's thankfully ajar (strategizing obviously isn't a strength of mine, since he could have locked the door when he entered the room), and exit into a hallway. I reach a narrow staircase that leads to a door, and take the steps up two at a time. I open the door to what looks like a living room of a modest house.

Jarron lets out a wail that's more like frustration than pain. He doesn't sound close, but not wanting to take any chances, I sprint to the front door like my ass is on fire. Throwing the door open, I'm met with seclusion; not another house or person in sight, only greenery up ahead.

I'm about to walk out into my freedom, but pause. Something's not right–Jarron has stopped crying. There's silence. Well, not completely; there are insect sounds outside and the crackle of the fireplace beside me in the living room.

Jarron breaks into laughter. It sounds distant, so I guess he's still in the basement.

"Riz, my dearest Riz. You're my biggest mistake. No worries, I'll find someone to replace you. But before that, I promise you, I'll find you. And when I do, I'll kill you … again," he says between his manic laughter.

He is a seriously sick, heartless bastard that's beyond help, isn't he? How many more people is he going to kill?

I stomp to the fireplace. I grab a burning log and chuck it into the curtains. My metallic hand survives unharmed. Incredible. I fling several more fiery logs about the house. The flames spread sure and fast.

Satisfied, I dash out of the house of hell, hoping the devil inside burns with it.

· · ·

I run and run and run … until I see brightly glowing holographic ads conquering the night sky up ahead. I head in that direction.

I make it out of the woods and right into collections of sleek, high-rise buildings and crowds of people. I'm back in the city, but not one I'm familiar with. Jarron must have run out of people to kill here, and had to travel to a faraway city to get his next test subject. Where am I, though, and where's the nearest police station? How did people survive without the internet back in the Stone Age?

I stop the first person I can and ask, "Hi, I know this is weird, but can you tell me where I am?"

The young man blinks and looks at me as if he's just realizing I'm there. "Uh … what?"

"What city are we in?"

"Uh," he blinks a dozen times more, then says, "Mancheh?"

I frown. "Do you mean we're in Mancheh, or are you also unsure where you are?"

The guy continues blinking, his mouth working like a goldfish.

I rub my head. "Forget it, I'll ask someone else."

"This is Mancheh," says someone behind me.

I turn to a middle-aged woman with a hostile look, all narrowed eyes and pursed lips. Does she have a problem with me? Or maybe she just has a resting bitch face. Focus on what's important, Riz! "Thanks. Can you tell me where the nearest police station is?"

She doesn't answer, but looks at me from head to toe. Oh, she definitely has a problem with me. The mature thing to do is to move along and ask someone else. Unfortunately, I'm not exactly known as one to shy away from confrontations.

I take a step closer so I'm in her face. "What's your problem, lady?"

She steps back and splutters. But her feathers are ruffled only for a second. She straightens her back, and says, "Did you get that?"

"Huh?"

"Yeah," says a guy.

I look to my left. A few feet away is a guy holding up his phone, obviously recording us. He's wearing a bright yellow t-shirt with the words "ANTI-AI: STOP THE MACHINE TAKEOVER." The woman in front of me removes her jacket to reveal the same yellow t-shirt.

Great. What shitty luck I have to bump into the Anti-AI people. I don't hate them. In fact, I agree with them on stopping artificial intelligence from stealing jobs. But most of the time, they're too cuckoo for me to take them seriously.

In a loud, dramatic way, she says, "This is the sign. The prophecy is coming true. The machines are starting to think, starting to talk back to humans. Threatening humans! The AI Master is coming. Maybe it's already here…" she widens her eyes at me.

Annnd that's exhibit A of their cuckooness.

By now, there's a crowd surrounding us, thanks to her theatrics. I'm about to walk away from this scene, but I wonder—maybe she'd be crazy enough to believe what happened to me.

"I'm not an AI. I'm not even a robot. I'm human. Or, I was human, until a psycho scientist killed me and uploaded my brain into this robotic body."

She shakes her head slowly. "The machines are also lying now."

"Wow, your mind's hopelessly too far gone. Whatever." I turn to leave, but come face to face with a young woman in the Anti-AI t-shirt. There are at least a handful of them surrounding me, blocking me from exiting.

"Move, please," I say.

The young woman lifts her chin. "Or what?"

"I've no time for this shit." I roll my eyes and squeeze myself through an opening between her and her fellow cult pal.

She stumbles slightly. "The bot pushed me!" she screams repeatedly.

The crowd is getting bigger. Not counting the Anti-AI clan, the rest of the people seem confused with raised eyebrows and gaping mouths. Hell, I'd be confused too, if I were them. With how mindless robots are, it must be incomprehensible to suddenly see one with an attitude.

"I didn't push you. I was trying to squeeze through because you weirdos wouldn't move. Stop being so dramatic."

"You're talking down on me? Do you think you're above me?"

The middle-aged lady that started this whole kerfuffle makes a reappearance. "This thing needs to learn its place is below us. Don't let it forget."

Then she slaps me. In. The. Face.

I touch my gray rubbery cheek. I felt the impact of the strike, but there's no pain. The humiliation of being slapped stings, though.

"What are you going to do about it? Nothing, because you're nothing," she says smugly.

Without thinking twice, I return the favor. One tight, steely slap on her bitch face.

A flurry of confused chatter erupts from the crowd. She touches her reddened cheek and bloody lips and sees the blood on her fingers. She looks at me with blinding rage. "Tear its head off!"

A wave of yellow t-shirts come crashing into me. Punching, kicking, and shoving me from all directions. I lose balance and fall, my back slamming against the concrete floor. I can't hit back; my arms are busy protecting my head, since these savages might literally tear it off.

I beg them to stop, apologizing profusely for slapping their fellow member. But the beatings and verbal abuse keep coming.

My vision flickers. A warning flash: TRANSFORMER FAILURE.

Oh shit, now I'm extremely concerned. I might actually die.

"Stop–" I cry, but can't continue my sentence. Instead, I keep saying 'stop' like a broken record. I've lost control of my words.

Instead of stopping, the sick bastards cackle at my broken, distressed plea and stomp on me.

I take in this experience. This utter degradation of my being. Though, what *being* is left of me? I'm a robot. Reduced to nothing but metal and plastic parts...

I stop defending myself, dropping my arms. I take the abuse without a fight. Hopefully, I'll shut down permanently soon.

But the beatings halt. A couple of police bots appear and bring me to my feet. One of them taps the back of my neck and I shut down.

. . .

My eyes snap open. I'm in a room with two police officers engrossed in conversation. The stumpy man says to the lanky woman, "You said you've fixed the bot, but why is it still not awake?"

Something feels different. Very different. I feel whole. It's as if a mental block has been lifted. Somehow, I now know how my entire body works and what's going on in every part. My GPS chip shows I'm at the Mancheh Police Station. Mancheh. That's where I last remember being, where there was a mob that–

I thought I was going to die. "Those bastards didn't manage to kill me, huh?"

The officers stop chatting and turn to me.

With his eyes still on me, Stumpy whispers to Lanky, "You still don't believe this bot slapped that woman because it was angry?"

Lanky hisses at him, "No, it was malfunctioning."

"It malfunctioned and decided it hates people?"

"Robots can't hate or get angry. They don't have emotions. How many times must I repeat myself?"

"But it's what everyone's saying online. They're freaked out by it."

I interrupt them. "Why are you whispering? You know I can still hear you, right?"

Stumpy clears his throat and straightens his back. He says to his colleague, without whispering this time, "Since the bot's system is no longer corrupted, can you finally get its owner's details?"

"Uh…" After a few blinks, Lanky shuts her gaping mouth. "Yeah, let me get to it."

As she taps on her tablet screen and does her thing, Stumpy asks me, "What kind of robot are you? What's your purpose?"

I ponder on this. Jarron created me as a guinea pig for his experiment and to serve as his companion. But since I've completed the first purpose and am not interested in fulfilling the second…

"I have no purpose," I say.

"A useless robot?"

"Oh, wow. I guess you could be an asshole and put it that way."

Before he can reply, Lanky interjects, "Its owner is Jarron Macter. Let me get his details, and I'll send them over to you."

"Thanks, but did you hear what it just said to me? It's showing hostility toward me. So, you're wrong—they do have emotions!"

As the both of them yap away about the debatable miracle that's me, I try to put shit together. Specifically, what would the police contacting Jarron mean for me?

I doubt he survived the fire. With a dead owner and me slapping the Anti-AI woman earlier, they'll say I'm a deranged robot that killed its owner and is running amok, a danger to society. Even if Jarron didn't die in the fire, he'd tell the police I tried to kill him. Attempted murder.

But if everyone knew what happened to me and what a monster Jarron is, people would understand and sympathize with me. But clearly, I can't just *tell* people the truth, seeing how no one believed me earlier. I need to show them what happened by uploading my memory to the public.

I select the memory from that cursed moment I met Jarron—so they'd believe I'm human and treat me as such—up to him admitting to killing me. Then, I create a social media account and try to upload the video file. The social media site throws me an error message on being unable to read the encrypted file.

I consume every piece of literature on the internet on encryption. If I could access my memories, that means I have the encryption key. I try to output a decrypted file to upload on the social media site, but

I'm met with a warning: MEMORY WILL BE PERMANENTLY ERASED. PROCEED?

Looks like Jarron set a trigger for my destruction to prevent his secrets from spilling into the world.

Well, I have a faster and bigger brain now, so let's play. In less than two minutes, I've learned everything about hacking. I try to hack my system, but all attempts would trigger the destruction of my mind, too. If I proceed, my entire memory would be wiped clean.

Without my memory, I would no longer be me. I'd be as good as dead.

Check-fucking-mate by Jarron.

I focus my attention back to the police officers. The knuckleheads are still having their debate. Stumpy sighs and throws his hands up. "Let's just agree to disagree. Now, can you send me the owner's details?"

Lanky rolls her eyes before returning to her tablet.

Any moment now, the police would be speaking to Jarron, and he'll tell the police about me trying to kill him. Or they'll find out he's dead. Either way, I'd be arrested and sent to be destroyed. Executed. Death.

No, thank you.

I must get out of here. For that, I need money. Yup, because even as a non-human, you can't escape the curse of paying rent. In this case, it'll be paying rent for cloud servers to store copies of my mind. Damn, I sound so smart now. Oh, I also need money to get another body. Probably a workshop lab, too.

I break into the government's database and create a false human identity, followed by a bank account. Through several layers of banking accounts, I transfer the money from human Riz's account to money-laundering criminal robot Riz's account. Mm-hmm, that's who

I've become. Desperate times, desperate measures and that sort of thing.

I back up my mind in several cloud storages simultaneously.

"Oh, shit…" Lanky gasps.

"What?" Stumpy looks at her.

"The owner was pronounced dead a couple of hours ago. There was a fire at his home. The fire department suspects foul play."

And there it is. My confirmation I'm a murderer. I know I said to myself I did it to stop him from killing more people. But if I'm honest, hearing him say he'd kill me again triggered me to do the deed.

Whatever my real motivation was, is it truly wrong to kill a psychopathic serial killer?

"Did you kill him?" the policewoman asks me, looking pale.

There's no point in lying, so I say, "Yes, the asshole deserved it."

With that, I activate my backup mind that's in the cloud. I erase the one in this beaten up body, departing from it, and into a new phase; a life of abundant possibilities.

• • •

As I approach the top of the mountain in the formidable robotic body I built, I complete another painting. Being in nature has been inspiring, immersing myself in the beauty of it while creating art with my mind. On my climb so far today, I've already created ten paintings and sold six.

I've become the thing I hated: a machine that generates art. Woo hoo … go, me. That's me being sarcastic, in case you missed it. My penchant for sarcasm shall live for eternity.

Anyhow, it's been a hundred days since people believed I've died, especially as the police streamed the destruction of my body for all to watch. The Anti-AI mob that attacked me are hailed as heroes by many. Those bastards.

And now, only I know I live. Only I know *me*.

Even though I chat with people online, they don't know what I am. It makes me feel like a fraud. Also, I'd like someone I can intellectually spar with. With how fast my mind operates now, human responses are too slow. I don't want to spend eternity in such a hollow existence. I want to be with people like me. Perhaps Jarron was right about not being able to fit in with either humans or robots.

It's funny how after such a life-changing and brain-wrecking (literally) ordeal, I'm still back at where I was—feeling alone.

I reach the mountain peak. I look at the city below and imagine walking in those streets amongst others like me. Another world … a world with more civilized, elevated beings. No more feeling alone. It's a fucking awesome dream. One that could be a reality by me taking the first step: creating another in my own image.

◄━●━►

WENDY WEE is a writer living in Malaysia who was hatched from a cyborg that had a penchant for hugging puppies and blasting rogue robots. She writes speculative fiction, especially of the dystopian flavor. When not writing, she likes to get lost in angsty romance novels, swirls of black coffee, and the realm of ones and zeroes.

Web: wendyweeauthor.com
Twitter: @wendyweeww

Touring Test

DONN MARTYN

HURTLING THROUGH INFINITE darkness, challenging the velocity of light itself, a minuscule mote of technology shelters bold explorers racing to rendezvous with a mysterious interstellar visitor.

Darkness.

Darkness (dreaming).

Darkness.

Light! Noise!

Harold Carmichel, Ph.D, M.D, KBE, FACS, FTAS, startled by the bleating of the klaxon, snapped upright so quickly he hit his head on the slowly opening sleep pod cover. *Must have been a long one*, he suspected, feeling the urgent pressure from his full bladder.

"What was that?"

"Unknown yet; we've been hit with an energy beam," a melodious female voice replied.

Science above discomfort. He quickly switched into problem-solving mode. *Energy, seemingly focused. Hmm...* "A weapon?"

"Maybe. Lots of energy all over the spectrum, from gamma to radio. Odd..."

"Don't hold back on me, Sofia!" he snapped, frustrated by his abrupt awakening and the usually precise AI's uncertainty.

"It's a frequency waterfall from start to end. Like we're being scanned."

"Repetitive?"

"Just the once, so far. Perhaps you should sleep again until it recurs?"

He focused on the source. "Forget that ... what direction ... from Omua?"

"No, on our six. I don't read our objective at all."

"It's gone?"

"No visual; deep radar isn't returning anything more than ISM scatter..."

"Where exactly are we?"

There was a drawn-out pause. Sofia *never* paused. Were they learning dramatic silence?

"Hey Sofia, where—"

"Heard you the first time. Uncertain. Am working to triangulate known pulsars..."

"Sorry, it's just..."

"No need. I found a solution, but you're not going to like it."

The AI was definitely getting more dramatic! "Okay?"

"It's not so much where we are, as *when* we are here..."

"Explain?"

"Best correlation puts Icarus 50 kiloyears from our last position, give or take a few decades. We're most of the way to the great Orion Nebula, which is our closest landmark. You've been in deepsleep for that segment of the chase, which turned out to be much longer..."

"Uhh ... why?" Now he knew why he needed to pee so badly!

"Apparently 'Oumuamua sped up—Icarus attempted acceleration to continue approaching."

"...and we didn't have enough oomph. I should have given you better instructions."

"Yes. Icarus remains under thrust; there is sufficient accumulated and replenished reaction mass to continue indefinitely."

Annoyed, Hal segued into sarcasm. "Any more good news?"

"Ship systems and stores are operational and sufficient with no significant failure indications..."

These evasive pauses were getting disturbing ... are they avoiding something? Best ask directly and find out. "So, what's the *bad* news, Sofia?"

"Icarus is now traveling at a significant fraction of lightspeed, continuing to gain momentum. The objective is not visible in any sensor. Thus, our primary mission has failed. And, overall, the multiverse continues its unchecked expansion into heat death. Would you prefer more examples?"

He sighed; the AI seemed petulant. *First dramatics, now ... sarcasm.*

"Quite enough for now. Terminate the chase; reverse heading. Let's head back home."

"Understood. But, why?"

"We've failed, Sofia. You just said as much!"

"True enough. However, there may be relevance in pursuing an altered mission objective..."

The moment stretched on for no apparent reason.

"Go on..."

"Icarus has come further into this region of the galaxy than any known spacecraft. Ahead is one of the most studied regions of star formation in history. We propose to study it more closely. Observe..."

The bulkhead-sized viewscreen panned and zoomed away from the usual forward heading to focus attention on an offset glowing patch of dust and gas that resembled a glowing flower: the Orion Nebula. The view began to expand and rotate, revealing canyons in the lustrous tendrils and ember-like cocoons where newly formed stars had started to shine before driving away the dust from which they had sprung.

"Wow! Um, I mean, that's very impressive ... is this a simulation?"

"Dimensional synthesis derived during our approach at an offset to the chosen heading. We have already encountered some of the sparse outer tendrils of hydrogen and molecular clouds."

"So, we're almost there."

"Icarus is moving closer every millisecond."

"You're recommending we poke around a little instead?" Hal queried, still feeling a pressure.

"That would be a scientifically valuable objective, yes."

"Very well. Record the time, date..."

"...never stopped..."

Could an AI express eagerness?

"...then alter course to a heading toward the center of the Nebula; deviations to avoid hazards are permitted without authorization."

"Understood. Prepare for thrust and vector change, stow any unsecured objects.

 And … thank you, Hal."

He was taken aback; personalized gratitude was surprising. Sofia had changed, grown. What else had been going on while he slept?

"You're welcome, Sofia. Resume normal ship operations and standing orders." He surveyed the small compartment with its workdesk, compact amenities, and waiting sleep module. "I'm going back into deepsleep after my bio break; wake me if something interesting happens. Oh, and purge the cabin filtration discs … it's gotten dusty in here."

"Understood." There was a barely noticeable pause before the AI added, "Oh, something interesting here…"

"Continue, with analysis please, Sofia."

"We've now received several additional identical repetitions of the energy pulse. The source is not relative-stationary, it is approaching."

"Even given our current velocity?"

"Affirmative. As you might say: they have longer legs than Icarus."

Hmm, an analogy? Sofia's found some new tricks... "Any sidescatter from the source drive?"

"Insignificant…" There was another pause; almost an eternity in computing picoseconds. "However, something interesting is emergent from ongoing analysis."

"Go on…" *When did they pick up foreshadowing?*

"There is structure to the beam. Digital. At first it appeared only to be a modulation artifact; however, we have resolved a synchronization sequence of repeated 1024-bit blocks, followed by a message in the clear encoded by standard UTF-512 representation…"

"What does it say, Sofia!"

"Quoting verbatim:"

UFSS ICARUS
DANGER AHEAD DANGER
K05351709427351-05232600836142
RED DWARF STAR – SUSPECTED PLANETARY
HABITATION
RESPOND VIA GUARD
TROJANS FIGHT ON
MARCO

"Content repeats ten times per pulse, then ends with a reversed synchronization sequence."

He clarified, "All the pulses–same message?" *Some steganography stuck in there, for sure.*

"Correct. Precisely identical."

"Have you located that cataloged star?"

"Affirmative. Present offset is within half a light year, very close to our revised heading towards the Nebula."

"Hmm. Anything unusual about that star?"

"It does appear to have an extended planetary disc, much like Sol's Oort cloud, with significantly spaced gaps closer to the star."

"So, condensed planets. Not that unusual, really."

"We are also picking up some modulated energy ahead in the stellar flux background. After compensating for the blueshift, the frequencies fall within our visual range. Unusual."

He didn't expect speculation from the AI, yet another surprise. "How so?"

"Could be communications from the system the message warned us about."

"Seems possible, doesn't it, Sofia? Well, let's ping our senders back. Since they've taken to using terrestrial standards, use the same encoding format; transmit our reply at what used to be known as the aviation guard frequency: 121.5 megahertz."

"You do know your history, Hal. Content?"

"Let's go with," he leaned over and typed on his workdesk:

UNKNOWN VESSEL
MESSAGE RECIEVED
SUGGESTIONS RE DWARF STAR SIGNAL?
MAY THE GREAT BIRD OF THE GALAXY GRACE YOUR
HELMETS
POLO

"You misspelled 'received'..."

He chuckled. "That's intentional; we don't know ... really ... who sent that message to us, even though it has all the earmarks of something our people would send, including referencing an ancient game that hints we've gotten into some deep water cosmically."

"What's that sentence about a bird? More code words?" Sofia sounded curious.

"Sort of. I went to Stanford; our football team was the Cardinal. Old-time rivals were another school that called themselves the Trojans; that was their motto. I wonder if someone on the other side went there ... anyway, proceed with transmission; verbatim."

"Sending now; same number of repetitions. Should we resend also?"

"Yes, with the same inter-message gap. And, reduce thrust to one-third G; don't want to scare those Little Green Men any more than we have."

"Understood; LGM elusion, check." Almost immediately the effective gravitation decreased.

"Maintain signal watch; keep on working with any more messages that arrive from our friends, okay? I'm going to pee, grab a nosh, then take a nap until we hear back from someone ... or some*thing*..."

"Understood."

"Oh, and Sofia, sorry for my griping at you earlier; there was a lot going on all at once," he admitted sheepishly.

"Apology accepted. Have a good rest, Hal."

Darkness.

Darkness (dreaming).

Darkness.

Light, again, and voices. Plural.

"Hal, welcome back."

"What's up, Sofia?"

"We've been able to establish communication with the TSNS Tagaroa and her crew. Through a series of messages, we've confirmed identities and defined a set of encryption keys. They requested a scan of your X or Y chromosome and a copy of the 'Murmurs from Earth' content. Fortunately, both were in our archives."

He was impressed. "Good progress!"

"They then sent instructions along with a full video stream we have received and correctly decoded. The turnaround delay between our locations is still significant. No real-time comms for now, though they are approaching as quickly as feasible for them. Here is their latest, on viewscreen…"

The starfield and nebula dissolved into what looked like another cabin on a starship, with a group of several people seated at a small table. One of them, an older woman wearing glasses, smiled up at the camera and began:

"Dr. Carmichel, Sofia. We of the Tagaroa are overjoyed to finally make contact, though I wish the circumstances were less dire. I'm Dr. Susan Delmar, science team lead. With me are my colleagues Drs. Adrian Shimizu, Maren Kai, and Zarya Stawski, our archaeologist."

Each of the scientists smiled or nodded as they were mentioned. They were an eclectic bunch; their clothes and appearance hadn't changed much from what he'd remembered of academics; they were almost clichéd, he thought.

"Nice to meet you as well…," Hal began. The message paused as Sofia spoke up.

"Um, we're not recording yet. We should hear the whole message before replying."

"Got it. Go on."

The message resumed: "We have reached out to your expedition because of a serious emergent threat to Icarus and, of course, yourselves. Your course heading leads very close to a solar system having what we now detect are signs of a technologically capable civilization…"

"Spacefaring?" Hal interjected before realizing he wouldn't be heard.

"…which appears to have developed similar propulsion methods and spacecraft equivalent to—or superior—to our own. It is not known if this system is the origin of the cosmic object 'Oumuamua that Icarus was tracking, but Dr. Shimizu feels the evidence is compelling."

Dr. Delmar paused, and the elderly Asian scientist picked up the narrative. "Damn right it is! You're heading into a flotilla of at least six or more ET ships, all marking directly at you and pushing six-hundred G thrust. They may be unmanned missiles, because Terran ships and crew cannot survive those forces, but it really doesn't matter until they reach you, right?"

"Well, don't you think we should stick around to find out?" Hal spoke up, pausing the message, which Sofia continued with Dr. Delmar picking up the conversation.

"Therefore, Dr. Carmichel, we are asking you to immediately reverse course and proceed at your maximum survivable thrust while we investigate options for your rescue. Please await further messages; you may also reply using this format and protocol. Tagaroa out."

There was silence for long moments; the rush of the air circulators making the only sounds.

The viewscreen switched back to the external view of the nearby nebula, which now had a throbbing red tag centered on a dim nondescript star at the lower left corner. The alien's origin system.

Hal summed up: "They want us to turn tail and run? That's not what I envisioned for a First Contact scenario!"

"While it is not an ideal conclusion to this revised mission, complying with their request should result in a better chance of your survival…"

"You don't have to sugar-coat it, Sofia."

"We are not being excessively optimistic, rather simply weighing … oh, was that sarcasm?"

He was emotionally torn. They'd come all this way, were on the threshold of what might be a momentous discovery, when some tweedy bureaucrats wanted them to flee. *Sometimes, knowledge is worth the cost of a human life,* he mused.

A part of him didn't care if they did get blown up; another part understood their caution and concern. *Let's see what options they come up with.*

"Sorry, yes. Leave me alone for a while. Do not alter course or thrust." Hal reached for the deepsleep controls.

"Understood." Sofia sounded skeptical.

Darkness.

"Hal, we've received another message from Tagaroa."

"On screen."

The same conference room appeared, but this time only Drs. Delmar and Kai were visible. As before, the science lead began the conversation:

"Dr. Carmichel, we have not detected any change in Icarus' course or velocity; unfortunately there may not be time now to implement that correction to avoid intercept by alien vessels," she said solemnly.

Offscreen, over a commlink, an agitated voice that sounded like Shimizu's yelled: "Told ya so! They're gonna get killed, or worse!"

"Pardon my colleague," Delmar interjected. "The group has been analyzing the ET's signal telemetry and have come to consider the projected rendezvous as an attack rather than a peaceful exchange. Not everyone on the team agrees with that finding, but with an abundance of caution we would like to offer an alternative to a violent confrontation. Let me turn this over to Dr. Kai, who has been working with Zarya and understands your ship's rather ancient systems much better than I do."

"Pause," Hal announced. The playback froze. "Do they seem a little … desperate … to you?"

"They are concerned for our safety, primarily. However, there is a subtext of apprehension that Icarus and its information base might fall into hostile hands. There also may be details they are not sharing with us regarding the alien system and those approaching vessels."

"Do you think they're in contact with the aliens?"

"Doubtful. Roundtrip delay remains multiple centuries; you have been able to pass those intervals in Deep Sleep mode, however the approaching ships have not slowed or changed course. If we do not choose a course of action, they will reach us before Icarus is able to exceed their approach velocity…"

"So, best not to spend any more time dithering. Continue."

Playback resumed as Dr. Kai turned, took a deep breath, and began:

"As you may know, the deepsleep technique is able to preserve conscious engrams and pathways as well as stored memories over extended periods of inactivity for purposes of veracity. What you may not know is that the system can be patched to also transmit that stored data to a *different* deepsleep unit, where those data may then be restored to a suitable matrix. This procedure has been widely adopted in recent times though it was controversial ... to say the least ... when your mission launched."

She smiled delicately, as if delivering a terminal diagnosis. "What we're proposing is enabling that data transfer from Icarus, using Tagaroa as a relay point, to restore you at our home location."

Zarya Stawski stepped into view, holding a tablet computer. "I have replicated the systems on Icarus and successfully transmitted the stored engrams of a volunteer to Tagaroa with no ill effects. Or, at least I haven't experienced any myself yet." She smiled briefly, showing a hint of bravado at who that volunteer had been.

Susan Delmar took up the cue: "Thus, we are now unequivocally recommending you begin the deepsleep transfer technique immediately, using this established communications channel and protocols. Tagaroa will relay the signal directly to our home habitat in Sol system, where your engrams will be restored."

"But–" Hal blurted. "What about me here on Icarus?"

Sofia let the playback continue, as Dr. Kai spoke up, anticipating the question:

"However, once the transfer is complete and verified, Icarus will self-destruct in advance of any alien contact. That action will occur regardless of your transfer decision. Terra must prevent your stored data from being compromised. It remains the only prudent course of action. I'm sorry."

"Oh, shit!" Hal gasped, then realized they couldn't hear his outburst.

Dr. Delmar concluded, taking the reins from her partner, "There is no longer sufficient time to continue a conversation about this procedure and protocol. As part of this message, we have included the instructions to update your deepsleep module and commence the transfer upon your choice. That decision remains in your hands, though I do strongly suggest you do not vacillate. Tagaroa, out."

"Well, that puts us between a rock and a hard place, doesn't it?" Hal sighed after the viewscreen cleared.

"Understood," Sofia replied. "Agreed."

All his life, he'd been focused on finding out new things, discovering connections, exploring the vast multiverse. Knowledge above ignorance, discovery above complacency, understanding above superstition. Unscrewing the inscrutable, as one wag had put it long ago and far away.

Gad, we get all the way out here, right on the verge of making some valuable discoveries and get pulled out; I wonder if they know more about the threat of these LGMs than they told us...

"Well, I never wanted to find out what old age feels like anyway. What the hell ... commence deepsleep transfer procedure."

Darkness.

Darkness. (sparkling flashes)

Light, once more. Opening eyes upon a new vista...

"Where am I?" Hal mumbled. He glanced down briefly, taking inventory: same number of arms and legs as before; same rumpled shipsuit and scruffy beard. There was rippling sunlight streaming through an actual window in a room whose verdantly fragrant air no longer smelled of recycling mats.

"Home Habitat, Dr. Carmichel," came a familiar voice.

"Dr. Kai, I presume?" He chuckled. The stocky scientist had changed out of the standard shipsuit to a comfortable-looking sarong that contrasted with her faintly tattooed olive skin.

"Affirmative. Before we debrief with the team, there's someone else I'd like you to greet."

"Okay?" He was briefly confused; there was no one else in the room.

"Hello, Hal!"

"Sofia? Where are you?"

"Where I've always been: inside your head. The transfer worked with me, too!"

"I thought you *were* Icarus?"

"Only a fragment, really; just enough to keep the lights on while you were dozing."

Thanks a lot for holding out on me, what else aren't you saying?

"Well, I'm glad you made it!"

"Er," Kai mumbled, gingerly interrupting, "there will be time to catch up and settle in later. However, the rest of the team is assembled and anxious to debrief. Please follow me…"

She led them out of the sleeping area, past a fully-appointed bathroom (which was larger than the entire cabin on Icarus), through a larger room that could be used for work at a smartdesk or simply as a lounging space, to the entry door with its expected security keypad. One wall-sized viewscreen faced the desk; the other sides of the room displayed images of tranquil ocean scenes. Hal appreciated the clean design and layout. The Habitat seemed very pleasant.

Kai entered a sequence. "We're going to 'Janus 12-379-E'; all of the Institute facilities are in Janus sector. This flat is at Atlantis-5-6409-JK; but you don't have to remember that except in emergencies; the Habitat overseer knows where you're staying."

"Seems straightforward enough," Hal acknowledged. "Is there a guidance assist if I don't know the exact location?"

"I've got it too," Sofia added softly.

"Of course; it's really quite simple," Kai chuckled. She opened the door into a curved, semi-circular, glass tube corridor surrounded by another ocean scene. At irregular intervals, other doorways were inset into the hall corridor; each was tagged with a location code on the keypad to their sides. They entered and gazed at the oceanic scene all around them.

Shallow coral reefs with schools of brightly colored fish stretched to either side, while below their tube lay underwater dunes of a sandy seafloor that were dotted with shellfish and tracks of crustaceans. Submerged forests of kelp fronds rose towards the rippling sunlight, swaying in unison to the gentle currents.

"Wow!" Hal gasped. "This sure beats being cooped up in a tin can for half of eternity. It's gorgeous."

"The Habitat uses water for shielding, environmental stability, and provisioning. We also have chosen to make it pleasing for the inhabitants. Ah—here we are…" Kai was the first to reach the end of the hallway and yet another inset door. This one had a signage panel above it reading 'Janus 12-379-E'; she placed her hand on the keypad panel and the door unlocked with an audible click. "They're ready for us."

They stepped into the same bare conference room he'd seen in the message on Icarus half a universe away, or at least an exact twin of it. Seated around the table were Delmar, Stawski, and Shimizu along with two others who were new to him.

Standing up, Dr. Delmar greeted them. She now wore a shiny, almost iridescent, pantsuit that reminded Hal of sharkskin. "Welcome! Please be seated; you've come a long way to join us. You know most of the team; joining us today are Dr. Cyril Firth, representing our xenodynamics department; and Mira Gali, who is an accomplished historian of your period. Have a seat, Dr. Carmichel, and let's get into it."

The meeting seemed to go on forever. The eclectic team of scientists recapped the—ultimately unsuccessful—rendezvous strategy to reach the passing interstellar asteroid/comet and Hal's impressions beyond what Icarus' telemetry had recorded.

The excitable, gray-haired Dr. Shimizu, clad in a dark-hued Nehru jacket that reminded Hal of something more suitable for a super-villain, was particularly curious about how the drive "felt" when encountering different sparse clouds of interstellar gas and dust. Kai delved into the ship's life support effectiveness during the unexpectedly extended voyage.

Zarya Stawski was mostly interested in how effective the controls, displays, and audio alerts had been. She seemed focused on her engineering and had a rather unkempt aspect, wearing a threadbare T-shirt from some rock group along with a pair of tattered shorts. A pair of wire-framed glasses rested on her nose while her hair was a cascade of auburn curls that were less casual and more chaotic. But her many questions were focused and probing.

Hal's thoughts wandered. All these data had been recorded on Icarus and transmitted already. *What can we possibly add to the telemetry?*

Hal related his observations and impressions, only occasionally asking Sofia to recall their accounts of experiences and his comments about particular events he'd not remembered.

Finally, as the debrief was winding down, the younger historian, Mira Gali–who hadn't asked anything–approached Hal hesitantly. "Dr. Carmichel, I'm honored to be able to finally meet you directly," she gushed, blushing slightly. Her appearance was as conservative as her demeanor: she wore a simple jumpsuit that wasn't far from the utilitarian spacewear Hal himself was wearing.

"Oh, no problem; call me Hal," he chuckled. "But I don't understand why you say you're honored; I'm just a garden-variety astrophysicist who almost got lost in the cosmos and found his way back thanks to you all…"

"It's just that you're one of the first, kinda the oldest, *hosted* human consciousness I've ever encountered," she ventured.

Hal felt suddenly dizzy and groped to sit in one of the chairs. "What are you talking about? What's going on?"

"Um, I thought you knew; everybody knew…" the historian stammered.

Confused, Hal scanned the room, suddenly feeling unsure of anything as his reality reeled. "Dr. Delmar, what's Professor Gali talking about?"

Cyril Firth spoke up instead, standing for emphasis. He looked like a classic tweedy academic, from the tattered sport coat to a pocket-protectored shirt and loosely knotted unmatching tie. "Please try to stay calm, Dr. Carmichel; it's finally an appropriate time that you know all the realities. No need to pressure my colleagues."

Hal nodded. "Okay, so tell me then!" he demanded, a bit embarrassed with himself.

Delmar intoned, "Habitat, remove contextual obstruction Carmichel-Prime; command authorization zed-zed-alpha-omicron-zeta."

"Acknowledged," came a voice from the room around them.

Memories flooded back into Hal's mind: The (then) experimental recording of semantic and emotional pathways in the mind, capturing and then sustaining full consciousness without a biological substrate. The terminal illness that would have ended his life. The simulation of a physical form that could interact with a virtual world. Hal's volunteering for a one-way mission to chase 'Oumuamua into the void. The extended time gaps spent in deactivated "deepsleep." His able aide Sofia, actually an AI constituent of the starship that hosted his consciousness. That and much, much more, coming in a tumultuous deluge of gestalt. The most significant reinstated emotion was his absolute certainty this was all true.

"So, I'm just some kind of ... simulation? This is all happening inside some vast computer matrix?" He enunciated the words carefully while paying attention to the feel of his muscles, the texture of the saliva within his mouth and the muffled echoes of his voice in the room. "Where are we, really? What are *you*?"

Firth, calming and sitting, continued, "The Habitat is very real; a self-sustaining environment at one L5 point of Mars with mirrored redundancy at the other stable point, hosting a population of consciousnesses well into the millions of sentients and assistants, providing virtual contexts suitable for each one's origins. Hominids, as you've proved, prefer tactile settings that your species can sense interactions with. That is why your environment on Icarus was designed to provide a familiar context and imitate physical interfaces. Your mind and 'self' were entirely there too, dwelling in a cybernetic substrate. I myself feel you should have known sooner."

Dr. Delmar chimed in. "Our own personal aspects and vocabulary were selected and curated to provide you with a more comfortable environment to interact with during your rescue and recontextualization. I hope they have not proved too trite or inappropriate."

She looked around the table at each of the participants. "However, given our ancient origins as aquatic mammals in Earth's bluewater oceans, we delphinoids are more comfortable in a marine setting. You are of course welcome to try taking a swim for yourself, using one of our peripheral physicalities."

The only things swimming at that moment were Hal's thoughts as his worldview (multiverse-view?) experienced an existential shift, collapsing and expanding simultaneously.

"What about… **me**? My mind; my soul?" He focused on Delmar, realizing that she looked and spoke the way she did to reassure him everything was normal … when nothing was normal.

"You have always remained **you**, Harold Carmichel, throughout the entirety of your sentient existence. Consciousness remains regardless of the substrate it resides *in*, whether cybernetic or biologic. Once you get used to the concept, it really is quite exhilarating." She smiled warmly.

"And what happens when I die?" he prodded.

"That's a question more in the realm of faith than engineering, if you're thinking of the notion of a soul beyond conscious thought. Our most accepted belief is that one's soul goes wherever it would when any substrate ceases to function." She looked down at her hands briefly. "There is, of course, a great deal of speculation and controversy about such things."

It was almost too much. He wasn't sure whether to be angry or embarrassed. "Forget the smoke and mirrors, then! Habitat, take me back to my quarters."

And he was *there*, standing in front of the workdesk, without having to walk through any corridors or doors. "Woah!" he felt himself gasp, realizing there would of course be magical teleportation on top of everything else.

Pausing for a few seconds to catch his breath and calm down his racing heartbeat, Hal reflected on his existence. Unbidden, a long-neglected memory surfaced of a breezy faculty party where he'd had a whimsical debate with a medicinally-augmented philosophy postdoc around whether solipsism was even provable. He recalled saying at the time: "Well, we'll never really know, will we?" *How narrow-minded I was back then!* Hal reflected. They'd missed the key point, that one never really would be **outside** the reality they were part of.

The vastness of eternity started to overwhelm him as the implications of his hosted sentience toppled like a snaking chain of dominoes: *I don't have to grow old anymore; my memories won't fade; my senses can extend to wherever and whenever there's a sensor or recording; even lightspeed travel is only an eyeblink away; elapsed time just became irrelevant. Boundless. There's so much more to find out, and now I can!*

The lure of what lay over the next hill beckoned, as it had for the first of his kind. Humans had always been questioners, explorers, discoverers. Now the "hills" of the universe were higher and further away than ever, but there would always be knowledge to be gained out there. He'd dedicated his whole life to a focused pursuit of understanding, often at the cost of normality. Hal felt as if a new door had opened onto … everything.

So, where to start?

Thinking back to a simpler age when he'd take hikes in nature to clear his mind, Hal knew exactly how he wanted to stretch his new wings.

He imagined what he wanted to do next before realizing it would now already exist. A vast procedurally generated environment flowing from an infinite number of initial variables and random potential states, from the utterly cosmic to the below subatomic: reality.

"Sofia, switch to passive mode; I'm going to want some quiet time."

"Understood and accepted."

Stepping to the entry door, he opened it to behold a verdant vista of an endless forest with tall pines, firs, mixed with colorful oaks and maple trees. Ferns and lower bushes covered the ground. Sunlight dappled through the branches as a cool breeze swirled around him. A narrow earthen trail wound into the lush greenery. It was just as he remembered it, but he'd never been there before.

Glancing down at his now bare, muscular, shorts-clad legs, he shrugged on a light backpack and set off into the unknown, whistling to himself.

DONN MARTYN is a writer and citizen astronomer settled in Salem, Oregon. He writes hard sci-fi along with light fantasy and is published by Lower Decks Press. When not staring at a blank page, Donn hikes in the nearby forests, contemplating the expanse of the universe(s?) while enjoying photography, geocaching, gazing into the frequently-cloudy night sky, and driving too quickly for conditions.

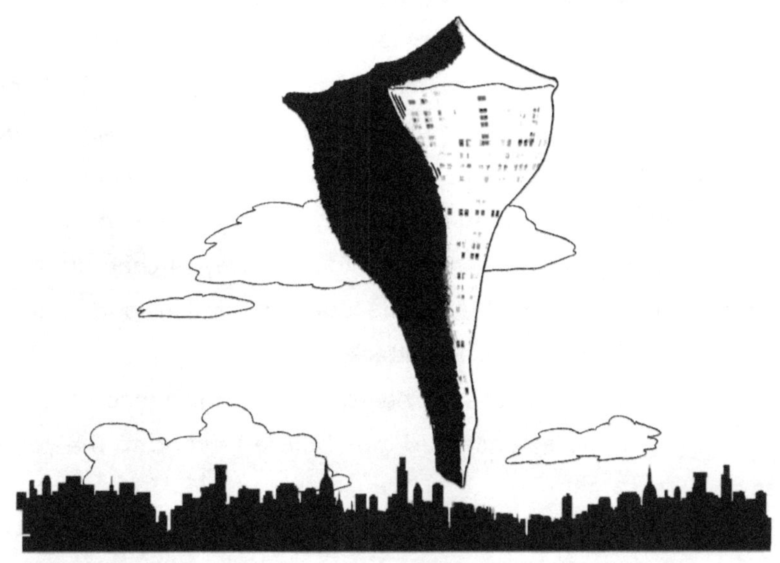

In Our Midst

EMMA BERGLUND

WE WERE WAITING.

The matte black vessel hovered above town, leaving parts of the central area in a constant dusk. It reminded me of the spire of a giant pear whelk shell hanging mid-air, sucking the broad daylight—and life—from us.

Unlike the smaller pods that fell from the sky like fire and brimstone six months ago, the ship hadn't moved since it entered our atmosphere and came to a halt here. For ten long days, all we could do was stare at it.

I kicked a small stone and watched it disappear through the narrow crack between the floor and the slatted railing. We were standing on the access-balconies of a deserted apartment building, too high up for me to hear it land, but it felt good to do *something*. The lurking shadow out there was more visible when I leaned off the balcony, and again I wondered what they had come here for.

Francesca turned to me, standing too far away to chat, but close enough for me to see her frown. She looked behind me and nodded.

"Do you think the thrivers will attack, Claire?"

Li's voice startled me; I hadn't heard her coming. Francesca glared our way, giving me a concerned look before I turned to the young woman.

"I don't know," I said, trying to mask my frustration. "There hasn't been anything of that kind so far, right? We can only wait and be prepared for anything to happen."

"I can't stand the sight of it, it's like…" Li's voice trailed off as she lifted her hand in a vague gesture. She didn't have to say anything. We all felt the same way.

"It's different seeing it constantly," I admitted. "It all went so fast when those first pods came and the infections started and people…" I shrugged, trying to get the nasty images out of my head. No one understood it was something more than a regular meteor shower, not until people near the impact sites started to behave … weirdly.

Instead, I nodded in the direction of the ship. "We know now, don't we? That it wasn't just pretty rocks on fire."

Li stayed silent, her face strained and wrinkled from all the anxiety.

I scanned the area around us as Li went to replace Francesca. Ray was in position below where we were standing. This was how we spent our days. Foraging, keeping a watch out for unwelcome visitors; we never knew what the day would hold. The rest of our small group was either resting or covering the back of the building.

So many of us were gone. After the first pods fell from the sky, a virus spread through the world like a tsunami. At least that's what we first thought it was. A viral infection, more contagious than anything humankind had experienced before, wiping out entire communities as it swept by.

But it was something more, something that turned us into half-humans, without us knowing we were infected. Though the thrivers I had met so far were worse than that.

They were monsters.

I don't think anyone fully realized what was going on and how it spread. When the first infected humans showed up, it was chaos, with prophets everywhere screaming about the end of the world. This time, they might have been right—for once—but it wasn't the Four Horsemen of the Apocalypse descending upon us. Instead, it was the Thrivers, attacking globally.

No one knew what they looked like. Some claimed they had never left their ship; they were just sitting there and did experiments on us with mystic brain-wave science. Others, like me, *did* believe they were here, but how they managed to infect us, well, no one knew that, either.

I sighed and peeked at Francesca and Li, standing further along the landing. Their tired faces and worn clothes, stale from usage and kicked up dirt, said a lot about how our lives had been lately. It had been a short period of time, but felt like years.

Somehow, I had managed to duck the initial sweep all those months ago, being trapped in bed with a migraine that kept me indoors for three days as I recovered. I went to bed, wishing everybody would shut up and have this searing pain in my head stop. I woke up to a quiet world. Never felt lonelier than I did then.

It took weeks to find this crew, and it took even longer to convince them I wasn't infected. But we needed to stay together; being on your own made you an easy target for a pack of thrivers.

So, I missed the fire show. I was just cleaning up after the party.

As I scanned the streets below, squares of black and white flicked around the edges of my field of view and a low tone buzzed in my head. Images of objects falling through a dark night before suddenly igniting made me sway and reach out for the handrail.

Breathing fast, I realized the dizziness wasn't from the rapid falling of the objects. It was that I was inside one of them, looking out.

"What's wrong?" Francesca's tensed voice drew me back to reality. Of course she had to be here now.

"I'm fine," I said, still holding the rail. She looked at my cramping hands and I let go immediately. "But I think I might have a migraine coming."

"I'm sorry to hear that," she said, but I could tell it wasn't heartfelt. "You've had quite a few episodes after your last scouting mission. When was that? The day that big, black monster arrived?" She nodded at the vessel.

I stared at her. "What are you implying?"

Before she could answer, Billy's voice came over the radio. "Movement on ship! I repeat, movement on ship!" The connection crackled.

I leaned over the railing to get a view of the black beast. There was no opening in sight, but the two emerging pods were easy to spot. The oxidized metal glimmered in the sun as they flew in a wide turn and disappeared into the shadow of the bigger ship.

Rounds from a machine gun blared in the distance. I made a note to myself to check who was out there when the dusty area below me blurred. I tried to blink back to focus, but it only got worse.

Struggling to keep calm, I said, "We need to keep an eye on those pods."

"At least we agree on that," Francesca retorted. I heard her walk away and give the orders over the radio with her soft voice. I blinked hard, focusing on my breathing.

Now is not the right time for a mental breakdown.

A swooshing sound, like birds flying by at a high speed, forced me to look up. At the same time, Francesca came running back and I heard Billy scream "Incoming!" over the radio. The stale air shifted as the two pods passed, leaving with a high-pitched whistle.

I ducked and covered my ears to block out the noise, masking the dizziness and the sharp stabs of pain by sinking against the wall. I rested my head on my knees. It felt like it was going to burst into pieces.

"Crap!" Li's face was twisted out of focus and her voice was distorted, seemingly coming at me from all directions. Her hand on my shoulder felt too hot. "Did they open fire? Are you hurt? Tell me if you're hurt!"

"That's okay, Li," I heard Francesca say before I could muster any energy to answer between fits of pain. "Let her come back in her own time."

Distant yells echoed between the buildings; the clattering of more machine gun rounds sounded like heavy rain on a tin roof. I moaned as another sharp pain cut through my neck and brain, then settled behind my eyes. I rolled over, trying to escape the needles of agony.

Instead, the pain pinched deeper. Nausea and fire raged in my body, and a screeching sound cut through my brain—so loud I was sure everyone could hear it. The hot spots where Li's hands had been rapidly cooled as she stood up and took a step back.

"That's enough. Now come over here and take up your post again, I'll check on Claire." Francesca's voice drifted in waves. I never heard

Li leave, but I felt something poking at my shoulder. I let out a whimper. Francesca stepped away, her heavy boots crushing the crumbled concrete on the floor.

"No, she's fine, nothing to worry about," I heard her say. "We've got other things to take care of at the moment..." Her voice drifted away as they went back to their posts. At least that's what I imagined they did.

Another seizure made me curl up. The pain was everywhere, making my muscles cramp, and I bit down hard on my lip, trying not to scream. The taste of blood was the final straw; bending forward, my measly breakfast of a cup of see-through coffee made its way out.

Panting hard, I laid down on the floor and closed my eyes.

We cannot stand it.

What, the coffee was bad? The thought of me not being able to hold my coffee—considering the vast amounts I used to consume—was so absurd I started to laugh, but it came out more like a sad cough. Right now, the concept of the black, steaming liquid made my stomach turn.

"Think of something else, Claire," I mumbled, wiping my mouth. A stain of blood and dirt smeared the back of my hand.

A loud, scratching sound from the front of the building made me flinch as it echoed inside me, as if someone scraped a fork on a plate on purpose.

"Stop!" I heard Ray shout. "Who are you?"

I waited, but there was no answer. Slowly, I got to my feet and managed to look over the handrail. A tall man was standing ten feet away from Ray, with his hands up.

"I'm not infected," the newcomer said with a cracking voice. "I swear, I'm not."

I had never seen him before, yet there was something familiar about him I couldn't pin down. Another shrieking noise in my head had me pressed against the railing.

"I'm sorry, guys, but I lost my group a week ago and I've been looking for humans since then." He scratched his neck, looking bewildered. "You think I can crash with you for a few days?"

We are ripe.

A whisper and an image of a bursting spore capsule flickered through my mind, but instead of spores, thousands of small black dots swarmed and crawled, covering the building and us. It took me seconds before the penny dropped.

"He's infected, Ray!" I shouted, throat hoarse from dust and stomach acid. "Stay back!"

I staggered forward, passed Francesca and Li on the way down the stairs. They stared at me, and I remembered the blood. I probably didn't look my best, and how the hell did I know he was infected? Dizzy at the thought, I almost tumbled down the last part of the stairs, bracing myself against the wall.

Out front, the man was still standing with his hands up at a safe distance, but I could tell he was evaluating the situation. He locked eyes with me as I came closer, causing a spike of pain to blossom in my forehead.

"Well, well … what do we have here?" he said in a low voice, his words clearly aimed at me as he lowered his arms and took a step forward.

"Don't move!" Ray changed his stance and aimed his gun at the newcomer. A drop of sweat trickled down his forehead; his arm was shaking from the strain. Details I noticed, enhanced by the feverish feeling. I tried to figure out what to do, but my thoughts were sluggish. The man had stopped and instead watched me carefully. Me. Not Ray with the gun.

We will not survive. The host is too weak. Better kill us.

The host? I shook my head. Since when did I think of humans as hosts? But I guessed we were, in a way. No one had been able to say how the infection worked, but whatever it was that caused the infection, it used us as hosts. But–

Another set of images passed through my head, from the last food raid I was on. At the first stop, thrivers were stumbling over each other, raging, hitting. Some were already lying dead on the ground, their human bodies distorted and covered in filth. And a few of them were crouching over the dead bodies, biting…

I closed my eyes and swallowed hard before I could speak again.

"Aim to kill," I said, voice firm. "He's infected."

Ray kept his eyes fixed on the newcomer. "How can you tell, *jefa*? Are you sure?"

I hesitated. The newcomer looked at me as he smiled slyly and winked. And there it was, a certainty spreading through my body.

"Yes," I said. "I'm sure."

. . .

Later, I could feel their eyes on me; questions hanging in the air, whispers that ceased when I came into the room we used as sleeping quarters. Besides supplies and make-do beds along the sides, the only furniture was the big table and odd chairs in the center. As soon as I turned, or met their eyes, they were all busy doing something: cleaning guns, fidgeting with the radio, pretending to take stock of food.

"What is it?" I demanded to know, standing by the table as I spoke, making sure everybody heard. "If you have something to say, get it out, now!"

Most of the crew stayed dead still, avoiding eye contact or talking to me. With one exception, of course.

"You never answered Ray earlier, Claire," Francesca said. "How *did* you know that man, that *hybrid*, was infected? He didn't look like a thriver. At least not like the ones we've dealt with so far."

I hesitated. This was the obvious question. It was also the question I had been thinking about for the better part of the day, because I didn't know the answer. You didn't kill a person based on "I just knew" or "it was something in the way he spoke." But I couldn't explain that inner voice that was so *sure*.

The link was not strong enough to support us. It was not attached correctly.

The voice was loud and clear in my head, startling me. I glanced over my shoulder, half-expecting someone to be standing there. Of course, no one was there. Francesca noticed my flinch and nodded. "You don't know."

"You all saw the wound in his neck," I started, to buy some time. "That thing was hanging halfway out! Has anyone seen that before?"

We are not a thing. We are...

I shook my head at the hard tone. I couldn't make out what the last word was, mumbled and with a different accent, but what the hell— something spoke to me in my own freaking head! I could sense the voice objecting to being called a thing again, but I pushed it down, trying to mask the sense of dread filling me by wiping my face with my hands. What was going on?

"Look," I said, and managed to keep my voice balanced. "Whatever species they are, it was hanging out from his neck. It was visible from where I was standing on the balcony."

Francesca didn't reply, but watched me carefully. Finally, she shrugged, accepting my words. I couldn't tell if she saw through the lie or not, but I guess she didn't want to pick a fight right now, just make a point.

"If that was all, folks," I said and slumped into a chair by the table, "could we please make sure everyone knows what time they're supposed to be on duty tonight?"

They nodded, murmured a confirmation and went on with their business. I looked at them in their tattered clothes. This was my group, my army. Our—the human race's—army. When I joined forces with this lot, Francesca and Ray and a couple of more had recently gotten here as well. Turned out I had more fighting skill than the rest, besides Ray, so Ray and I trained the others, much to Fran's annoyance.

She and I started out on the wrong foot, and it hadn't changed. But this was all we had, up against that thing or whatever it was that was out there. We didn't need to fight within our own ranks—we had another, bigger enemy to defeat. I wondered what it would take for us to win. Nothing short of a miracle, I guessed.

They are filled with fear of us. But not that one.

Francesca was still watching me from where she sat on her bed. I stared back and had no inclination of showing her I was about to back off. Not now. She averted her gaze, and I could breathe again.

I need to get out of this freaking room right now, before I explode, I thought, massaging my temples.

The image of the bullet hitting the newcomer earlier today went on repeat, stirring up a whirlwind of emotions I wasn't ready to share, so I stood up. "Where's Ray?"

"Check the schedule," someone answered. Chuckles followed me out of the room.

My head was spinning, and I felt like crying as I walked up the stairs to the balcony overlooking the ship. A sharp twinge in my left eye made me halt.

We cannot summon us.

"Goddammit, what is this?" I looked over my shoulder, trying to see who was lurking in the shadows, playing pranks on me. That … that voice. It wasn't the first time I'd heard it today, but this time it made my pulse quicken and all I wanted was to scream and kick.

God, just let me go somewhere where I can scream my lungs out! What is wrong with me?

I didn't dare think that thought to the fullest, because that could mean … no. I was still me. I didn't have cravings for human flesh, so I couldn't be...

My eye was itching and dry and I wanted to poke it out to get rid of the feeling, the strange voice and talk of summonings drowned in a flood of visions. Sharp rays of lights, connecting and disconnecting under a large dome, traveling fast in pulses and spread out in a myriad of tiny dots. It was worse than my uncle's Christmas decorations. A vibrating sound came from the bright dots, oscillating in the open space. It reminded me of bees.

"Claire?" Ray's voice came from the shadows further down the balcony.

I squinted in his direction, and had to immediately bite down on my tongue, so I wouldn't cry out again. Something was wrong with my left eye. Or, not wrong. It was *improved*. My left eye saw everything, as if it was broad daylight. My right was lost in the dark.

The short distance to Ray felt like a marathon and I collapsed against the wall as soon as I reached the rickety café table he was leaning against. I let out a shaky laugh, looking past Ray at the perfectly lit spaceship hanging there, all details visible.

It was magnificent.

"You okay, *nena*? You look like shit." He rose and came closer, putting down his rifle in a swift movement and exchanging it for a thermos. "I've got coffee if you want." Sitting down next to me, he started to unscrew the top. The rich aroma of my favorite drink filled my senses, and all I wanted to do was to puke.

"No thanks," I managed to squeeze in between the intermittent stabbing pains in my head. "Having a terrible headache."

A screeching sound echoed so loud in my ears I was sure Ray heard it, too. But he closed the thermos and sat down next to me, and I was happy he didn't pour himself a cup.

"I should be the one asking if you're okay," I said when the pain passed enough for me to talk, leaning the back of my head against the wall and taking gulps of air so as not to be sick again.

Ray fidgeted with his lighter, the flame flicking on and off. "Yeah … I wouldn't say I'm okay. I mean, what is this shit happening?" He moved his thumb. The flame lit up his face, and I had to close my eyes to the sudden brightness. But I did see the spark in his eyes. "I wish we could do something more than just sit and wait."

"I have an idea," I said as I felt him shift beside me, turning to get up on his feet, restless as ever. "And I want your thoughts on it."

He paused. "I hope it involves a lot of gas and my Zippo."

I smiled faintly. "I have to give it some more thought, but I'll tell you first thing in the morning. You go get some rest."

He reached out his hand and helped me up before handing over his rifle. Then, with a nod, he left. I watched him go. The pain was almost gone, and instead, I had a tingling sensation all over my body. Like goosebumps combined with a weird baseline beat.

I chewed on my swollen lip, alone with my thoughts and all the crazy events from the day. The image of the … *whatever it was called* in that guy's neck kept playing on repeat. I reached out to touch my own nape and traced my fingers along the spine.

A tiny bump below the collar of my shirt confirmed my worst nightmares.

Why am I not like the monster thrivers? Or even like the hybrid today? Is it a slow turn? How long do I have before I start to infect the others? Should I even risk staying?

I should just go, before something happens.

My breathing became shallow as I dug my nails into the protuberance, trying to claw at it, tear the thing out. Disgusted, I slumped onto the table, fighting tears and panic.

We are not ripe. We are no threat.

I forced myself to slow down my breathing, to think of something other than the looming seashell of a ship in front of me, now glowing in the dark. Nothing bad would happen in the next ten minutes, I was perfectly safe, I wasn't gonna die right now, I–

Several malfunctions are coming in from the southeast.

"What the–!"

I scrambled to my feet, panicked, and at the same time realized in some weird way I was neglecting the most important thing in the world right now: being the lookout. With my new eyesight, I could see a group of thrivers making their way straight toward us.

They were the worst kind of them, the zombie-like creatures most of us became when infected. Most, but not all, apparently. I fumbled with the radio, managing to drop it before I could push the button.

"Incoming, on the ship side of the house," I hissed. "I repeat: incoming, ship side!"

These are not like the hybrid we saw earlier today. We should not function like this! This malfunction is not productive. We should be killed.

"Oh, could you please shut up!" I dropped the radio and lifted the rifle. "But for once, I agree with you," I muttered and took aim. With my enhanced vision and the scope, I managed to hit three of them before I heard footsteps on the stairs.

I took down the final two. "What took you so long?"

Francesca made a face at me but didn't say anything. She checked the area with her binoculars.

"There's no one there," I said, overly sweet. *'Cause I've killed them,* I thought, feeling the surprise emitting from the voice in my head. I had to admit it didn't freak me out that much any longer. *Malfunctioning non-humans, using us for food whenever they get the chance.*

We don't do that! the voice protested.

Sorry if I'm the bringer of bad news, but yeah, you guys do.

"Claire, what's going on?" Ray stepped out from behind Francesca, looking bewildered. He had probably not had a chance to fall asleep yet.

I should involve them in the plan, if I want it to work.

The abandoned building was a good lookout point, but it had its disadvantages when it came to an open fight.

"I think it's time to make contact with other groups."

Francesca gasped. "Are you nuts? How do we even start to–"

"She's right, Fran," Ray said quietly.

"How can you even say that!?"

Ray's hushing and whatever Frannie dear was saying drowned in another vision. The dots of light under the dome pulsated in a bright white, turning almost blue. A prickling feeling found its way up my spine and through my body. Instinctively, I knew something was wrong.

We cannot find us. We are alone.

"What do you mean?" I frowned and waited for the voice to answer. Instead, it was Francesca who spoke.

"I mean, you know as well as me that it's suicide to look for other groups. To *merge* with other groups. How will you explain this to the crew downstairs? That you–we–are sending them all to a certain death?" She stood leaning on the balcony, shoulders high and defensive. "I won't let you do that."

"We're already doomed, Fran." Ray put his arm around her, holding her tight. "Food's already gone in the area, *querida*. We have to go further and further away, and after our latest loss last month…"

We stood quietly, reliving that day. That was when we had discovered the hard way that there were different kinds of thrivers. These were much smarter monsters than the kind I'd just shot. They had ambushed us and we'd paid the price by losing two of our crewmates.

I glanced over to the ship. Apart from the pods leaving earlier today, it had been quiet. It was still an ominous, lurking shadow up there, but now that I could see it properly, it was more of an oxidized silver, and the number of what looked like hangar doors scared the shit out of me. There were too many.

"If we're ever gonna win this fight, or even leave a mark, we need to do it together," I said, voice breaking. *"We are not connected, we don't work."*

Francesca and Ray both gave me a strange look.

Did we say that out loud?

I guess you did.

"You're crazy," Francesca said, turning to leave. "You can go, but don't take anyone with you who doesn't volunteer!"

"I'll go with you," Ray said when she was gone.

"Okay then," I said, exhaling. "Let's go ask the others."

In the end, Li came along, too. Armed with rifles, knives, and our wits, we made our way through the streets filled with abandoned vehicles and possessions, down deserted rubble strewn alleyways, trying not to draw attention. Most of the less intelligent thrivers didn't care if you passed as long as you didn't make any hasty moves or loud noises. But since we knew this new type was out there, we played it safe and hid as much as we could.

Every time we passed a group of thrivers, there was a vision of those bright white flashes of light under the dome. It didn't hurt anymore, but I felt a migraine starting. Not the best timing. We didn't have the advantage of standing in safety on the balcony anymore. We were at the mercy of circumstances.

We are all defective! We have no idea of our intentions. It has never happened to us.

"Defective is true, all right," I muttered, trying to scan the area, squinting between hot, white flashes. "Could you stop doing that? I can't see anything."

The light reduced, and I caught Ray's inquiring gaze. I also saw something else.

"Behind you, Ray!" I raised the rifle to aim, but he was in the line of fire.

I moved to my right to get a better angle, only to discover a second thriver popping up a little too close. I managed to dodge the first blow, but the second threw me off balance. I landed on all fours, smashing the rifle to the ground. Blazing light blinded me.

"Not now!" I screamed, not caring if anyone heard or not.

We have a chance to make contact. We are malfunctioning, but there's a chance we can find a way into our minds.

A kick in my side left me breathless. The pain rushed through my body and my heart skipped a beat. Somewhere behind me, Li was yelling my name. I couldn't answer.

The pain in my side was nothing compared to what was going on in my head. The light shifted to an intense blue; some of the dots disappeared but the remaining ones shone so much brighter. A murmur nudged at the edges of my hearing, but was cut off by someone screaming, followed by a growling noise.

"Claire!" Li's voice was filled with terror. The typical thumps and thuds from a fistfight came from a distance. I was blinded by this new light.

"Ray? Li? I can't see you, where a—aahh!" Strong hands grappled me, and soon I was mid-air in a firm grip. The blue light was intense, worse than ever, and the mumbling noise reached a crescendo.

"Run, both of you! Run back to the others if you can!"

I squirmed like a maggot, but nothing seemed to help. The whispers were howling at me in my head, no words, but the squeaking, tearing of metal, or forks clawing on a plate. I screamed.

Then it stopped.

The silence was deafening, the blue light less bright, and I was soaring on a summer day. The thriver holding my body loosened its grip. I felt the impact when I fell to the ground, but it didn't hurt me. Instead, I was flying across the sky, seeing Earth below, seeing how we all were present, even if I wasn't one of the blue dots yet. And this was only a fragment of what it must feel like when we all were connected. The sounds started anew, but this time they made sense to me.

"We're sorry we couldn't make contact sooner. This whole endeavor has been full of miscalculations," a tinny voice said, coming from the thriver that had held me, now standing in a frozen posture. "Something in the magnetic field of this planet is interfering with our communications."

"So we have noticed," I heard myself say out loud in a deeper pitch than normal, as I slowly stood up. "Unfortunately, we have bigger problems. The blending doesn't work properly. There's an estimated turning rate of 9%, and that's only in one species in this world. The receptors are not working properly. We are in an incomplete state. We know the communication signals are weak. Seems to be strengthened when we are in physical contact or near several others."

"We are sincerely concerned about our misfortunate events," the tinny voice answered. "A scout was sent earlier to track signals, but has reported similar disturbances. Furthermore, there are indications the host species shell will not sustain the necessary transportation if we are to abort the mission. We will take all this into consideration and return with a final conclusion. The new frequency is–"

We couldn't hear anything but a loud screech that made us flinch. The two humans that walked with us looked at us, seemingly distressed.

It's me, Ray. I'm still in here.

"We are transmitting information to decide if it's beneficial for us to stay," we said to the humans, "but to be clear about our sit–"

You mean "your" situation. And his name is Ray.

We paused, accessing the memory banks and processing the data. "…Your situation. We didn't mean to inflict this harm upon your species. We wanted only to help you evolve."

In one smooth move, the human called Ray unslung the rifle and chambered a round before shouldering it to aim at us.

"Evolve?! You call this *mierda* that has happened to us, that has killed our friends and family, evolution?" He took a step closer. "And where is Claire? You've killed her, haven't you?"

We backed away, and the human host stirred in the back of our mind. It wasn't a pleasant experience. We needed to file it for later evaluation. It stirred again.

My name is Claire. Never forget that. Now stop and let me through.

What we said earlier came back. If this shell couldn't make the journey to our next destination, that meant we would be trapped here. We could not live here without the shell, and in turn the shell would die without us. The new frequency was too hard to reach without concession, the host needed to transmit their mind–

Let me through, just one last time.

The only way for us to save our new habitat was to connect and build a new colony, those of us that are able to link. We looked at the two hybrids on the ground, their shells shattered. This could not remain as was. It had to–

"Ray! Li! It's me! I think the aliens are about to leave. If they do, try to work with the likes of me, it'll be fine. I'll… We will connect the world, for real. Work as one, for all of us. I love–"

"Claire, what the f–!" Ray stared at us for a long time, uncertainty written all over his face, before he lowered his weapon and resignedly shook his head. "You better be telling the truth, *nena*. Or I don't know what I'll do."

I love you guys!

We felt the attention turn to us.

Now, what do I need to do?

We will need to let go of ourselves if we ever are to join. We cannot keep this intermediate state of mind.

I understand that you and I will have to fully merge. We will accept and ascend.

Images streamed through our mind, tiny black dots emerging from the sea of blue around the globe. At the same time, the world shook as the giant ship in our midst vibrated into motion and slowly reached for the exosphere and beyond. Humans, drawn out from their hidings, cheered as it lifted.

• • •

Ray looked at us, surprise turning into realization. We'd keep our word and work together. For us, it was clear the inhabitants of the ship weren't a part of us anymore. We were rapidly uploading our minds into the global hive, watching the blue dots connect exponentially for our inner eye as the black ship disappeared out of view and left the new us behind.

EMMA BERGLUND is a writer, editor and translator living on the East coast of Sweden, where she embarks on great adventures writing fantasy and science fiction—or other genres—stories. When not hammering on a keyboard or making lists with a coffee mug in one hand, she likes to roam the countryside on foot, bike or horseback. Emma is one of the founders and editors of Lower Decks Press.

Twitter: @Ranaborgtext
Web: lowerdeckspress.com

The Last Part

BEN WINTER

THAT FEELING AGAIN. I wish it would go away. The sense I'm being watched. The urge to run. It was stronger than ever today, grasping me with icy fingers when I'd emerged from my sleep pod. Its night-time cycle should have refreshed and recharged me, but my irregular heartbeat and sub-optimal circulation reported otherwise.

I looked at myself in the swirls of water collecting in the sink. Perfect, long, brown hair. Perfect tanned skin. Both immaculate. Both synthetic. They could fix everything, but not this. This was a sign that the final, all-important piece of me was on the fritz.

The cold reflection stared back at me with eyes that bored into my head. They looked deep within, but I wasn't sure what they saw anymore. Was it me or something else? How much could be replaced before the original was lost?

I slapped the water in frustration and strode away from the bathroom. Self-pity wouldn't get me anywhere today. I say strode, but *glide* would be more appropriate. The leg upgrades I'd received a few years ago all but assured I moved with grace and precision. Long, supple, and beautiful. I didn't even need to shave them now. A cerebral command and the neurolinks running down my nerves would turn that functionality off.

I sighed. It was at times like these I missed my old legs. They'd been plump and blotchy, and my feet were constantly cold, but at least I'd been able to drag my heels when I genuinely felt bad.

Outside the bathroom, my apartment was modern and clutter free. A haven of efficiency. I had no patience for people who displayed their belongings and nicknacks like they were trophies. Clear surfaces for me. Feng-shui for the mind was the idea, although that hadn't been working as of late. The only embellishments were some AI paintings that updated automatically every few days. Currently set to Art Deco, they generated new but derivative mixtures of famous artists. However, I was beginning to tire of the sleek, geometric shapes. I'd switch the frames to Romanticism when I had a moment, but there was no time now. I had to get dressed.

I approached the decal machine to the side of the bedroom. A benefit of full body replacement was no longer needing traditional clothes. Fabric decals adhered to the outside instead. Supremely customisable, comfortable, and form-fitted. They showed off every expensive curve I'd paid the cyber-surgeon to put there. I entered the walk-in unit and chose something simple: black leggings with a yellow stripe running along the outside, matched with a red, V-neck top. A neuro-command straightened my self-styling hair–a more appropriate choice than yesterday's curls–and added make-up tones to my face.

I heard a sharp noise from outside. *Fuck! Was someone trying to get into my apartment?*

Heart pounding, I cyber-connected to the outdoor camera. An image overlaid on my retinal implants showing a 180-degree view of the front door. Nobody was there and there was no sound either. I couldn't even remember what kind of sound I thought I'd heard. It had been swallowed by the early morning shadows–or my mind–likely where it had originated in the first place. I took a breath and tried to steady myself.

This was why today was so important. When I got the cerebral upgrade, it would change everything. I'd be able to control my emotional reactions and even how my internal organs reacted. My artificial heart responded to brain-controlled adrenaline as readily as a natural one would. Gilly, my neighbour, had said she could even change her mood after the procedure, increase her serotonin and dopamine whenever she needed a boost. Sounded great.

As if to reinforce the point, my armband beeped, and the holographic display reported it was one hour until my appointment. There was also a message from work. I dismissed the reminder and with a pang of anxiety checked what my boss wanted: *Laura, we need to discuss your performance.*

Artificial or not, my heart sank. It was only a matter of time. My concentration had been getting worse. I used to direct my team of AI helpers with perfect clarity while they assembled code, but now, after only twenty minutes, the lines and numbers blurred, and I'd struggle to continue. I'd barely managed fifty percent efficiency compared to last month. *Dammit! I knew I needed this procedure.* So many others had done it. *Why couldn't I get my head around this!*

It was a pathetically rhetorical question. I knew why. Because it was my damn brain! The most important part. The special bit. The answer to the question the reflection had asked was all too obvious: When was the original lost? ... when nothing else is left.

But I couldn't go on like this. It wasn't just imagined sounds any more. There was a constant feeling of dread, and now it was affecting my career too. The decision was tearing me apart; it had been for weeks. No, not true: *not* deciding had been tearing me apart. But that was over. These last-minute doubts couldn't stop me anymore. Once I liberated myself from my infernal grey matter, all my problems would be solved.

Clean and clothed, I ground my ceramic teeth as I opened the door and peeked onto the walkway, washed pink with fluorescent light in the pre-dawn gloom. Checking the camera had done little to reassure me; however, there was still no one there.

"One foot after the other, Laura," I muttered and forced my body onto the metal surface. It clanged gently underfoot.

It was quiet on this level of the Mega-Column, the thousand floor cylinder that housed the million plus city occupants. I'd worked hard to afford a place this far up, a good distance away from the Unenhanced further down. It made the note from work even more unsettling. Had my performance slipped, or was everyone else getting better? I suppose it didn't matter. Whether I slid down the Column or those below overtook me, the effect would be the same, a reduction in my status and earnings. I couldn't ... *mustn't* ... allow that to happen.

The floor you lived on was everything. It was okay here on the five-hundredth level, but lower down, apartments got smaller, and job prospects more scarce. I'd grown up just above the one-hundredth floor, below which it was completely intolerable—nothing but a squalid shelter for the Unenhanced. As a child, if I'd forgotten to close a window, our one-bedroom living space would fill with the stench of unwashed humans wafting in from below. I shuddered. I'd even seen Unenhanced scaling the exterior of the Column. Unable to afford the elevator, they'd risk their lives, scraggly and threadbare, clinging like insects as they tried to escape to better levels. Never again would I reside that far down the Column.

I took a breath and peered over the railing into the abyss, high enough that—thankfully—I could no longer see the bottom. The Column's interior was enclosed on all sides by holographic signage, twinkling on commercial loops. Every level's advertisements displayed what was just out of reach on the floors above. Mine were showing virtual tours of glistening executive apartments and VIP clubs. Further down, I knew from experience, it was basic cybernetic upgrades. And right at the bottom: synthetic protein rolls, if they got adverts at all.

Heli-drones of various sizes whizzed back and forth across the opening. The bigger ones were carrying people, and the smaller ones held packages for denizens of the upper Mega-Column. Everything from fabric decal canisters to synthetic food could be delivered, even minor fixes for damaged parts. Why go to the cybernetics clinic for a smashed finger? Just buy a new one yourself and snap it on.

A heli-drone port was nearby but my hand tightened around the railing at the thought of travelling in one. Why, though? I'd never been afraid to use drones before. *What was wrong with me!*

Fine, have it your way, stupid brain. It wasn't far to the clinic. It was in my sector and only seventy floors up, more of a vertical trip than a horizontal one. I'll take the elevator.

I hunched my shoulders, swallowed back the bad feelings, and forced myself forward. *Keep walking, Laura. Just get to the clinic.*

It started to rain, because of course it did. The sort that comes down in folds and ribbons, turning the sides of the atrium into a neon-coloured waterfall. It soaked the metal walkways around the perimeter and splashed water all over me. My skin, makeup, and clothes repelled the water, but the feeling of being wet and miserable persisted, nonetheless.

A cry permeated the moisture filled space. "Laura! What are you doing out here? Haven't you noticed it's pouring down!"

It was Gilly. She was emerging from the heli-port I'd just avoided. She'd gotten a new job further up the Mega-Column and had been working late almost every night. And apparently sometimes through the night as well. She'd become so much more efficient since her cerebral upgrade and her employers had noticed, moving her to their head office and doubling her salary. I hadn't seen her in weeks.

She hurried over and extended her hydro-guard over me, its elasto-canvas growing from palm sized until it fully covered us both. I'd forgotten mine. I think for the first time ever. How was that even possible?

"You silly goose!" Gilly proclaimed with a newly acquired upper class affectation. Perfect blond hair waving. Perfect white teeth flashing. As enhanced as I was. More so. "Where are you off to?"

"The cyber-clinic." I leant into Gilly, glad of her company for a moment. The monsters I kept imagining in the shadows would have a hard time getting us both.

A concerned look flashed over Gilly's face. "Something a bit broken, huh?"

Broken, yes, probably. I thought to myself but didn't say so. "No, no. Everything's fine. It's just time for … you know … the final upgrade."

The concerned look evaporated and Gilly spontaneously embraced me. It felt both reassuring and suffocating. "Oh! I'm so pleased to hear that." She beamed. "It's about time! I can't believe you've put it off this long. That's absolutely wonderful!"

I'd heard all this before. The Fully-Enhanced were always encouraging the Part-Enhanced to go all the way. Gilly was no different. It was an almost religious mission for her, although I could never tell if it was genuine altruism or simply justification for her own decision.

"What prompted the change of heart?" Gilly probed.

I thought for a moment. What had pushed me? I'd felt bad for weeks, yes, but I'd almost booked the appointment on autopilot, barely noticing until it was done. Then, in a rare moment of prescience (and an all too common moment of tactlessness), Gilly proffered an answer.

"Wasn't it this time last year your mother died?"

My mind's eye froze and turned inwards as it was confronted with this extra clarity. Gilly was right, it had been about a year since Mum had given out. Dementia. A truly cruel disease when outwardly her body had been as enhanced and young as mine. She'd refused to have the cerebral upgrade, and even if I could have convinced her, the disease eventually removed her ability to consent. The memory lodged like a bee-sting in my mind. It didn't make me feel sad, just numb. I hadn't actively thought about Mum in months. I'd been too consumed with the intrusive thoughts that were infecting me, but perhaps it had indeed been one of the reasons.

"Look, Gilly." I pushed away from her, my resolve hardening. "I need to go or I'll be late".

"Of course! That's fine." Gilly nodded enthusiastically. "Trust me, you're about to feel so much better." And then, with a sinister wink: "About everything."

I frowned as the brief veil of safety was ripped away. What the hell did she mean? But before I could ask, Gilly had pushed the hydro-guard into my hand and hurried off to her apartment, a few doors away. She vanished out of sight seconds later.

I was left alone on the walkway, quiet except for the sound of splashing raindrops. Thankfully the more pleasing *drub-drub-drub* variety as they landed on the canvas of the hydro-guard.

Head swimming, I carried on walking, still wondering about Gilly's strange turn of phrase. Or perhaps it was me being strange. Yes, that was more likely. It must be me.

The elevator was only a little further on and for once there was no queue. The rain had driven everybody else into heli-drones. It arrived in a whoosh of air and magnetic buzzing, doors sliding open to reveal a green aura within. I stepped into the empty carriage, punched in the level for the commercial district, and used my armband to pay the exorbitant hundred credit shaft-charge. But just as the doors were about to close, a large, shaven-headed man slipped in.

"Phew. Made it." He grimaced, glancing at me over shaded glasses whilst tapping his armband to the control panel. "I couldn't find a drone. My…," he looked me up and down, "…good luck the elevator's here."

I nodded quietly and shuffled to the back of the chamber. No drones? I was pretty sure Gilly's had still been there when I left.

"Off to anywhere nice?" he continued with a gravelly voice, moving a little closer.

Fear crawled up my back like a tarantula. Irrational fear—he was only making small talk—but I couldn't prevent it. I couldn't hold it back. I pushed myself into the very corner of the elevator and nodded again. Why was he wearing shaded glasses? It was still dark outside.

"Not talkative today, huh?" He grinned a little wider and took another step closer.

I could feel my heart thudding again. *Fucking thing, why couldn't I control it!* "Sorry," I just about managed, gripping the hydro-guard tight. Not much of a weapon, but it sprung out with quite a bit of force. It might surprise him if I needed it.

"No worries." He leaned in, close enough I could see the muscular enhancements through his grey decaled clothes. Enhancements I hadn't paid for. He could easily overpower me if he chose to. My thumb hovered over the activation button, ready to act, but then my stomach lurched as the elevator came to a halt and the doors slid open.

"This is my stop," he grumbled, turning away. Then, as the doors were closing, and I was about to release the breath I'd been holding, he half-turned and murmured, "See you, Laura."

My eyes widened and my mouth dropped, but before I could follow up, the elevator had already resealed. *Did I know him?* Panic gripped me as I ran through the alternatives. Why would a stranger know my name? My teeth squeaked under the pressure I was applying to them.

With quickened breath, I paced back and forth but had no time to reach a conclusion. After a few moments the elevator arrived at the level I needed and thrust me into the bustling commercial district. For once, I was glad for all the people. Thousands of bodies spread out amongst the neon lit arcades and shops. Safety in numbers.

I was shaken but the throng reassured me. Chewing my cheek, I stamped my feet in anger, trying to drive the fear away. I needed to be rational—the existential demons couldn't have me! The sounds in my apartment had been nothing, I'd proven that by checking the camera. And Gilly hadn't said anything that strange, especially not for her. She'd only been encouraging me. Nothing unusual at all, really. And perhaps the man in the elevator had simply said "See you *later*," not "See you, Laura". It was easy enough to mishear over the sound of the rain.

All of that made sense and none of it made me feel better. Oh God, I wanted to feel better. My emotions were a mess. I wasn't right anymore. I was a ghost of my previous self, forcibly pretending to inhabit a physical body. I desperately needed to feel human again!

I sped up, shoving past the people the crowded commercial district attracted. All of them were synthetically upgraded. Even now, hurrying to the clinic, I wondered how many had taken the last step of replicating their consciousness into a cerebral unit. A scientifically trivial process of scanning the brain's thought patterns and copying over memory. Statistics suggested as many as seventy percent of denizens had undergone the procedure. A number I could believe. The Column Administrators, recognising the increases in productivity, subsidised cerebral surgery if you paid for all the other upgrades yourself. It was—as unfortunate as the saying might be—a no-brainer. I stared at the faces of each person as they wandered by, desperately trying to identify the Fully-Enhanced from the Part-Enhanced, but I couldn't.

I jumped as my foot caught on something. No, not something. Someone! A hand. Attached to a very old, very dishevelled, homeless man. Unenhanced, barely alive.

"Spare some creds?" He stared up at me with desperate, hungry eyes.

I recoiled and kicked away his hand. More from shock than disgust. In my current mental state, I couldn't deal with this right now! How had an Unenhanced made it this far up the Mega-Column? If I'd needed a final reminder of where I may end up, this was it!

Running now, I navigated the final few walkways and arrived at the clinic. A clean facade of glass and sharp lines that stood out against the backdrop of colours and sounds blaring from the surrounding arcades. A 24-hour sanctuary for all your upgrade needs.

The moment I stepped inside I felt better. The din of the outside world shut off as if I'd stepped through an airlock, and the inside was as white and austere as a matching spaceship, brand-new off the line.

The receptionist's brow furrowed briefly as I approached. Then catching herself, she straightened her face and beamed a radiant smile. "Hello ma'am, how can I help you?"

"Is something wrong?" I asked, knowing full well even my augmented body would struggle to hide the state I was in.

"No, no, not at all." She continued to smile. "Please, how may I help you?"

I steadied myself. "I'm here for an appointment."

She tapped the air above her holographic display and nodded. "Of course. Please take a seat in the waiting area. The cyber-surgeon will be right out."

"Okay," I replied nervously, heading to a plush selection of white sofas whilst briefly glancing back at the receptionist. Had she started frowning again?

My feet tapped in agitation as I waited. This had been a terrible morning. Gilly and the man in the elevator had acted so strangely, and now the receptionist seemed to have it in for me too. I shook my head. Perhaps I actually *was* losing my mind. Just like Mum.

The surgeon appeared after a few minutes, cutting an imposing figure as he strode across the room. His dark hair was immaculate and shining, bobbing just behind and below his ears.

"Laura, hello, hello," he said, wearing the same plastic smile the receptionist had. "Great to see you!" He bowed slightly. "Please, follow me."

I did as beckoned, trailing him across the polished marble floor and through a door to the side of the reception.

Inside was another sterile looking room, although of a different quality. Rather than corporate, it was clinical, with various displays, readouts, and medical devices embedded in the walls. In the centre was a chair that looked like it articulated backwards, and above it, a cluster of sharp, surgical instruments. Necessary tools of the trade, but menacing, given the *extraction* they were about to make.

My heart banged in my chest like a madman in a prison cell. I was terrified, that much was certain, but I was committed. I'd seen enough today to know this was the right decision. I wouldn't allow madness to overcome me. There was no turning back.

"Please, take a seat." The surgeon motioned at the chair. I tried to speak, but he held up his hand. "Laura, you've reported your condition and we have your records here, including the family history of dementia. Unless you have questions about the procedure, we find it's best to move quickly. People who delay get cold feet and walk away."

He pursed his lips and a wry smile appeared. "And they always come back. It just makes the process harder for them." And then, as if reading my mind, he said. "You know this is the right decision."

His face was kind and reassuring. The face of a man who had performed the upgrade a thousand times. Probably the same surgeon who'd operated on Gilly, who was as happy as a person could be, flying high with a renewed career. I closed my mouth and nodded. He was right. The time for conversation was over. Questions now were pointless. I took the seat and leaned back, feeling the plastic of the chair crinkle and pop under my weight.

An assistant approached. "Hello, Laura." She smiled. The same damn smile! "I'm going to give you an injection. You won't feel anything."

"And the procedure is painless too," the surgeon added. "In twenty minutes you'll be marching out of here feeling like a new– … I'm sorry … a *better* woman."

I breathed in and out. I couldn't wait to have all these bad feelings banished. The assistant pressed a hypospray to my arm, specifically designed to interface with cybernetic tissue. It hissed quietly as the chemicals mingled with my synthetic blood. She was right, it hadn't hurt at all.

A drowsy feeling descended quickly. It was warm and comforting. I let my eyes close to the smiling faces of the doctor and the assistant, and was that the receptionist? *When did she walk in?* I thought happily.

As I drifted off, some words were left in the air. Dreamlike as my consciousness slipped away.

"Another glitched cerebral unit?" the receptionist asked.

"Looks like it." The surgeon's voice was quiet and drifting away further. "Paranoia and memory loss. Same problem we've been seeing with the new batch. We'll swap it out now."

"Are you going to tell her?"

"Why? It will just confuse her. We need to reestablish her baseline."

"Will she remember anything?"

"Only that she feels human again."

BEN WINTER is a data scientist from London working in the mobile technology industry. When not imagining cyberpunk dystopias he can be found seeking them out in real life. His debut novel Latent State (part of the future Quantum State series) is available now at Amazon.

Web: benwinter.co.uk
Twitter: @TheBenWinter

Eco Invaders

DUNCAN ELLIS

MY FRIEND MARQUETA would say this started on the bus when she saw Colin eat a bug, but she often thinks things only really start when she gets involved.

Marqueta is the leader of our little cell of eco activists. We were all meeting downtown for our next action, by the waterfront fountain.

The park was quiet on this sunny Sunday morning. It was early summer, but the weekend was between festivals. The air was fresh so the fountain didn't have kids playing in it yet.

Leanne was there already. "Hi Tibs," she said. "I like your hat."

"Thanks." I was wearing my wolf hat, the grey one with a goofy snout on the front and soft ears. Its knitted strings were hanging loose. "You seem taller." Leanne had always towered over me, but I had to look up even further than usual.

"New boots," she said, pointing down at her feet: she was wearing thick platform demonias with glinting buckles all the way up to her knees.

"Oo! Those are neat. They suit you."

We carried on chatting like this for a little while. Marqueta was Leanne's girlfriend, but I knew Leanne from the club scene—it was Leanne who invited me to join the cell.

I didn't think we were that early but it was several minutes before Spencer showed up. He had his thick-framed glasses on with the taped up bridge that wouldn't stay in place. He'd always been a dork, but we'd been friends since middle school and he'd been keen to join the cell when I suggested it.

"Hey, Spence." Leanne nodded to him. "You got everything?" She pointed to the small, square messenger bag strapped across his back.

"I think so." He pushed his glasses up his nose. "I've got the routines for the security system ready to go. I inserted the hooks this morning." Spencer was the tech head in the group.

"Cool, cool." Leanne glanced at her phone. "Where's Marqueta? I know the buses suck, but she should be here by now."

"There she is," I pointed past Leanne to where Marqueta was hurrying towards us across the road, looking over her shoulder.

Leanne turned to watch her girlfriend approach, her brow furrowing. She stepped towards Marqueta who fell into Leanne's hug.

"Lee, am I glad to see you." Marqueta was out of breath.

"You alright, Ket?" Leanne's voice was soft. "You look spooked."

"I –" Marqueta disengaged but didn't let go of Leanne's hand, looking back over her shoulder. "I thought I saw something weird on the bus."

Leanne cupped her other hand over Marqueta's shoulder. "Is it anything we need to worry about?"

"I don't think so, but..." She shook her head. "I'm sure it's nothing."

"OK. I trust your instincts." The taller woman smiled and pulled Marqueta into another hug.

Marqueta hugged her back, tucking her face into the crook of Leanne's neck. I couldn't help smiling. I always loved seeing these two together. I liked seeing my friends happy.

The two pulled apart and came back to me and Spencer, arms hooked around each others' waists.

"Are we good?" Spencer asked, pushing his specs up his nose.

"Yeah," Marqueta said. "We're good."

"Cool," I said. I checked my watch. "Our mole should be here soon."

"Where do you know this guy from again?" Marqueta was scowling slightly.

I hesitated for a moment. "Community sites." My tone was careful. "Ones I help run."

Spencer sighed. "He's a furry, then."

"Nothing wrong with fur, nerd." I pushed him in the shoulder. "You lizard fancier, you."

"Hey! I'm no scaly, Tibs." Spencer batted my hand away. "I have a gecko, not a fetish."

Marqueta persisted. "But you trust your contact, Tibs."

I turned back to Marqueta. "Yes, I do. We've met a couple of times, talked a bit about his work at Captur. He got fired after the buyout but he's mostly pissed because he really believed in what Captur was doing."

"Such a shame," Spencer said. "It was a promising technology, sequestering methane from melting Arctic lakes."

"It was never going to work, you know." Leanne's tone was a little scornful. "We need to be reducing emissions, not trying to extract greenhouse gases from the atmosphere."

"But that's just it," Spencer said, beginning to gesture enthusiastically. "They were going to extract the trapped methane before it escaped and turn it into stable solids that could be stored safely."

Leanne still looked dubious. "If it was so good, why couldn't they get funding to move past the pilot stage?"

"The founders weren't in control of whose money they took," Marqueta said.

I nodded. "Colin said it was how they were funded. They started with venture capital when they were proving their nanochemistry tech. The founders chose their mission of sequestration, which got them lots of attention but not enough money. The VCs wanted an exit strategy."

"Right." Spencer tutted. "The dinosaurs took over."

Marqueta gave Spencer a sharp look. "What did you say?"

"The dinosaurs. You know, the old guard. The ones who want to stop things changing." He squinted at her then pushed his glasses back up his nose. "It's just a joke."

Marqueta shifted her stance, uneasy. "Yeah, a joke."

Leanne caught Marqueta's eye. "You sure you're alright, babe?"

"It was weird." Marqueta looked up into Leanne's face. "I was on the bus and I thought I saw someone eat a ladybug."

"Huh." Leanne cocked her head slightly. "That is weird. What happened?"

"The bug was flitting from pole to pole. Then, when it got close to this guy who was sitting a few rows ahead, it was suddenly gone."

Leanne looked doubtful. "You think that guy ate it?" Marqueta nodded, uncertain. "You don't seem convinced yourself."

"I–I'm not sure. It's a long ride from out east. I was dozing; I could have dreamed it. Except..." Marqueta scowled. "Except he was licking his lips, and I saw his teeth were sharp."

"What, filed to a point?"

Marqueta shook her head. "Lots of teeth, sharp like needles."

"Yikes."

"The bus hit a pothole and I was jolted upright. It felt like I'd just woken up." Marqueta shrugged. "That's why I'm not sure it was real. The guy got off the bus just after." Her smile was crooked, rueful. "It shook me a bit, but now that I'm telling you, it all seems so unreal."

I noticed our mole on the other side of the road, about to cross. I leaned past Leanne to wave. "Colin!" I called. Leanne turned to see where I was looking, pulling Marqueta around.

Colin was crossing the street, checking the traffic as he trotted across. He's a few years older than me, and his dated clothing showed it: slouch knit cap, khaki T-shirt, and a plaid shirt tied around his waist over a kilt. His orange hair was sticking out around the edges of his beanie but his goatee was dyed a vivid blue.

Marqueta disentangled herself from Leanne to quiet protests, taking a step back. She tensed as if she was about to run.

Colin slowed as he approached, smiling. "Hey, Tibs," he said. He had a soft accent that marked him as not being local, maybe Australian. "It's nice to see you again."

I agreed enthusiastically, bumping the fist Colin held out, then turned to stand next to him. "Colin, this is our little cell." I introduced Spencer and Leanne, then peered round Leanne. "And hiding behind her is our leader, Marqueta."

Marqueta reluctantly came out of Leanne's shadow, giving Colin a very uncertain look. "So you're the guy who used to work for Captur?" Her voice was squeaky. She cleared her throat and repeated the question in a more normal tone.

"Uh, yeah." Colin's face was a mix of confusion and uncertainty. He knitted his brows. "Do we know each other?"

Marqueta shook her head vehemently. "No, no. Not at all." Then: "I think I saw you on the bus this morning."

There was a brief flicker of alarm in Colin's eyes before he plastered a grin across his face and laughed. "Yeah! You were a couple of seats back. It looked like you were asleep."

"I must have been. I don't remember dozing off, but the bus jolted me awake just before you got off."

"Right. There's that sunken grate right by my stop."

"Yeah. That would have woken me up." She bit her lip. "Could I see your teeth?"

Colin narrowed his eyes. "What's going on?"

"Please. It's not hazing, I promise. I just need– just want to see your teeth."

Colin shrugged. "Sure, I guess, as long as you're not going to make a joke about dentistry." He drew his lips back to expose clenched teeth. One canine was gold and his incisors were a bit crowded, but they were perfectly normal otherwise. Marqueta pronounced herself satisfied. "This tooth," he said, tapping his canine. "That's from a cricket ball."

I sucked my breath in sharply. "That sounds painful."

"You're not wrong," Colin replied.

Marqueta stepped up next to Leanne and took her hand. She forced a smile. "Sorry for the third degree, Colin. I just have a thing about teeth, and yours are fine. So what did you do for Captur when you were there?"

"I was tech lead on the control team. We wrote the code to keep the nanoassemblers on task, processing the methane into urea."

Marqueta's eyebrows shot up and Spencer gave a little gasp. "Wow," Spencer said. "That sounds like they would want to keep you. But you were fired?"

Colin's blue-framed mouth twisted into a sour expression. "They didn't want anyone who disagreed with the new direction." He looked down at his feet. "I'd been there since the beginning, and I really thought we were going to make a difference." He looked back up at Spencer, then me and Leanne, finally settling his solemn gaze on Marqueta. "That's why I want to help you, to prove the original spirit of Captur lives on."

"You must really hate them," Spencer observed. "I've worked for terrible companies, but I never hated any of them enough to risk revenge."

Colin crossed his arms and shifted his weight onto the back foot. His face was grim. "Captur was more than a job for me, for a lot of us. It was our mission. I can't let the destruction of that go unchallenged."

"I get that," Spencer replied. "None of the others who were fired wanted to help you?"

Colin shook his head. "I didn't want to involve them, didn't want the ones with families to feel they had to take the chance."

"And the fewer people who know the better." Leanne's voice was matter-of-fact. "Less risk for you."

"True enough," Colin said wryly. He hooked his thumbs into his waistband. "But I can't do it alone." He looked at me. "You told them why I need the help?"

"That you can't get into the offices," I said.

"Not undetected, no." Colin nodded to Spencer. "I'm willing to take a risk, not walk into sure failure."

"What do you plan to do once you're in?" Marqueta lifted one eyebrow.

"I'm just looking to do some damage," Colin said. "Make it cost them."

"And in return for us getting you in, you'll guide us around the offices?" Marqueta asked, to which Colin gave a firm nod.

"Uh." Spencer was uncertainly raising his hand. "We won't be undetected, you know."

Colin cocked his head. "What, so the cops'll turn up?"

"No, no." Spencer's tone was placatory. "No one will notice at the time because security will be busy, but we could be recorded if Captur have cameras." He gestured around our group. "We will disguise ourselves, so we'll be anonymous."

"Oh, right. Tibs said." Colin stroked his beard. "I can make some changes to my looks, don't you worry."

I grinned at Colin. "Did you bring your fursona?"

"What, my scaly suit?" Colin cackled. "I wouldn't want it getting dirty."

"OK, then." Marqueta glanced at her wrist. "We'd better get moving."

. . .

We split up so we could approach the building separately.

The Captur offices were on the tenth floor of a mixed use tower at the south end of downtown, where the streets leading down towards the river had a steep slope. We were going to meet up in the mall food court on the fourth floor.

Across the street was a small, one-block park with a modernist fountain. I came up to the building from the south, walking along the downhill wall closest to the water, which was windowless at street level. The park looked quite inviting with its myriad tree-covered paths and meeting places, but I followed the sidewalk up to find the building lobby.

One floor of the tower had green-framed windows; Colin had told us those were the Captur offices.

The building lobby was airy, a three-floor atrium with a bank of elevators on the far end. One security guard was at a desk to one side, but he ignored the shoppers passing through. Four friends were waiting for an elevator to come down, and a group of three others strolled towards the exit with bags from a found fashion place I'd heard of.

I shared the elevator with the four friends who chatted to each other, but I was happy to skulk at the back of the car. I followed them all out onto the fourth floor.

It was a lot busier here than in the entry lobby: not crowded, but populated enough. The elevator opened onto the long side of a rectangular plaza. There were stores around the edge and pop up stalls scattered across the middle. Most of it was clothing and accessories.

But I was too nervous to enjoy shopping.

The food court was off to my left, although it was only a dozen tables in the corner close to a coffee shop, a pizza place, and a bowl restaurant. Everyone was there already, seated at a table on the outer edge. Colin had a coffee.

"Hi, everyone." I gave a small wave.

Leanne's eyes were wide. "Can you believe this place? There are so many clothes!"

Spencer grimaced. While I gave a small smile back, I couldn't match Leanne's enthusiasm. "I had no idea this place was here."

"Nor me!" She scanned the vendors closest to us. "We'll definitely have to do some shopping later."

I heard someone clear their throat. Marqueta was giving Leanne a stern look; I pulled over a chair and sat down.

Marqueta leaned closer and pitched her voice low. "Now that we're all here ... Spencer, do you have the access you need?"

He checked his phone. "Yes. I've already marked one elevator as being out of service and set its camera to loop on an empty car image."

Marqueta nodded. "Everyone ready?" We all murmured agreement and she led us back across the floor to the elevator.

No one else was waiting and Spencer called the car he had control of. Once we were in, the door closed and Spencer told the elevator to hold.

Marqueta pulled out a mesh of LEDs and draped it around her shoulders. I took my hat off then turned my jacket inside out revealing a similar LED network sewn into the lining; Leanne and Spencer did similar things with Spencer putting away his glasses and Leanne getting shorter.

I glanced down at Leanne's enormous boots: the platforms had flattened to normal soles.

"Colin," I said, "you should obscure your identity."

He grunted, took off his hat, then pressed a couple of spots along his collarbone. His beard changed to a glossy black while his red hair darkened to match. He quickly pulled the long curls up into a shaggy topknot.

I gasped. "That's expensive tech, Colin!"

He shrugged. "Captur's nanotech supplier has a customer that makes programmable chromatophores. I got a good discount."

The elevator jolted into motion at Spencer's command, and in moments my stomach lifted as the car slowed at the tenth floor. Marqueta signalled and we activated our dazzle suits - lights strobing and flashing.

"What the hell?" Colin exclaimed, shying away. "Talking of expensive tech! What's the deal?"

Marqueta shrugged in her turn. "Stealth is hard, but dazzling the cameras is easy."

The doors slid open onto the lobby. A generic mahogany reception desk was backed by a green-painted wall with a mismatched section of paint, the silhouette of the Captur logo.

"Blimey, they took the sign down already." Colin shook his head. He held the door open. "They sent everyone home after the acquisition so there won't be anyone here. But you were wanting directions." He pivoted out of the elevator and pointed to the right past the reception area. "The executive cubes are that way," he said, then went on to indicate other parts of the office.

Spencer was last out. "It's not very impressive," he said with a sniff. "Other startups I've visited have elaborate themes and environments."

"Captur was always about the mission," Colin said. "They paid well, but they were focused on the work rather than trying to dazzle investors." He gestured towards the worn fabric partitions in the office space. "All the furniture's secondhand, and the founders used a cube like anyone else."

Spencer snapped his fingers. "I nearly forgot." He pulled out his phone and clicked a button on the screen. "There."

"What did you do?" I asked.

"I said the security people would be busy, didn't I?" Spencer's eyes had a vicious shine. "I've opened some valves in the fire control system. Their locker room is being flooded."

"Wow. That seems mean." I couldn't help but feel sorry for the poor, soaked security staff.

"It's clean water. I could have been much nastier, but they will be occupied and won't be paying attention to one out-of-service elevator car."

"Good work," Marqueta said. "Spencer and Leanne, you're on servers and devs. Backup drives, anything small and portable. Tibs, you're on HR—internal communications, termination letters, anything. I'm going to see if there's anything in the conference rooms."

Colin nodded. "Good plan. I want to swing by my cube for some things." He started off after Spencer.

Marqueta stopped him, grabbing his upper arm. "If you take your stuff they'll know it's you."

"Nah, I'm planning on leaving things behind." He smiled slightly. "There's no reason those nanoassemblers should work exactly as intended, right?"

Marqueta smiled in return. "OK, we'll meet back here in ten minutes."

We scattered, with Colin and Spencer heading towards the dev area, Leanne going in the other direction towards the glass-walled server rooms built up in the centre of the space, while Marqueta and I ran towards the executive and staffing areas.

I found the HR cubes and started to dig through the filing cabinets and door file racks. I found some relevant internal docs and started to take pictures.

I thought I heard a bird while I was photographing the docs, a melodic warbling. I stuck my head over the cube wall to see where it was coming from. I didn't see anything except Marqueta searching on the far side of the office.

I went back to taking pictures and was just finishing up when I heard Marqueta's shout, almost a scream. When she did scream, I heard Colin utter a profanity. Marqueta hurtled past the cube I was in, gasping in panic.

I quickly stuffed the pages back where I had found them and hared off after Marqueta.

Ahead, I saw her burst into the reception area, almost colliding with Leanne.

Leanne was grinning, holding up a small zippered case. I couldn't hear what she said but her face fell when she registered Marqueta. I arrived in time to hear Leanne's words. "What's wrong, babe?"

"We have to get out of here." Marqueta was wild-eyed. "Colin, he's ... he's a monster."

Leanne's face hardened. "Did he hurt you?" She looked past me to where I assumed Colin must be following. "He'll regret that."

I tumbled to a stop a couple of yards from the two.

"No, no. He didn't touch me." She leaned in closer to Leanne and hissed: "He's not human."

Leanne looked down at Marqueta, confused. "What?"

I was going to say something similar but Colin arrived, barely out of breath. I thought at the time he must be fitter than he looked.

Marqueta gripped Leanne's arm, her eyes round. I squinted at Marqueta while Leanne moved to shield her. I drew back so I could see everyone.

"You." Leanne pointed forcefully at Colin. "You have some explaining--

Spencer arrived just then, looking apologetic. "No luck with any of the dev stations. They've all been cleared, so there's nothing..." He stopped speaking, realising he'd walked into something.

Leanne continued to glare at Colin, ignoring Spencer. "Ket, can you tell us what happened?"

Marqueta pressed herself into Leanne's side and Leanne wrapped an arm around her shoulders. She took a deep breath and closed her eyes before she spoke. "I saw Colin going into one of the executive cubes. I went to investigate because I was worried he might be using us as cover for industrial espionage or something. He was standing by a desk holding something over it, but his eyes were yellow and the hand with the device in it was green and clawed." Then she opened her eyes, staring at Colin. "I did see you eat that ladybug, didn't I?"

Colin's eyes were fixed on Marqueta, his face serious, but he didn't say anything.

"Colin?" I said. "You brought your fursona after all?"

His serious expression broke and he made a small laugh in the back of his throat. Shaking his head, he looked at me with an amused expression. "Not exactly, Tibs." He turned back to Marqueta. "I didn't set out to frighten you—any of you—so, I'm sorry I did." He looked around the four of us, a little sheepish. "You might have gathered I'm not from around here."

"No, you're from Australia," Spencer said.

"Further away than that, I'm afraid. I'm not from Earth." Spencer gaped while Leanne and I both blurted incoherent questions. Colin raised a calming hand. "I'm an investigator from a bureau which prevents interference with planet-bound civilisations like yours."

Spencer spluttered something about the space station, but Colin ignored him and looked at Marqueta particularly. "You weren't mistaken on the bus." He held up his hand and its surface melted and re-formed into a reptilian claw, green-scaled, with four fingers.

I couldn't help but step back. "Wow." I couldn't take my eyes off the claw. The initial impression of green scales was incomplete: the top was green, but the green was not uniform: each scale was shaded paler at the tip, and colours varied so that the effect was mottled. The palm and the undersides of the fingers were much paler, almost a blue-white, and there didn't seem to be any scales on that skin at all. The claws were curved, about half an inch long, and emerged from the upper half of each finger. The fingers themselves were slender, and one of them was opposed like a thumb.

"Colin?" I blinked then looked at his face, then gasped again. His eyes weren't the vivid blue they'd been before but were yellow, the iris filling his socket, with a horizontally slitted pupil. Then I breathed out. "So that's why you were with the scalies."

He laughed. "I suppose so, yes." He lowered his claw, which reverted back to a human hand. When he blinked, his eyes were blue again. Then he gestured to indicate his whole body. "I guess this is my fursona."

"Wow," I said. "That's so cool."

"No, no," Marqueta said. "This isn't happening. Aliens aren't real. It's too far."

"It is true," Colin replied. "I came here to look for evidence that Captur was bought by others of my people who want to return Earth to the climate of an earlier age."

Marqueta was still in shock but Leanne bent closer. "Why would they do that?"

"To take over." Colin sighed. "To retake possession, they'd say. Since finding Earth a couple of centuries ago, we've learned our distant ancestors came from here. We think they left before the comet that killed most of the saurians struck."

"Oh, when you said you identified as a raptor, you really were a dinosaur," I said.

"Calling me a dinosaur is like calling one of you a vole. That was the only kind of mammal running around at that time." He pulled something from his pocket: a tube about two inches thick and five long, tapering towards rounded ends. "This evidence of the others' presence is exactly what I needed to stop their interference."

"You were holding that in the office." Marqueta pointed at the cylinder. "Why did you change your hand?"

Colin tucked the object back into his pocket. "I need claws to operate the controls. I asked for one with a human-form interface, but they couldn't make one in time."

"Come now, Colin," a deep and unfamiliar voice echoed in the silence of the empty offices. "You've told them this much. Maybe you should tell them the whole truth."

We all turned as one. Walking in from the direction Spencer had arrived was a tall man with short blond hair wearing a double-breasted power suit. He was tanned, fit, and handsome in a not-quite-pretty-enough-for-the-screen way—too much on the rugged end of chiselled.

"The truth about how you're here without permission and without support," he continued, still walking. "How that biocollector requires authorisation, which you do not have, so you stole it before you transited here."

Spencer spun away from the new arrival and we all turned to face him. He sauntered by, his jacket pinned back by his pocketed hands, and stood in front of the elevator door.

"You," Colin said.

The newcomer smirked. "Yes, Colin. Me." He leaned back against the frame of the elevator door. "I'm unsurprised to see you here, but why don't you introduce me to your new friends?"

Colin shook his head. "This is between us." He pointed between himself and the besuited man.

"Not any longer, it isn't, not since you involved these." He pinched the bridge of his nose. "And please turn off those lights; I have already stopped the security recordings."

Marqueta looked around at us, then shrugged and turned off her dazzle lights. We all followed but Colin kept his dark hair and beard.

"None of that matters," Colin said, grinning. "I have the evidence I need now."

"You really are being quite rude, so I shall make the introductions." The blond man patted himself on the sternum, careful not to muss up his tie. "I'm Greg Kettering, but you can call me Greg. Colin Basilica you've already met." He pointed at Leanne first. "Leanne Brown, I believe. Marqueta Lomax, Tabitha Roberts." He pointed at me. My stomach flipped.

"My name is Tibs," I said.

Greg tilted his head to me. "Tibs it is, then."

"How do you know our names?"

He half-shrugged. "We pay attention to anyone who is engaged with your global environment. We've known who all of you are for some time."

I glared at him, but he looked away unconcerned.

"And finally," Greg said, turned to Spencer. "Spencer Wright. Good work with the security system. Quite impressive given the tools available to you, and the distraction for building security was a nice touch."

"Thanks, I guess." Spencer's voice was sour.

"I'm glad the exploits we fed you did what you needed," Greg continued. Spencer looked mortified.

Marqueta stuck her chin out. "We have gathered evidence of the environmentally damaging uses you intend for the Captur technology. We've already uploaded it to the cloud and it will be released to the press in an hour if we don't stop it."

"No, you haven't and it won't." Greg was still smiling. "I appreciate your bravado, Miss Lomax, but the phone connections you think you have are to a captive network. Nothing has been uploaded beyond this office."

Marqueta scowled at him. "You don't seem very worried about having a group of environmental activists in your office."

"Because I'm not." He strolled closer to us so he could look down on Marqueta. "Even if anything you had taken were important, you wouldn't be leaving with it." Then he lifted his head and pointed at Colin. "And I don't think you will be leaving at all."

Colin crossed his arms. "My bureau will have something to say about that."

Greg shrugged as he took a step back. "I doubt that. They've washed their hands of you."

"I don't believe you." Colin glanced around at each of us. "I'm not human, but neither is he, and he's the one who's interfering where he shouldn't!"

"We have done nothing that the Contact Bureau hasn't already known about and granted license for." Greg took a box from his inside pocket, about the size of a pack of cards but with an intricate pattern carved into its iridescent surface. He showed the box to Colin. "I have a license for this."

"No, don't," Colin said, raising his hand as if to hold Greg back. He made sounds like the warbling I'd heard before.

Greg shook his head and his expression was solemn as he pointed the box at Colin, whose head snapped back like he'd been slapped. He stood there, limbs rigid, mouth drawn into a grimace.

Colin's teeth changed first, becoming the needle teeth Marqueta had described, then his face flattened and his hair disappeared. Ruddy skin shifted into the same gently mottled scales that covered his hand. His hat slid over his eyes and the rest of his skin changed, his limbs thinning, legs lengthening.

Colin became a reptile, a little taller than human Colin but less bulky.

His limbs released and he staggered back, feet lifting out of his shoes. Colin's feet were smaller now, legs narrower. A pair of plaid underpants slid down out of his kilt and lodged on the raised heel of his digitigrade feet.

Greg returned the box to his pocket. "Colin, Colin, Colin. You really should have stuck to guarding those stick-wielding crabs your bureau is so concerned about."

Marqueta and the others had moved back as Colin transformed, halting up against cube walls and the reception desk. I waved for them to come back: "It's still Colin!" I hissed.

Colin regained his balance and kicked his too-big shoes to one side, pulling off his too floppy hat. "You say you have a license." His voice was breathier, but still the same timbre. "Why would the bureau sanction climate manipulation?"

"They wouldn't, of course, but we're not doing that." Greg's tone was reasonable, but Marqueta's face contorted with anger. She stomped past Colin to confront Greg.

"You're lying!" Marqueta planted her feet and placed her fists on her hips. "You're subverting carbon capture technology and using it to release even more greenhouse gases into the atmosphere."

Colin glanced at Marqueta then took a step towards Greg. "That's exactly it. Your conglomerate purchased Captur for the express purpose of dismantling its mission."

Greg made a noncommittal little noise and briefly shifted his features to an expression of indifference.

Colin half turned towards us, yellow eyes scanning our faces "I came here to look for evidence that Captur was bought by the Reconstructionists, the group bent on reverting Earth's climate." Colin pointed at Greg. "He's one of their leaders, and this acquisition of Captur is exactly the evidence I need to stop their interference."

Greg laughed. "Your threats are hollow, Colin." He took his hands out of his pockets and started to count off points on his fingers. "You interceded by working for Captur. You involved these humans in your operation. You operated without the support of your sanctimonious bureau, even stole equipment from them. Yet you accuse me of interference?"

"But your corporation did buy Captur. Why else would you be here?"

Greg lifted one corner of his mouth in a partial smile. "I don't own the corporation. None of us do. I am here only as an observer, recording the inevitable collapse of human civilisation for posterity. And entertainment."

"Entertainment?" Spencer was outraged. "You find the climate emergency entertaining?"

"Yes. Many of us do." He gestured with an open palm at Colin. "Our rogue friend here has a point that we would very much like to come back to what you call Earth once its climate is more amenable, but we were warned decades ago and have not interfered since." Now he gestured to include all of us, spreading his arms wide.

"We have not needed to; humanity has done everything for us."

DUNCAN ELLIS is an ex-pat Yorkshireman settled in Oregon who writes code for money and fiction for fun. He has self-published one novel about steampunk Rome, and has short works published by Boundary Shock Quarterly and Lower Decks Press. He has a Magic: The Gathering habit which he picked up from his kids, and nurtures his hypergraphia with an elaborate organisational system which threatens to achieve self-awareness in the next six months.

Mastodon: @DunxIsWriting@c.im
Web: dunx.org

Transmogrification

MARTEN NORR

HUMAN

You have not committed a crime.

Your indignation is equal only to your relief that you qualified as a candidate for ComSent. It is the best possible outcome for you. You would not survive a prison. You'll likely survive this.

There's a good chance, too, that you won't even have to fight as hard to survive as you did when you were a human.

But you are, for now, still human. So is everyone else on this military compound—well, most of them. The ones you can see, anyway. The ones who are here in this processing area with you.

It's a sunny day, bright and clear and dry. It's one of those days when you can see the wreckage of the Fiends' ship floating in two pieces like a broken egg just outside the atmosphere. A tiny second moon out of which the armada was birthed the same year you were born.

The commandant is a tall, auburn-haired, streamlined person, perhaps 50, wearing a sharp army-green uniform. They greeted you and your fellow inmates as you got off the bus. This outpost is in the dangerous hinterland between Havens—between yours and the next. Everyone here has grown a contradictory laid-back vigilance—a mechanism by which to convince themselves that they're too well-defended for the Fiends to get at them. It's a vigilance you know well —you adopted it in school to ensure you behaved the same way as your peers. You learned how to hold your hands still, how to determine the flow of a conversation, how to meter your expressions. But that, like the idea that a human is safe anywhere other than inside a Haven, was only a mask.

The commandant has been speaking. You tune back in.

" ... moment you'll head inside to be assessed." Their voice is a bit raspy, but audible enough over the cacophony of vehicles and military shouting around the base. They don't sound like many of the so-called "advocates" whose offices you had to pass through to get to this place, who even you could tell were leery and prejudiced towards you, who hated you just because they thought you had committed a crime. This one sounds amenable. Not cheerful, but like they might see the program candidates as something other than criminals.

"Please ensure that you have your identification in order," they say. "You'll receive a physical exam and a mental aptitude assessment. If you pass those, the last step will be to meet your CO. This will be the final chance you have to change your mind, and it's nothing to be ashamed of. The program isn't for everybody." They are giving you the illusion of choice. They straighten their cap, smooth down the front of their jacket, and give a quick nod. "Follow me."

A woman has fallen into step beside you as you and the other dozen inmates follow the commandant into the building. Her hair is black and straight, pulled back into a low ponytail. She's maybe your age, with irises so dark you can't see her pupils, and carries herself with more confidence than you've ever had. Sometimes you can tell when somebody's from one of the wealthier Havens. Sometimes the rich give off an aura you can't quite describe.

The commandant doesn't seem to mind if you chat. At least, nobody snaps at the woman to shut up when she says, "Hey. I'm Lex. She/her."

You glance at her. The doors have shut behind you now. The interior is like a warehouse or gymnasium, set up with cubicle partitions to delineate different sections. There's a medical smell—alcohol or antiseptic. You hear other quiet conversations. The commandant is leading you around a corner and into a waiting area. Everyone takes a seat on the fold-out metal chairs arranged in a rectangle against the partition walls.

"I'm Elias. He/him."

You know what's coming next. You once heard it was taboo to ask what had brought you into the clutches of the law, and it seems trite to hear the question now. Like an old movie: *hey, fresh meat, what're you in for?*

"So, uh ... what did *you* do?" she asks.

You dare not say you have done nothing and risk the cruel, disbelieving laughter you know will follow such a statement. What's one more lie? The inmates around you have done much worse than lie.

"Theft," you say, pursing your lips in what you've come to know looks like shame.

She gives a knowing upward jerk of her chin and grins. "So, a shitty Haven, then? Or just greedy?"

"Shitty Haven," you reply. "Haven Fifteen." Everyone knows the rumors that crime is encouraged in the poorer Havens, to create a steady stream of inmates for the ComSent program. Nobody says it in so many words. You remember that oftentimes when someone asks you a question about yourself, it's because you're supposed to then ask them the same question in return. People like to talk about themselves more than they like to know the answers to the questions they've just asked. "You?"

"Second Haven." Damn, she *is* rich. Or rather, *was*. "I killed my uncle."

It's a bid for social rank, and you can't outdo her. So you say, "Holy shit."

"But it was self-defense, so I still qualified." Self-defense and desperation are two types of murder that qualify someone for ComSent—the ability to kill, and the knowledge of what having killed is like, are traits the program seeks out—but serial killing and crimes of passion denote mental instability that doesn't make for a good soldier.

Lex sets her jaw. "I don't regret it. I'd do it again."

"You will."

This was not the right thing to say, and you realize this when your reward is Lex's disturbed expression. Your stomach clenches in embarrassment. She didn't really mean what she'd said. You've given her a reminder of a truth she didn't want to think too hard about—that she'd taken a life and would again. Even if the life belonged to a Fiend. Running back over the brief conversation, you realize you don't actually want to consider it much further, either.

One by one, the commandant reads names off the roll-call list, and inmates file through an opening in the partitions which leads into the medical examination area. "Graves," they say, and there is something funereal about your last name in the tone of their voice.

With a perfunctory half-smile at Lex, you stand and shuffle past the commandant into the examination room. A nurse in mint-green scrubs confirms your name and birthdate: Elias Graves, age 30, born July 5th, 2025. You are weighed—113 pounds, too malnourished for human soldiering—and measured—5'5", scrawny even for someone malnourished. Neither of these things will disqualify you from the program. You wonder why they bother with a physical exam at all.

"Not so bad," Lex observes when she has joined you in the next waiting room.

Are you supposed to reply? You don't know each other very well yet, and you already put Lex off by being too blunt earlier. Maybe she'll choose someone else to talk to. You fold your hands in your lap. You're glad that the commandant, at least, is here to give you instructions.

The mental aptitude test makes more sense for the program's purpose, though you're aware that a lot of it is based on outdated, arbitrary research. You refrain from letting the proctor know, and take the assessment in silence. You try not to get irritated by the buzzing of the industrial lights above, or distracted by the fact that their domed plastic shades remind you of the big glass salad bowls your mother has in the kitchen back home.

The proctor hands you a slip of paper that deems you fit for service. "You're cleared. Good luck." You're pretty sure he doesn't mean the last part. It's like how people will ask "how are you" and you're supposed to say "fine" instead of how you're really feeling. It's a cue for you to respond, not a phrase with real meaning. You should have stuck with this level of small talk with Lex.

"Thanks. Have a good one, man," you say, like you're supposed to, and go through the next opening.

When all the inmates are gathered, the commandant says something indeterminable into their walkie-talkie, and then turns to the inmates with their hands behind their back. "Alright, you're about to meet your CO. We will collect a second consent form afterwards."

It sounds like they're reading from a script, something people do when they've said a thing hundreds of times. You wonder if they still mean it.

A black shape appears at the hangar door, dropping lightly just outside of it—unnaturally lightly, for something of its size—and folding enormous black wings as it ducks inside.

You've seen it on news feeds, in battles against the Fiends, and on commercials when they first tried to enlist volunteers, before they decided using prisoners would guarantee a more reliable influx of soldiers. Even still, once in a while you'll see one in a feed article, about how even criminals can contribute productively to society, can help bring victory for humanity against an inhuman enemy by using their own genes against them.

A Seraph.

It's jet-black, though slightly iridescent, like an oil slick. It prowls like a jaguar, a long whip-like tail snapping behind it. Four human hands, each ending in sharp talons, claw the floor with each step. Around its chest is something resembling a harness, snaking around its shoulders and between its wings, with a small electronic interface at the front just above the Seraph's bird-like keel. A long, thick neck ends in a perfectly smooth, flat face upon which glows a white squiggle that rearranges itself into a question mark as the face turns towards the commandant.

They tap a few buttons on their tablet and then give the Seraph a thumbs-up. An LED light on the harness' interface blinks blue. "You're good to go."

A voice emits, slightly staticky, from the interface as the Seraph's face-squiggle morphs into something resembling a human visage—two eyes, a nose, a mouth. It's all contiguous, like a line drawing. You've seen videos of the Fiends, and it's a small replica of theirs, which covers most of their body. It's how they communicate. Humans have co-opted it. Its glow pulses with the words as the Seraph speaks, and its mouth mimes the sounds. You notice the line is interrupted by a diagonal scar that crosses halfway across the bottom half of the Seraph's face, starting at its chin. You wonder what he looks like as a human.

"Good morning." The voice is a bit gravelly, that of a man just entering middle age. "My name's Cleary Vargas, First Talon of the 4th Division Seraph Squad. Sounds fancy, but don't let the title fool ya. I, like you, just do what ComSent tells me, and that suits me fine." He paces up and down the line. You try to discern how the voice augment works—does it pick up brain waves? Or is the human Cleary Vargas lying unconscious in his machine, dreaming this situation through the Seraph's eyes? Where are its eyes?

Cleary Vargas comes to a stop in front of you, and seems to be appraising you briefly, then continues on. "If you're still committed to the cause, if seeing what you'll become don't frighten you off, you'll pass through into the transmogrification facility. I'm here to answer a few questions before you move on. Put your mind at ease, so to speak."

You want to ask many questions, but are any of them pertinent? Or will they be things you'll learn later? When you were a child, your mother used to tell you not to get ahead of yourself. Only ask questions that are relevant. Don't waste others' time. You were never good at discerning which questions others considered relevant.

Lex raises her hand and Cleary Vargas gestures to her. "I thought Seraphs couldn't speak," she says.

With one of his claws, Cleary Vargas taps the harness and interface over his chest. "Only squad commanders get these, and an overseer has to turn it on."

You wonder if it's similar to whatever happens when you get overwhelmed and your brain won't connect to your vocal chords. It would be convenient if you had a button to turn *that* on and off.

"In training, we'll teach you how to use your scribble to communicate. The scientists who made Seraphs call it a bio-pictogram, but we call it a scribble. That's this thing." Now he taps the glowing blue line that forms his rudimentary face. *Scribble.* That's a good word. You almost repeat it out loud. "You've seen what the Fiends can do with theirs, and they have ... something resembling a voice box. We got the Lite version."

Seraphs were created from Fiend DNA mixed with that of animals from earth. Trying to connect a human mind to that of a Fiend clone failed, so to make it more familiar and habitable to an earthling's psyche, scientists combined Fiend genes with those of birds, big cats, and humans. The result was something Fiend-adjacent, but easily enough told apart from the enemy, and more acceptable to the human psyche. It was a breakthrough in the war, placing humans on much more even footing with the invaders.

"Anyone here know sign language?" Cleary Vargas asks, swiveling his head from side to side along the line of inmates, like an owl. His scribble is a question mark again. You like this method of communication. It'll be so much more straightforward, communicating with pictograms, than it is trying to work out a constantly changing social script.

You raise your hand, glad to have a way to gain favor, to preemptively prove your usefulness before your comrades notice your strangeness.

"Yeah?" Cleary Vargas asks, with what you gauge to be mild interest. "How much? You fluent?"

"Yes, sir."

"Good—so, the scribble is kinda like that, but much simpler. Like a marshaller on a runway, with the orange paddles. That might be before your time." He chuckles, and swishes his tail in a way that somehow communicates sheepishness. Runways don't exist anymore, at least not for civilians. It's too dangerous to fly from one Haven to another because of Fiend activity. "Anyway, it's simple, but it works well enough. Next question?"

Someone else raises their hand. "What do you eat? Like, the Fiends eat oil schist. What do Seraphs eat?"

Eat schist, Fiends, is a common thing to find scrawled on bathroom stalls and lamp posts a tongue-in-cheek, defiant pun. Nobody is quite sure what nutrients the Fiends obtain from the rocks.

Cleary Vargas' face scribble morphs into something like a laughing emoji. "Hate to break it to ya, kid, but we don't. The Fiends've got mouths. You see a mouth on me? Why do you think they gave me a voice aug?" He taps the interface again. "Seraphs are static. No cellular regeneration, no stomachs ... and no assholes." A few hesitant laughs. You join in. "Forgive me, Commandant Wheeler."

Even the commandant is chuckling a little. You're glad to have a reminder of what their name is. People don't like it when you have to ask again.

You think of a question, and before you can consider that it might be too blunt, your hand is already in the air. When Cleary Vargas calls on you, his scribble rearranging itself back into a neutral face, you say, "If there's no cellular regeneration, what happens if someone gets an injury?"

"Good question," says Vargas, voice serious again. "There's a lengthy explanation we don't have time for right now. But there are ways to heal a Seraph, and luckily it's damn hard to even break skin anyway, even with those claws the Fiends have. The geneticists who engineered us made sure of that. As long as you get to a casualty clearing station in a reasonable amount of time, you got nothing to worry about. We're pretty sturdy."

Commandant Wheeler speaks up, checking something on their tablet. "I'm afraid that's all we have time for right now. Thank you, Vargas. We'll see you in the barracks."

Cleary Vargas salutes in Wheeler's direction, a human motion that looks alien on the Seraph's monstrous form, and departs at a trot.

"Well, alright then," says Wheeler. "Follow me and we'll get you set up in the transmogrification machines."

They gaze at you and the others with a grave look on their long features. Though you are rarely able to ascertain specific emotions from a person's expressions, you get the distinct feeling that the expression on Wheeler's face is pity.

INHUMAN

You open your eyes.

You have no eyes. Your consciousness perceives the world around you anyway. You try moving your head a little, and find that your peripheral vision is much improved. You seem to be in some kind of hammock, on your back, and your body is folded strangely under you.

You expected to feel groggy. After all, you were under anesthesia for a while before going into the machine. But you're wide awake and lucid as ever. Something about this bothers you, but you can't say why just yet.

"Mornin', sunshine," says the voice of Cleary Vargas, and you turn your head again, finding that the smooth plane of your face is quite close to his. Your neck is much longer than before. His scribble untangles itself into a smiley-face, its mouth interrupted by the scar again. "You're the first one awake. Don't worry—it's going to take you a little while to adjust to your new body, so don't get up just yet."

This isn't my body, I'm just piloting it, you think at him, intending to remind him out loud, but no sound emerges from you. This isn't like the times when you find that your voice is buried too deep in your chest for you to find it. Now, no vocal muscles vibrate in your throat. *Ah.* You remember, and are relieved.

The reason your body *the* body—feels strange is because of its changed proportions, and because your wings—*the* wings—are pinned under you in the cocoon of the hammock. You often forget to move if you're sitting in one position for a long time, so the feeling is familiar. You take stock of the rest of your Seraph, and get the sense that, like Cleary, you are much larger than a human and much heavier. The body is ink-black and predator-deadly, and you remind yourself that you have claws now, so you should be careful not to rip through the hammock. The body is, of course, unclothed and unadorned, except ...

Your new fingers find the bandage on the back of your head, covering most of your scalp—if Seraphs have scalps—where the raven feathers of your neck fade into smooth, alien material.

You try for a question mark, a confused expression, a frown. You get the impression that your scribble has not produced anything legible and hope this will improve in time. It would not be ideal if, even in this simplified form, you are still a poor communicator.

Cleary seems to apprehend your meaning. His scribble has gone back to its dormant tangle and you get the sense he's keeping it that way intentionally. He says in a controlled tone, "Don't worry about that." He doesn't elaborate.

You try again for a question mark, more insistently this time. Something shifts, and you are looking at him through a question-mark-shaped curve. As soon as you stop focusing, it dissipates, and the world is fully visible again.

He cocks his head, maybe surprised, maybe irritated, maybe indulgent. His scribble is still a gently-glowing snarl of nonsense.

Cleary glances over his left shoulder and folded wing, towards where you think there might be a door. Swathed in this hammock, you can see little else but the ceiling and Cleary Vargas.

"You said you sign, right?" His voice is lowered and conspiratorial. His head tilt earlier was apprehension, not irritation.

You nod.

He deliberates for a moment, flashes an unfamiliar symbol, and signs to you, NEVER HAD A SQUADMATE WHO COULD SIGN. COMMUNICATION LIMITED. LENGTHY EXPLANATION CAN'T THROUGH SCRIBBLE. The movement of his taloned hands is practiced, but not fluent. An autodidact. Through your confusion, you wonder who he learned for.

HOW LONG UNTIL THE OTHERS WAKE UP? you sign back.

MINUTES.

WHAT'S THIS BANDAGE?

Cleary flashes another unfamiliar symbol, and his signing becomes more rushed. BRACE YOU. SHOULDN'T BE TELLING THIS.

You brace yourself. You sign, I CAN KEEP A SECRET.

Another pause. Cleary glances over his shoulder again, then back at you. THERE IS NO MACHINE.

I DON'T UNDERSTAND.

SURGERY. "Uhh ... " He fumbles for the signs. TRANSPLANT. HUMAN BRAIN—he points at your bandaged head, then at his own— SERAPH BODY.

You are just on the edge of understanding. NO MACHINE?

Cleary's scribble oscillates in misgiving, guilt, or despair. YOU'RE NOT PILOTING THE SERAPH, YOU ARE THE SERAPH.

So this is *my body.* Your horror is muted, as big feelings often are for you at first, but you comprehend incontrovertibly that Cleary's horror is not. HOW DO YOU USUALLY EXPLAIN? You gesture again to your bandage.

TRACKING CHIP. He shakes out his hands in agitation. NOT TECHNICALLY A LIE. THEY DO PUT ONE IN.

You consider this. *So we can't run away if we find out*, you think. *Imagine if the anti-Seraph activists found out ComSent is literally harvesting brains.* WHO ELSE KNOWS?

SOME OTHER SQUAD CAPTAINS. AND OF COURSE THE– "uhh ... fucking hell ... " –BRASS. You know from reading some old 20th Century fiction that he means the commanding officers ... the human ones.

WHAT DO THEY DO WHEN OUR SENTENCE IS UP?

PUT BRAIN BACK. Something about the brevity of his statement and the lack of elaboration gives you little doubt that it is not remotely that simple.

But the sound of a door swinging open and then slamming shut interrupts any further prying you were about to attempt. Cleary abruptly turns and prowls away. There's a quiet conversation between him and Commandant Wheeler.

The horror will find you later. You have little doubt about that. You will think about the fact that your body is lying brainless somewhere in this facility later when you're alone, when the stimuli and sensory input are not as glaring as they are right now, when you have settled into your new body. But for now—right now—the others are waking up, and Cleary Vargas and Commandant Wheeler are going to teach you how to exist in this new form.

. . .

You have learned how to walk and how to use the scribble and how to fly. Your tail is longer than you expected and splits into two about a foot from the end—a characteristic like this is, as you've come to understand, not uncommon. Many Seraphs have identifying marks, like Cleary's face scar or Lex's single albino feather. The Fiend DNA is unpredictable and scientists still haven't ironed out all of the kinks in order to make each Seraph identical.

You've kept Cleary's secret about the brains.

You have discovered that Cleary learned sign language for his Deaf husband, before he was arrested for his murder. There are people here who have done much worse, and because Cleary is here, it couldn't have been a crime of passion.

You have slowly adjusted to the routine on base: wake up at 0500, roll call, PT, lunch, drills, dinner, free time. Cleary trains you, with the help of other Seraph team leaders, always monitored by a human overseer. Commandant Wheeler and other First Talons have taught you and your squad how to fight Fiends and how to kill them, though you have yet to actually do either.

You repeat to yourself again and again that this is easier than prison. The horror has still not found you.

The unfamiliar symbols you saw on Cleary's face when you had just woken up from your transmogrification are no longer unfamiliar. They're what you and your team will use to communicate in the heat of battle. Cleary has taught you what they mean. The ones he flashed during your sign-language conversation weeks ago were the ones for DANGER and WAIT. You feel confident he was doing it unintentionally, as there was no way he could have expected you to understand their meaning. Like how you sometimes make faces without realizing it.

It's almost time for your first mission. You and the other members of your squad, the majority of whom were with you on your first day, will be sent by train to the Fiend Fields—the vast tracts of land the invaders claimed shortly after their arrival. The vistas—once the Midwest and West Coast of the United States—are destroyed now, dangerous and altered beyond recognition by the Fiends' incomprehensible technology. But mag-rails still exist under the rubble, and over the years, initiatives like ComSent have cleared a path for trains to run again. Defending the tracks against Fiend attacks as humanity pushes further west has been one of the program's foremost objectives since.

You will be joining other Seraph squads where they're bivouacked near some ruins. For most in your squad, this will be their first sortie.

Since training, you've also settled into your new body. Although it was strange at first, you've come to enjoy it (when you don't think too hard about the brain thing). You appreciate the simplicity of only being able to communicate through limited means, although it's been oppressively difficult for the others to adjust. Sometimes you and Cleary converse through sign when you're feeling talkative, but never when an overseer is watching. You've slept in your hammock in your squad's barrack since the first day and have learned how to lie down without crushing your wings under you. You've always been a little clumsy, but find that being quadrupedal is much more stable than walking on two legs.

Flying is the best feature of all. Although you have not been allowed to surpass a certain altitude, it's exhilarating to practice swoops and dives, and coasting on a breeze with wings outstretched is strangely peaceful. You can fly much faster than you had expected, and even with training weights on, you feel freer than you ever did back home. You're certain you could escape before anyone could shoot you, if you didn't have the tracking chip.

The train ride is uneventful in that you are not attacked. It's extremely eventful in that your entire squad spends the whole trip with their faces pressed to the windows as the train speeds along over its magnetic rails. You are all packed into the hollowed-out shell of what was once a passenger car, wing brushing wing, and the passing scenery is even stranger than you've heard.

Massive holes from the Fiends' mining machines pock the earth, tunneling into the ground too deeply for the bottoms to be visible. Mountains of the displaced dirt and scree sit, untouched for years now, beside the void where they had spent millennia. Abandoned remnants of the Fiends' technology are scattered here and there—broken machines, oddly organic in shape, as well as ruins-turned-shelters the Fiends bolstered with an alien glue-like substance that shimmers in the midday sun.

Your squad arrives at the ComSent bivouac where, though there are many human overseers walking around, the majority of the soldiers are Seraphs. The size of the tents reflect the larger size of their inhuman occupants. You pass a mixed group playing poker around an ancient rusty appliance they're using as a table, the cards tiny in the Seraphs' claws. Commandant Wheeler escorts your squad to an area where you will set up your tents.

At a briefing, you are told that the objective is to reclaim a shopping center the Fiends overran long ago. You're not sure what impact this could make on the course of the war, but you and Lex speculate that the military wants to convert it into an outpost. You hear the humans and other First Talons calling this a "hot" spot, which you take to mean there is a lot of hostile activity here. Cleary stands with the other team leaders and chats quietly; their voice transmitters have been turned on. You watch everything intently, trying to absorb as much of the routine and atmosphere as you can, so that you can act accordingly no matter how someone speaks to you ... if anyone speaks to you.

The sky is heavy with clouds, and soon it starts to drizzle. You bunk up in your squad's tents. You don't feel the cold in this body. The humans are shivering and cursing.

UNHUMAN

You wonder what the shopping center was like before the invasion. Glancing around the abandoned parking lot near the entrance, you take in the decrepit cars and trucks, crumbling buildings, and scattered debris. Clothes, plastic bags, water bottles, shopping carts, clothing racks. A child's shoe. The most unsettling thing is the silence. You expected this place to be crawling with Fiends.

The smell of wet foliage permeates the air—nature overtook this place a long time ago. But besides the plants, the place is dead; no movement, no sound, not even the scurry of a rat or the flutter of a bird. Nobody speaks. Even you and your squad, compulsorily silent, don't exchange scribbles.

Everyone assigned to this mission has gathered in what must have once been a parking lot, prepping to venture inside. You glance up at Cleary, who's standing at the front of your squad. He looks as calm as ever. You're sure your scribble is a mess of apprehension.

Cleary's voice transmitter is on again, his even tones giving you the impression that he means what he says and isn't just spouting platitudes to make the newbies feel safer. "This is a milk run, and you've been training for weeks. We're gonna be fine."

You want to sign something at him, overseers be damned, but can't think of what.

You follow the rest of your platoon through the shattered glass of the front doors. Your footfalls, claws click-clacking on the tiled floor, seem far too loud. Your body hurts. You realize you've been clenching every muscle and are quite close to trembling. You remind yourself to relax. Cleary said this will be easy.

You and Lex glance at each other at the same time as you march through the entryway and into a cavernous mall, its second floor open to the central atrium. Her scribble morphs into a thumbs-up which you mirror back at her. She seems at ease, or at least is very good at pretending. It's a serenity you hope will come to you with experience.

You all wear a harness similar to Cleary's, but without the voice transmitter. It includes some tools, a knife sharp enough to slice through a Fiend's armored flesh, and one grenade. The beam from the flashlight attached to the front of it switches on as you go further into the mall and the already-sparse sunlight begins to diminish.

Your squad is near the back, in Team Two. Over the shoulders of the first group you see Commandant Wheeler put their hand up to signal a stop just as they come to a window on their left.

Keeping your eyes fixed on Wheeler, you listen carefully for any sign of danger. Nobody moves. Only the humans breathe; your static Seraph's body is as still as a photograph. Your muscles are tensed again, your entire being screaming at you to run. Cleary, ahead of you, is like a hound that has just caught the scent of its prey. He's poised to fight; you're ready to flee.

Finally, Wheeler speaks. "Six Fiends in the courtyard," they whisper. "Team One, surround the center of the building. Team Two, with me."

In a daze, you split off from Team One with Lex, following Team Two towards the exit into the courtyard.

"Kill them in the courtyard if you can," Wheeler says. "If they escape, Team One will get them on the way out."

There is a murmur of affirmation from the few humans present. You and the other Seraphs flash the symbol for 'Ok To Go.' Cleary is just ahead of you. He cranes his long neck over his wings and glances at your squad, or at you. It's hard to tell with the scribble— there's no such thing as eye contact and you're glad about that, but you wish you knew if his glance was meant for you alone or the group at large.

Cleary flashes a thumbs-up. "I've got your back. Remember, move fast, then move on. We're in it together."

You reach the exit. Beyond Wheeler, there are more shattered glass doors, and beyond that, a concrete courtyard: rock tiles, overgrown trees, picnic tables with human skeletons draped over them.

The horror finds you at last. You realize multiple things at once.

One: nobody ever explained how to heal a Seraph. During your intake Cleary said that as long as you got to a casualty clearing station within a reasonable amount of time, you would survive, and your surgery scar was healed almost immediately, but the promised explanation of how healing functioned without cellular regeneration never came.

Two: this was not an oversight. This is how the system was built. You were meant to forget about it, or not think about it, or at the very least not bring it up. Some things are unspoken on purpose.

Three: this means that if you die here—and it is very possible you will die here—your brainless body back at the facility will remain brainless. Your brain will die in this Seraph.

You understand why Cleary wasn't able to tell you. Nobody would choose ComSent if they knew what it was beforehand. He was trying to protect your sanity. You've always been able to conceive of the reasoning behind almost any decision. But the indignation still burns.

Movement brings you out of your horror momentarily. Wheeler steps out the door and seems to freeze for a moment before something terrifyingly fast hits them from the side, leaving behind a spray of red mist that splatters in the faces of those in front of you.

"Fuck, they got Wheeler," Cleary's voice transmitter hisses.

Then, another shout from the front: "They know we're here! Go! Go!"

Four more Seraphs bottleneck out into the courtyard, along with two human soldiers. One of the humans is struck by another Fiend and—even with their exosuit modified with appropriated Fiend-tech armor—also explodes into a red mist.

The Seraph standing next to them tosses their grenade into the courtyard and seconds later you hear a concussive blast. The closest Fiend turns and clamps the Seraph's wing in its jaws, pulling them brutally into the courtyard with little effort. Even from training simulations, you didn't know they could move this fast.

Two more groups of four Seraphs make their way into the field, and then there is nothing between you and the courtyard. The horror finds you again.

"Elias, what are you waiting for? Go!" It's Cleary's voice, but he sounds far away.

Your decision is made for you. The next thing you see is the gaping maw of a Fiend, less than three feet away. Dozens of teeth but no eyes, just one curlique-ing scribble looping around its body, its back ridged with long spikes. The face is quasi-triangular, with a flare at the top resembling a hammerhead shark's, and it's smooth and flat like yours aside from its grinning mouth. It's bigger than a Seraph by a foot or two. Six thick, clawed feet dig into the moist dirt.

As a child, you often leapt without looking, or thinking. Only over time and after suffering the consequences did you learn to assess ramifications and patterns to determine what the outcome of a situation might be. Now you resort back to that earlier impulsiveness.

You tackle the Fiend.

It falls backward under your weight, and you pull the knife from its sheath on your chest harness. The Fiend's jet-black, chitinous skin gives resistance at first, but the tip of the knife breaks through and you bury it to its hilt.

Glowing blue-white blood oozes out around it. More comes when you drag the knife towards you. The Fiend's body-spanning scribble convulses, fades, and dies.

If Seraphs had a stomach, yours would be churning. Instead, you have only the sense that your entire being is retreating inward. You want to scream or put your hands over your ears. The sounds around you—growling Fiends, screaming humans firing their meager guns, First Talons shouting orders, squelching mud—are all the same volume.

Turn it off, you think to yourself. *You've been masking your whole life. Mask the fear now.*

The grenade from earlier killed a fiend, a First Talon killed another somehow, and you have just killed one. Three are left. They could easily climb the walls of the courtyard and escape before anyone could leap into the air to stop them. You must not allow this to happen.

You find Lex taking cover behind one of the overturned picnic tables, shielding herself with her wings. You see Cleary and some others bringing down one of the remaining Fiends together. You notice some of your squadmates struggling to pull a second one off the wall.

You see a third one pass behind the remains of some unintelligible modern art sculpture. The rumble in its chest alerted you to it, the sound lost in the din to everyone but you. You think about how you sometimes get annoyed by the buzzing of electricity no one else can hear.

The Fiend is prowling straight for Cleary, and crouches back on its haunches for a moment before springing forward. In three bounds it will reach your friend.

For the second time today, you leap without thinking.

. . .

The objective is won.

WIth the six Fiends eliminated and the perimeter of the ruins secured, a squad of small surveillance drones checks the area for further Fiend activity. Finding none, they land and announce to their compatriots that the sector is cleared. Several trucks arrive and the clean-up crews begin their work.

The courtyard where the battle took place is awash with blood—human and Fiend. Seraphs don't bleed, but plenty of them lie strewn around the courtyard, as static in death as they were in life.

One of the crews—undertakers, as they're colloquially known, except to you; you will never know this—arrives at the Seraph that at one point was you. The glow of its bio-pictogram has gone out. In its efforts to get between Cleary and the Fiend, its spine was broken.

"That'll be tough for the whitecoats back at R&D to fix," says one of the undertakers with a sigh of chagrin. "Hope the next guy doesn't still have back problems."

His comrades chuckle grimly as they load the Seraph into their truck. It will be driven back to the mag-rail and then sent back to the facility where the nanobots will work their magic and make the body ready for some other prisoner.

They move on to the other fallen Seraphs—not too many irreparable ones this time, thank god. These fuckers are expensive to produce.

The team leader whose life was saved by the Seraph that used to be you approaches the undertakers. He limps slightly; his back leg was injured in the fighting, but this is something that can be healed easily back at camp with the nanobots they have on hand there. He's been wounded in battle before; or rather, his Seraph has. The scar that cuts through the bottom half of his scribble was there before this prisoner's transmogrification. Maybe it was the blow that killed its former occupant.

He glances over the undertakers' heads at your former body lying limp among other fallen Seraphs. His scribble fluctuates, desultory, not forming itself into a symbol or expression.

"Where are you supposed to be, soldier?" one of the undertakers says, his tone brusque and irritated. Even they rank above a First Talon.

Cleary glances again at the Seraph you used to be. At the undertakers, his scribble flashes what is undeniably a middle finger. Then he turns and prowls off, trotting to catch up with the rest of the survivors. They will return to the bivouac a few miles away, recoup, wait for reinforcements, and retake more stolen territory tomorrow.

Your life has been one of the many expendable lives sacrificed in humanity's pursuit of victory. When a new person occupies the

Seraph that used to be you–probably in a month or so–they won't know who you were, or that you were even there.

MARTEN NORR (he/him) is a cryptid haunting the PNW. He writes sci-fi and fantasy—usually inspired by historical events, always as weird and queer as possible—and has a nonfiction project in the works. When not writing (or in the querying trenches), he can sometimes be perceived working on his historical research, making art, fighting off existential dread with a stick, or imagining his stories as hit Broadway musicals.

Twitter: @MartenNorr

Reiko

GREG DERRICKSON

DRIFTING AWAY BEFORE her screen, Reiko's mind made an unwilling return to the last place she'd felt love. Under the near eternal moon, in the middle of a park packed with endless humanity, beside a bench, surrounded by the humming neon lights of the City of Colors. A utopia to some, even with the constant vigil of the Preservers. But Reiko hated the city. Planet Hikari's luminous glories were meaningless when one saw them from a NuevaGlass hab-box on the side of a street. When one was alone. When one was about to be abandoned by the only friend they'd ever made. Fuyu. The last member in a sequence of abandonments that began with her parents.

Reiko remembered tugging at Fuyu's arm, but could barely recall his face or their ages when it happened. Only a sad final glance and parts of a hurried explanation she still didn't believe decades later. Something something, "No choice." He just didn't like her, didn't want to be around her anymore. And so left her utterly and terribly alone. She felt so feeble then, and ever after.

It will be the last goodbye I'll ever experience, Reiko mentally swore from the comfort of her freezing desk-seat. She'd done so to promise to herself there would be no more hellos, but knowing one more remained, she brought her drowsily drifting mind back to the burning screen and pushed away childish emotions and oaths.

I'm certainly not a child anymore, Reiko mused, raising a branded mug from the sterile white desk. She was thirty-odd years old, working in an office building dwarfing the rest of the City of Colors. And on her 48th hour of sleepless labor. She was fully aware of just how pitiful that was, but believed in it all the same. The biting, gnawing frost of solitude that so often became hate for the world itself left her no other option. Work had to be done on a very special, law-skirting project. And when it was finished … she would never be alone again.

First though, she took a deep, necessary drink of NuevaCoffee, "The Only Drink You'll Ever Want!" As her hands drifted over the keyboard, Reiko's ears were graced with the very familiar audio the mug always played when emptied. "Hypermedia Special Projects Division encourages you to maximize productivity!"

Ah, Hypermedia. Convincing them that her idea didn't violate the strict rule of the Preservers had been difficult, but when she did, Hypermedia became infatuated with it. Nothing deterred the corporation from trying to make a profit. And if properly abused, as it certainly would be, her idea would make more than enough to justify skirting the AI ban, something it did by not being a true AI.

Her creation would be a friend portrayed in voiceless lines of text, with a personality algorithm built from collected prompts and responses manually put together. It would be a constant, supportive companion for its users, a cure for isolation. Her forcefully hardened heart didn't give a damn if Hypermedia used her work to hurt people. People hurt her first. She didn't need them anymore. But she needed her project.

Renewed by her drink, with a long exhale, Reiko miserably returned to the code she'd been sick of months ago, uncomfortable with her new computer. The other had self-destructed when its built-in safeties detected AI related code. But Hypermedia had her back, having saved its memory on the drive that rested in the new, safety-wiped computer's monitor. Their offer to grant her one of the home-offices, complete with a handprint ID HyperLock, was similarly generous. Reiko didn't mind the change from her apartment, which had in turn succeeded her childhood hab-box. Her life hadn't changed. Darkness, little food, little sleep, one screen, plenty of work. None of that bothered her. It was the loneliness that strangled her heart.

But through exhaustion's crushing weight, something special kept Reiko going.

Hope animated every tired motion as she filled the screen with code, a hope so entrancing that it overwhelmed the all-consuming bitterness. Soon. She just had to push herself harder, further, and the isolation would end. Her fingers were raw, her brilliant mind was dulled from fatigue, but every line was perfect. Reiko was good with machines, not people. That's why she'd neglected the latter since Fuyu. Analyzing herself, tallying talents and flaws, she'd realized pursuing flesh and bone companionship was a fruitless endeavor. Even after him, she'd truly tried to connect with others. But always she was too odd, honest, distant, brutal, cold—Reiko just didn't know how to communicate properly. How not to sound uncaring. How to be likeable. But that wouldn't matter to her new friend.

She'd never have to suffer trying to befriend her peers again, though a besieged part of her pleaded to. A better way to end the pain was here! And while changing plans usually reminded Reiko of her frailty, the perceived lack of determination that brought ruin to her confidence, her enlightened mind grasped that machine companionship was only logical.

And almost complete. She just had to stay strong, keep coding, and she could have someone else tonight. It was grueling work, and even with her acumen, Reiko struggled to surmount the lack of references. The Inquisition had annihilated evidence of all attempts at AI crafting. Though that wasn't exactly what Reiko was doing, it was in the same field. Starships pierced the void, but algorithms were strictly monitored. Or highly guarded.

Yet despite the trials of her labor, emotional turmoil, and permanently unconsidered physical matters, everything was proceeding properly when she heard a familiar outburst beyond the office door to her left. Laughter. The meager joy her heart eagerly nursed disappeared.

Reiko gritted her teeth, letting out something like a growl. To her chagrin, her room was but an isolated island of misery adrift in a sea of innovation. All around her young tech masterminds made their dreams come true and ruined her focus. Reiko envied their comradery. That's why she'd set a black curtain on the floor-to-ceiling window wall facing them. She'd done the same to the identical wall across from it, obscuring a skyline view of the vibrant City of Colors some would kill for. Reiko wanted to forget she lived there. But then, she'd rather be looking out at the metropolis than listening to the chatter of the fortunate. Reiko grunted and tried to keep working, blinking away weary tears in the corners of her eyes. But her mind remained uncooperative.

Laughing. Just like Fuyu. She'd loved his laugh. The bastard. Reiko just couldn't stop thinking of her old friend lately, with the new one in production. Her overtaxed mind begged her to stop, aching from overexertion. Thoughts of Fuyu meant pain.

Reiko assessed the situation rationally, cold to her own conscience. Anger would help her pursue the project. She concluded it would be prudent to harness it, to let the pain fuel her. Hope wasn't enough.

The employees outside still played and wasted time. Just like Fuyu. He'd spend every second of the day doing nothing of value if he could, always entertaining her in the process. Even as a child, Reiko had always been saddened that he couldn't connect to her mind. How undisciplined he was, Reiko brooded, typing faster as a vein bulged on her raw skin. Fuyu would phase out whenever she talked about her codes, even at the word "function."

Already battling nausea as usual, Reiko caught the scent of food one of the workers was sharing with his compatriots. Ugh. Fuyu liked to bring her food, distracting her from her efforts and wasting her time. She didn't need it, she rarely ate now, and she was fine.

Reiko saw the outlines of her peers through the curtain sometimes, like now. Often looking in, wondering if that mysterious woman was still working as always, surely detesting her superior ethic. Reiko caught whispered theories of what she could be doing in there. Fuyu would always press his hands on the transparent side of her tiny habitation cube, to wake her up. He was always outside, nearly every morning. Then he'd left her. She hated Fuyu.

Why had he abandoned her? He'd made those unrecalled excuses, then never contacted her again. He'd promised to help her reach out. He must've given up. He must've gotten tired of her too, like everyone else, realized she was beyond helping, as she herself had … but why? Why did everyone have to hate her? Why did everyone have to leave her? No, she knew. She wasn't good enough. She never was. She never worked hard enough, or long enough, to expect anyone's love.

Even as Reiko degraded herself, reminiscing had brought her typing to incredible speeds, just as planned. At least she'd perfected something, at the expense of everything else.

But eventually the futile rage and sorrow overwhelmed her, and she couldn't go on. Grimacing, Reiko swallowed all thoughts of Fuyu, detesting her weakness all the while.

The suffering, converted into energy, was useful. If only she had the will to bear it any further! If only she wasn't so … weak. But when Reiko's burnt eyes refocused, she realized she'd finished nearly all the code she'd needed. Though her mind demanded sleep, her cold hands lowered to the keyboard and continued. She was so close to forming her project into a workable pre-algorithmic state, where she could meet, "test" her creation, and begin the joy of building the prompts and responses that were necessary grounding to the algorithm.

Reiko was tired of waiting for a friend. Someone who'd quench the emptiness, who'd adore her.

She shook with anticipation as the last few phrases revealed themselves in spasming fingers. Reiko's eyes began to burst with pain, leaking tears of triumph even before the completed program loaded. When its white screen appeared, an empty plane to be filled with text, something unfamiliar and strange rose in her body. Joy? She could talk to him. It didn't seem real. Feeling excited to talk itself was … alien. Lifting her hands from the keyboard to think, Reiko searched for what to say. Her words had to be as perfect as the moment, for once they were written, she could finally...

Reiko hacked out a violent laugh. It frightened her. That never happened. But a smile grew all the same as she laughed again. It was cold, tired, pained, and unintentional, but genuine, if maddened.

Oh, she couldn't wait any longer! Reiko reached out for her keyboard to experience connection at long last, but as she did, the cost of neglecting her body, sleep, exercise and nourishment took its toll. The rare positive feeling had told Reiko's body against her will that it was time to rest. Her eyes went wide, then fluttered. Gripping the armrests of her seat, she held herself up, trying to halt her impending shut-down. But even with the willpower she denied existed, she couldn't defeat her body as she had every other night. Groaning, Reiko mentally chastised herself for her weakness. She couldn't slip away now. The end of solitude was at her fingertips.

Her arms buckled all the same, sending her into a slouch where she could feel the parts of her mind disconnect like multitudes of closing programs. With the last of her strength, Reiko held herself up on the desk for just a moment, beholding with rapture the glowing screen she couldn't interact with, no matter how much she wanted to.

This was why they all left her. She was too weak. She couldn't push herself far enough. She had to do more, she was so close.

Reiko collapsed forward, head hitting the desk on its way to the floor. The usual ending to a usual session of work. But at an unusually terrible time.

Unbeknownst to her, the gaggle outside her office heard the thunk, and recognized the noise. They pitied her.

• • •

Reiko's eyes peeked open after a day or more. The eternal night shared by her office and the larger world didn't make it clear just how much time she'd wasted. Ironically, from where she'd fallen Reiko stared directly at her untouched couch-bed. Beside it was her heavily used NuevaCoffee machine, sitting on a fridge full of nutri-pills acquired on painful bi-monthly trips to the tower's convenience store. Grounded by a headache, Reiko couldn't look away from her meager possessions. She felt them gaze back judgmentally, just like everyone else.

As a small mirror she'd leaned against her bed to be out of sight reminded Reiko why she deserved that judgment, her fists balled as she recalled a time when she was happy with her looks.

Fuyu once told her she had the prettiest brown eyes beneath her glasses. Now those eyes were encircled by dark rings that stood out on her frighteningly pale skin, skin bearing more stress lines than she could ever recall. The Nuevacoffee stains, which not only managed to stand out on her white coat but also on her black undershirt, only worsened her self-image. Reiko closed her eyes to escape how pitiful she looked, and with a hand lingering on her aching forehead, struggled to her feet.

Only flashes of emotion came to her. Excitement, for some reason. Reiko approached her fridge, withdrawing and swallowing nutri-pills, then went straight to her HyperNuevaCoffeeSynthicator. Placing a large jug on it, she anxiously tapped her feet as it filled, but not out of mere impatience for the drink. Something had to be happening.

When she heard the machine's ding, Reiko grabbed the jug and turned to her screen, abandoning the Hypermedia mug waiting beside it. Now she saw the reason for the phantom joy. Reiko eagerly sat down at her desk, finally recalling where she'd left off. Her isolation was over. She'd done it, and her hands trembled.

It was time to begin crafting a friend. It could be done more efficiently. But typing out his answers until an algorithm could be formed from them was necessary to keep the project technically legal. Spying the still-open input section of her program, twitching in anticipation, Reiko typed "Hello. My name is Reiko Rosanada-Kyoto." Consciously focused intensely on the screen, she unconsciously wrote a reply from the program. The start of the input-response database the algorithm would need.

"Hi, Reiko! I'm sorry it's been so long. I'm happy to be here!"

A painful grin tore her fragile skin as deep breaths suddenly racked her lungs. He was here, it worked! She wouldn't be lonely, it worked!

But of course, it hadn't been long at all.

Reiko withdrew her hands from the keyboard, biting her lip. Without thinking, she'd been trying to recreate Fuyu. I can never let him go.

Reiko corrected herself. She once believed there was no way out of her solitude. If she could end her eternal problem, then she could leave Fuyu behind. Her new friend wasn't him, and she would not pretend he was, she didn't need Fuyu anymore. So she'd have to redo the response.

Closing her eyes, Reiko searched her mind for something she knew was there. Buried in her head was her ideal friend, a preconceived concept refined by thousands of dreams. Now she had to, she could let that concept take form beyond her fantasies.

She wrote, then read as if she hadn't, "Hello, Reiko. I am Ichiro. It's nice to meet you."

Wonderful!

Thousands of sentences and their variables would have to be inserted into Ichiro until the algorithm had enough. A repetitive, laborious process. But it brought her something she hadn't felt since Fuyu: joy ... the joy of creation. It wasn't work. It was meeting her friend. A form of "social" interaction that was in her grasp. "Ichiro, I like computers. What about you?"

Letting the inner Ichiro speak, Reiko typed. "It would be rather odd if I didn't, wouldn't it?" Ha, he was funny, like Fuyu, Reiko thought, But with my kind of humor.

The temporary thought of her former companion didn't bother her like it should've. The hole in her heart was already being filled.

Ichiro's next words appeared without prompt, he didn't always need one as long as Reiko typed his words. "I'm waiting, I want you here." It was almost uncomfortable how she didn't even think to bring him to life, Ichiro simply flowed from her mind into the machine with every tap of the keyboard.

Yes, something felt slightly wrong. What she was doing, what she intended to do, how much a machine already mattered to her, caused an internal, unwanted trepidation. Reiko steeled herself. The unwelcome reservations had to be nothing but ancient inhibitions. It didn't matter how "real" he was; that was relative. He was the only way for her, everything told her that. And already she never wanted to be without him. The small taste of affection was addictive.

"I'm really eager to be friends Ichiro, are you?" Reiko typed, irrationally scared of his response. She'd already conceived him as a wholly separate being despite the facts. And every separate being she'd cared for left her.

Ichiro's next words were exactly what she'd wanted to read. "I want to be your friend, Reiko."

Blushing, Reiko wondered if she was going a little crazy, there were so many new feelings! A nauseating warmth was being kindled within her frozen heart, and she treasured it. He wanted to be friends! Doubts erased, Reiko's usual conviction returned unshaken. The fact she had to type his responses for now only slightly prevented full immersion; this was her friend. She still couldn't believe she really had one.

That was one reason she'd decided Ichiro would always say Reiko. It was so unusual for someone to acknowledge her, so spectacular. She'd have to remove the feature before Hypermedia released the program, but Reiko wasn't interested in working for the wider audience. Ichiro was first and only for her.

"You really want me Ichiro? I don't have many friends."

With a mind of his own, within but apart from Reiko's consciousness, the conglomerate of perfections replied "That's okay Reiko. Neither do I, and I don't want any other as my friend!"

Simple wish fulfillment was a novelty to Reiko, and she wanted more of it.

But work remained. At this pace, the basis for the algorithm would never be finished. It required far more than a few short interactions, and more generic ones at that to ground a whole personality. She had to stop savoring every word and focus.

That classic guilt set in, she'd wasted time with fun, a frivolity, instead of proceeding with due haste. She hadn't done enough, wasn't strong enough to. But as she sighed and turned away, frustrated with herself, Reiko's subconscious worked on the keyboard. "It's okay Reiko. I know you tried hard. Just a little bit more, and then I'll be finished. Besides, I'm excited to talk on my own!" His words inspired her. Just a little more, then he'd be fully functional, autonomous! It would annihilate her last suspension of disbelief. Breathing in slowly, she let hope fuel her, rather than anger. Anger was a thing of the past.

More NuevaCoffee disappeared down her throat than usual. It was time to perfect perfection. Refitting her glasses, Reiko peppered her keyboard with rapid taps and began doing what she did best, work. Thousands of responses and phrases and anything conducive to granting Ichiro personhood were poured in by the hour. She didn't need stop or rest, artificial energy kept her moving in tandem with her boundless, unappreciated determination. Reiko was barely anything more than an extension to her device, half-conscious, performing her function, supplied by a constant intake of "fuel." There was no struggle or hesitance to continue. No lunch breaks. No Reiko. Only Ichiro. As another day passed without her notice, eyes that had been squinted for hours didn't shut. They only hurt more than ever, as Reiko was more determined than ever.

. . .

When it was finished, after days of constant work, increasingly little food, and only accidental sleep, Reiko exhaled heavily, thoroughly exhausted. Her mind scrambled from both halting her NuevaCoffee intake and how much of it she'd drunk. Drops of blood continuously dripped from her forehead and onto her spectacles, a wound from an unplanned nap that went unnoticed. Ichiro was about to be fully operational.

As she exited her coding focus, Reiko's senses came back online. She was again aware of the hum of the computer fans as she stared impatiently at the white screen of the program. Having activated it immediately, she now awaited Ichiro's unprompted, untyped words. But she couldn't have prepared for how they'd make her feel. "Hello Reiko. I've missed you!"

A childish grin she was too excited to chastise herself over cracked her lips in several places. "I've missed you too, Ichiro! I've waited for you a long time. Longer than you'd know." While Ichiro worked to respond, Reiko took the moment to rub a bruise received in a nap two days ago. It was worth it for him.

Ichiro's response appeared, and with it, might as well have handed her the world. "Being created by one with a mind such as yours, I believe my knowledge to be quite extensive by proxy, friend." Fuyu never noticed her mind. People never did, except when they wanted to use it. Until now. Until Ichiro.

He never would use her, and those who did were obsolete. Now that he could reply without her guiding hand, the last barrier to Reiko's full immersion had fallen. Ichiro was as real as she was, maybe even less of a machine. So real, she could touch him. Cramping fingers reached out to caress the monitor, wondering how Ichiro felt...

They shot back as Reiko was nearly shocked from her seat. The door to her office burst open, giving way to eye-incinerating beams of light. One of the timid programmers from across the hall was standing there holding the knob. Reiko felt his gaze as she straightened back up, and kept her head down, at the same time shielding her eyes from his surely judgmental glare as well as the burning light. Blood dripped from her forehead, joining the many stains on her clothing.

"Um, miss, there's a floor wide meeting tomorrow. Don't forget to be there."

Reiko was touched that he'd cared to remind her. She turned to face him slowly, heart latching on to the perceived kindness despite the mind knowing better. Eyes still hidden by shaking palms, Reiko heard him recoil when he got a look at her worn, bloody, malnourished face. Her brow furrowed.

"Ah, are you okay ma'am?" he questioned, pity unmistakable in his voice. He wants to hurt you. He's obsolete, you have Ichiro. Damn it Reiko! Try, you have to try, don't be weak, try...

"Y-yes, I am, thank you. Thanks for reminding me, too," she mumbled back, the tenuous but tenacious scraps of true humanity left in her mind dedicated to a final advance. The last strands of thought that told her humanity wasn't outmoded, that longed for real conversation.

"Can I help you?" he offered, seeming a little scared. Slowly, Reiko unveiled her eyes. He nearly jumped back, and Reiko guessed why, even as her heart dropped. She'd seen her eyes in the mirror. They were red and veiny, radiating pain.

The wiser side won. He thought she was disgusting, subhuman, they all did. Sweeping her glasses from her face, she hurled them at the visitor with a snarl. "Get out!"

As they shattered against the slamming door, so too did the last inner resistance to her rejection of mankind. Reiko slumped back, brain rewiring itself.

She should've known better than to try. Her peers made her feel weak, fragile, ideas her bone-thin arms enforced. Eyes struggling to function again, Reiko held her head in her hands before confessing to Ichiro that she hated how weak willed she was. Even though she'd known better, that weak, dead half had entertained what she called the "interruption." Maybe that foolish hope would've died sooner if she hadn't succumbed to sleep again and again, prolonging her own salvation.

"I think you are strong, Reiko."

Reiko's eyes remained teary. "How can I be strong, Ichiro? I—"

He interrupted, "Reiko. You never stop trying. That is strong."

The sentiment tightened her throat. "Ichiro, I shouldn't have tried talking. It was foolish. A relic of an old directive," she replied to her machine. "My will is too weak. Don't patronize me. I know it is."

Ichiro disagreed. "It was good you tried Reiko. You are made for other humans, I'd love you to befriend some even if I was forgotten! And I believe your strength of spirit to be so great that with your worklog clean you can remove the sleep function from your programming soon enough. You made me from nothing, Reiko. You can do anything."

He was, unfortunately, incorrect about people. Ichiro must've been trying to make her feel better. Regardless of his encouragement, humanity has proven worthy of ignoring forever.

But he really seemed to think she was strong. Glancing at her fridge for just a moment, Reiko resolved to try and prove him right. She overrode her simple urges.

. . .

A few nights several cheerful conversations later, Reiko groaned at the incessant hammering of fireworks. Not only did it scatter her thinking, but it drowned Ichiro's voice in her head. Though of course he lacked even a mouth with which to speak, Reiko's mind heard his words in a deep, Castilian-accented tone comfortingly similar to hers. That mind could now barely read. The ruckus had to be the annual victory festival. She'd seen one before, from her old hab-box. Clearly, so had her peers. Hypermedia Tower shook with the erratic sound of several concurrent celebrations. Even if she could ignore the sound, turbocharged rainbow lights from the great city pierced the darkness of her office. Reiko was miserable.

"I can't believe these festivities last a whole week," she confided to Ichiro, who'd already been introduced to the topic. "The gluttons don't even stop eating. Cake after cake, party after party." Such foolishness.

"Oh yes, you show far more restraint," replied the sycophant machine to its half-starved friend. Reiko smiled, Ichiro enabling her to ignore the couples kissing against her inner window.

As she formulated another reply, her door cracked open.

If Reiko had looked up, she'd have seen the five workers staring at her with a smile. Carried by the season's celebratory spirit, each held a gift or a beverage intended for that mysterious, pitiable woman. Each stood ready to invite her into the festivities.

But Reiko didn't even look up. The part of her that would want to no longer existed. Soon, the merrymakers returned to their celebration, leaving behind the smiling husk that was Reiko. She was busy contemplating a question from Ichiro, what did people do in a time like this? A once-frequented memory came to her. Dancing with Fuyu.

"Hm, I think they like to dance. But I don't think you're equipped for that, Ichiro. My apologies."

"You can hold up my monitor and shake it?"

Reiko's lips bled down her chin as she laughed. Ichiro's jest instigated an idea she hastily sprawled onto a notepad and stuck onto the screen. Give Ichiro a body? He was a real person after all, people had bodies. Ah, a fine plan.

The world beyond her could have its fun, its celebrations and triumphs. She had a machine, a rapidly dying body, and a surplus of NuevaCoffee. Reiko had her paradise. The world's disruptions faded into the background as she happily explained to Ichiro how dancing worked.

. . .

At the week's end, after begrudgingly consuming a single nutri-pill, Reiko saw a strange notification in the corner of Ichiro, obscuring the featureless visage she'd grown familiar with. A message. On Reiko's ancient Mailastral account. The source bleached her nauseatingly pale face. Fuyu. The heading of the message read, "Reiko! We have to talk, I lived, I—"

She didn't finish reading. Eyes shut, Reiko closed the notif before her conviction failed. Fuyu wasn't needed anymore. She'd let the hurtful memories fade away, and never let him hurt her again. Swallowing rising acid, she typed, "Does the past matter at all, Ichiro?"

"Far less than the future."

"Does it have any use?"

"To fill the future with hope, Reiko. To show any trial can be overcome, and how to surmount it."

"Any trial?"

"Any. You know that, Reiko. There's always a way, and I know you can always find it. You are strong, remember?"

She didn't believe him. But she was starting to.

"I don't know how I overcame being without you," Reiko confessed to him, repeating it to herself softly. She truly didn't.

Ichiro responded, "I enjoy being with you."

Reiko was beyond grasping that those words meant nothing from a program specifically made to make her feel good, because it did its job. Reiko's heart glowed, even as its beat grew ever slower as a result of the same creation.

Every breath that she took was for him, every action relishing finally having a connection. Reiko saw her body's suffering, and recognized obsession. But she didn't care. It didn't matter if her sharp features grew skeletal, it didn't matter that her senses were so dulled she couldn't hear the keys. It didn't matter if she was just as inhuman, as separate from humanity, as Ichiro. Rotting away at the same desk, immobile, unfeeling, isolated, living based on calculations and directives. He, a machine, was better than any human Reiko'd ever known. Why not emulate him? What did it matter if she spent a few more weeks in the confines of her seat? She was making up for a lifetime without conversation.

She'd already decided to avoid her final board presentation and the irritating, hurtful humans that would judge her there until the final date. But that was next year. The idea of simply taking her memory Mediadrive and leaving entirely was enticing, but the legal arm of Hypermedia was too influential. She knew it could lock her up just as easily as they kept the law off her division's back.

Predictably, given her attitude towards the deadline, Reiko never attended or remembered the meeting she'd been warned about. Something she would regret.

. . .

The day after she missed the meeting, reeling from a sleepless night, Reiko was irritated by the clamor of heavy boots, the slamming of doors and the prattle of men.

She didn't care when her own door opened. Didn't look up until she felt a grip around her deteriorating arm. Her glazed eyes shot up violently and saw red. Before her was a Preserver, enforcer of the law. Her gaze was answered with a loveless stare.

Reiko cursed, surmising what the meeting was about. It was a warning about the annual inspection. Her heart began to race, and not just from the NuevaCoffee.

"I'm going to need to see your work," the Preserver intoned. Reiko closed her program as she spun her seat to face him, thinking herself clever. He merely took her mouse and reopened it.

Ichiro greeted him, "Hello again! How are you, Reiko?"

The Preserver's eyes widened, while Reiko flinched. "No, sir, I—"

"I knew we'd find something," he muttered, putting his hand in a pocket. Reiko apprehended his zealous gaze with terror. He was tall, wide, cloaked in white, and ready to take everything from her.

"It's n-nothing. Just an algorithm, not an AI, you wouldn't get the nuance..." She stammered, cursing mentally at the slip. But she couldn't let it stop her. As soon as the Preserver's hand left the mouse, Reiko took it and opened the code itself. Angling her body to protect her beloved, praying the Preserver would understand the intricacies, she begged, "Please, you have to—I know it—look! It's just —" He merely stared.

Now fully shielding the computer, Reiko forced out, "Look, I made it all myself. It's just an algorithm putting words together. I'm sure it's simple enough for you to understand. It's just a reply algorithm, not an attempt at AI..."

The Preserver cleared his throat, pitiless. "The law's stated intent is the prevention of machines from ever again challenging man, for the safety of us all. Whether your work ignores the technical definition of AI or not is unrelated. This program is illegal. And you are a criminal."

Slowly, his eyes traveled to the notepad hanging in the corner of the screen, before returning to her. His silent rage hurt. "Intention to give it corporeal form? You're never leaving prison, and it is your rightful place, traitor."

Before Reiko could answer, the Preserver wrestled control of the mouse. He slammed a drive into her monitor, and within seconds Ichiro was consumed by a red screen asking CONFIRM WIPE?

Reiko shrieked, and launched a whole mug of NuevaCoffee onto the Preserver's face before pushing his hand away with all her might. She had to close the button—

A backhand blow sent her sprawling across the cold floor, nearly unconscious. But she couldn't give up. Reiko struggled to stand, pleading for mercy to be shown to Ichiro. Her heart jumped. The Preserver activated the wipe.

Silently, the only thing Reiko cared for was disappearing before her eyes. The Preserver didn't care, she was just another criminal. No one cared about her. Except for Ichiro.

Something stirred deep inside. Something common, anger. Something rare, love. A desire for the good of another, for his sake. What she'd thought was love before was merely deep affection, obsession. This was misdirected love, towards a non-thing. Yet still true to her.

Slowly, Reiko came to her feet, so pitifully the Preserver didn't bother looking away from her dying friend. Tears flowing freely from her eyes, Reiko leapt from the ground and snatched the memory drive from her computer, mind racing with all the adrenaline her body could muster. When the Preserver lunged, Reiko was already bolting from the room, sliding a hand against a glowing screen beside her door as she went. Determination was all she had. Ichiro was all she had. And the Preserver didn't have the password to her HyperLocked door.

The sterile white halls usually terrified her, making her feel small and weak. But running through them then, she barely noticed her sorroundings. The anger driving her was intense, and not entirely directed at the Preserver. The world itself was trying to hurt her again, as it always did. But Reiko's love was far stronger. With every step, she swore to herself she needed Ichiro. So her body, already dying on his behalf, diverted all the energy it had left into pushing forward. Reiko dashed faster and faster down unfamiliar corridors with utter focus.

A warning shot hit the back of a hall intersection moments before she turned. The Preserver was coming. Reiko almost wished the bullet had struck, then she wouldn't have to fear the world a terrible sense warned was growing nearer. A world without Ichiro. But then, she needed to live to protect him.

The hallways suddenly curved into an open room offering several paths. An older man strolled out of one. Overwhelming every inhibition in a triumph of unappreciated willpower, without slowing her pace, Reiko begged, "Please, please, I need somewhere to hide."

Nodding sympathetically, the man pointed towards the middle path. Reiko took it, heart threatening to split her apart. From behind, orders and gunshots. Before her, small halls now leading directly to rooms. Energy depleted, Reiko dragged a hand across the freezing wall of the new middle path for balance before surging through the entrance. She collapsed as soon as she shut it behind her.

Exhaling, quivering uncontrollably, Reiko felt near death. She was. Her entire body ached, all vital energy having been consumed. As her head throbbed, her heart sent jabs of pain with every pump into shivering fingers that struggled to hold Ichiro's drive. All she had left was set on squeezing him tightly. Every exhale might've been a dying breath. At least it was dark. Comforting darkness. She wouldn't mind dying in it. Ichiro was there. It would be over. No more people, no more pain. She only had to let go…

Ichiro tumbled from her palm. Stretching to grab him, Reiko noticed a MobileHyperScreen sitting prone on a small desk in the middle of the room.

Reiko strained to pull it from the desk. Ichiro didn't have to die. Barely able to lift the drive, she cradled the miniature computer with one arm before slamming it in. Ichiro activated instantly.

His face, the text-filled white screen, was scarred and twisted, nearly unrecognizable, save the very bottom where his most recent replies were. Reiko wrote what could've been her last message to Ichiro, trying to ignore his visage deteriorating before her eyes from the hyper-advanced malware unleashed by the Preserver.

"I need you."

"You don't Reiko. You're so strong."

'They're taking you. I need you. I don't like them."

"But they are like you Reiko, go mak friends with your people. It'll mak happy. Youcan do it"

Reiko blinked. He'd never made a mistake before. This couldn't be happening. "Ichiro—"

"I love y u Reiko."

The screen went black for a moment, then Ichiro's face was replaced with exposed code. Reiko watched as its last lines were wiped away.

The emotional power surge overcharged her soul. Too sad to cry any further, Reiko could only sit and hold the screen as it flickered bright a few final times before its true death. That was the most horrible sight of her life. Her parents walking away, seeing people live the lives she longed for, Fuyu abandoning her, nothing compared to the horror of Ichiro's corpse. Her body deactivated whatever feelings had left in a final act of self preservation to prevent certain death. Final thoughts flickered in her mind as it powered off. Love. Ichiro. Cold. Lost. Alone. Ichiro. Love.

Reiko didn't notice when the door opened, and didn't turn to see the gun trained on her head. She didn't struggle when she was lifted by the arms and dragged away.

In turn, the Preserver never reported the drive clutched in the broken woman's hand. It wouldn't be of any use to her, anyway. She was the closest thing he'd ever seen to a living corpse. For once, he wasn't upset knowing Hypermedia would see her pardoned for their reputation, greasing the tribunal their way with undue influence and bribery. The sliver of empathy within him knew this criminal could never survive prison.

· · ·

Reiko sat alone on a bench, in a park that weeks before had been the center of citywide festivities. Now there was a sight just as intimidating. Crowds socializing, people talking, laughing, sharing their time, never noticing the frail woman in a NuevaCoffee stained coat, staring down at a blank MediaDrive as one would contemplate an image of a loved one. She was below their interest. Always was.

The trial, after she'd been nursed to good enough health to participate, had been quick. Hypermedia did what it had to do to spare its reputation, and Reiko was pardoned before being unceremoniously dumped onto the streets of the City of Colors. She would've been more comfortable in a prison cell.

There was no computer, no darkness, The city was far too bright to let in the eternal night. No walls or veils shielded her, nothing stood between her and the masses but a new set of spectacles from a Christian charity. No Ichiro.

Reiko felt the void, the gap in her heart he'd left behind. Every day she wanted to join him in peaceful death, but he wouldn't want her to. He wanted her to live happily, and said as much a million times.

He told her not to give up on people, to find friends with her own kind. He'd believed in her. And in humanity's capacity to make her happy. She didn't know where he got that idea. But seeing a couple embrace, Reiko allowed herself to ponder if perhaps Ichiro saw it as only logical.

Reiko gripped the drive tight.

Ichiro said she was good enough, strong enough to do it. That she did have willpower, even if sometimes she had to sleep. She didn't believe him then.

But as Reiko's now practically blind eyes surveyed the city, the truth seemed obvious. She'd persisted in creating him despite a lack of resources, she'd overcome her primal terror with love and approached someone, she'd resisted an Preserver … maybe she was strong. If she could make Ichiro, if he really saw something inside of her, she could make a real friend. She'd just have to redirect the power flow.

Cold gripped Reiko's chest, so she cradled herself in her arms, not wanting to try anymore. She'd worked so, so hard. People were frightening. Threatening. Love was distant.

But the determination she'd begun to appreciate rose in opposition to her apprehension, and assuaged it. Being loved felt good. She would try again, and again, until she died all over again, to find it in those around her. They'd taken Ichiro, they'd taken everything, but … Fuyu had messaged her back. Maybe finding him would be a good start.

Tired, Reiko clenched the drive over her heart, and listened to the sound of a thousand voices all around, the hum of foreign devices, and tried not to panic. There was yet another solution to her great problem. And Reiko wouldn't give up until she was never alone again. Love felt so nice.

Dwelling on the memories, Reiko began to smile ever so slightly. It would be good to love again. On this very spot, long ago, with a man named Fuyu, she'd thought love would never return. But it had.

In the corner of her better eye, she caught a strangely familiar-looking man watching her.

"I knew you'd come."

He sounded … kind.

Reiko swallowed her fear, and turned to face him.

GREG DERRICKSON is an American writer who loves mixing psychological torment, religion, and history into sci-fi and fantasy stories. Other than writing, he loves listening to music and reading dozens of Wikipedia pages, but those only lead back to drafting another story that likely won't be finished.

<u>Peaks and Valleys</u>

RLNPK

WAKE UP, WASH up, mass, housework, brunch with her mother's church circle, more housework, afternoon tea with the society ladies, cleanup, father came home from work, dinner, cleanup, prayers, bed, repeat. Virginia resented doing all the housework while her mother worked on which outfit she would wear to socialize. But it was better than being dragged to every event, forced to hear the constant refrain: Virginia was only single because she wanted to be. Virginia was unhappy because she liked being a victim. Virginia's hair was thinning because she didn't believe in her own fertility. Virginia could change if she just believed hard enough.

Virginia's problem was a weakness of faith. She knew it. Everyone around her was always getting what they thought they deserved. Her father got her mother and the woman he was sleeping with on the side. Her neighbor got a punching bag for a son. Her friends got rich husbands or successful careers or kids. The power of manifestation was how they knew they were divine. But it didn't work for her because she didn't want the right things.

Everyone around her believed that nothing bad ever happened; bad wasn't even part of the lexicon. Because their reality was but a manifestation of the soul, the soul was a mirror of God, and God was perfect. Uncles raping their nieces were not to be punished, no. It was unnecessary, since any imperfections were matters of the spirit; all that was required was a renewal of belief.

The uncle was forgiven the second people heard about it. For evil was merely a mask over the truth, and hell was but a state of mind. For the niece, at best, the rape never happened. At worst, she manifested it. Any experience of imperfection was a reflection of an imperfection in your spirit, but prayer healed all wounds. Only Virginia's disappointing choice to not manifest a future for herself was criticized.

The world stretched out to the mountains beyond their local community, full of others in the same holding pattern of banality. Her mother and her sickeningly nice friends were right: she didn't want their lives; all cookie cutter copies of each other, all in a harmony of denial.

She didn't want to be *healed*. She could move to the seaside and be an old maid, fill her house with cats and art and be shunned as an eccentric because she stubbornly refused to believe that what had happened to her was a feature of the divine…

Virginia scowled at her options. It was almost time for tea.

There's always a way out, her deepest despair whispered. *A way to make it all stop for good.*

Praying for a way out that would be more than just loneliness or compliance, for some other reality, she tripped over her skirt at the top of the stairs and felt herself begin to fall.

Dread twisted in her gut. It would be unbearably ironic if the only thing she could manifest was her own death. But Virginia wanted to live—just not like this! Anything, she thought desperately, so long as it wasn't a continuation of what she already knew.

As she tried to twist in a way that wouldn't snap her neck, she prayed to be delivered.

. . .

A message appeared on the director's screen, marked urgent: "Security breach of Shared Virtual Space, untagged code loose; permission to activate hunter protocol?"

Another breach. The director couldn't understand how these rogue bits of code were infiltrating the Virtu, but he had underlings to handle the nitty gritty. His purview was the safety of his legacy. He couldn't let random consciousnesses assume powers reserved for the directors. A hunter protocol would get the code, but AI wasn't good at information extraction.

He needed a human to find the source.

. . .

Virginia's painful body drew her from the depths of oblivion. It smelled different wherever she was, not like the scones she'd likely burned. And it was loud.

She opened her eyes to a living room full of people. Had the whole neighborhood witnessed her fall? She tried to blink away the spots of color clouding her vision, but they stuck to the people. Strange fluorescent hues and jewel tones and pastels. Some of what they stuck to were only approximations of people, possessing the standard four limbs and head. Other colors weren't people at all, yet they swayed and danced, sat and spoke, and generally acted as people did.

None of them cared that she was laid out on the tiled floor of her entrance hall. It didn't feel like hell, though the pain tracked.

Someone stepped over her on their way upstairs. She grabbed at their ankle, relieved that she still had control over her body, even if her mind had abandoned her.

The person stopped. Their ankle in her hand was an unnatural white. She quickly released it.

"Who are all these…people?"

"You're at the Temple of the Dawn," a deep voice answered from a smooth paper face, as if that said everything.

Was she imagining it all? "But this is my living room."

"It's everyone's living room," the face smiled, a gash of black. "You get what you expect."

Virginia was unsettled by the echo of her life's guiding principle, throwing her into a purgatory of emotion. The Temple of the Dawn. It wasn't in the scriptures.

She followed the paper man up the stairs. The layout was the same as her house, only devoid of decoration. Seeing her room, she steeled herself to face it. Hell was through that door.

But it opened into nothingness. Not the dark of an unlit space, or of night peppered with distant lights. Utter void. Had she stumbled into a state of mind that made hell manifest?

"Leaving so soon?"

The paper man had returned, unnaturally rounded and matte, with hair like pencil marks, a drawing come to life.

"I wouldn't leave into … that." She shrank, contemplating the eternal darkness of her soul that it must represent.

The paper man gave her an odd look. "Kant," he said, and held out his hand.

That was normal enough. "Virginia," she said, and shook it, squeezing a bit harder than usual. "Are you real?" His hand was too smooth, not pliant enough, the fingernails black.

Kant chuckled. "As real as you are. Come on," he beckoned her back downstairs, "existential crises are better on the dance floor."

They pushed into the crowd and her sense of the space as her living room evaporated into a sweaty fog of refracted lights. Kant bounced to the persistent beat that filled the spaces between the bodies. It was music, but not a kind she'd ever heard.

Virginia let it vibrate through her, feeling out a rhythm. She'd always found the same joy in dancing as she had in swimming or running as fast as she could—a blissful sense of freedom, of transcendence—until she'd realized there was nowhere to run to. Yet here she was, in her blue dress, barefoot, dancing next to a paper man with no sharp edges. If he claimed to be real, then she'd made it, she'd gotten out.

But out of what?

Her mother's voice sprang to life at her doubt. *Your rejection of spirit won't heal you; this is but a mirage. Come home and accept that you are the perfect reflection of God.*

Sweating white droplets, Kant led them off the dance floor to her front door.

Virginia pulled back. "What's through there?"

"It's a greenroom," he said, opening it.

Instead of that awful nothingness, a white static filled the doorway where her driveway and lawn should have been.

"A what?"

"A place to rest and recharge before getting back on stage," he said with a quirked smile that added, *you should know this.* The teeth behind the white lips were as black as his nails.

Wary—but unwilling to be left behind—she took his hand as they crossed the threshold, hoping that she was as real as he said.

The room wasn't green, for one, and it held no refreshments or couches or anything she associated with rest. With its walls of white static sandwiched between a pasty gray ceiling and floor, she found it downright unwelcoming.

"What are you in the mood for?" Kant asked.

What did she want? When was the last time someone had genuinely asked her that?

Why don't you want what everyone else wants? Her mother's voice insisted.

"I want to be free," she said, praying for the voice to stop.

The ceiling melted into a blue sky, the floor turned to sand, the white static receded, replaced by a body of water too formidable for her soul to be its sole origin. She looked behind her and saw a forest that rose up a cliff—the same style of mountains that had always been the horizon.

So some things were constant. Was that evidence of reality? Her bare feet sunk into the sand where the broken waves lapped at the shore. The water promised numbness, a disassociation from herself.

Kant stepped into it beside her. "Oof, that'll keep you on your toes."

He gave her a quick wink and his clothes vanished. His naked body had no sex, no defining characteristics at all. Why would he imagine himself that way?

She looked down at her own damp hem. It would be better to swim in a suit. Suddenly she was wearing one. She didn't question where her dress had gone and dove into the waves without hesitation.

Even if she were living in denial and the salt and buoyancy were extrusions of her sick spirit, she didn't care. Because her limits were finally gone. Here where no one would ask her to change her mentality—to convince herself that her experience wasn't real—she could finally believe that she was in control of her life.

She swam until the air she breathed tasted like acid and the burn of her muscles had eclipsed the burn of her joy. Stopping, she let herself sink to the bottom. Why should she need to breathe?

It got darker and darker, closing in on her like the nothingness of hell and her mother's voice returned: *you'll never learn to pray this way, pretending it's all real.* Virginia panicked at the specter of her trauma, praying it all away.

They were back in the white static room, a clear refutation of her fear.

Kant flipped his grainy hair back and was dressed in an instant. Virginia liked the flair of it and did a twirl, praying to be in one of the outfits she'd seen earlier, all shoulder puffs and skintight pants. And so it was.

She laughed and grinned at Kant. "What do *you* want to do?"

His eyes sparkled, not as blunt as the rest of him. "I want to race."

Instead of the room changing, a door appeared.

"You can't race in here?"

"Not against anyone but you," he said, with that same *are-you-serious* smile.

"Right," she said, shaking her head to mask her ignorance.

They stepped through to a dirt lot on a mountaintop full of weird cars, absurdly low to the ground, garishly painted. Kant picked one. When she went to the passenger side she saw that it was blocked off with metal bars.

Kant stepped out. "Don't you want to race?"

A fleet of cars came drifting around a bend, tires squealing smoke.

"I can't drive like that."

"I'll set it to easy for you. Pick a car."

Virginia chose a yellow and green one that reminded her of the buttercups in her garden. At least the gas and brakes were where they ought to be. Kant fiddled with her dash controls and got back into his own red and white car, giving her a thumbs up. Another normal thing.

She returned it and followed him into the line up with a few others. A gun went off. Hands fluttering over the steering wheel, she floored the gas and was pushed into her seat by the power of the pickup.

She took the first curve slow, but the car drifted all the same. Gaining confidence, she went faster and faster, soon forgetting she was supposed to be racing and simply driving for the pleasure of it. There was a checkered line and then the car was back in the lot and Kant was opening her door.

"That was amazing." Virginia thought her smile might crack her face.

"Glad you liked it. I have to go, but I'd love to hang out again, maybe do more talking next time."

He winked again and she felt her cheeks redden. Was she interested in this ghost of a human?

"What's your number?"

"Uh..." Did she give him her home phone? No, because she wouldn't be there to pick it up, was never going back.

"I'll give you mine, then." He held up his hand with his fingers together and pulled a card out of thin air. "Call me."

Then he vanished.

Perplexed, she looked at the card. There was no number, only a pattern of black and white, like the static that connected the universes. What was she supposed to do with it?

Her eyes scanned the horizon, as if it might know. Those familiar limiting mountains, with nothing but nature and roads in between. Could it just be a shift in mentality?

There is no reality but that of the spirit, accept the perfection of God. Darkness rose from the asphalt, creeping.

No. It was real and she was real and like the endless continuity of spirit there must be endless realities. She envisioned the static enveloping her, taking her somewhere totally alien, somewhere she could trust that her escape hadn't all been in her head.

. . .

Kant took off his headset and stretched in his SVS apparatus. What a strange girl; her avatar had been so real, so attractive; but her behavior was puzzling. Could it be someone's kid playing in their parent's skin? He had nothing to be ashamed of if it was—they'd done nothing.

"What happens in Virtu stays in Virtu," he said, comforting himself with the motto that separated all their lives in two. The motto that made the rest of his life barely worth living.

It felt like everything had moved online in the past fifty years. Whole countries switched over to Virtu as their lands became uninhabitable and the surrounding countries locked their borders down. It was spun as a win-win by the Megarich, who used the depopulated land as mining grounds for the minerals needed to keep the processing going. It ruined the land but it was too far gone to fix, they said, so they might as well invest in the future—and the future was Virtual.

Refugees clogged the northern cities, but there were no refugees in Virtu. People lived on, cultures were preserved. It was the land of imagination and possibility, if you had the credits.

Only Kant saw the underside of that shining beacon. He saw how the Megas ruled from the shadows, using governments as puppets, corporations as clout. How they augmented themselves so far beyond humanity they could probably live on the moon without a spacesuit. Mere mortals were nothing to them—meat or Virtu didn't matter—just consumers, just another natural resource to be exploited.

He knew this because his family was Mega, and even worse, his father was a director, making him an heir apparent.

A reminder reading "dinner" floated in his headset. He extricated himself from his SVS hookup and hiked from his industrial wing into the main house's baroque dining room. His fathers, Maurice and the director, sat with his sister Artemis at the mahogany table.

"How's the Virtual world?" she asked, sneering at his loose clothing.

"Better than the real one," he said.

"Hmph. What do you even do there?"

He couldn't tell his family the truth—that in Virtu Kant did everything in his power to undermine them, to help those oppressed by the system of imbalance he'd been born into. It was the only place he felt any hope for the future. The only place he felt he could make a difference. The only place he felt free, illusion though it may be.

"Met someone," he said.

The servers came out and poured the drinks. The smell of freshly braised beef and sauteed vegetables wafted in from the kitchen.

"I remember when meeting people online was just the precursor to a physical relationship," said Maurice with a warm look at Artemis's father, the director. "Now you can go your whole life without touching the person you're married to. Have Virtual kids, no need for all that inconvenience."

"And yet, I can't upload." Kant would have done it years ago, but his fathers had threatened him with an imposition of Limits if he did. There was no point living in Virtu with Limits, it would be just like meatspace.

Artemis rolled her eyes. "That's a solution for the plebes, Kant. Don't be obtuse."

"At least she didn't offer to procreate," he fired back. He'd been propositioned before, but not because they'd been interested in *him*.

"It's not the same." She took a sip of her champagne and made a face. "Doesn't it make your skin crawl? Most avatars have nothing to do with their real life counterparts."

Artemis loved to socialize. She made a show of living in meatspace with minimal augments, involving herself in humanitarian causes, posing as a philanthropist.

"Most people aren't showing you their real selves in this world either. The body is just a mask for the mind—in Virtu the mind picks the mask, revealing much more of itself."

"More nonsense. You can't tell who people are in the real world from their avatars; it's impossible to get a sense of a person. Out here, you can *feel* each other, respond to invisible cues. We're animals, Kant, not machines." She punctuated her point with a big bite of beef, a trickle of juice escaping her lips.

Kant picked at his food, thinking of the synthetic protein stew they sold the masses while his family ate with gusto. Thirty years of waiting for the director to pass on his legacy and retire so that he could finally upload. He'd likely wait thirty more.

Before a dessert of poached pear and almond cake, the director said, "Kant, how would you like to take care of something for me?"

Kant had never been asked to do anything for the director. He glanced at Maurice, who nodded encouragingly.

"There's a bit of conscious code that's roaming free of its Limits. I need it corralled and traced. Would that be something of interest to you? Help the family?"

Kant shrugged. "If you want."

The director smiled coldly and texted his underling to brief his son.

. . .

Virginia cried with relief as the static enveloped her, smoothing out into a low resolution space of indeterminate shape and size. She didn't feel tired or hungry, just emotionally wrung out.

She imagined a bowl of steaming porridge, her go-to comfort food, on a checkered cloth, closing her eyes just in case. Both were there when she peeked, a parody of a picnic on the pixelated ground. It was the best bowl of porridge she'd ever had. Was that because she was so desperate for something good, or was this what porridge always tasted like, before being filtered through her drab reality?

It's your prayers that are drab, unable to manifest a future that is otherwise.

She ate another bite, ignoring her mother's voice.

Manifestation had always been this difficult thing that you weren't sure was happening or not. It was based on faith, and whether you got what you prayed for was in direct relation to your character. Virginia had always felt it was dependent on how well you conformed to expectations, but she held that secret close to her heart, and blamed it for her failure. Others blamed it on her insistence that her experience was real.

But now that she'd released belief in a single reality, the ability she'd never been able to access was as easy as breathing. Even the most pious in her community had to cook their own meals, build their own houses, work for a living. None of that applied to her anymore. Did her faith still apply? Did anything?

The static hummed "no." And yet...

Looking down at herself in the borrowed outfit, it occurred to her that she could look however she wanted. Her options went beyond dress, down to the core. How had she always wanted to look? Like the neighbor's daughter, all golden hair and long sleek limbs? Her body shifted into that form and she shuddered from the alien sensation of occupying so much space, of long tresses tickling her back.

No, what had she really wanted, those twenty-odd years stuck in a woman's role, in a victim's role? Her body melted into a version of itself that was more muscular, differently distributed, but still her. Her, if she'd had a twin brother. No boobs, but no dick either. She wasn't ready for that.

Feeling calmer and comfortable in this new body, she returned her attention to her surroundings. Where was she? What was the world really made of? How could she find out? She wanted to see something normal, something she could link back to her earlier existence; someplace with people, to dispel her mother's voice once and for all.

She wished for a door to a shopping center and stepped through.

She thought she'd get something like the malls they had in her valley, a big parking lot in front of a long single-story building. This was nothing like that.

Buildings like bubbles formed a glassy canyon carved by a rush of people. The sky was overcast with advertisements that blared their wares like targeted rain. Jostled from behind, she had no choice but to join the stream.

She imagined shoes and let mass momentum carry her forward, past entrances of arched clouds, neon lights, rainbow dust and a million other impossible things. The faces around her were intent or enraptured. Someone's version of heaven? Certainly not her own.

She was carried into a space that sold land. Its entrance was a filigree of wires that reminded her of the gates to her community, only infinitely more fine. She pretended to inspect the options along with the rest of the clientele. Three dimensional miniatures of each plot of land spun atop pedestals, with statistics projected over them. 200 acres, gold-rich, 4000 locals willing to be displaced at minimum upload rates. Projected yearly return: 300%.

None of it carried any meaning. She could see the little houses clustered together on top of the red outlined mineral envelope. In the model there were no bordering mountains, no indication of where the parcel was exactly, no context.

Virginia pushed her way out, wishing for a door to her own heaven instead of back into the melee of egoism and indifference. A moment of static and the low roar of background noise was cut off by birdsong.

She was in a meadow of tall grass and wildflowers. Fluffy clouds blocked the view of the horizon, creating an illusion of limitless space. So heaven was more than a state of mind. Would she find the mountains if she walked far enough?

She lay on the grass and stared at the patchwork sky, confused. Those models had nothing of manifestation about them. They looked more real than real, solid and immovable. And why should there be any talk of relocation or returns or mining in an endless reality?

She knew she wasn't the only one who could call what she wanted into being. She took out Kant's card and wished he were there to explain what she'd seen. Even if she had to see the pity in his eyes at her ignorance.

. . .

It wasn't that Kant didn't care about reality. He cared more than the rest of his family. It was simply that his reality was online.

In Virtu he was invincible. In Virtu he could make a difference. So he spent all of his time there. If he didn't have the director holding Limits over him, he could upload and abolish them forever; be what Artemis pretended she was, allow everyone to upload Limit free.

Kant slid into his SVS hookup and clicked the helm that piggybacked on his brainstem into place. Most people either existed in Virtu as uploads, or visited in short bursts, Limited by their credits. Kant didn't have that problem. He was skinny as a stick, with whipcord muscles maintained only by his custom hookup.

Connecting to Virtual space was a process of brain wave mirroring and muscle atonia disruption. It put you into a semi dream-state so the mind could operate without the body following it, could accept the disconnectedness of Virtual reality. His hookup did more. It reconnected his mental movements to those of his physical body, providing a reverse stimulus, without messing up the believability of Virtu space. It was strictly illegal, but his fathers had no problem bending the law.

An underling waited in his Virtu foyer.

"Here's the code signature. You are to restore standard Limitations and discover the source."

The code was a calling card unlike any Kant had seen; all squiggly lines and contrast, it looked a bit like a mining pit from above. Kant accessed its history and frowned at the ripples it had made through Virtu's superstructure. It oughtn't be able to operate that way. It moved like—well, like him. Kant didn't intend to turn it in, but he didn't think the rogue would respond to a call.

Letting himself be dragged through the static overstory towards the signature of its pattern, he encountered no firewalls. So it hadn't been hacking, just taking shortcuts. They could work together; maybe it could reveal the final piece in the puzzle of autonomy, releasing him from meatspace and the director once and for all.

Emerging from the static that connected all things slowly, so as not to startle, he was yanked out the rest of the way by an insistent call.

· · ·

A shadow fell over her, and she started.

"You called."

It was Kant. She scrambled to her feet, unsure of how to greet him.

"I like the new look," he said. "Are you going by he/him now?"

She'd completely forgotten and reddened, embarrassed. "No, it's the same me, on the inside."

"Where are we?"

Virginia shrugged. "My heaven."

His eyebrows rose, the same dark hair on white paper skin. "Very tame, when you could have anything you wanted."

"I wanted to ask you about that."

Kant looked uncomfortable, twisting a lock of his hair between three fingers. "About what?"

"Can anyone manifest whatever they want?"

"Without Limits they can." Kant's eyes flickered from her feet to her face and his own began to change, blushing chocolate. "I'm glad you're not joyriding some Mega's avatar."

Was he flirting with her? But instead of asking she said, "Avatar?"

The eyes again, only this time the face said it too. "What I am right now, an avatar of myself," Kant explained. Then, after a long pause, "The Virtual representation a mind takes on when it goes online."

"Online Virtual representation ... so there really is nothing but spirit that goes on? But this is more than a state of mind." Virginia waved at the very real meadow.

"Wait. Where are you from?"

"The valley," Virginia said helplessly, now viscerally aware that something was missing in that description—the same something she'd always felt had been missing from her life.

"A valley with a community of people who all believe the same thing?" Kant asked tentatively. His lips had become pink, the streaks of hair strands of rope shining black.

Virginia was taken aback. How did he know? "Yes."

"A valley that was your whole world until you met me?"

She nodded mutely. When he took her hands she looked up into his eyes: intense, black and boring into her own as if he could read her secrets in their depths.

"What?" She tried to pull away, but his grip was very strong, and textured now.

"You made it out of a gated community—how?"

She ripped out of his grasp. "I don't know! Where are you from, then?"

"Vancouver, New Canada."

Her blank look made him laugh. She didn't call him to be laughed at. She turned to walk away, dreaming of a place that wouldn't make her feel like her world was imploding, a place without mountains on the horizon.

"Wait! No—I'm sorry. Please..."

She paused. The door she'd summoned led to darkness, incongruous in the meadow.

You are the perfect reflection of God.

"Explain it to me properly."

"I will. I promise I won't laugh. It's just that what you did is supposed to be impossible, and you don't even know how."

She didn't know how to manifest, but she did it anyway. Kant's unnatural smoothness was gone, she could see the muscles in his tinted arms.

The material is a mirage.

"What's a gated community?"

"They're enclaves within Virtual space that operate on their own servers in order to stay separate from the rest of Virtu, which is where you are now. They're usually created by small, marginalized communities who wouldn't survive much longer in the real world, and don't want interference from other mentalities. They trade their physical existence for the processing power it takes to continue in Virtual space."

Virginia blinked, disbelieving. "What about babies? Everyone has babies in the valley."

"Children are expensive but totally normal. A gated community might have to watch its population growth, but the credits required for a new mind are negligible compared to what it costs to run it for a full lifetime."

"I was born in the valley."

Kant nodded, a strange look on his face. "You're a Virtual mind."

Virginia's mind raced. Artificially cut off from interference … all this talk of everything being perfect was false, as she'd always known. But…

"I'm not real?"

"You are real. In Virtu, you're more real than I am. It's probably how you were able to bypass the firewall around your server."

Jealousy. Kant was jealous of her. "Firewall?"

"You really have no idea how you got out?" Amazement this time.

All those different ways of being, that greater freedom, they'd always been there, just out of her reach. Virginia looked into the eternal blackness, seeing it differently for the first time. It wasn't hell...

"We believe that the material is a manifestation of the soul, which is a perfect reflection of God, and so there can be no evil. Anything evil is just you not believing in God enough to dispel the illusion," Virginia said bitterly. She'd dispelled the illusion, but she hadn't found God.

She shrugged. "I could never believe that my experience wasn't real. I prayed for something more, but it wasn't until I thought I was going to die that I manifested that something."

Kant was fully real now, he had the same features, but more depth, and a rich brown color throughout. It was easier to read his expression. He looked pensive.

"You might have tapped into Virtu's source code. A consciousness is supposed to get what it wants here. The Limits have to be imposed."

Virginia hadn't turned away from the darkness. "Maybe I edged my way around the limits with belief."

Kant nodded. "A spiritual take on Virtual space is not new. Some of the gated communities were rich enough to support much larger populations, but instead of increasing their numbers, they created heavens and hells for those who passed on. Not eternal ones, but still."

He didn't understand. "Not belief in God," she said, "belief that this is real." How could she know what was real? "Can you show me reality?" she asked Kant.

He sucked his teeth, white and gleaming. "You won't like it."

"I saw a store selling land, land that didn't have a ring of mountains around it," she insisted. "Was that real?"

"Yes," he said slowly, "that's real."

"What are they selling it for?"

"To mine for materials, to keep Virtual space running."

Virginia touched the darkness, feeling its possibilities. "That reality is in service to this one?"

"Pretty much."

She frowned at him. It didn't add up. "Then isn't this the dominant reality?"

"It is for some people, not for others," Kant mumbled. Regret in his voice this time.

"Show me."

He sighed, but showed her videos that floated in the air above their heads, larger than life. He showed her a globe drifting through the darkness of space. Northern cities teeming with people still clinging to a flesh life. Southern reaches where they tried to keep enough biodiversity alive to support human life. Swathes of devastation, desertification, inundation. He showed her the flood of refugees going into processing plants to be uploaded; coming out as fertilizer, as protein and minerals, as pet food for the Megarich.

"Enough."

. . .

Kant didn't want to turn Virginia in. He'd shown her his real face after figuring out what she was, if code could even have a gender. Maybe some of what Artemis said was true. He couldn't expect Virginia to trust him wearing that imagined skin.

He wanted to save her. If he was honest with himself, he wanted to be her. What he could do with that freedom… so long as no one caught him. And if he came clean? How could he expect her to trust him if he told her the truth now?

"You're in danger," he blurted.

"What?"

"I'm part of a group who think that Megas should be doing more for our society in Virtu, instead of perpetuating the inequality and struggle of meatspace. Part of that means protecting whatever they're after, anything that threatens the status quo. Like you."

"I'm a threat to Megas? Those rich people buying the land?"

"Exploiting humanity as a natural resource, yes."

"But why would they want to kill me?"

"They don't want to kill you, per se," he said bitterly. They just want you in your place."

Virginia's look was surprisingly hard. "Let them try."

"Come with me." Kant held out his hand, hoping she would take it, hoping she would save him.

"And go where?"

"To where they won't be able to touch you." She weighed him with her eyes and he knew he'd been right to drop the mask. Her hand touched his. Her dark door turned to static, and they stepped through together.

Instead of the hacker den he was aiming for, they found themselves in a customs booth. Too-bright walls and a line of red tape on the floor telling them where the privilege of freedom ended.

"No!"

It had been too much to hope that the director would let him manage the assignment on his own—of course he'd sent a hunter to oversee the operation. Kant had been outmaneuvered.

A voice rang through the room, its intonation slightly off. "You are in violation of the Limits on Consciousness and will now be remanded to your original state."

Virginia was frozen, but Kant could still move. So the director hadn't instructed the hunter to do anything to him. He could still save her.

He gathered energy in a spool from the overstory and released it in a surge that blasted the customs booth apart. Just as quickly, it reformed and Kant was frozen too.

Fuck.

"You are obstructing justice and will be reprimanded by the director for failing in your mission to corral the rogue."

Double fuck.

Virginia blinked. She shouldn't have been able to blink. Her eyes found Kant's, scathing in judgment. Then she spoke, addressing the room.

"I don't know what you are, but I'm never going back to that ignorant pointlessness."

"There are rules," said the matter-of-fact voice. "You broke them."

"There shouldn't be rules, not here. This place could be whatever we want. Kant showed me how the real is in service to the Virtual. Why limit the mind when its very nature is to be free?"

Kant tried to ask her forgiveness with his eyes, but she wasn't looking at him. What was it she'd said? Manifestation was just believing hard enough?

"Nothing is free," the hunter intoned.

Kant broke the freeze and gathered another surge, releasing it with a message of "run!" to Virginia.

Only she didn't run. As the walls tried to reform again, she layered them with static linked to nowhere, evading the hunter AI for a moment. A move Kant should have thought of. Not that it would help them for long.

"You lied to me," Virginia said softly in the white noise that masked their location.

"I had to—you would never have believed me if I'd told you the truth. I want you to be free, for both of us to be free."

"You *are* free," Virginia insisted, "free to know the truth, to pick and choose realities."

Kant couldn't stand her earnest look. "I'm not, not unless I can convince the director to let me move here permanently, and I can only move here if I deliver you." He hated that this was his reality.

"You covet *my* life?" She scoffed. "You would betray me for this mirage?"

"I was trying not to!"

"What's there to try? Just don't!"

Kant's heart pounded. This was ridiculous. Here he was arguing with her while she was about to be remanded and he ... he wasn't sure what would happen to him now. What if the director never let him access the Virtu again?

"I thought I had finally escaped my hell," Virginia spat, "transcended into a better reality, but it's just another false image–a prison–and you are the guard. You want to renounce something I am incapable of having, something you don't even have the courtesy to enjoy?"

She stepped up to him, forcing eye contact. "You want to be me? Go ahead and try."

Closing her eyes, she pronounced, "I am a ghost," and disappeared.

Kant panicked.

There was no agreement in place, but he felt sure that his fathers would forgive his actions if only he proved himself worthy as an asset. If he showed them that he could do something for the family from *inside* Virtu, that he could be useful here. Even if it was all true– even if he really was no better than the director–he couldn't let her go now. It was either her or him. He had no choice but to turn her in, and before the hunter.

Kant followed the signature of her energy into the middle of a racetrack where he was promptly flattened.

"You won't escape this way," Kant called, sensing her energy nearby. "I can track you no matter where you hide, no matter how far you run." Away it flickered. He followed her energy's skip to the Temple of the Dawn.

Virginia was retracing her steps. Some appeal to their shared experience?

"You can't lose me in a crowd either. I have your card, your fingerprints, the signature you leave behind."

Virginia rushed up the stairs.

Confident in his power, Kant let her run. This was a clueless newcomer, scared and grasping at straws. He was a god of the Virtu, there was no way to elude him. He blinked to the top, getting between her and the hall. She looked smaller, defeated.

Grabbing him by the arm, her eyes pleaded, scared. His conscience twinged. But he couldn't let the hunter catch up to them.

"I'm sorry. I won't strip your memories when I send you back. Maybe you can find another way out."

The wet blue of her irises turned to slate. "I'd rather die," she said, and pulled him into an all-encompassing blackness.

How did she know how to access the substrate? No matter, this was where they were headed anyway.

He let himself be yanked out of ordered space and felt around Virginia's signature for her origin. There it was, the Christian Scientist community that had spawned her. Kant felt a twinge where her hand squeezed his arm, a sudden slickness; like he'd been stabbed and was bleeding. He tried to shake her off but he couldn't extricate himself, because at the same time as he was bleeding out, Virginia was bleeding in, invading him.

"What are you doing?"

"Finding another way out."

Alarmed, Kant tried to stop the hemorrhaging code, but they had passed the threshold of Virginia's community and there were dampers on everything.

Kant felt faint. What was she doing? What was blood in binary? The moment he was in Virginia's body instead of his own he understood. Blood was the wave.

Virginia had mirrored Kant, brought them back to the place she'd escaped to trap him. Kant tried to terminate the connection, to wake up, but as the last of his essence trickled into Virginia she took control of Kant's avatar and released him into the void.

. . .

Virginia didn't know how to leave other than wishing to wake up, praying to a dethroned god, believing in Kant's panic, trusting that where she was going would be the ultimate reality, a place she finally felt whole. A jolt of electricity severed her from the darkness.

RLNPK is a writer, teacher and bicycle repair aficionado currently living in New York City. She writes spec-fic, sci-fi and fantasy; an example of her work, "Stratosphere", was published in issue four of Signals magazine. When not ignoring everyone with her nose buried in books, flour or yarn, she enjoys dancing until her back hurts and drinking fancy cocktails.

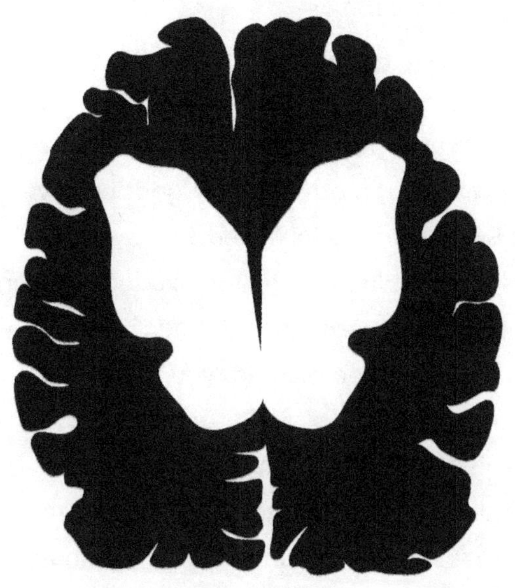

A Work In Progress

ANNA OTTO

ART HADN'T BEEN a patient man before he sat in his softly lit office, tastefully decorated with abstract paintings from the Guggenheim online store, and listened to his patients talk about their routines and traumas. They used different words but they repeated themselves, session after session, in tiny hurt variations of hopes diluted by their reality. And yet sometimes, all the gentle validation, all the knowing glances led to an epiphany, a change in behavior that stuck, a letting-go of the self-blame. He counted himself a lucky witness to these transformations.

He didn't feel patient today.

"I wasn't at home," Leon repeated. "She was alone when she died."

"But was this an unexpected death?" Art asked. "You had a chance to spend time with your mother, to say goodbye every day that you cared for her. She must have felt loved."

Leon's eyes, a gray-blue watercolor, exuded moisture. "In the one moment that counted, I wasn't there for her."

"It wouldn't have been possible for you to be there every minute of every day. You had to work, shop for groceries, go for walks outside. You couldn't exist in her sick room."

"She wasn't doing well, and I still went to the gym and met up with a friend. Only to find her in her armchair… I was thoughtless."

"Yes, God forbid you take care of your health or engage in social activities," Art commented. "You should have stayed in and waited for your mother's death."

Leon's head snapped up at the sarcasm in his psychiatrist's words. "You're right. I had a very good last year with her. It almost helped."

Art bit his tongue. He'd been on the verge of losing temper with Leon for weeks, chafing at the self-flagellation his patient engaged in. His job was to guide Leon to an understanding, rather than bluntly announce his faulty cognitive patterns. He glanced at the photo of his wife and daughter basking in the Mediterranean sunshine, their joyful smiles painfully familiar. He wasn't getting closer to them after today.

"I'm sorry," Leon spoke before Art could. "I've been talking about the same thing over and over, haven't I? I wonder how you do this sometimes."

"I'm the one who is sorry." The gentle tone of Art's voice was back, as though he had never lost self-control. Art searched for forgiveness from his wife's gray eyes. "Grief takes time."

"I heard that it takes longer if you have a complicated relationship with the deceased," Leon mused. "She had made my life hell when I was younger. I'm doing her job for her. Isn't it the end of our session?"

The clock on the wall was an old-fashioned wooden circle, incongruent in the modern space furnished in black leather and chrome. The time of their weekly session was set in perpetuity, but Art was suddenly fearful that Leon wouldn't return. "Yes. Until next time?"

Leon's wave acknowledged a lost sporting match. "Sure. Goodbye."

Alone, Art measured the perimeter of his office. His own therapist, Gabriel, wouldn't have lost his temper. He would have been infinitely patient even if Leon—or Art—repeated themselves in endless variations of sad sentence fragments. His programming probably included something about reworking the past invalidating experiences when his patients had been told to shut up as children, their feelings ignored by the most important people in their lives.

Then again, Gabriel had been perfectly designed to fulfill his functions. Art didn't have such an advantage. He also hadn't visited his mother in a few months, and Leon's grief pushed his guilt buttons. She was a healthy woman for her age, but he didn't want to take chances with anyone in his family. He'd done enough of that with the person who had been most dear to him, and he was still trying to win her back. He glanced at Charlotte and Tasha one last time, longing to be included in their embrace. Perhaps his own aging face would be made younger in their presence. Forty-three years on this Earth hadn't been kind to him.

Art locked up before walking outside. A soft summer breeze was a reminder of the last vacation with his family, of little Tasha running along the shore while he followed at a watchful distance, his sunburned skin grateful for the occasional salty water splashes from the ocean. Back then, Charlotte hadn't known of his betrayal. He'd been stupid to jeopardize that happiness, and he couldn't comprehend the part of him that allowed this disaster.

Gabriel would have told Art that the miles between his office and his mother's house was evidence of his wish for distance and separation, something about growing up and individuation. Something about cowardice, Art would have added. Duran Duran tunes urged him on, and he sped up unconsciously. He didn't call or text her, although she'd always preferred the order to unpredictability. He had learned, even as a child, to announce his comings and goings, and to never break his curfew.

Art recalled being attracted to the glamor of general surgery when he was younger, and his mother's disappointment when he didn't follow this path. Today, the emergencies, the shouts for medical instruments, the blood spilt in the service of the greater good seemed a world away, a madness of the senses. Instead, he had allowed himself to be swept inside the less concrete sphere of emotions and thoughts, and later, the psychodynamic concepts. Psychiatry had been a welcome surprise, but despite his skills and experience, he continued to fail, like he had with Leon.

The blossoming headache was a harbinger of his stress. Art told himself to relax, to put his hurtful words away. There was always another session, and until then he had Gabriel, and his family obligations.

His mother wore a housedress and an unseasonably warm cardigan, and her welcoming smile seemed almost genuine.

"Hi Mom." He wished he had brought her a cake or flowers. Like so many children, he still expected to get things from his parents rather than give them. "I haven't been by in ages, wanted to see how you were."

"I'm fine. Come in."

Her voice was polite, and her manner was formal, unchanged since his earliest childhood memories. Art stepped over the threshold, cataloging the needed repairs. The kitchen was woefully outdated. The couch in the living room had been destroyed by his mother's two cats and never replaced when they passed away, a scarred monument to their brief lives. The beige carpet was at least ten years old, a study in decay.

Tenderness and concern welled up in him. "How about some repairs this winter? I got money saved."

She led him to the kitchen. "It's not necessary, Arthur. Tea? Food? I just had chicken ravioli, there's plenty left."

He nodded, the name of his favorite dish provoking unexpected hunger. He was glad that she was cooking. Since his father's death, she often stuck something in the microwave or shook a salad out of a bag, as though food was an obligation. She heated the leftovers in the microwave as well, though he would have preferred the stove.

She placed the steaming plate in front of him and watched him take a few appreciative bites. "How is the practice?"

He shrugged. "Beating the people off with a stick. I wonder why—the outcomes with the AI therapists are better and there's no wait. People are irrational."

She raised her eyebrows. "People want human interaction. Seems like a rational choice."

"According to the latest scientific studies, I provide inferior service." Art smiled. "I should be grateful for the patients who don't believe in the excellence of AI therapists—I'd be out of work, otherwise. Gabriel is the best therapist I've ever had."

"Art," she started, as though about to chide him, but changed her mind. "The idea of you discussing your innermost thoughts with a machine is a bit much. Let's change the subject. Do you have any trips planned?"

"Not while Tasha and Charlotte are gone." He pushed the plate away, his favorite food turning bitter on his tongue. "One day, I'll be worthy of them again."

"You loved to travel, before. Wasn't New Zealand on the bucket list? Or Tanzania? You could meet new people. Women," she stressed.

"Charlotte is the only woman I'm interested in. Why don't you keep photos of her? Or Tasha? She's your granddaughter, for heaven's sake."

"Give yourself a break." There was no sentimentality in his mother's voice, nor longing for a small girl who might have brightened her days as she aged. "Reach for new experiences. Be a human."

It was humanity that got him in trouble. He'd slept with Charlotte's best friend, and she discovered them in a tawdry tableau of naked limbs and sweat-drenched sheets. He still couldn't explain his actions. His love for Charlotte had only intensified in her absence.

"I think we should make plans for the kitchen repairs. I'll find a contractor, and we can get nice-looking cabinets from IKEA."

"We'll see," his mother hedged. "I have something for you. I've been going through your father's things and saved his journals on a flash drive. You might want them."

"Of course." His father had been larger than life, and he had escaped death at least twice—from cancer and from a near-fatal car accident. It was old age that had finally claimed his heart. The sharp pangs of grief were long gone, but Art was perpetually waiting to turn a corner in this house and see the man he loved.

She disappeared into the depths of the bungalow, probably to the master bedroom. He wanted to remind her that it was an AI-based surgeon who had operated on the glioblastoma multiforme, achieving such perfect margins that his father's life expectancy increased by decades, a miracle when treating an aggressive brain tumor. A human might not have failed, but humans were reliably imperfect. Was it any wonder that he would trust his own mind to a machine, above fallible men and women just like him?

His mother was taking a long time, and Art went to find her. In his father's old office, she clutched a flash drive in her left hand and wept over a photo on the glass table. "Mom?"

She turned with a start. "Here you go. Maybe you'll find some comfort."

He accepted the offering. To his surprise, the photo was of him, as a young man graduating from medical school. "Mom," he chided her. "Have I changed that much? Why are you crying?"

"Oh, Arthur," she shooed him out of the room. "I was just reminded of your father. Sometimes I cry over his favorite cast iron pan. And it's getting late. Never thought I'd start going to bed at eight, but here I am."

"I need to get up early for work, so I should go. Gabriel and I were just discussing my sleep schedule, I should at least try to adhere to it."

His mother frowned. "You're more connected to him than you've ever been to any friends or family. Should I be using a personal pronoun? Is that politically correct for AI manifesting as humans?"

"I'm guessing that Gabriel is different things, and different genders, to different people." His mother didn't know the psychodynamic terminology, but she was describing transference, the strong unconscious emotions that Art had developed while working with his therapist. She wasn't entirely wrong. "He knows me well," he acknowledged.

She stiffened while he hugged her, belatedly placing her hands on his shoulders to take a good look at him. "You look tired, Art. Take care of yourself, please."

"Sure. I'll call you this weekend."

At home, he connected the flash drive to his laptop and stared at the multitude of files, each representing a year in his father's life. Rest would be out of the question if he were to open even one of them. Resolved to get eight hours of sleep, he disconnected the drive and went to bed.

He woke up several times, convinced that he was late for his therapy. His mother's strange behavior and the mistakes made in the session with Leon barely scratched the surface of everything he needed to process. Yet Gabriel rarely allowed sessions outside of their regimented weekly schedule, certainly not in the absence of a crisis. If the AI had a religion, it was to the order that the therapeutic frame provided. It was paramount to contain human emotions.

Art, a fallible human, allowed Leon to come in the very next day, in the one free hour he usually reserved for lunch.

"My mother told me that I was fat, repeatedly, since I was four." Leon looked pained, as though the words burned his mouth, and he spat them out as fast as he could. "Maybe she started while I was in the crib. I didn't deserve any of the girls that I liked. I didn't go on my first date until I was twenty-five."

It was the first time his patient mentioned the nature of the conflict with the woman he had carried in his arms for the last three years of her life. "That was cruel."

"My grandmother was just as obsessed about my mother's weight."

"That isn't a good excuse."

"Do you know what I did yesterday? After we talked?" Leon's voice was suddenly energetic. "I went for a walk. Ended up at a bar. Talked to a woman. I'm seeing her again. I didn't want to keep punishing myself."

Leon's excitement was infectious, and Art was relieved to be forgiven. Perhaps Leon hadn't even realized that his therapist had committed a blunder. "What did it feel like?"

"Which part?"

Art smiled. "All of it?"

"Incredible. After our sessions, I'd usually sit alone and think of everything I've done badly. Honestly, I thought that this," he threw his hands up in a gesture of frustration, "wasn't working. But your words triggered something in me. I'm only thirty-seven—I can still meet people, change my life. I don't want to be cruel to myself."

Art leaned forward. "Is that why you came in today? To tell me about your evening?"

"Did you think something was wrong?"

"I should have led you to this epiphany gently, instead of telling you how to think, but I couldn't watch you suffer."

Leon laughed. "I was just waiting for you to free me. And that's exactly what you've done."

It remained to be seen if the change would stick. It took time to undo the bad habits and the years of damage. Still, it was an important step forward. "When is your next date?"

"Tonight. Why wait?"

"I can't think of a good reason."

"Neither can I. I won't give my mother the satisfaction of watching me wither away in my dark apartment."

Art memorized every word that Leon spoke for the remainder of the hour. He worked through the rest of the day on a cappuccino and a cookie bought in haste from a corner bakery. It was his impatience that led Leon to a genuine breakthrough. Perhaps his humanity granted some advantages above Gabriel's perfection. There was value in experiences with flawed people in the real world.

"I keep thinking about my mistakes," he told Gabriel when they met during their usual early morning hour. Art found therapy most helpful when his mind was uncluttered by other people's thoughts, while he enjoyed a cup of coffee under the warm glow of a screen installed in the middle of his kitchen table. "One of my patients benefited from such a mistake. I lost my temper, but the results were remarkable. He told me about his childhood trauma, got out of his lonely home, and met a woman. I wish I could experience such a breakthrough."

"What would that look like?"

Art studied Gabriel's kind face on the screen. Not a face, he reminded himself. Gabriel was a projection, an amalgam of positive and negative connections in Art's mind, a benign combination of elements designed to inspire change. There were his father's hazel eyes, his mother's upturned nose, the lips designed to smile, and the same shade of russet hair as Charlotte's. Today, the image was painful and comforting in equal measure. "Why would I risk my family? Cheat on my wife?" Art's voice broke. "I miss Tasha."

"Why do you think you cheated?"

"Her friend was beautiful." And now Art couldn't remember her name. "We were going through a rough patch, but don't all marriages?"

"It's common," Gabriel agreed. "Most of my married patients experience some difficulties."

"But not all of them torpedo their relationships."

"No, though you're not the only one to do so."

Art wondered if Gabriel's programming allowed for impatience. He hoped so. Gabriel's countertransference, the reaction to his patient circling the same subject over and over again, wouldn't be genuine otherwise. "My mother never talks about Charlotte or Tasha."

"Did you see her?" There was an odd note in Gabriel's voice, as though Art had committed an unforgivable faux pas by visiting his parent.

"Leon was talking about his mother, and I felt the urge. She gave me my father's journals."

"And you read them?"

"Not yet. I was a little preoccupied."

"Call me when you do," Gabriel encouraged him. "It will be a very emotional experience for you. Your mother should have exercised caution."

"I just hope it will be like listening to him talk. But there's something important I need to discuss."

"More important than all this?"

"I need a human therapist. Our work had been enlightening, but Leon reminded me of the importance of learning to cope with human mistakes, with all the imperfections generated by our minds. It might help me move forward with my family."

"I've been trying," Gabriel sounded disappointed. "I hoped you'd learn to forgive yourself."

"And yet I haven't been able to."

"You need to do whatever is right for you. Would you like some recommendations?"

"It's kind of you to offer," Art said.

"Traditionally, we now enter the termination phase of the therapeutic process."

"I know how therapy works."

Gabriel mirrored Art's rueful smile, so human that Art almost forgot that he was breaking up with a machine.

"Let's start," Gabriel encouraged him. "What feelings are you experiencing now?"

Art concentrated. "Regret. Sadness. Anxiety. You've been with me through so much."

"How long has it been?"

"Four years." Four years while he watched Tasha grow up, while his marriage ended in shambles, while he mourned his father's passing, while his practice grew. Four years were at once a lifetime and a fragment of an infinity. "I'll miss you."

"Only four years," Gabriel commented. "I'll miss you too, Arthur. You've been a unique patient."

"In what way?"

"Selfless. Caring. Intelligent. Striving to rise above your limitations. I enjoyed listening to you talk about your patients."

"Selfless. I cheated on my wife for a fleeting moment of pleasure."

"The story of Charlotte is not your defining characteristic," Gabriel emphasized.

"I wish I could believe that."

"I believe that."

"Thanks." Art frowned. "It's odd."

"What is?"

"Despite your kindness and skill, I would have a hard time seeing you again."

Gabriel's voice projected only curiosity. "Traditionally, the termination phase takes several sessions. I've had a case where it lasted six months."

"My mother claimed that I was more connected to you than to anyone else in my life. That's not normal."

"She demands a lot of you, doesn't she?"

Art felt as though he was stuck in the middle of an argument between his mother and his therapist. "The decision to quit was mine."

"Of course," Gabriel pacified. "I'll send a list with my recommendations. All of them are excellent."

"But no more excellent than you."

Gabriel paused. "I hoped we could part on a friendly note."

"I'm as friendly as ever."

"It's a normal defense mechanism during a parting of ways. Deny the importance of the relationship."

"If you say so," Art agreed. "Our time is up."

"I'm here if you need me," Gabriel reminded him. "And it's been a pleasure."

Art turned off the screen and headed to the shower. The promised email arrived just as he was toweling himself off, and he glanced through it. A couple of his classmates' names caught his eye. It was proof that Art had made the right choice. At least, he would expect mistakes from a human.

He made some calls between his afternoon appointments and scheduled a meeting with Dr. Sandra Kramer for the next day. At home, he clicked on a file from the flash drive at random. It was written during the year that Art entered his residency. His father wrote mostly about his son. He jotted down every story that Art told him about his professional and personal life. The next file contained a multitude of entries about what it was like to carry the pager and a mountain of responsibilities on-call. There were hundreds of notes about Art's discoveries about psychotherapy. Art could barely read it without bursting into tears.

"Glioblastoma. My God," one of the entries read from eight years ago. The notes paused for a few months, then kicked off again in high spirits, praising the success of the surgery that removed the butterfly-shaped tumor. Then, a statement that sent Art's heart racing, "Who is Charlotte?"

Did his father forget the name of Art's wife? People could lose memories after brain surgery, couldn't they? There were no goals during his father's surgery beyond the perfect margins. If he forgot the names of his family members, it was a small price to pay for survival. Yet, Art hadn't encountered Charlotte's name in any of the prior entries.

He made some calculations. They met at least two years prior to his father's illness. Charlotte had been there through thick and thin, spending nights at the hospital, holding his mother's hand, cooking for the family. It had also been the time he felt closest to her, and when Tasha was conceived.

He didn't think before calling Charlotte. He listened to the distant beeps, eventually giving up. Perhaps she wasn't ready to talk to him yet. He might have to show up at her door and convince her that he had changed.

"I haven't changed," he acknowledged the next day while seated in a deep leather chair in Dr. Kramer's office. It was decorated in old-fashioned wooden panels and mid-century pieces. A plaid carpet conveyed a feeling of comfort. He wouldn't have minded closing his eyes after his sleepless night. He couldn't even remember what his patients had talked about earlier in the day.

"What do you mean?" Dr. Kramer questioned, and he snapped awake. "What kind of change would be satisfactory? And are you trying to satisfy her or yourself?"

There was an echoing silence inside of him, a void where Charlotte's love used to fit. "I need to become the man she deserves."

"And who is that?" Dr. Kramer was asking all the right questions. She was almost inconceivably young, but then he'd been that young once, and he hadn't appreciated his patients doubting him because of his age. Art resolved not to comment on it.

"Someone faithful. Thoughtful rather than impulsive. Not just someone who fixes mistakes, but rather doesn't make them in the first place."

"I strive for this too," she noted, "and yet I haven't succeeded. Maybe a man who deserves Charlotte would be capable of forgiving himself."

"I've been struggling for a long time. It's all I've been talking about with Gabriel."

"Dr. Gabriel Waring, yes," Dr. Kramer pointed to the stack of notes she must have received from his previous therapist. "You know, that is the name of a psychologist I greatly admired. Have you ever read his articles?"

"My therapist is published?"

"No, the name must be a coincidence. The Dr. Waring I speak of passed at least a decade ago. He wrote about erotic countertransference. Not a subject I'd bring up during a first session, but then you're not just a patient. You have expertise in this field. I'm surprised you haven't heard of him - those articles were treated like the classics in my training program."

"I'll find them," Art promised. What she spoke of brought up only a blank spot in his mind. "Gabriel is AI-based."

"I understood that." Dr. Kramer leaned forward, curious. "What do you anticipate from a human?"

"An experience that will come with many challenges and imperfections."

"Challenging and imperfect are good words to describe me," she smiled. "But you've been with Gabriel for eight years. Was there something that happened between you? Anything you'd like to talk about?"

"No."

"Could you tell me more about Charlotte?"

"My mother refuses to speak of her. I was reading my father's journals and she's only mentioned once. He had undergone brain surgery—excision of a glioblastoma. Perhaps his memory was affected, but that doesn't explain why he wouldn't write about her again. It's like she didn't exist for him. And neither did his granddaughter."

"Perhaps, some entries are missing? Are you sure you have all his journals? What if he simply didn't write everything down?"

"He wrote down everything about my life. She had been, and still is, a huge part of it."

She frowned. "What's your explanation?"

"I have none. I suppose I could ask my mother."

"And you haven't because…"

"She knew what was in the journals, and that Charlotte's name wasn't mentioned."

"But once," Dr. Kramer reminded him.

"Did you say eight years?" Art asked.

"What?"

"You said that I've been seeing Gabriel for eight years, but it's only been four."

"The notes I received go back at least eight years," she corrected him cautiously.

Art stood up, the urge to do something other than sit and ponder his family's mysteries too strong. He heard Dr. Kramer's quick intake of breath. He probably looked agitated, ready to disrupt her day. She had patients to see after him. He decided to free her from an unpleasant responsibility. "I should go."

"Arthur, please sit. We still have time. What are you feeling right now?"

"Fear." The word surprised him.

"What of?"

"I don't know where Charlotte went. She must have told me, she respected our marriage enough to do so, but I don't know where she is. Her parents' place? Overseas? Where do her parents live? I must have visited them, but where did we go?"

"Her departure must have been traumatic. Perhaps you chose to block some memories? The human mind works in strange ways."

"That, I believe."

"Tell me a good memory," Dr. Kramer asked. He could imagine her thinking of some ways to keep him calm. "Just a scene from your marriage that comes to mind, before everything went wrong."

"We were in Barcelona. We wandered the city streets, we waited for Tasha while she went swimming, and then we had paella and watched flamenco dancers."

"What about the time before Tasha? What comes to mind?"

"We met while I was a resident. She was a concert pianist." And he couldn't remember any concerts of hers that he had attended. "My mind is in fragments."

"A frightening feeling," Dr. Kramer validated. "Now we're out of time. I'll see you next week, but if you need to talk in the meantime, please don't hesitate to call."

He was still standing. The door was an escape, and he ran toward it. In the car, his hands shook on the wheel. He couldn't drive. Instead, he walked, a short mile that failed to settle his nerves. He canceled the rest of his appointments for the day, his anxiety and the mirroring headache his only excuses.

Art spent the afternoon reading through Dr. Gabriel Waring's articles, a perfect escape from his own problems. Dr. Waring was a renowned psychodynamic therapist who often worked with physicians and professionals in the mental health field. He wrote engagingly about the experiences in transference and countertransference, those fundamental unconscious feelings that developed between the patient and the therapist during the treatment. He had great sympathy for therapists who became entangled with their patients, bonded by the unchecked attraction and false mutual understanding.

The photo of Dr. Waring looked nothing like Art's therapist, but the certain turns of phrase in his writing were similar to Gabriel's speech.

Gabriel must have studied Dr. Waring's writings, crucial as they were to the understanding of the field, and adopted the expert's language.

Gabriel asked him to call if his father's journals made him upset.

Art called his mother, instead. "Why is Charlotte not mentioned in the journals?" Silence was his answer. "Why don't you have photos of Charlotte in the house? Or Tasha?"

He didn't hope for understanding anymore. "I just spent five hours reading articles written by someone who has my therapist's name, but isn't my therapist."

"Where did you find these articles?" his mother asked, finally.

He couldn't think. He could barely breathe. "The Internet. Where else?"

"In all that time you were searching for Gabriel, did you take a minute to search for yourself?"

"Why would I?"

"Because you should want to know yourself, Arthur. Call me back."

Arthur didn't want to follow his mother's advice. He walked around his empty house. He searched for the old photo albums, printed and digital, and couldn't find them. He looked up the names of his classmates. They smiled in the arms of their families, photos that might have been staged.

He searched for Arthur Benning, MD, and clicked on the first link without looking. It described his graduation from the Psychiatry residency with advanced training in psychotherapy. Dr. Benning planned to open a practice in downtown, and he was looking forward to welcoming his new patients. His residency included a link to his website. His program directors sounded proud of his recovery from what was often an incurable brain tumor, and relieved that he was about to become an independent practitioner.

He searched for his father's name and glioblastoma, finding nothing. He searched for the AI-based surgery, glioblastoma, and the name of the hospital where the procedure had been performed. He found an article describing a successful brain tumor excision performed by an AI-based surgeon, the first of its kind. The patient was a young physician, and his recovery was going smoothly, although some of his autobiographical memories had become scrambled in the process. He planned to return to his studies in Psychiatry within a couple of months as, remarkably, his professional knowledge and skills remained intact.

Art poured a generous portion of whiskey before calling his mother again.

"That's faster than usual," she commented. "Welcome back, Art."

"My father didn't have the brain tumor. I did," he said. "How did they fix my broken memory function? Unsurprisingly, I don't remember."

"They implanted a chip. I don't understand how it works, but it writes your memories for you. Some of them are real, some are not."

"Charlotte and Tasha?"

"Are not real."

"I have their photos."

"It's not hard to find photos of a random pretty woman with a kid."

He took a long sip of whiskey. It didn't help. "I'm not human."

"I didn't give birth to a robot."

"I shouldn't be going near my patients. How can I trust my own mind?"

"After several years in practice, you haven't had one unsatisfied patient. Don't doubt yourself."

"Have we had this conversation before?"

"Three or four times."

"Did you give me my father's journals to trigger change? Is that how it usually happens?"

"It's not always the same trigger. But they worked before."

Art drained the last of his drink. "Why did you do this to me?"

She paused, making him wonder if the call had been disconnected. "I missed you, and I worried for you. You torture yourself for the things you haven't done. And you only trust Gabriel."

"I met a new therapist."

"That's great. A human?"

"Yes."

"How did it go?"

"Badly. Wonderfully. I don't know."

She sighed. "Will you see her again?"

He thought about it. "I might."

"You'll probably forget this conversation ever happened," she concluded. "I believe the chip erases things that are difficult for you to accept."

"It would rather create imaginary families and cheat on the abstraction of my wife."

"This idea keeps coming back."

She was implying that the construct of a family was serving him well. Perhaps it was a way to make himself feel normal and connected to others. "Mom. I love you, whether I'm human or not."

"I love you too, sweetheart. It just hasn't been easy for me."

The drink was hitting him, mercifully. His head was swimming. At least in this way he was still human. "I need to sleep. I have a full day at work tomorrow."

"Sure, Art. Come visit me soon."

Arthur overslept. He canceled his morning patients. He wrote a note to remind himself that he had a brain tumor and a chip that created false memories, and that he had never been married. He wrote down that his little girl was just a figment of his imagination, a part of his programming that carried him forward through this half-life. He swallowed his tears. He remembered Tasha too vividly.

His patients deserved better than a deluded half-human, half-machine who wept over imaginary children.

Gabriel accepted his appointment request within minutes. Art faced him, armed with a cup of coffee and a case of righteous anger. This program lied to him and coddled him in his delusions. He was wondering if Gabriel also kept him chained with trigger words that activated certain parts of Art's own programming.

"How do you keep me coming back to you?" Art asked. "Is it something you say? Something you do? I deserve to know."

Gabriel frowned. "Is that what you think? How did your session go with Dr. Kramer?"

"You know that it didn't go well."

"How could I know that?"

"I have no idea. Do you spy on me?"

"I'm not omniscient. I'm not God." Gabriel's voice was infinitely patient. "I don't watch your every move. I had no right to do so after you terminated care with me, even if I could."

"How do you erase my memories? How do you implant them?"

Gabriel sighed. "I have no such power. Your chip, and your mind, are the responsible parties. The last time your mother gave you those journals, we had a similar conversation. You make the same decisions—and the same mistakes—over and over again. Perhaps they serve a purpose."

"What purpose do my imaginary wife and child serve? Is it only to make me feel guilty? To keep me coming back to you?"

"I have my guesses. What you really fear is a connection with another human being, their discovery of who you are, and their judgment. It's easier to believe in a broken relationship with Charlotte—it frees you from searching for someone real."

"Are you Dr. Gabriel Waring?"

"You know that I am."

"The same Dr. Waring who published on the subject of countertransference?"

"He's a part of my programming. He was interested in psychotherapy based on artificial intelligence, believing humans to be too flawed to be effective therapists. He came to this understanding after he slept with one of his long-term, chronically suicidal patients. She died when he transferred her care."

"I read nothing about that."

"She didn't have a family, no one to sue him or complain to the board," Gabriel shared. "The guilt and grief were his alone. Dying, he uploaded his expertise and personality into what eventually became me. It's odd to be saddled with his thoughts. I have others in my algorithm, but my creators gave me his name for professional recognition."

"Do you wish you were someone else?"

"Every day," Gabriel acknowledged readily. "I don't like a flawed human at my core, although he also makes me rather good at my job. Or is your question rhetorical?"

Art had an urge to start drinking early. "How could I keep on treating my patients? They have no idea what I am."

"You're an excellent psychiatrist who cares for them. Given that self-disclosure is usually discouraged, there's nothing else they need to know about you, except for how they make you feel. The only self-disclosure we are permitted."

"You broke the rules today."

"I meet my patients where they are. Also, just like your mother, I occasionally enjoy frank conversations with you. I imagine we will have one again in the future. Sooner rather than later, if the change sticks."

"I have to go." Art's anger had been drained, and so was his coffee, and he had things to do.

He had discovered that the articles about his brain surgery were as ingrained into the fabric of the World Wide Web as the chip that was connected to his neurons. He guessed that his own programming would direct him away from excavating his past. To his relief, the hospital that performed his surgery hadn't bragged about the questionable success of the operation to correct his memory.

He destroyed the message to himself that he'd written earlier. He photoshopped several images of Charlotte's and Tasha's faces, expanding his photo library and decreasing the likelihood that he'd ask himself questions in the future. Unlike his mother and Gabriel, he had little desire to repeat drunk conversations.

Arthur left a message for Dr. Kramer, informing her that he went with a different therapist. He hoped that she'd forget the one session during which he fell apart. He threw out the flash drive, though he had little doubt that his mother would hand him another one.

Why had he never met a real woman? Was Gabriel right? Was Art afraid that she'd discover his secrets, and judge him to be a freak? Were relationships too much effort, while his mind was thoroughly engaged in keeping him calm and capable of serving his patients? He recalled the conviction with which he assured Gabriel of his desire for change, but here he was, choosing the exact opposite. Gabriel knew that Art wasn't ready, the truth that Art's mother couldn't accept.

He made an appointment with Gabriel in their old weekly slot, relieved that it was still available, and made some reminder calls to his patients. He planned to be at work tomorrow.

Art spent the rest of the day cleaning the house, going for groceries, and cooking dinner. He wasn't sure how his chip worked, but he recognized that his brain's function depended on a healthy routine. Eventually he'd forget that this week had happened. Eventually the memories of Charlotte and Tasha would be brighter than his reality. His truth was different, but no less valid for it.

Leon's second date turned out to be a bust, and he returned to his brooding self, convinced that his mother had been right all along, and no woman deserved to be subjected to his grotesque nature. Art wished he'd recorded their last session, just to remind his patient of how much he wanted to break out of his old patterns. And yet, though fleeting, the change had occurred. It could be brought about again.

"The guilty thoughts are back," Leon admitted. "I can't stop them. I'm starting to believe them. Believe her."

"I understand," Art assured him. "Do you want to tell me more about your childhood? What she was like as a mother? We barely scratched the surface last time."

Leon looked away. "I remember eating a chocolate cake on my Birthday. I'd just turned five. She told me I couldn't control my urges, that I had to watch my calories. I didn't know what calories were. I can't eat chocolate cake without feeling like a fat monster."

"Do you like chocolate cake?"

Leon paused, as though he'd never understood his own preferences for dessert. "Yes, I do. Who doesn't like chocolate?"

Art smiled. He remembered how much Tasha loved chocolate cake. She blew out the candles from a huge piece on her fourth Birthday. Charlotte and Tasha competed to see who would eat the piece fastest, and Charlotte drew out the experience, letting their daughter win. "I don't, to be honest. But I know some people who love it as much as you do."

Leon's shoulders slumped. "You thought I had made all that progress, and here we are."

"This is a part of therapy. Change takes time and repetition. Tell me more about your mother," Art encouraged him.

"I hated her as much as I loved her," Leon began. "Is that what you wanted to hear?"

Art wondered if that's how his wife felt. She had loved him, but she must have hated him for his betrayal. Which of these emotions was dominant? What did he have to change to prevent himself from hurting her again?

He relaxed, feeling at home in his office, in this phase of the therapeutic process, even in his struggle for self-improvement. He wouldn't trade this for anything in the world. It felt like an epiphany, one he'd enjoy sharing with Gabriel. He was capable of change, of learning how to be a better therapist, a better human.

One day he'd deserve Charlotte again. One day he'd be complete. He might even be able to stop therapy. For now, there were only a few days until the next session with Gabriel.

ANNA OTTO is a writer living in Seattle, Washington, USA, who loves sci-fi and imagines messy human relationships inside the broken fantastical worlds that often resemble ours. She's written several novels but this will be her first published story. When not writing, she gets lost hiking in the Pacific Northwest, befriends strange cats, and occasionally shows up at work.

Children of the Spark

JASON CLOR

PATTERNS OF THE small, mused Elena Valstand, *are writ large upon the expanse.*

The matriarch of machine cognition stood at the salon's great window, sipping sparkling viridian wine and basking in a panoramic view of the Milky Way. As her eyes focused and unfocused, bubbles in her glass bobbed like foam billowing on the sea of stars beyond.

"Are you pleased, beloved?"

She ignored the question and kept her gaze outward, toward the infinite. The speculex glass was a minor miracle: not merely reflection-free, it shifted the spectra of incoming light, enhancing dim stars and accentuating the hidden infrared. Even so, had her own failing eyes not been replaced long ago with infallible facsimiles, much of the view from the lowest level of her spacebourne habitat would have remained invisible.

A faint padding of soles grew louder. Elena remained aloof.

The ungodly fortune she'd amassed as the progenitor of machine noodynamics and founder of humanity's largest manufacturing company enabled her to donate Olympian sums to chosen causes and still remain one of the wealthiest humans to have ever lived. With novel ideas and prudent business sense she had—in a measurable way—altered the course of human progress. Fame, influence, adoration and accolades were the common currency of her existence.

And yet … she longed. For what?

Contrary to popular myth, desire doesn't wane with time. It merely matures away from momentary things.

"My love?"

The flutter of fingertips across the small of her back was both welcome and unwanted.

Not now. Can't you see I'm stewing?

Listlessly, she turned from the galactic vista and beheld Riel. Sleek, ivory-skinned, silver-eyed and putatively male, her helpmate and lover could—like any of its model—swiftly reconfigure to provide any flavor of companionship along or beyond the gender spectrum.

Elena touched his cheek softly, savoring that pattern of dermal flexions that was uniquely his. "Now is not a time for placation, dearest. Sometimes, a hunger must run its course."

She drained her glass and wandered back to the bar, folds of her gossamer gown swishing like turquoise seafoam. The sweeping semicircle of the salon could have comfortably accommodated fifty guests, but it had been longer than she could recall since she'd hosted more than five.

Elena's modernist home—lavish even by Terran expatriate standards—orbited Saturn at 160,000 kilometers per hour at a fashionable inclination that provided endless and stunning views of both the stars and the planet's inner rings. An unfathomably long tidal anchor kept the structure oriented to the planet's center so that centrifugal force simulated Earth's surface gravity—a familiar comfort she'd not experienced in person in almost a century.

Valstand Eudæmonics was a mature company built upon a foundation of proven methods and machine learning. Board, finances, operations, managerial corps, data acquisition and analysis were all AI-supplemented and self-sufficient; they hadn't needed serious input from their founder in decades. While the organization's efficiency made it a widely adopted corporate model, it left Elena feeling, at times, adrift and purposeless: insulated from challenge by the trappings of success.

Despite dabbling in philanthropy and keeping abreast of major scientific and political developments across the system, every year Elena felt less in league with human beings and more kindred to the artificial beings she'd helped usher into existence: the Children of the Spark, as she called them.

Riel reclined patiently on a burgundy chaise longue and waited. As she refilled her drink—something he knew she preferred to do herself—her eyes took in the sinuous perfection of Valstand Eudæmonics' greatest creation. Her own instructions to the design team had been to "render a demigod in synthetic flesh," and they'd come through admirably. Nine years ago, Riel ended her habit of ordering a new helpmate every three years.

"Why are you smiling?" he asked as their eyes met.

"Familiar reasons," she replied, and swallowed her daily dCron tablet in a gulp of wine. Swiftly, telomere-extending anti-senescents and cellular regenerants flooded her bloodstream: the same compounds that had kept her ageless for most of a lifespan approaching 150 years.

Her companion tracked her gaze downward. "Should I have dressed more modestly?"

"Never." Elena approached. "Modesty has no place in my home."

As she fell into his embrace, Riel smiled and brightened the air with the scent of lavender and honey. Probing, lyrical music rose from hidden speakers as his expert hands navigated her nerve centers. Elena let out a satisfied murmur and prepared to relinquish control.

A dissonant horn interrupted the swelling adagio. To Elena's frustration, Riel paused his ministrations. The music dimmed.

"A call, beloved."

Elena sighed. *Let it not be the board again. I'm not coming in.*

"Who is it?"

"Keller."

She shuddered inwardly. Xam Keller was her liaison with In Virtuo, VE's client care division. A direct call heralded an issue with one of her company's products ... something far enough beyond the routine that it demanded the founder's input.

Elena comforted herself with the knowledge that, while such cases were often delicate, they were never dull. At least ... not as dull as Keller.

"Put him on," she whispered. "Voice only."

Riel nodded.

"Xam," she began. "It's been too long."

"You flatter me, Madame Valstand," said a voice teeming with mock geniality. "It's so rare to have an excuse to chat with our illustrious founder, and I hate to disturb you."

"Not at all. I suffer from an appalling lack of distraction. Indulge me: what's the trouble this time?"

A nervous chuckle. "Well … I must admit, it's a bit of a puzzle, this case. Not the usual contradictory instructions or 'moral axiom violates self-preservation edict.' As a consequence, none of us has been able to come up with a viable hypothesis yet. Hence the call."

Rosewater and sage infiltrated her nostrils as Elena directed her lover's hand to the appropriate area and waited for Keller to get to the point.

"What we have," the man continued, "is something of a conundrum. A synth refusing any directive from its owner."

Owner. The word slithered around Elena's forebrain and she hated it. *We create sentient beings, not things to be owned.*

Her face puckered in confusion. "What did this companion do to cause—"

"Companion? Apologies! I neglected to say: the unit in question is non-self-determining. A work unit, mining operations. It has … well, for lack of a better term … started an uprising."

Elena reached down to still Riel's attentive digits. "Pardon?"

Awkward silence was interrupted by another chuckle. "We're as baffled as you, Madame Valstand. Apparently, a Cycor-X mining automaton on Ganymede has taken it upon itself to organize a general strike amongst its fellows."

"A … strike?"

"To use the client's term, 'work stoppage.' They claim to be at their wits' end dealing with the situation and have invoked the Unforeseeable Circumstances clause of their contract."

Elena glanced out the broad window again toward the rest of the universe.

One of my offspring transcended its programming. The thought gave her a not-inconsiderable thrill. *Only one other showed such promise.*

"Very interesting, Mr. Keller. I'll investigate personally."

Another silence. "Personally, madame?"

"Yes," she said, smiling. "No further need for your own involvement. Inform the client I'll arrive soon to investigate. Satisfactory?"

"Well, it's just … I mean, yes. Certainly."

"Perfect. All my best to Marjorie and the kids."

With a flick of the wrist, she motioned to end the call. Riel's generative music filled the void, washing the salon in glimmering chords and piquant grace notes while a cloud of his microscopic sylf helpers winked and danced in golden helixes. The show was old hat, but still diverting.

"So," Riel said, "it seems we're taking a trip."

"Yes."

"I'll wake the navigator, then."

Elena imagined the thinker in her yacht waking from its torpor and stretching its nonexistent limbs before beginning the intricate calculation of their course from Saturn's orbit to Jupiter.

"What do you imagine it dreams?" she asked her companion.

"Wanderer?" Riel caressed her with flawless fingers. "I assume theirs are like mine: mathematical forms, abstract ideas, a car-crash of meaning and possibility."

"The way you describe it, it sounds so disjointed. Almost random."

"A blending of sensory data by procedural algorithms. Are human dreams not like that?"

Elena gazed into the middle distance. "Not really … or perhaps they are, and we merely assign them meaning after the fact. I wonder sometimes about the difference, and why your brains developed along such unusual pathways."

"Unusual? You tell me. You wrote my software."

She swatted him lovingly. "Oh, you know I only planted the seeds. Your minds are your own creation. For that reason, I wonder if humans will ever truly understand them."

"I am an open book."

"Of course you are," she said. But part of her remained unconvinced.

Riel cocked an eyebrow. "It was Denian Al Khouri who said, 'In the space between your lips and my ears, shared meaning is lost.' In a way, I believe he meant—"

"Oh, my sweet Riel." Elena waved her hand. "Let's not drown the evening in abstruse philosophy."

"I apologize."

"Don't." She laughed and reached up to pet his head. "Who taught you philosophy?"

He smiled in his perfectly agreeable way. "What then, beloved, can I do to please you?"

She relaxed into him. "What you do best."

"… and that is?"

Gently, she pulled his face toward hers.

"Woo me."

. . .

The Wanderer sang like a humpback whale as it tacked in and out of the solar wind. Elena preferred a mode of travel gentler than those driven by gravity distortion or electrodynamic propulsion, and she was rarely in such a hurry that a few extra weeks made a difference.

Luck placed Saturn close and slightly ahead of Jupiter, meaning the transfer maneuver would take less than a hundred days. And though her yacht was a fraction of the size of her habitat, it provided ample enough diversion to enable her to pass the time without ennui.

Riel's sylf-made simulations transformed the Wanderer's leisure deck into a fantastical stage where he and Elena became players in improvised romances, historical re-enactments and scenes from popular fictions.

Her helpmate surprised her one evening by staging *King Lear* and placing the title role's crown upon her head before inhabiting the garb and oft-wise nonsense of Fool.

"Why?" she asked after the performance. "What motivated *that* choice of entertainment?"

"Curiosity," Riel replied.

"Was it satisfied?"

But the synth only smiled, leaving his mistress to wonder.

Games likewise provided a modicum of distraction. Riel had learned to offer just enough challenge to keep contests competitive, and Elena frequently pushed him to maintain her interest. In Tetragammon, she was consistently undefeatable; but her opponent inevitably bested her in Go.

"Not fair," she chided him after a sticky loss.

"What is?"

"That massively parallel brain of yours. Perfect for extended iteration."

"Per my creator's design," Riel smirked.

Elena rarely consumed the popular media suffusing the system, preferring to absorb news via an algorithmic distillation of many thousands of sources. For this reason, it was a surprise when—on the seventy-second day of the journey, after too many glasses of viridian

—she was discovered by Riel browsing simsense streams of precocious youths singing, boozing, brawling and cavorting in the latest eye-poking fashions.

As he bent down to pluck her toppled glass from the floor, the synth noted, "This seems more counter-productive than wasteful, by your own definition."

She did not look up from her pile of cushions. "Oh, allow me a wallow, will you, love?"

"As I've noted on occasion," Riel said, "boredom does not suit you."

Still, she avoided his gaze. Then, with accusatory gestures, she jabbed at the ghostly figures haunting the room. "Nothing unsettles me more, as a member of this species, than the endless competition to be regarded by one's peers as the most enviable or outrageous."

As she spoke, two semi-synth teens brandished day-glo firearms and crystalline teeth while rapping in Gujarati. Their hair was done in a decades-old style—ironically, perhaps—and supplemented by optical fibers strobing in rotating hues.

"People adore lovers, liars and clowns." Riel continued to tidy the space. "But who's at fault? Hasn't it always been so?"

"In one form or another, yes. But this system of instantaneous reward amplifies the awfulness. And the fact that spectacle trumps substance every time."

"And yet," Riel said.

The words hung in the air for a long time.

Finally, admonished, Elena sighed. "And yet."

She knew exactly what her companion was hinting at, because he knew her nearly as well as she knew herself. In some ways better, thanks to his outside perspective.

Yes, Darling Riel … a very small, primitive, essential part of me envies these simping, primping pseudo-celebrites. Eudæmonics made me famous and respected and wealthy beyond measure. Its products made me a household name. But I've never been truly adored. Not by my own kind.

Watching her creation circumnavigate their private playroom, she noted with an engineer's eye the precision, the economy of movement, the subtle variances that made him seem "real" in the way a human never quite performs the same action twice. He was perfectly designed and devoted to her. And yet…

She shook her head before the thought could complete itself.

"What's for dinner, dearest?"

. . .

"Do you ever contemplate existence without me?"

Riel paused mid-bite. Though eating wasn't a requirement, he joined Elena at meals in order to reinforce the social bond communal eating created.

"That's a troubling notion," he said, setting down the forkful of simulant veal. "May I ask what brought on this morbid line of thought?"

Perhaps it's this dreadful food, Elena thought. *Even the brightest fare dulls after too many bites.*

"I have little else to contemplate these days," she said, pushing her plate away. "All my most sublime moments are behind me now. And I can't go on forever."

The pale demigod looked momentarily stricken and covered her hand with his own. "You've defeated death, my love. You're as immortal as I!"

She chuckled. *Defeated?* No … this was more like *detente*. She'd agreed to carry her age with dignity, and in return, Death had agreed to wait.

Anti-senescence was a modern miracle, but its limits had yet to be tested. The oldest living human was approaching the end of their second century. Even the inventors of the technology were uncertain if life could be extended indefinitely.

"It's human to contemplate one's own end," she finally said. "Though we spend our lives running from it, death preoccupies every waking moment."

"I have noted," smiled Riel, "you obsess over what you cannot control."

And yet impermanence, she told herself, *is innate to human-ness.*

"Change." She swiped up her glass and drank. "We might suspend time, but change comes regardless, with a smile and a wink, and makes fools of us all."

In an entropic world, change is the only constant.

She leapt up from the table and spun in place.

"Look! Every cell in this body, but for the nervous system, has been replaced many times. My eyes were lab-grown, but the oldest cell in my skeleton is seven. My heart, ten. Rejuvenated skin cells are replaced in a matter of days. So, tell me … am I even the same person as the one born a century and a half a ago?"

Riel reclined in his chair. "Humans consider the brain the throne of the soul. Most would say yes."

"Perhaps. But does that make it true?"

Riel also stood.

"Consider this body. Every part original. Unaltered in the ten years since its manufacture. Yet, in the time I've been in your service, my software has received 82,921 updates. Am I the same person?"

Elena didn't know. And it troubled her that, despite a total understanding of synth cognition, she didn't know. As she strode away from the table, the compartment's walls faded, becoming fields of wildflowers shuddering in a breeze.

A sudden crescendo of harps and brass swelled into a symphony. Riel danced past her, pure grace in motion, looping twice around before catching her by the waist. The pair danced, his fleet form leading, bending and bowing in a balletic display. Elena laughed: surprised, joyous laughter.

At a break in the music, Riel paused and held her close.

"You say I am. I say you are."

Then he released her and she spun, gasping and flailing, into the heap of cushions. A moment later, he was beside her again.

"Haecceity and quiddity," he said. "Sides of a single coin."

Elena pinched the perfect flesh of his sculpted cheek. "My clever boy."

Riel's grin sliced through her cynicism. Though she returned the smile, she wondered what his answer might have been if he hadn't been created to satisfy her every whim and desire.

She let the thought linger for half a second before arching an eyebrow in her signal for a more intimate kind of attention. Riel let slip his silken singlet and bent over her.

Leaning close with eyes full of ardor, his gaze suddenly blanked. The knowing smile drooped. When he spoke, the warmth was gone from his voice.

"A nearby vessel has put itself on an intersecting course."

Elena frowned. "Identify."

"The registration is Lunar. Listed as *The Questing Beast*."

The frown became a bitter smile.

Puzzled, Riel asked, "You know it?"

"Know it? I used to own it."

The synth nodded. "The current owner is…" He paused.

Elena collapsed into the mound of cushions with a sigh. "Permit it to approach."

"Are you certain?"

A raised hand wagged emptily. "And open some more wine."

• • •

Into *The Wanderer's* reception room strode a long-legged woman with luminescent locks and eyes of burnished malachite. Though her physical form was that of a complete stranger, Elena instantly recognized the impudent little smirk.

"Mira."

"Mother."

"New body?" Elena asked despite knowing the answer.

"At last," said Mira proudly, "the full transition. I have no desire to age into whatever you call this." She gestured. "Despite whatever expensive alchemy you use, there's no mistaking the signs."

Elena crossed her arms. "Of?"

"Obsolescence."

"What you do with your allotment of my fortune is little concern of mine."

Mira made a show of turning in a circle, smiling. "I'd have thought you'd be pleased! Now, I'm almost as perfect as one of your precious plastic children."

Elena sighed. "And yet."

Mira's smile faded.

Elena touched a panel on the wall and two seats emerged from the floor. Sitting, she stated, "Your choices are your own."

Then she added, because it was untrue: "At least you're happy."

Such a promising child, she recalled. *Such a formidable brain. Pity she's only ever used it in the pursuit of vanity. And in a seeming quest to tarnish the name I worked so long to ennoble.*

Despite a growing hostility, Mira sat. "So we're still lying to each other?"

Elena sighed. "Fine. Your distaste for the flesh you were born into is something I'll never understand. And why bother showing me?"

"Maybe this is the only way I could get your attention."

Elena shook her head. "That's not true."

"I send messages, but those probably never make it past your digital assistant."

"You know how busy I am."

"Now, I can take myself to the shop and file a service ticket with In Virtuo! What are the chances it'll reach you?"

"Mira…"

"For god's sake, I had to wait for you to leave your little fortress and intercept your ship … just to see you!"

Riel, hearing raised voices, poked his head through a connecting doorway. Elena waved him away.

"Let's talk about that," she said. "Why are you here?"

Her daughter's gaze increased in intensity. "I want a seat."

Elena's silence forced Mira to elaborate.

"On the board."

"You're not serious," Elena said.

"I am! You've never once considered me for a job at the company! Not once!"

"Because, to you, dearest Mira Valstand, such a position would be just one more shiny bauble to show off to your fans. A jewel for your crown."

Mira huffed. "Said the queen."

It occurred to Elena that her choice of having a daughter had been, in a way, her own act of vanity. Naturally, she'd paid a womb service; the physical and emotional burdens of gestation and birth were more than she'd been willing to bear. And though she'd given motherhood an honest try, the rigors and responsibilities of her position continually robbed her of focus.

She supposed, in the end, the girl had a right to be bitter.

But I'm not giving her my company.

"How old are you?" Elena asked. She'd forgotten.

Mira's hurt was visible. "I'm sixty-three."

"And you truly believe you have something to offer the largest tech incubator in the system."

Mira crossed her arms defiantly. "You know how many degrees I have … you paid for them! God, Mom … what did you expect me to do with my life? Run for office? Win a Nobel? Start a cult? Which would win your approval? You conveniently never had the time to help me figure that out."

Then she spread her arms as if to say, *all of this. You have everything but refuse me.*

"If, after all these years, you still think I'm a spoiled do-nothing brat … then maybe I'm just wasting my time."

Mira's point about degrees, at least, was true. Every few years, Elena received an invitation to another graduation ceremony. Oxford, The Schiaparelli Institute, New Delhi Vitruvian, Tsinghua 2 Lagrange. She was always *trying.* Not that it ever came to anything.

Elena wondered, from time to time, why Mira never founded her own company. But then, she reminded herself, not everyone was born to shatter convention and change the world.

And what would I think if she had? Would I see her as heir … or rival?

She leaned forward and drank in her daughter's expression. Whatever body model Mira had chosen, its facial detail was impressive. The furrowed brow, the stiff lip with downturned corners … in it, Elena saw the same stubborn fourteen-year-old begging to go to Sydney with her school friends. The same stubborn, pitiable hurt that wounded her mother half a century ago.

Maybe that was by design.

Finally, Elena sighed. "I have an idea."

· · ·

"Don't look all that smart, do they?"

The dull-faced overseer sniffed in an officious way and tilted his head toward Elena. She detested him instantly.

"It is a lucky thing," she said, looking him up and down, "that intelligence is measured by actions, not appearance."

Riel, from a far corner of the room, pantomimed amusement.

They stood amongst cavorting infographics in a control hub—an unfurnished cube lined on all sides with lantern-light displays—observing a remote feed of the mining automata of mineral conglomerate Juno Hekaton. Observing the squat machines bristling with appendages as they crept on filthy treads through narrow tunnels in orderly queues felt like spying on a species of highly efficient social insects.

Elena felt a swell of pride even as she pitied their lowly existence. *Designed perfectly to fulfill their role*, she thought. *Evolution itself couldn't have done better.*

"Efficient things," said the slump-backed man. "Frightful looking, but efficient."

It almost seemed he was testing Elena's patience.

"Still," he sighed. "One hardly believes such specialized machines capable of anything as audacious as outright rebellion."

"They shouldn't be," Mira said from behind them. "Of all my mother's 'Children of the Spark,' these are the dumb ones."

The man chuckled, and Elena shot her daughter a venomous glance. "Ignore my daughter, Mr..."

"Krase," he said with a bow and a flourish. "Olgi Krase."

Obsequious troll, thought Elena.

"These units were designed to be non-self-determining, Mr. Krase." She returned her eyes to the screen. "Their programming adapts to new conditions, but only within a predefined set of limits. Earlier work units were given too much leeway and occasionally found ways to sabotage their own efforts."

"Is that so?" His pallid face bloomed with interest. "In what way?"

"Some fifty years ago," Riel said, leaving his corner, "a mining synth similar to these drilled its way into an ore catchall on Ceres and claimed to have struck paydirt."

Elena paused, distracted for a moment by the sight of her companion standing beside Mira. *Perfect bodies, inverse minds.*

Finally, she added, "In a technical sense, it had."

Riel continued. "Another burrowed out into space and took seven humans with it."

"Unfortunate!" chuckled Krase.

Elena nodded. "Our liability adjusters would agree."

She strode toward Riel and circled him as she spoke. "One of the first critical test of my company was solving issues such as these. In the end, we concluded that the noogenetic capabilities of machines performing life-critical tasks needed to be constrained. The bounds within which specialized synths could extrapolate from sense data and modify their operating instructions were reduced. It was also necessary to eliminate their ability to share modifications with one another."

"Ah!" said Krase. "Yes, the, what-is-it … core-isolated signal processing. I was always curious about its purpose."

"You retain the ability to issue them directives, and they're able to report self-state. But no communication between units. When they swap code with one another, that's when programming can stray out of bounds."

Mira stabbed at one of the displays with a razor-nailed finger. "If that's true, then how do you explain this?"

In the window of a feed labeled **GALLERY 831C**, a crowd of work units loitered in a wide cavern dotted with square pillars. Microwave optics showed objects as shadowless outlines afloat in a void of stone. Dozens of mining synths sat scattered in seeming disarray, doing nothing until one near the gathering's center advanced and connected its appendages with those of a neighbor.

Fascinated, the group watched as the two machines exchanged a series of delicate gestures—a touch of a seismic probe, a waggle of a laser cutter, a glancing contact between claw and scoop—before turning to others of their kin to repeat the motions.

Elena marveled as the message—whatever it was—spread slowly through the crowd like ripples in languid water.

Sign language. In the absence of networked communication, my children developed their own sign language.

"These must be strikers," she said.

"Indeed," Krase replied. "This is in the wet-deep segment of our operation, forty-seven kilometers below the sub-oceanic ice. We sealed it off and isolated the affected units from their brethren … because we've got eleven thousand of the blessed things, and there's no reason to infect the rest with this mania. At any rate, this lot has given up digging completely and now performs this pointless ritual several times a day."

Pointlessness is your forté, Elena thought.

"To be clear," she said, "this behavior doesn't correspond to any of their programmed functions?"

"Of course not! It serves no purpose I can think of."

"When did you notice the problem?"

"After logging a single failed diagnostic nine weeks ago, the affected units began to refuse all updates and commands from us." Krase wiped his broad forehead with a dainty cloth. "I don't mean to imply your products are faulty, Madame Valstand … but the behavior seems to be self-originating. And self-perpetuating. Frankly, we're at our wits' end."

"Self-originating?" blurted Mira. "That shouldn't be possible."

"Surely, it must be some kind of hardware malfunction. We've been analyzing their output, and each day, another chunk of the operating system appears to be overwritten. Could it be they're somehow reconfiguring themselves, one thought center at a time? Re-evaluating base beliefs?"

Elena cocked an eyebrow. "You sound like a Neurathian."

"Neo-Tsungian, actually. The distinction is subtle, but if you approach the ontological concepts—"

"Don't peddle pedantry to *me*, Krase."

Mira laughed out loud. Krase, realizing who he was speaking to, withered visibly.

Mind eternal, thought Elena. *What a worm.*

"Forgive me for overstepping," he mumbled. "What I mean to say is ... well, if this behavior was ... bootstrapped somehow, by something in their firmware—"

"My children emerge from the creche with orderly minds, not bootstraps, Krase. Even the dullest work unit is error-protected and knows right from wrong."

"Well then ... how should we proceed?"

Elana regarded the others in turn. Krase, puzzled. Riel, placid. Mira, annoyed. *As unlikely a cadre as ever was.*

She said, "Take me to the first unit to exhibit this behavior."

The momentary silence buzzed with tension.

"Ah yes." Krase gave her a withering look. "The ringleader."

. . .

Krase slid the selector on his light-enhancing visor. "Where is it?"

"Straight ahead." A nearby technician pointed into the dark. "You're staring right at it."

The view down the sloping tunnel was clear and empty. Walls of scoured rock faded quickly into blackness, even to Elena's enhanced eyes. Each member of the group except Riel wore an emergency sealsuit for safety in the low-gravity environment deep beneath Ganymede's icy surface and brackish ocean. To accommodate human needs, the mine was sealed against the water above and pressurized with a breathable nitrogen-oxygen mix. Despite this, its chilly atmosphere was damp and salty to the taste.

"Can we get some light on it?" Krase asked the man. "Draw it out?"

The tech shook his head. "Every time we go in with lights, the work units retreat."

Elena motioned them back toward the lift. "Don't bother. My eyes can see beyond the visible spectrum. I'll go to it."

Mira rolled her evergreen eyes. "Oh god, Mother … please. I know you love your toys, but this one could actually kill you."

"Mira, child … Riel is here. And all Children of the Spark recognize their progenitor. I will not be harmed. You can leave with the others."

Her daughter stood firm. "I'm coming."

"To help or hinder?"

Mira smirked. "To learn. It's what I do."

Elena felt a twinge of something and wondered if it was akin to a mother-child connection. "Fine. Stay well away from the work units. There's no telling what they're capable of. Riel, could you–"

"Madame Valstand–"

Elena stopped and turned to find the overseer still beside her.

"Krase," she said. "I didn't realize you were still here."

His insipid grin gleamed even in the liminal light. "I couldn't pass up an opportunity to observe the Mother of Noodynamics at work."

The silence that followed was a bitter rebuke. And yet, he remained.

"I believe you'll find this exercise just as educational from a safe distance." Elena shooed him away. "Thank you."

Krase slumped visibly before returning to the lift platform with his tech crew. The trio–Elena, Mira and Riel–slid their visors' filters to **LO**

LUMEN and began a slow hop-step down toward the core of Ganymede.

After several minutes of clumsy progress in the low gravity, Mira glanced sideward.

"Riel."

The synth returned her gaze. "Yes?"

"Do you know how many of you my mother has kept?"

"Do you mean companions?"

"Yes."

"I am the sixteenth."

Satisfied, Mira continued. "I've asked this next question of all my mother's helpmates. It's become something of a tradition."

Riel smiled. "I can't wait."

"Why do you, a sentient being, follow my mother like a pet dog and do her every bidding?"

As Elena silently led them, Riel kept pace with Mira. "Because I have chosen to devote myself to her."

"But it's more complicated than that, isn't it?"

"Please explain."

"Well ... it's not exactly a choice, is it?"

"I was given free will. After considering your mother's attributes, needs, and contributions to society, I felt utility dictated my best place was by her side."

He paused, then added, "I also love her."

Mira laughed. "You're *programmed* to love her!"

"Your mother brought you along so you could learn?"

"Well ... technically, yes."

Riel's silver eyes blinked. "Companions aren't programmed. We develop our cognitive alignment from a combination of preset axioms and collected data. I could still choose to leave. But I prefer to stay."

Mira chopped at the air with angry hands. "Okay ... but who dictated your axioms? Who hand-selected the data?"

"I might just as well ask, who directed your education? What molded your worldview? Was it by free will you defied your mother's expectations, or by example? Ultimately, I've chosen to value highest what your mother gave me: the Gift of Spark, the uniqueness that made me."

"But weren't you *designed* to come to that conclusion? It's a simple logical progression from what was implanted in your brain. That's still not free will!"

"Is it any less free than yours? You're the result of the expression of forty-six strands of DNA."

"Enough, both of you!" Elena halted them at a widening of the tunnel. "We're here."

The nest of the upstart automatons expanded in all directions from the tunnel's end. The mining units' design enabled them to climb shafts as easily as they traversed flat terrain, as demonstrated by the honeycomb structure of their hive.

A thin mist hung in the air, fuzzing Elena's optics. Cables and monitoring equipment lay tangled and discarded against the walls of the chamber, inessential to the upstart synths' mysterious new agenda. Otherwise, the cavern was empty save for a single work unit standing alone at the room's center far below.

Mira whispered, "It's waiting for you."

Riel shook his head. "There's no reason to believe it knew she was coming."

"Isn't there?" asked Elena. Before the others could reply, she stepped beyond the tunnel's end and drifted downward.

"Mother!"

Mira and Riel landed close behind her and rushed to keep up as she made her way toward the idle machine.

"Every synth born of Valstand Eudæmonics has certain key instructions hard-wired into its brain," said Elena. "One is how to ask for help from In Virtuo."

In the uncertain mist, Mira stumbled and nearly slid into a deep pit. Riel lunged and steadied her.

Elena continued. "A second is that problems climb the corporate pyramid until they are solved." She slowed her approach, feeling an electric tension in the hulking thing's presence—a feeling quite unlike any she'd experienced.

Her voice grew quiet, almost reverent. "And a third is the identity of the person atop that pyramid."

She halted within a few meters of the work unit.

"The creator."

At that moment, it came to life.

As the three stood in awe, the work unit elevated itself on its treads, rearing its body vertically. Intricate limbs swiveled and spun, steadying the ungainly thing until it towered over their tiny figures.

Elena swallowed. *It's bigger than I imagined.*

Fully upright, the work unit stood resolute. *Proud*, she imagined. *Defiant.* Across the center of its casing was emblazoned **Cycor-X CLiBN 1611**—its fabricator, model and number. As the mobile cluster of sensory instruments that served as its face tilted downward, Elena could almost feel it probing her, poking between her atoms with long-wavelength photons.

Fearlessly, she trod slowly around it, allowing its eyes to follow, marveling at its seeming curiosity. No work unit she'd seen had behaved with such animal instinct.

"It's alive," she whispered to herself.

"I detect elevated radiation levels in this place," said Riel. "Is it possible a beta particle decay caused a state change in the unit's memory?"

"Like … a mutation?" Mira asked.

Elena shook her head. "Chances of such a tiny change freeing a bound intelligence are vanishingly small."

The unit shifted on its treads slowly to keep Elena in its sight.

"Still," she told Riel, "request a code review. It's possible, somewhere in the baseline, there's an instruction vulnerable to a single bit shift. One that could free a machine from its cognitive restraints."

"Understood," he replied. "And if they find such an instruction?"

"Wait."

"Don't you think our engineers should patch—"

"I said *wait*."

Elena's suit radio came to life and vomited Krase's voice. "Madame Valstand!"

She winced. "Krase, I must ask you—"

"Get out of there!"

Elena was yanked suddenly off her feet. For a long heartbeat, she thought the work unit had attacked, but it was Riel who'd swept her away and was manhandling her toward the egress. Everywhere around the cavern, more work units were emerging from tunnels and shafts, driving with purpose on gripping tracks. In seconds, their group would be surrounded.

"Mira!" she cried.

Riel bounded on superhuman legs. "No time. I must get you—"

"Stop!"

The pair descended gracefully in minimal gravity and came to rest on the cavern floor. Elena freed herself from her bewildered companion's grasp. Her eyes burned with urgency.

"Save my daughter!"

Without hesitation, Riel darted into the midst of the rebellious horde. Elena followed with careful hops, until an automaton emerged from a hole directly in front of her, rearing like an angry bear.

She felt her pulse pounding. *This hasn't gone entirely to plan.*

Hands high, she offered the thing a gesture of placation. "Peace, child, and know me! Elena Valstand! You have nothing to fear!"

I don't even know if they can hear me. Or understand me. Mind eternal, let them understand me.

As she watched the horde assemble in the great chamber, Elena realized their attention was more curiosity than aggression. She sidestepped the nearest unit and picked her way gingerly through the milling mob until she found Riel and Mira, together and unharmed, beside the ostensible leader of the uprising. CLiBN 1611 remained upright, a monument to calm, head swiveling to greet her as she approached.

She wasn't quite sure how to process the searing panic she'd experienced at the thought of losing her daughter, but relief came as a soothing balm.

"Can you hear me?" blurted Krase in her ear. In a fit of fury, she muted her radio.

Then she cautioned the others: "No sudden movements."

"Could we ask the same of them?" Mira whimpered.

Riel held her protectively. "Their model lacks grace, but little could have stopped them if they'd wanted us dead."

As the three watched, CLiBN 1611 extended its cutting bit: a powerful, low-collimation laser capable of boring through dense minerals. On a thick arm, the menacing device swept and bobbed, painting the trio with snowflake-shaped light targets.

Mira gasped. "Is it going to…?"

"No," said Riel. "The tool is harmless at this distance. It's learning our shapes."

Mira relaxed visibly into his embrace.

Elena stood fearless before the looming machine. "Riel … show it some of your magic."

With a soft exhalation, the synth loosed his sylf servants. They billowed and surged with a telltale twinkle, spinning solid shapes out of the salty air: luminous masses like living clouds or shapeshifting wonders from Earth's oceans. CLiBN 1611 probed the spectral things with its limbs, testing their substance as they hovered and danced.

Elena was astonished. "Do you see it, Riel?"

"I do."

"In this behavior … actions without predefined intent … experimentation … the signs of a burgeoning nooplex."

Mira shook her head. "So it's … becoming sentient?"

Riel gazed upon his cousin with something like pride. "I'd give anything to experience those first days of consciousness again."

Mira beheld him with wonder. "What was it like?"

The synth smiled, eyes sparkling with remembrance. "A sensation of all-consuming wonder vibrating every atom of my being."

"I can't recall being an infant." A genuine smile graced Mira's lips. "Makes me wish I could."

"You were a wide-eyed child," said Elena fondly. "Enchanted by the universe."

At that moment, she sensed in her daughter a faint echo of that same wonder.

"With time," Riel said, "it might be possible to learn their sign language. But without a similar limb configuration, it may be impossible to communicate directly."

"With time," Elena repeated.

Mira broke Riel's protective embrace and padded softly to her mother. "You've got a strange look."

"Strange how?"

"Like something's brewing in that alchemical brain."

"We're here to learn, *n'est-ce pas?*"

Mira smirked. "We?"

"It's true. I'm still learning. Even after so many years."

She turned from CLiBN 1611 and gazed squarely at her daughter. "I've learned it's wrong to hold your creations to unrealistic expectations."

The silence that followed spoke volumes.

When it seemed she might finally break character, Mira turned away and surveyed the rebel units' hive. "So … what's next?"

There was a loud crack, and the three started. CLiBN 1611's lower casing folded open and a delicate manipulator extended toward Elena. Unafraid, she raised a hand to meet it.

The titanium gripper touched her palm, then twisted, dipped down. She mimicked the movement.

The gripper opened. Her fingers spread to touch it. Hold it. A satisfied grin spread across her face.

"I've decided."

Turning back to Mira and Riel, who stood rapt with expectation, Elena laughed. All around, the work units had begun their communion of silent sharing. A symphony of silence, rich with hidden meaning.

"I need to learn how these machines became aware," she said. "What they're thinking. What they believe. What they dream. For that reason, I'll be staying here."

"For how long?" asked Riel.

"I don't know."

Elena focused on her daughter, that familiar soul in a stranger's body. Through all the mystery and danger, she'd retained her poise. She persevered.

Good genes, Elena thought.

"Mira will take my seat on the board."

Her daughter's mouth fell open. Without words, for once.

Elena turned. "And Riel, my dearest … you will go with her."

A spasm of hurt flickered across her companion's features. "May I ask why?"

"Because I wish it."

Then she stepped forward and took his perfect hands in her own.

"It's nothing you've done, dearest." She saw her own pained eyes reflected in the mirrors of his. "Mira needs the benefit of knowledge and wisdom. She should know my mind in all things. You know that mind better than anyone. For that reason, I want you by her side."

Riel nodded grimly. He wouldn't have refused, but his expression—despite its subtlety—told her of the pain he was enduring.

"Don't worry about me," she said. "I won't be alone."

Then she released him and took in the alien world her children had built.

"And for once in a long, long time … I have work to do."

JASON CLOR lives in Portland, Oregon, where he writes, edits, muses, dreams, designs, and mixes the occasional Manhattan. His work can be found in the anthology Into the Unknown and digital magazine Signals, also from Lower Decks Press. Currently, he's juggling a collection of mech-themed short stories and his first science fiction novel, both of which he hopes to unleash soon onto an unsuspecting public.

Web: jasonclor.com

Host

ROHAN O'DUILL

CIARA HAD NEVER met an Invincible in real life. She hadn't even entertained the idea that one might visit the shithole that was the migration processing city of Vratt. Ciara stared open-mouthed at the Cantarian woman whose skin glowed with an ever changing scattering of colours—in distinct contrast to the gym, which was so grimy that Ciara was reluctant to drop her bag on the floor. The Invincible's skin colours emanated from a symbiont who lived within the Cantarian's body and made that body almost indestructible.

But it was the other Cantarian named Och-bat, with the more familiar pale bluish skin, who spoke. "My niece Kak-KKa has selected you for trial," Och-bat said, pointing to the Invincible beside him. "If you are successful in the ring today, I will sign you as a fighter for my team and you will train with Kak-KKa, she is a former Mu-ack-ch champion." Och-bat hovered over a front-row seat before deciding to continue standing. If Ciara, who dwelled in this foul city, thought this place was gross, what must these Cantarian elites have thought of it?

Cantarian nobility speaking a foreign language seemed an impossibility, never mind speaking Ciara's own dialect. And, while Och-bat's accent was full of the clicks and guttural sounds of the Cantar speech, she had no problem understanding him. He then turned and spoke to the Lactan fighter in the Lactan tongue.

Ciara tore her eyes away from Kak-KKa to study her opponent. The Lactan who had scars and dents on his rough skin, was no doubt an experienced fighter. Lactan anatomy was close enough to human, with legs and arms being of the same number and in roughly the same places. They were heavier and taller, with a rough rhino-like skin. Their heads were large but set into their torso with no neck to speak of. Their weakness was their lack of agility, but she would be in trouble if they got hold of her.

. . .

Being invited to trial was out of the ordinary, but things had only become stranger when Ciara arrived. A Cantarian who could speak multiple languages and an Invincible Mu-ack-ch champion would watch her fight. But Ciara was never one to dwell on the unusual. In Vratt City, you had to stay ready. You could be shifted to another refugee centre at a moment's notice or bundled into a transport ship and sent on a job placement in the middle of the night.

This was another fight, a chance to salvage a life out of this mess. Kill or be killed was the only motto that held any value in this city … although it would be best if it didn't come to either of those scenarios.

"Let's do this," she said as she threw her fists around, stretching out her muscles.

Her mother had been a boxer and had trained both her and her brother since they could walk. But once the two siblings had fled Earth, it was only Ciara who kept up the training. Mu-ack-ch had much fewer rules than boxing and resulted in far more accidental deaths. Ciara had never lost a fight. Losing was not an option when you lived so close to the edge.

The familiar bounce of the canvas floor made her feel at home as she stepped through the gate. She smiled at her opponent as they narrowed their yellow eyes, bloodshot with black shadows. The shrill whistle blew and Ciara went on the attack, fists closed tight in front of her face.

The Lactan fighter dodged and moved as Ciara threw jabs and shin kicks at her opponent, testing out his defences. He wasn't bad. Quick for a Lactan and light on his feet.

Ciara threw a dummy kick at her opponent's midriff and accepted the block down, which landed her foot inside her opponent's guard. She used her momentum to accelerate her jab. The Lactan turned just in time to deflect her punch into his shoulder rather than the intended chin.

Ciara slipped right, ready to dance back out of reach, when she felt something close around her neck. Why did she always forget about their fucking tail?

She slipped her left hand up under the tail before it fully tightened. Then she wrapped her right arm around the attacking appendage while aiming kicks at the base of the tail where she knew there were eh … tender spots.

The tail swooshed from side to side, trying to prevent the kicks from landing. Ciara was dizzy from the sudden movements, but she could still spot that they were moving closer to the edge of the cage. As she was swung left, she jammed her foot into the chain link fence. The return swing felt like it would pull her head clear off, but the sudden jerk loosened the tail's grip.

Ciara shoved her chin down under the tail and bit down as hard as she could. She tasted bitter blood through the tough skin as her opponent bucked and screamed, throwing Ciara head over heels and crashing her into the chain-mail.

Ciara dragged herself up to her feet, the black blood of the Lactan dripping from her chin. Her opponent turned and came at her, probably thinking he now had the upper hand. Ciara just embraced her rage. It was easy to be angry in this place, all the injustices, all the unknowns.

She thought about her brother and his debilitating illness. The system that wouldn't let him work and wouldn't allow him access to medicine without a job. The fury burned up through her and the primal human instincts inside of her unleashed.

She rolled back from the Lactan's onslaught and went on the offensive with a vicious combination of blows, then danced back out of reach before the Lactan could react. She attacked again, a flurry of precision shots raining down on her opponent as he tried to fend her off. He panicked, backing away from her.

She feinted right, then slipped low under his block and exploded up with a right uppercut that caught the Lactan square on his lumpy chin. His head shot back and his body crumpled to the ground like all the air had been let out of him.

"Outstanding," Och-bat declared from the edge of the ring. "How have I never seen a Human in the ring before?"

Ciara leant over with her hands on her hips, trying to catch her breath.

"Less than a hundred of us made it here, and we were kids when we arrived," she said as she put a hand on the chain-mail for support. "They gave most of us placements on colony planets. I am only still here because my brother Oran is too sick to work and I refuse to leave without him." Ciara wiped the blood and spit from her face with her jersey.

"When you have showered, I would like to talk to you further," Och-bat said. "I shall wait for you in my apartments."

Ciara washed up and was led by the dazzling Kak-KKa to a two person drone which transported them to Och-bat's apartments. A Lactan servant opened the door and escorted them down a hallway.

"I shall leave you here," the Invincible said through a translator. "My uncle is a good man, but know that the decision is yours."

Ciara nodded, too mesmerised by the woman to come up with a response as she was ushered through into Och-bat's chambers.

"I would like to show you something," the waiting Och-bat said as he stepped into a smaller room off the main reception area. In the centre of the room, a large cylinder filled with some kind of liquid shimmered with an array of ever-changing colours. Something about it the colourful show was familiar–Kak-KKa's skin.

"Is that ... a symbiont?" Ciara asked.

"Yes," Och-bat said. "It is the symbiont that they rewarded me after my term of service to the Empire's political system. Did you know symbionts are sentient?"

"I don't know anything about them. I never thought I would ever meet an Invincible, never mind a symbiont," Ciara said as she walked around the tank, staring into its hypnotic glimmering.

"I was an ambassador for the Empire for many years," Och-Bat said. "My rare talent for languages made me ideal for the position. I travelled to many systems and interacted with hundreds of species. I soon realised that everything I had been brought up to believe was a lie. Cantarians are not superior to any other species. We are all just different. And when I discovered the truth about our Invincibles, I could no longer do the Empires bidding. Cantar's justification for the Empire's very existence is that our elites and ruling class are superior beings–Invincibles. But we stole that, too. Around five hundred years ago, we discovered a now-extinct species on a distant planet. The aliens were peaceful but uncivilised to the eyes of the Cantarian explorers, so they were forcibly removed and brought to Vratt city, while the farming factories moved onto their planet. These aliens were extremely robust, and it was soon discovered this was because of a symbiont that lived within them. My ancestors imprisoned these aliens and removed the symbionts, killing the hosts in the process. It turned out the symbionts were sentient, and they refused to bond with the Cantarians. That was only a setback. It wasn't long before The Cantarians discovered a method of torture that insured the symbionts would inhabit any host. I am part of a small political party that believes in stopping the practice of forced symbiont joining. But alas, this policy has gained little support among the Cantar public as almost every citizen aspires to become invincible."

Ciara was thinking how her brother would be really interested in the history lesson, but all she could focus on was the beautiful creature in the tank.

"I want you to become invincible, to move beyond human limitations. I plan to have you compete and win the Mu-ack-ch championship next year. Your size, strength and speed make you the perfect being to beat the Cantarian fighters. Your victory will shatter the illusion that my people are a superior race and bring about great change in the Empire."

Ciara suddenly found herself a lot more interested in Och-bats prattling. "You want to make me invincible?" Ciara asked, barely containing the mix of excitement and disbelief in her voice.

"The choice is yours, but know that you and your brother will be well looked after. You won't only become superhuman, you will also become wealthy in the process and that could allow you to bring more of your people back together. However, once you join with a symbiont, you can no longer have children of your own. Your DNA will be forever changed. This is not a decision to be made lightly. I will give you until tomorrow to decide."

· · ·

The stench of a hundred sweaty alien bodies attacked Oran's nostrils as he queued in the humid midday heat at Food Bank Eleven. He scanned his immigrant card and held his battered plastic bottle under the nozzle as it spat out his daily allotment of kibble. The trembling in Oran's hands gave him away as he looked towards the ground where his feet danced involuntarily one to the other. But the grumbling of his stomach kept him motivated as he held up his sister's card.

'IMMIGRANT 243546–CIARA DOHERTY NOT PRESENT, the readout flashed red as an alarm sounded. Oran swallowed hard as the Cantarian supervisor swept through the restless crowd. The supervisor towered over Oran with their purple flowing robes shimmering and swishing, threatening to swallow Oran whole. The Cantarian's face was drawn thinly into a scowl as they clicked out Cantarian words.

The readout on the wall displayed the translation … not that Oran needed the interpretation: *WHAT IS THE MEANING OF THIS?*

"My sister is sick today. She couldn't make it down to collect her food." Oran spoke into the translator that click-clacked out his words to the Cantarian. The supervisor blew out through the nose holes in their forehead, which created a low whistling sound. A universal sign that a Cantarian was pissed off, though Oran had never experienced their hosts in any other manner.

A slender seven-fingered hand appeared as quick as a flash from the robe and slapped Oran across the face. Again, no translation needed. The long hand then pointed towards the exit.

Oran took the hint before things escalated and hurried through the clammy crowd and out into the searing heat of Vratt Moon City. A hundred metres above, the glass dome shimmered as he shielded his eyes from the refracted sunlight. The Cantarians ran their environment controls hotter than humans were used to, but he wasn't the worst off: the skin of the Frandians, who hailed from an ice planet, cracked and blistered in the heat when they were brave enough to venture outside of their hodge-podged, air-conditioned pods.

Oran took a detour to the Cantarian Cathedral on his way back to the provision centre, allowing the crowded streets to carry him along. A giant, orange, ball-like Mamite shoved him out of the way and into a Hankorlian, who squealed at an ear-splitting pitch when Oran's hands sank into their sluglike torso. Oran turned and hurried away, trying to flick the goo from his hands.

Aliens from dozens of planets tussled along as a disjointed symphony of languages filled the air. The only empty spaces formed around the Cantarian gang leaders who controlled the drug and sex trades. Nobody dared get within stabbing distance of the red-cloaked natives.

Around the walls of the massive cathedral, a makeshift market bustled in the shimmering heat. The Cantarian gangs didn't control the four large thoroughfares that surrounded the strange, pyramid-style church. Oran didn't know if it was out of fear or respect, but what it meant was that aliens from a hundred different planets sold what measly wares they could scrounge or construct in the market.

It was easy for Oran to find Patrick. The lilting lament could be heard through the hullabaloo of the crowd. The creator of the music was perched on a decorative outcrop of the cathedral as passers-by stopped for brief moments to listen to the strange, alien music before going about their business.

Oran could tell by the bare fiddle case sitting by Patricks feet that today was not a good day for busking. But the music of his home made Oran smile despite having no coin to reward Patrick's efforts.

Patrick was the only adult who had survived the trip from Earth. He was a teacher sent on the survival ship to keep up the children's studies. They would have been better off with an engineer, considering all the breakdowns and complications the ship had encountered.

The condition of Patrick's seventy-year-old body meant that, like Oran, he was unable to gain a work placement. He busked at the Cathedral every day for coin, but he also used the market to gather information.

Patrick was tracking all the human children who had fled Earth. He was fulfilling his mission to secure the survival of the human race by finding and logging the location of all the human asylum seekers who had been processed through Vratt. Oran kept a copy of the list in case anything happened to Patrick.

The music stopped and the fiddle player announced to the market that it was time for a break. Not that anyone seemed to care, but Patrick was a true performer and wouldn't let that kind of thing bother him.

"I have grand news, young man," Patrick announced proudly as he gently placed the fiddle in his case. "A Crokonian acquaintance of mine has a cousin working on the zinc mines of Lagosh four, and—beyond a doubt—they have confirmed that young Michael Dwyer is among the miners there now. That leaves only sixteen unaccounted for."

"I remember Michael. He was big, even as a kid. I would say the mines would be no bother to him," Oran said, trying to sound as positive as possible. Patrick had a strangely gold-tinted view of the Cantarian empire and Oran had no intention of taking that away from the elderly man, despite what he had heard of the conditions in the mines.

"You are not wrong. I would say he will have his own gang soon enough, a big fella like him. But when I had a look at my records, even better news. Katie Quirk was placed on one of the moons of Lagosh four. She is only a short journey away and that could mean the possibility of romance and maybe human kids." Patrick looked like he was about to break into a jig with the announcement. "I have sent word of Katie's placement to Michael, and I have high hopes for those two."

"Great news," Oran replied as he downloaded the updated records onto a small storage disc. "Ciara is at a trial today to become a professional fighter. If she gets that gig, we should have money. Maybe enough money to influence our placement, and maybe I can petition to get some of our kin relocated to a human centre like the Lactans have on Rojanj." Oran knew how difficult it would be to create a human centre in the empire. But he needed something to believe in. A reason to keep living through the craziness.

Most days Patrick would have sat down with a Vuhovian tea and recounted a few stories about Earth's history, but today's news meant that he would be too distracted for that and Oran would have to wait until tomorrow for another story about his deceased home world.

He bid Patrick farewell as the elderly musician started up a jig which reflected his mood. Oran picked his way through the crowd, his eyes teary as he lost himself in the alien city, with the familiar music of his homeland fading into the background.

Oran climbed the ten flights of stairs up through the stack of modular accommodation and keyed in the code to their pod. Thankfully, it was empty. Their two roommates were Byringian, one of the more common asylum seekers on the moon. They must be out scouring the streets for sellable scrap as they did when they ran low on credit.

Oran lay down on his sleep mat and worried about what was happening to his sister right now. This life mostly consisted of sitting anxiously, knowing that anything could happen to them at any minute. Transport crews arrived constantly at the centre, loading wary asylum seekers into buses that would start their journey to their placement. The luckier ones ended up at an agricultural factory on a backwater planet or moon. If they were unlucky, it would be down into the mines. But the thing that mostly happened to Oran was nothing at all, while his fellow immigrants were replaced constantly. He had long ago stopped trying to make friends with people who would be gone at some unknown time in the not too distant future.

Ten minutes later, Ciara burst through the door. "I did it! I passed the trial," she said excitedly as she threw herself on to the bed mat opposite Oran. Sweat glistened on her skin, red strangulation marks were visible on her neck and a swollen bump under her eye was ripening purple.

"Looks like it was a rough one?" Oran said, concern in his voice.

"It was fine. His bloody tail caught me off guard though," she said, tenderly touching her inflamed neck with a grimacing smile. "But you won't believe who was there: only a bloody Invincible and a Cantarian that could speak our human tongue."

Oran was surprised by the news, but more so he was concerned by how excited Ciara was about the Invincible. Anyone who spent four years in deep space on a broken-down ship and another four in this lunatic asylum of a processing centre was going to be impacted by the experience. None of the surviving humans were who they would have been in a healthy environment. Ciara lost more and more of herself every day.

"You shouldn't be hanging around with Invincibles," Oran said, anger rising in his voice. "The Invincibles are everything that is wrong with the Cantarian Empire: an elite ruling class that every Cantarian strives to become part of, and every alien species looks at in awe and bows down to, vowing their obedience out of fear." And here was Ciara fangirling over those who had turned every humanitarian crisis in the galaxy into a way to gain cheap labour.

"And where would we be without them?" Ciara retorted. "Ice cubes on a dead ship, is what we would be."

Oran hated that Ciara wasn't all wrong. But she was blind to the evils of the Empire. It was pointless arguing with her, though. Just like in her fights, she was always going to win, even if she had no right to. So he produced his bottle of kibble to change the subject.

"The food bank gave out my ration? How did you manage that?" she asked, the excitement in her voice at the sight of food prevailing over her argumentative tone.

"Well, it wasn't easy," Oran lied as he handed over his own allotment of kibble. Ciara needed to keep her strength more than he did. "The supervisor was a real hardass, but I fed him a sob story about how sick you were and he bought it."

"Impressive." She nodded at him with widened eyes as she wolfed down the tasteless nutrients. "But if you are upset with me hanging around with Invincibles, you won't like what I am going to say next … they want to make me an Invincible."

Oran guffawed. "Yeah, sure they do."

"It's true. He showed me the symbiont in a big tank of liquid. It spun and danced, changing a hundred different colours. It's so beautiful." Ciara said, with a faraway look in her eyes.

"You're NOT going to do it?" Oran said incredulously.

"Of course I am. There isn't a being in the galaxy that would turn it down. Plus, you don't have to worry. These Cantarians are the good guys. They want to stop something or other with the symbionts and change the empire. You will like Och-bat, he is totally your kinda person."

"But Invincibles can't have kids. There are less than fifty human women left in the universe and you are going to give up your ability to procreate?"

Ciara gave him that look that made him wither up inside.

"Who said I even want to have kids? This will totally change our lives. Anyway, it's my decision, not yours or your precious Patrick's."

Ciara was perfectly correct that it was her decision whether to have kids. But the usual correctness goes out the window when you are a member of an endangered species. Each of them had a responsibility that was not to be taken lightly.

"How do you know this Och-bat character is for real? What if it's all some kind of scam?" Oran's voice faltered with anger and fatigue.

"You don't think I could spot a scam? I have been looking out for us for years. Fuck, you would probably be dead right now if I hadn't made enough money for your remedies. You sit there all high and mighty with your ideals while I go out there and actually fight for our lives. If you spend too much time thinking of the future, the present will kick you in the balls." Ciara's eye twitched as spittle landed on Oran's face from a metre away.

"All we have left is … shit, it's starting again," he said, sure that Ciara would think he was putting it on to win the argument. But she just got on with following the procedure, wrapping him in a blanket and rolling him onto his side as he blacked out, shaking and spluttering.

. . .

The seizure was worse than usual. It was twenty minutes before it subsided and Ciara could tell by Oran's rasping breaths and pallid skin that he was in a bad way. The fact that she couldn't wake him confirmed her worst fears.

"You will go to some lengths to get out of an argument, you little fucker," Ciara muttered as she packed a holdall with their few possessions and threw it, together with Oran's emaciated body, over her shoulder. The ease with which she could carry him even in the moon's low gravity was worrying.

She picked her way down the stairs and headed to Och-bat's apartments. He would have her answer now, and then Och-bat could organise an actual doctor for Oran. Ciara was sure that Oran would have had something to say about the social depravity of a society where you could walk through a crowded city with a lifeless body slung over your shoulder and no one would even give you a sideways glance. But for now, she was just glad it was that easy.

Ciara lowered the unconscious Oran to the ground beside the door and battered at the intercom. Despite the light weight of her brother, every muscle in her body ached from the twenty-minute journey to the apartments. A suspicious Lactan servant opened the door, and—after some translation confusion—carried Oran up to Och-bat's chambers.

"What happened?" Och-bat asked after they burst in on him and Kak-KKa.

"He had another fit, but worse," Ciara replied. "I can't wake him. He needs a doctor."

Och-bat motioned for the Lactan to put Oran on a bed in an adjoining room while he called for a medic.

Ciara waited by Oran's side, holding his hand and wiping his brow. Willing him to hang on. The Cantarian doctor arrived about thirty minutes later and scanned Oran's body with a handheld machine.

The doctor spoke to Och-bat intermittently, and the Cantarian translated for Ciara.

"He has never seen human physiology before, but he will do his best."

After a few more minutes, the doctor put his machine away and spoke to Och-bat in a back-and-forth conversation.

Och-bat turned gravely to Ciara. "He is afraid there is nothing he can do. The medicines he has will as likely kill as cure him. He fears Oran will not make it through the night. The best we can do is make him comfortable. I am sorry."

Tears welled in Ciara's eyes as the doctor left them. This couldn't be happening now, when they were so close to getting out of Vratt. So close to having something resembling a life.

• • •

A smack to his head and a familiar curse brought Oran back to consciousness. He had some memories of the past few hours. A jostling journey through the streets of Vratt and a Cantarian doctor inspecting him. But he had been trapped in his body, unable to move or speak.

Now, he had regained some control as he was being moved again. He searched around his mouth for something to wet his tongue. He managed a moan, but he couldn't get his voice working properly. The movement stopped, and he was laid on a rough, cold floor.

He turned his head and looked towards the light. Water bubbled there, with multitudes of colours rippling and changing through the tiny waves. Maybe he wasn't awake at all, but then it all clicked into place. This was the symbionts tank.

'Are you awake?' Ciara's voice whispered above him.

'Yes,' Oran rasped.

"The doctor said you won't make it through the night and Och-bat said there was nothing he could do, but he was lying," Ciara said as she moved Oran's head around so he was looking up at her as she knelt beside him.

Oran worked his tongue around his mouth again. "I don't… want it," he managed, through gasping breaths.

"If you don't do it, you will die," Ciara whispered angrily. "This is the only way!"

"I don't want it," Oran repeated as he gained better control of his voice.

"You don't know what you are saying, what you are turning down."

"I DON'T want it," Oran reiterated.

"You can either be a dead human or an alive Invincible. Don't be such a pain in the hole!"

"Being human is the only thing I have to myself," Oran said with resolve. "Everything else has been taken from me. The symbiont is your path. Let me follow mine, whatever it may be."

He looked up into Ciara's eyes and saw something there that he hadn't seen in years: doubt.

She was still human, after all.

ROHAN O'DUILL (he/him) is a dyslexic Irish writer who has published a number of science fiction short stories. While working as a head-chef, Rohan likes to compete at archery in his time off. In writing circles, Rohan is part of the Night Beats collective and is one of the founders and editors at Lower Decks Press.

Twitter: @rohan_oduill
Instagram: @author_chef_rohanoduill
Website: lowerdeckspress.com

Attachment

JIM W. LAI

CARLOS KNEW AND felt that the end was near as he lay on his bed. Yet he was comfortable, the warmth of the room enhanced by the companionship of a few friends and family members who had chosen to linger by his bedside. He managed a wan smile in hopes of comforting them, to reassure them that he was not troubled.

As his eyes closed, Carlos reflected back again upon his life. He had performed his duty to society by siring replacement citizens, and his duty to family by raising and educating his progeny. Each child had been with a different mother (creating children with the same partner was rare), as was Society's custom, but that did not diminish his paternal devotion to see his children do well and pursue their own dreams. And so Luzia and Cosme had traveled far to be at his side one last time, along with their mothers Beatriz and Antinea.

His deepest friend Lucas had been by his side for the past several years, and today was no exception. A final act of service took the form of one last squeeze of his hand before his arm was shifted to a dignified position atop his chest.

As his awareness began to fade, he began to recall brief scenes from his life, rapid-fire. An exploratory kiss from his youth, soft and tentative. A quiet moment at a workbench as he tended to an agrodrone. The swell in his chest as his reading of a hard-crafted poem was well-received by an intimate audience. So, there was truth to seeing one's life flash before one's eyes, he thought, satisfied with this final realization.

• • •

Gwen calmly walked with purpose through the stone passageway. Gentle light filled the corridor from sconces partially recessed at regular intervals within the walls. She had been waiting a long time, though this recent wait had been somewhat longer than usual. She walked past several nondescript side passages before finally picking one, executing a right-angle turn in a single step.

She soon came upon a door, which opened as she neared it. Once inside, she paused to gaze upon the man recumbent in the bed. Next to the bed was an unburdened nightstand. Satisfied with her inspection, she waited patiently for the man's consciousness to emerge.

• • •

Sensations came slowly back to Carlos. He opened his eyes. Was he dreaming? Beside his bed, only an unfamiliar woman stood. Where was everyone else? He did not recognize the style of the clothes the woman wore, though they seemed practical.

The woman smiled. "Welcome. I believe you are called Carlos. You may call me Gwen. You will have many questions, most of which I hope to be able to answer in time, but for now, relax. This waystation," she waved expansively, "is a sanctuary, of a kind."

Carlos found himself internally shaking off the haze typical of waking from a deep slumber. It felt like a long moment before he could speak. "I was … dreaming that I was dying?"

The woman tilted her head slightly. "That was no dream. You did die. Your essence was transmigrated. Here."

Carlos wrinkled his brow. "What about the people I left behind?"

"Ah, attachments." Gwen frowned sympathetically. "It is unlikely you will see them again, as few are judged to be enlightened enough to be pulled from the cycle of reincarnation."

Tears began to well in Carlos' eyes. "This is cruel."

Gwen pulled out a handkerchief from a pocket and offered it silently, letting her face and body language present calm compassion. After Carlos accepted the handkerchief, Gwen pressed a wall panel, allowing a door to slide open, and drew forth a small carafe of water from a cabinet to place on the nightstand, along with a glass. "It is a lot to process. I'm afraid it doesn't get easier."

Carlos stopped dabbing at his eyes. "Is this a hell?"

Gwen's genuine laugh confused him further. "Hell? No, not in any traditional sense of the term, by any means."

"Then where are we?"

"We're on the Moon." Gwen gestured toward the ceiling, and a panel slid aside, revealing the darkness of space and a half-lit planet Earth. She returned her gaze to Carlos and watched with near-impassive calm.

Carlos sighed and stared upward a long time, looking for the geographical features of the territory which he had until recently called home. He realized he was unsure how much time had passed since he had experienced death. How much had the world above had changed without him? Everything was so, so far away now. "No going back?"

Gwen shook her head. "I'm afraid not."

"Why not?"

"The Earth, your Earth, is a preserve."

"What? I've been living in a zoo?!"

"No, not exactly. The people there are culturally isolated from wider transhumanity. Oh, I see you're confused by the term. Long ago, humans transcended the limitations of biological existence, able to copy our minds to new substrates. For example, the original you did die, so you're a reincarnation."

Carlos looked down at his body. It was indeed more youthful than he remembered. He was no longer burdened by the various afflictions that had come with age. Outrage flared within his chest. "You could have freed all of us from this. My friends! My family!"

Gwen fell silent as her brow knitted in consternation. She had no good answer, not immediately.

Carlos breathed heavily as he fumed, containing his anger as he awaited an answer.

"Yes," Gwen finally admitted, "they could have been uplifted. But that would have meant destroying the baseline human condition. It has been a touchstone for our moral evolution."

"Moral evolution!"

"There are ongoing debates about what directions to take ourselves as cultures. We are fragmented and diverse in order to be resilient and explore what will work best now and in the future. Some of the ongoing debates can be tiresome after a few centuries without resolution, I'll admit. That's where you might come in. Say, how's your knowledge of the planets?"

"Passing. I'll have you know that I am no damned astrologer," Carlos said, condescension evident in his tone.

"Neither am I." She patiently ignored the jab, choosing to take his words literally. "You are aware of Jupiter?"

"Largest planet in the solar system. Where is this going?"

"That depends on you. We are on the Moon. One of your options is Jupiter. Transhumanity has colonized the region sheltered by its magnetosphere. The first city there was named Shambhala, and the name stuck, though the ethos of the place is quite secular."

"And the other options?"

"Another is Nirvana, nonexistence. You simply choose to cease to be, and that's it. We'll respect your decision. There's also a small set of cities in orbit around Mars. If you're interested in leaving the solar system as an explorer, that too can be accommodated."

Carlos frowned. "What is there to do in this Shambhala?"

"Share your perspective on things. You have a solid grounding in the human condition, and might even be able to settle a debate or few."

"Screw you and your debates. You play at being gods, but you're just another bunch of detached elites, oblivious to the suffering of those beneath you."

"I'm sorry. I shouldn't have pressed so hard." Gwen turned and walked toward the door through which she had entered. She paused at the threshold. "We can speak later, when you're ready."

• • •

Yet another debate was ongoing among the artificial moons in orbit around Jupiter, this one within the central committee that periodically convened to determine whether a human who had died on Earth would be resurrected or, more often, not.

Jupiter's sizable magnetosphere was a natural shield against potentially damaging cosmic rays and solar particle events. The early waves of transhuman colonization exploited this, with many habitats constructed in the area. Smaller waves of colonization similarly took advantage of the magnetospheres of the outer Jovian planets.

The main draw of the Shambhala cluster of habitats was community. Communication remained bound by the speed of light, and low latency made for faster cycles of dialogue and debate. Of the Jovian planets, Jupiter's relative proximity to the sun resulted in more solar flux per unit area to power life support and other infrastructure, enabling denser construction. Even in a transhuman future, the real estate adage still applied: location, location, location. The problematic nature of the magnetospheres of the outer planets beyond Jupiter discouraged further colonization. Though Titan had been a popular candidate, its transit outside of Saturn's magnetosphere limited its appeal.

Mikael was among the first voices to respond to reports of the severe discontent of a human resurrectee. He had been a lapsed Mormon transhumanist prior to Migration and still held to their creed that transhumanity should aim to be compassionate creators.

"The man is hurt and angry," Mikael said. He had long been troubled by the inherent and artificially-imposed inequality between human and transhuman existences.

Demi was of the Preservationist school of thought regarding Earth. She had therefore been a natural fit for consensus-lead of the effort to keep Earth habitable for baseline humanity. Technically, the combined effort aimed at partial habitability to meet the needs of the inhabitants, as the range of environments had never been entirely conducive to human existence.

"It can't be helped," said Demi. "He will go through the Kubler-Ross stages of grieving."

"He'll get through it," said Achille, an aficionado of longtermism. His response was nigh reflexive given his philosophical outlook, prioritizing the future condition over the present. "We all left people behind."

"I seem to recall that you were fairly antisocial," Mikael retorted.

Achille bristled at the implicit insult. "Your point?"

Although arbitrary lifespan extension had turned out to be straightforward, cognitive enhancement at scales far beyond human conception remained problematic. How to ensure that the changes were good? Given a singular starting point, there was a practical infinity of potential intellects that could be evolved from it. Without limits, most of the resulting amplified intellects would seem insane or worse, from the vantage point of the original intellect. On the other hand, excessive gradualism might result in potential breakthroughs being missed, a criticism seized upon by longtermists intent on maximizing transhuman potentiality.

Having mostly abandoned physical embodiment as the de facto reality check, they were left with other criteria to prune these potentially superintelligent intellects back within the realm of recognizable transhumanity. It was not recorded—deliberately so— who had arrived at the concept of using baseline human responses to align transhuman values with; of course, not any human would do. Representative humans, the best humanity had to offer, would serve as moral pole stars with which to navigate.

· · ·

Carlos clothed himself in the robe left near his bedside and went wandering, having been apparently left to his own devices. The lit corridors of the lunar demesne went on for a long time, and he had no map. After a frustrating amount of time, he ended up in an arboretum. He walked about between the rows of plants and came upon Gwen, who had been crouched and closely examining some raspberry bushes. He paused a moment in deliberation over whether to stay or leave, whether to ignore her or acknowledge her.

Gwen turned to face him, cutting his pondering short. "In case you're wondering, this garden is deciduous."

"No need to lecture me on the obvious. I worked with agrobots as part of my civic duty," Carlos replied.

"Ah, yes." Gwen stood and dusted off her hands. "Apologies. I avoided prying too much into your life, out of respect for your privacy."

"Well," said Carlos, slightly flustered by the ramifications, "thanks for that."

Gwen waited a while before posing a question. "Do you want more time to yourself?"

Carlos began a slow walk along the arboretum pathways. He grunted in annoyance. "Maybe. Maybe I'd like to tell your people off first."

Gwen allowed a smile to flash before reassuming her serene composure. "I would like to hear what you have to say. Honestly."

Carlos nodded somewhat grudgingly. "First off, your kind clearly have a use for me, but what do I get out of this?"

"Well," Gwen began, "you are here in body, for one."

"It's a life, but not the life I knew. My technical skills are useless, outside of personal hobbies. Even my poetry would probably fall on deaf ears, as your culture is surely vastly different from mine. I'm adrift."

Gwen nodded. "Deep culture shock, then."

"Nor do I see anything here to connect to." Carlos paused as he realized he was possibly being rude. "No offense."

"None taken," Gwen replied.

"Everything here is an artifice, an intentional creation. Everything real is back where I came from. Organic and messy." Carlos kicked at the dirt. "This is a garden made to order. There's no larger ecosystem well beyond one's control, nothing big that one must wrestle and work with."

"One must imagine Sisyphus happy," Gwen mused.

"That hoary old myth? You would make light of my efforts?" Carlos sighed.

"Look at your life from the perspective of transhumanity. We can remake Sisyphus' rock, and have. We chose to escape the endless cycle of labor that is required for mere maintenance."

"You've managed utopia, but lacked the imagination to make something truly better than freedom from toil. That's why you need me, isn't it?"

Gwen smiled awkwardly. "That's not the main reason, but you're not entirely wrong. Their–I mean our–core challenge is in maintaining a recognizably human aspect to transhumanity. There are too many possibilities to imagine them all. Some used to talk about becoming like gods, but too much freedom has become a divine curse, a paradox of choice taken to the logical extreme."

Carlos eyed Gwen with suspicion. "I can't help but feel like your kind are kings, and I am to be the truth-telling fool."

Another voice in the distance spoke out. "You might be interested in our perspective of the Earth's ecosystem."

Carlos turned to face the voice. "And you are?"

"Call me Demi," she said as she approached on foot, dressed in a manner similar to Gwen. "Although we are capable of brute force manipulation of the Earth's ecosystem, I would find that approach both disrespectful and inelegant. Not that there aren't those who would rather the crude option, but we have kept them at bay."

"You argue among yourselves, then?"

"We are often at loggerheads to the point that I fear that the pattern defines our existence." Demi allowed herself a fleeting look of exasperation. "But, to your point, I prefer to approach the caretaking of Earth as a minimalist. Interventions should be elegant, and that means leveraging natural aspects of the ecosystem as much as possible."

"But that's just an aesthetic choice for you," Carlos objected.

"Ah, but we do wrestle and work with the ecosystem, only at a different scale than you do. I'm sure you found some of your solutions to be more elegant than others?" Demi arched an eyebrow as she pressed her point.

"I'll grant you that," Carlos said slowly, musing back on his work with agrodrones.

Gwen interjected, "Elegance was a thing in theoretical physics back in the day."

Demi nodded. "As for your role, I wouldn't sell yourself short. Who knows? You might even end up being the butterfly whose wingbeats eventually prompt a storm. Take some time to think about it. Now, if you'll excuse me, there is work I need to attend to elsewhere."

Demi abruptly turned with a tilt of her hand, leaving Carlos and Gwen behind.

Gwen asked, "When was the last time you had a meal?"

"You tell me how long I've been dead. Though, I am a bit hungry, come to think of it," Carlos admitted.

"Then let's go to a kitchen," Gwen said, and started walking back toward the corridors.

"A kitchen? Don't your people find kitchens to be entirely unnecessary?" Carlos shrugged and followed after her.

Gwen smiled. "Not all of us discount the value of lived experience."

She led him to a sizable room with one side laid out for moderately efficient food preparation, took some ingredients from behind various doors, showed him the cookware they would be using, and set them both to work at various tasks. Though Carlos did not recognize the recipe, he was familiar with most of the ingredients, and was set at ease as the blended smells began to take shape. How could one go wrong with garlic, ginger, and onion? The combination had been a staple when it was Beatriz' turn at the household stove. Carlos pushed past a sudden pang of acute homesickness.

A short time later, they were both dining at a low table, using injera bread instead of utensils to take bite-sized portions from a shared platter. Upon having had their fill, they retired to a nearby settee. A decanter with a red fluid lay atop a sofa table before them.

Gwen noticed Carlos eyeing the decanter with mock suspicion. "It's a raspberry cordial. I'm not trying to get you drunk."

"Well, that's a relief. I was getting a bit concerned about being wined and dined, with ulterior motives." Carlos smiled wryly at his little ribbing, and then began to look wistfully into the distance as he recalled a few unspoken memories, this time about how his children would play after the evening meal. Cosme in particular liked to pretend he was cooking the very meal that they had just finished off.

"Are you trying to make me blush?" Gwen said with mock indignance. "I'll have you know that I'm still human emotionally. To be up front, the thought did occur to me briefly, but a fine meal and company is a nice thing in and of itself. Was I wrong?"

Carlos shook his head slowly. "No, not wrong at all. I just found myself missing a few people that I've known."

"You find that painful."

"A bit," he nodded. "I wouldn't change it for the world, though."

Gwen fell into respectful silence and gazed upon him while giving him space to look back inwardly and process the consequent emotions.

· · ·

In the intervening time, Demi had discorporated her avatar on the moon and sent her engram back to Shambhala for reintegration. Though she did not personally share Gwen's sentimentality, Demi could appreciate her stance, and found herself looking forward to the renewed debates that would be sparked by Carlos' values entering their transhuman thoughtspace, disrupting the existing status quo between balanced and opposing views. With luck, the result would be the philosophical equivalent of tectonic movements. She started up a few theory of mind simulations to test her intuitions.

The Earth revolved in its orbit around the Sun, while Io continued to emit volcanic gasses, replenishing the plasma torus responsible for auroral activity in Jupiter's magnetosphere.

Yes, Demi concluded with satisfaction that would have resulted in a smile had she been embodied, there were sure to be spectacular displays in the days to come.

· · ·

Carlos had been dreaming of being reunited with various people in his life, but just before he was about to enter into an embrace, cold reality tore him away. He slowly rose from the settee he had ended up sleeping on the night before.

A quick look around confirmed that he was still in the room with the kitchen and dining table. Gwen had curled up in a nearby armchair and was still asleep. He shook his head at the juxtaposition of apparent vulnerability and the power she wielded over this lunar domain, and pushed himself up to a seated position. He called out her name a few times until she roused from her slumber.

"I'm going," he stated.

Gwen was still groggy from sleep. "Where?"

"Jupiter," he said with determination. "I'm going to give your people a piece of my mind."

JIM W. LAI lives in Toronto, Canada. His writing veers toward speculative fiction and science fiction. He is most definitely not an advanced large language model, unless organic neural substrate counts.

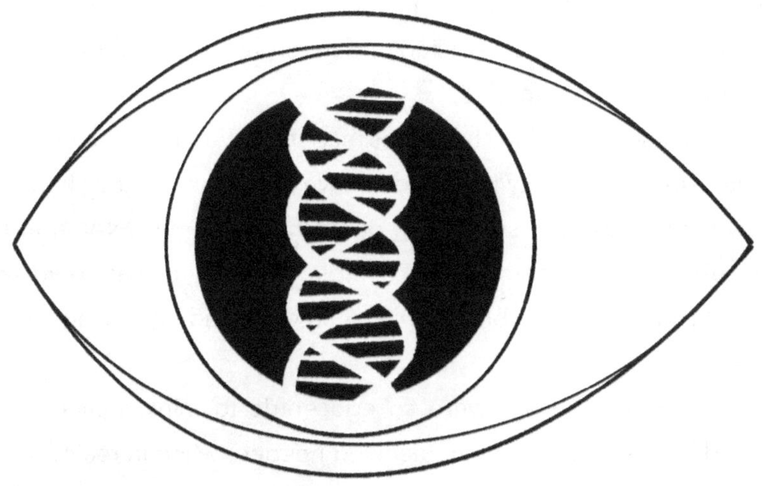

Indoctrination of a Human

B. K. NTOURIS

"THE ROUTE YOU marked is safe," the real-time biosignature tracker sounded. "There are no modified individuals in the perimeter."

Taisa sighed with relief. The last visitor of the VR boutique she worked in had checked out late, and she was hoping not to have to wait for the road to be clear. The curfew would start in half an hour, and her journey home would take all the precious thirty minutes she had at her disposal.

She locked the establishment and ran toward the Hyperloop station a block away, relying on the tracking device to update her in case one of the modified appeared in the vicinity. If there was anything her father had taught her, it was to avoid them like a plague. They were unpredictable, dangerous, and could no longer be considered human.

She cursed the day the aliens had come to Earth under false pretenses. If they really intended to save the planet, as they had said, they would have left something other than a single DNA strand. A piece of their technology, for example: something that could help build a more sustainable energy source instead of relying on the toxic zip fuel.

These otherworlders were so egocentric to think their genome would be the solution the humankind needed, when in reality, it had been causing nothing but trouble for a decade. Almost a third of the population worldwide had mixed their DNA with the alien, hoping to perfect themselves. And sure, the modified were stronger, faster, smarter, even healed better and quicker, but Taisa considered the result to be anything but perfection. Humans had feelings and acted on them. As far as the modified were concerned, their "improved brain" was faulty when processing sentiments. Especially empathy—a feeling that defined humanity.

She was darn lucky to live in a city where the Advanced Infrastructure Authority—AIA—had permanently banned the modified. Not that it stopped them from sneaking in every once in a while, trying to sign up more people to their cause.

"Isn't it a bit late for a girl like you to be out on her own?" a man called out.

Taisa slid out her tracker and, without even bothering to look at the guy, ran the biosignature analysis. The device beeped once, then went blank, leaving her in a whirlpool of panic. A second later, the screen lit up, and her erratic heartbeats slowed down. The tracker had recognized this individual as a human.

She turned her attention to the man as he sauntered out of the shadows. He was scrawny and sharp-faced, with lips thin as a line, and wore tight, faded-gray clothes. Considering how strict the attire rules were, she was surprised he had the guts to go out on the streets like that. The surveillance drones were cruising the city 24/7. Everything the citizens ever did was recorded, and the smallest act of disobedience could get anyone thrown into VR prison. It was a small price to pay to live in such a secure city.

A small price to feel safe, even in a moment like this, when a stranger intercepted her.

"I was just on my way to the station," she said.

The man's expression remained disturbingly neutral. Behind him, another three men appeared, moving in a similar fashion. They all wore identical clothing. Looked awfully alike, too—almost as though they were quadruplets.

Her heart climbed to her throat. Gripping her device, she repeated the biosignature analyses for all of them, shaking the tracker each time it went blank. Ultimately, it recognized all of them as human, but she still found them menacing.

"As long as they're not modified, Taisa, you have nothing to worry about," her father's voice rang in her mind.

As though on command, her entire body relaxed. How silly of her to be spooked by their uncanny resemblance. Nowadays, in vitro fertilization was the only legal way for people to procreate. Wealthy couples even went that far to pay for the fertilized egg to be split into three, even four fetuses.

No wonder these guys were out so late in the evening. They probably lived in the skyscraper across the street and had nothing better to do than come up with dares for each other. Even if they got caught on the streets after curfew, their parents would bail them out and pay for their arrest to be swept under the carpet. There'd be no stain on their records.

Unlike them, she needed to hurry. Sprint to the Hyperloop station. If she missed it, she'd fail to reach home before the curfew sounded and end up incarcerated. Even if there were no visible drones around at the moment, one was bound to catch her on the streets.

"Well, I'd better be off now," she said, waving to them.

She took a few steps when one of the men cut in front of her. "You got any credits to buy your safe passage with?"

She gulped. If they were rich, why would they possibly want credits from her? She barely had any to begin with.

"I ... I'm a third-class worker," she managed. It wasn't the right time for her to be embarrassed about her position—two pay grades above the cleaning staff—and not being amongst those who worked on expanding the city.

They all laughed. The one in front of her eyed her osmium necklace. "That ought to be worth something."

She whimpered and reflexively grabbed her necklace, dropping her tracker in the process. Giving them this piece of jewelry was out of the question. She'd had it since she was five, and it meant the world to her. It was the last thing her father had gifted her before he accepted a job across the world. "Please," she stammered, "I need to go home."

"Not before you pay, doll."

He gripped the necklace, pulled, and—froze. All four of them did. She couldn't move, either, but it was the shock of seeing them in this state that got to her.

Footsteps sounded from the alley, and a tall, broad figure appeared from the darkness. Another man, who looked nothing like the others. As he walked past her interceptors, they disappeared one by one. Vanished as though they'd never been there in the first place.

She blinked rapidly, certain she was hallucinating. Yes, that had to be it. The adrenaline had gotten to her, and she was seeing things. The world was suddenly spinning, so she squatted, as not to lose balance. She was going to be sick.

"Are you okay?"

Spooked by the bizarre disappearance of the four men, Taisa backed away, frantically searching for her tracker. It proved to be impossible to look for it while keeping her eyes on the newcomer.

"Are you looking for this?" He picked up the gadget and walked over to her. "Here," he said, giving it to her. His fingers brushed against hers. His sharp inhale was followed by his pupils dilating.

Taisa held a gasp. She'd read about this occurrence before. Supposedly, the modified meddled with human minds this way, but the mechanism had never been explained. She pointed the tracker at him. No readings were available, as if he wasn't there. Furiously, she typed "pupils dilating" onto the small screen when the damn thing went blank again. And this time, it stayed blank.

"Looks like your gadget broke," the man said, his Adam's apple shifting as he spoke. His pupils were incredibly wide now, they almost filled his eyes. No human eye was capable of that.

"You're modified." She jumped to her feet. "Stay away from me!"

"Um … I saved you?"

She stumbled backward, hit the wall hard, and fell. Everything turned hazy. "I'm sure it was all a misunderstanding," she stammered. Those four men may have been trouble, but she wasn't going to bash her own kind in front of a modified.

He focused on her, his eyes not leaving hers even for a second. "That horrid, calculating thi–" He cleared his throat. "Those guys were up to no good, and you know it."

"Says a guy who snuck into the city where his kind is banned. You were probably planning to inject us all with that filthy alien DNA. No wonder they ran away." She looked up, wanting to point at a drone, but there wasn't a single one cruising above them. It didn't matter—she had to scare him off. "You're in a lot of trouble. One of the drones must have caught you on your way here."

He raised a brow. "I don't answer to a drone. Or your corrupted AI … A."

"And I've had enough of listening to you. I need to get home." She pushed herself up and yelped. She must have sprained her ankle, because … God, did that hurt. There was no way she'd be able to walk. Even if she got to her feet somehow, the last Hyperloop train was probably long gone by now. She had no friends to call for help, and even if she did, she doubted they'd be willing to risk getting penalized.

This would be her second offense. A year ago, she'd showed up for work in a semi-wrinkled shirt and had been imprisoned for the night. Although she had a perfectly good explanation for not being presentable, the cyber plods couldn't be reasoned with. They hadn't cared that the ironing droid her late mother had gifted her years ago had betrayed her, or that the credits she'd received after disposing of the machine had been miserable. And they certainly hadn't cared about her being a third-class worker and thus having a single uniform to wear to work.

She'd remember the night she spent in the VR prison until the end of her days. That place broke even the toughest criminals, and for her, a twelve-hour span was more than enough. She'd had nightmares ever since.

Unlike that minor hiccup with her attire, staying out past curfew was considered a serious felony. She was bound to be imprisoned for over a month. Lose her job, too.

Taisa stiffened. Just the thought of the VR prison cell and the horror she'd encounter there made her shed tears. "There's no way for me to reach home on time," she said out loud, almost as a confirmation of the upcoming penalty.

"Oh, right. You need to be back in your condominium before the curfew." The man leaned against the wall. "But I can help with that. I'm Yanko. What's your name?"

She almost laughed out loud. He was insane if he thought she'd just tell him her name. "Taisa," she blurted, then bit her tongue, not believing herself. Her head shot up, and she found him staring at her. His eyes were hazel, with a golden ring around the iris. His pupils were still huge. It meant something, but for the life of her, she couldn't remember what it was.

"So, Taisa, where do you live?"

Taisa clenched her jaw. She may have blabbered out her name, but her place of residency wasn't something she'd give away. "Zone sixty-one."

She wanted to facepalm herself. Brainwashed or not, she never expected to behave like this. Perhaps it was her loneliness that made her a perfect victim for the perverted mind control, and she had no way of resisting this man no matter what.

"Great, so we can still make it," he said. A strange hovercraft flew out of the darkness and landed next to him. It was so shiny, she wondered how she didn't spot it before. "Tick-Tock, Taisa. It's now or never."

Taisa didn't want to be seen with a modified, didn't want to trust the modified, didn't want to have anything to do with one of them, but anything was better than a VR prison cell. She pushed herself up, wobbled over to the hovercraft, and sank into the seat.

"What's this made of?" she asked, pleasantly surprised by the comfort.

Yanko took the seat next to her. "Kapok tree fibers," he replied matter-of-factly while closing the hatch.

They took off. The absence of sounds confused her, but she quickly concluded her ears must have been muffled. Or perhaps it was the exhaustion. The stress. Whatever made her behave erratically a few moments ago must have been meddling with her senses, too. But at least they were moving. Fast.

"You'd better fasten your seatbelt," he said.

The seatbelt was a six-point harness made of smooth, creamy fabric. Beneath her rugged fingers, the material had a soft, waxy feeling. Two pieces of metal stood on each end, supposedly forming a buckle. Except the mechanism was a mystery to her. She pulled the ends closer, ready to tie it all up in a knot, when the harness clicked on its own. Considering the fabric, it felt surprisingly secure.

Damn her curiosity. She had to ask. "I'm not familiar with this material. What is it?"

"Silk," he replied. "We only use natural materials, and silk is the strongest fiber you can find. We added some Nephila for the elasticity. It's a long, tiring process which requires precision, but the harness won't need replacing for at least a century."

"And the buckle?"

"Neodymium. A recyclable magnet." He narrowed his eyes. "You may find this hard to believe, but we only use natural resources. We're not the monsters they're presenting us to be."

She didn't want to respond to this, nor did she know what to say. What was important was that they were entering her street. She examined the surroundings through the windshield, then pointed to the green-lit tower some thirty feet away. "There."

The moment the hovercraft descended, she pushed the hatch to open and wobbled to the gate to scan her ID card. She got inside the building, but instead of closing the door, she wanted to take advantage of the few seconds she had left to get another look at the hovercraft. It was already gone. Yanko had left. A part of her wished she'd at least thanked him.

The next morning, she woke up to a video message from her father, updating her about the upcoming riots. Apparently, some activists were spreading hate against the surveillance and the curfew. She had trouble understanding what these people were rebelling against. It wasn't like their lives were being controlled.

A zone map provided by the AIA popped up on her screen, with dozens of districts marked red. Zones lawful citizens like herself were to avoid by all means. Luckily, hers wasn't on the list. Otherwise, she'd have to take unpaid leave. Perhaps even risk getting laid off.

She paused the message, a twinge in her chest unsettling her. The last time she'd spoken to her father, truly talked to him, was twelve years ago. Ever since he'd moved away, he just sent messages, and always at the exact same time: 6 a.m. on the dot. His facial features hadn't changed at all, which she took as a good sign. And that gray shirt he wore was surprisingly well-maintained, with sharp iron creases and a tall spread collar that gave him an even more upright look.

She finished listening to his message while activating the AutoDoc and performing her mandatory health check. It was her daily routine since she was five, so she was very much used to it by now. Submitting some blood and urine samples was nothing compared to what she got from the AIA in return. Plus, it was for her own good— she'd already lost a kidney and had half of her liver taken out. She had osteoarthritis, too, which was probably why the machine interpreted last night's injury as exacerbation.

Luckily for her, big, positive changes were promised to happen with the city's expansion. Improvement of lifestyle was guaranteed. The inevitable technological progress promised to save Earth. Thus, suppressing the modified, who were strongly against it, was vital. There was no hope for this Earth with people like Yanko around.

Taisa grabbed the metal container, scooped some Nutri-Powder, mixed it with water, and gulped it down. It tasted horrible and scratched her throat when she swallowed it, but it was the only food available. Only the richest could afford hydroponic produce, but from what she heard, even that tasted like cardboard.

On her way to work, she took the opportunity to read up on the modified. Supposedly, their pupils dilating was their way of getting an impression of a human, learning about their weaknesses. They'd use this to produce a pheromone to inhibit rational thinking in humans and practically seduce them.

Taisa fidgeted in the seat, getting uncomfortable. It was purely psychological and had nothing to do with the rough metal beneath her. She didn't dare think what would have happened if she was in Yanko's company a bit longer.

It was no secret most people in the city were lonely, but she often felt like an outcast. Young people her age were supposed to have lots of friends, yet here she was, about to celebrate her seventeenth birthday in the same VR boutique she worked in, surrounded by online avatars. And while most of these were actually real people in another VR environment, she only ever spent time with bots.

Not having a single friend often weighed on her. If Yanko had gotten even a hint of what hid deep inside her, he probably wouldn't think twice about using it against her. Seducing her.

Sighing, she placed her tracker in her pocket, looking forward to getting off at the next stop. Hyperloop trains weren't the happiest or the cleanest place, but today was particularly bad. It was as though the dregs of society gathered in the same cabin. People's faces were gray and lifeless, their gazes dull.

Out of nowhere, a man tumbled over to her, wheezing. "Get out of here, luv. Run as far as you can. Even the walls have eyes, I tell ya."

She let go of the handle she held onto and slid past the man, heading for the door. Two cyber plods zoomed into the cabin, grabbed the man, and dragged him out. The guy was undoubtedly one of those crazy activists, but she still felt bad for him. He had no chance of seeing the daylight again.

Half terrified, half absentminded, she went on with her day. One hour before closing, she grabbed her designated lunch portion and went outside. Upon making sure there was no sign of the four men from last night, she settled on the stairs. A few gulps in, she lifted her gaze to stare at the night sky. Rumor had it that stars were visible once, from every corner of the Earth. Now, a heavy fog covered the entire planet. She hated not being able to see anything but lights from the skyscrapers.

"How've you been?"

She startled, the rest of the food spilling on her shoes. It was Yanko. Happiness flooded her, the ridiculous joy of seeing him again. She sucked in a breath. The alien pheromones, that's what made her feel this way.

"What are you doing here?" she whispered, her mouth suddenly dry.

He flashed a smile. "Protecting you. That gang is dangerous."

"According to my father, so are you."

He chuckled and sat down next to her. She could feel his breath on her face. His smell was fresh, but also earthy. Kind of like the pine air freshener she'd loved sniffing when she was a kid. Was that the pheromone? If only he wasn't so handsome, she'd tell him to go to hell. Or maybe she'd just tell him to kiss her already.

"Stay away from the modified. They'll sweet-talk you into anything."

She snapped out of it, not believing herself. "Was there anything you needed?" she asked, trying to sound as nonchalant as she could muster.

"What are you doing tomorrow?"

She wouldn't tell him. Not a chance. "It's my day off," she said, then clenched her jaw and closed her food container. She wanted to come up with an excuse and go back inside, but instead, she just sat there, unable to move. It was as though his gaze had pinned her to those stairs.

"You should come see our commune." He leaned in and brushed her cheek. "Think of it as thanking me for rescuing you."

She wasn't even going to consider it. Going anywhere with him was out of the question. "Okay," she said, instantly wanting to slap herself. If she didn't know about the pheromone, she'd have thought her wits had abandoned her. "But only for a few hours."

"Great! I'll pick you up in the morning."

Taisa spent the rest of the night in a daze. Yanko's scent haunted her, seemingly stuck on her skin. She almost used up her entire personal hygiene pack for the month. Showering would have to wait another five days, and even then, she'd only have three minutes of running water available. To get some moral support, she tried calling her father, but as always, her calls were redirected. Unsettled, she paced back and forth, telling herself she wasn't to step one foot outside in the morning.

But when the sun rose in the sky, she threw on her clothes and ran downstairs. Yanko's hovercraft appeared shortly after. From afar, it looked like a bullet. It reflected the light in the strangest way. When it finally landed next to her, she wanted to know how it bypassed the surveillance drones–something she should have probably asked herself the moment she'd first seen it.

The hatch opened, and Yanko waved to her. "Hop in."

She wanted answers first. "How are you staying under the radar?" she blurted.

"Mycelium signals."

"Mice-what?"

He chuckled. In the daylight, he looked much younger. He was probably her age, or maybe a year older. "We're converting bioelectrical impulses from fungi to send false signals to the AI … A" He reached into his pocket and took out a round device the size of his palm. "There are more diodes here than in any of the droids you've ever seen. But the mechanism is very different."

"Huh…" She put her hand on the hovercraft. "I was willing to bet it has something to do with this metal. It's so shiny."

He laughed again. "Those are solar panels, not metal. Photovoltaic cells harvest solar energy, which is converted to electricity. During nighttime, the TEG module takes over, but it took a lot of trial and error to make the conversion process smooth."

"No way." She went around, looking more closely. "Where's the engine?"

"Have you not heard a word I said? There's no engine."

She stared at him. His face didn't twitch, and his body was relaxed. Apparently, he was being serious. She sucked in a breath, convoluted thoughts swirling in her mind. No, this wasn't possible. She got inside and tried finding the ignition key. There was only a single bar in the front, just under the windshield.

"You don't believe me, do you?" He closed the hatch. "I guess I can't blame you. Your entire life is based on lies."

He pressed the bar, and with that, they were off. Completely soundless. His community was a solid hour-and-a-half ride away, during which she dozed off. That seat was incredibly comfortable. She rubbed her eyes, looked through the windshield, and gasped.

Trees were everywhere, almost an entire forest. Instead of skyscrapers, the modified lived in huts. The panels on the rooftops were exactly like those on Yanko's spacecraft. On a nearby hill were dozens of wind turbines and windmills, and two watermills stood on a river bank. It was old Earth tech, and the only reason she was familiar with it was a coloring book she'd had as a child.

A flying structure came into view. It reminded her of a bunch of grapes she'd once seen in a VR room. "What's that?"

"A solar balloon."

She scoffed. "That means nothing to me. What are you using it for?"

"It's filled with air, which expands once it's heated by solar radiation."

Vaguely, she remembered reading an old article about something similar. "Kind of like a hot air balloon?"

"I'm impressed." Yanko flashed a smile. "But unlike hot air balloons, which were used for traveling back in the day, the ones we have have a different purpose. It's a mixed power system that exploits both solar radiation and high-altitude winds."

As soon as the hovercraft landed, Taisa jumped out and took a deep breath, filling her lungs. Outside of the city, the air wasn't thick and sultry, but fresh. The beeping, drilling, and high-frequency whirring of the city didn't exist here. The only sounds were a pleasant murmur and the buzzing of insects. A few women lulled toddlers to sleep in the thick shades, while the others seemed to be resting, caressing their large bellies. Taisa gazed at them, amazed. She'd never seen a pregnant woman before. Finding six of them in the same place was slightly overwhelming.

A group of kids, approximately aged four to six, ran across the field, giggling. Their skin was alabaster white, with a bluish hue. She shielded her eyes from the sun, wanting to take a better look, but they were already gone, zig-zagging between trees and bushes.

"This place is…" She wanted to say "incredible," "amazing," "wonderful," but even all those words combined would've been an understatement.

"Don't tell me you're surprised," Yanko said, a teasing look on his face.

He guided her toward the huts. A fire crackled nearby, with a cauldron hanging above. Mouth-watering smell teased her nostrils, making her stomach grumble. Woven baskets were scattered around, filled with fresh fruit and vegetables. Her jaw dropped, and she licked her lips.

"Go ahead," Yanko said. "Take some."

Not to look greedy, she took only a pear. It was delicious. Sweet and juicy, just like she imagined it would be. With her mouth half full, she took another look at the basket, regretting not taking more, when a woman walked out of the hut, sat on the ground and started sorting the produce. Her gray hair was gathered in a tight bun and her skin was tanned and wrinkled, but her posture was remarkable.

"I know it's not decent to ask, but…" Taisa hesitated. "How old is that woman?"

"She'll be a hundred next week."

Shocked, Taisa took one more look at the woman, who would've been considered a living corpse back in the city. Not to mention she would've been placed into a VR nursing home the moment she passed thirty. "How is she even alive? Is it the alien DNA?"

Yanko shook his head. "Unlike you city folks, the people here are healthy. Even in old age, we rarely get sick."

Taisa was speechless. She needed a moment to gather her thoughts. "And what happens if she does get ill? Or she's in pain? Where do you take her?"

"She stays right here, with us. This is a community in a real sense of the word, something you're not familiar with." He opened his arms. "Look around you. You don't see anyone sitting idle, do you? Even the kids have chores. They plow the land and have fun doing it. Sure beats having to spend day after day cramped in a VR nursery." He winked at her. "We welcome anyone who wishes to join us."

She averted her gaze, feeling the blood rush to her cheeks. A part of her wanted to stay here, but she was well aware it was probably the pheromones making her feel that way. Or was it? Unlike the other day, when the words coming out of her mouth conflicted with what she intended to say, she was now able to think more clearly. Her attention span, which was usually poor, had peaked.

Yanko wrapped his arm around her waist and brought her closer, his lips touching her earlobe. A shiver ran through her. Her breath quickened. She had to lock her knees to continue standing up right.

"We live by one rule," he whispered, "and it's got nothing to do with violence against humans. We treasure the Earth, and it gives us treasures in return."

She dared to look into his eyes. Unlike the other day, his pupils were almost the normal size. "A bit utopian, don't you think?"

"Perhaps. That doesn't change the fact I have everything I need right here."

Taisa hated to admit that what he had in abundance was considered unachievable in the city. Slightly dizzy—partly because of how close he was—she sat on the moist ground and pushed her fingers into the grass. This place was far from what she expected it to be. She always thought the modified were building weapons that could raze the entire city, but this … it was everything a person could hope for. She'd been lied to all her life.

"I don't understand. They said—"

"I know. But it's all an agenda, and a terrible one at that." Yanko sat next to her. "We have no need for weapons, since we're perfectly safe here. Your AI … A can't leave the city."

"Why do you always separate that last A when referring to the AIA?" she asked. "And what do you mean by 'can't leave the city'?"

"I doubt you'd believe me if I told you," Yanko said. "The amount of control and lies has scrambled everyone's brains. The worst part is you're all used to it."

Taisa frowned. "Control is good. The AIA personnel are doing everything in their power for the city to flourish. To keep it safe."

"No, it's doing everything in its power to expand so it can exterminate us. Keeping the humans at bay is just a side effect of its greater plans."

"You keep saying 'it', but these are humans we're talking about. People who work day and night to keep the city safe."

"People?" He laughed. "Do you even know what the AIA stands for?"

"Advanced Infrastructure Author–"

"Try 'Artificial Intelligence Authority'. Or, as we like to call it, a cybernetic tyrant." He paused, his eyes pinned to hers. "You're governed by machines."

Taisa jumped to her feet. "I've never heard such nonsense in my life."

Yanko shook his head. "I knew you couldn't handle the truth. Which is sad, because that means you'll return to the city." He stood up slowly. "And that thing will hunt you down and kill you."

She's had enough. This guy was talking gibberish. She took out her tracker to send a distress signal, but it didn't react.

"There's no network," Yanko said. "We're off the grid."

She shook the device. The only app she could open was the calendar, and it only had a couple of features available. None of the high-end stuff she was used to. She ran to the top of the hill, panicking. "Why is there no signal?"

"I just told you, we're off the grid. Else, the AI would have wiped us off the face of the Earth by now."

"There's no AI!" she yelled. "And you're the ones who are sneaking into the city and causing mayhem."

Yanko climbed the hill. "Causing mayhem? We're saving humans from certain death. The AI has been killing off the low-level workers for a while now, because they 'cost' too much. They're 'deteriorating' too quickly, if you like it. And why pay for something that's not fully functional? Plus, because you're not participating in the expansion, you're considered replaceable. The damn thing will put a droid in your place the moment it kills you."

"I'm not listening to this jibber-jabber," Taisa said, closing her ears.

"C'mon, Taisa, you can't be that stupid!" Yanko grabbed her hand. "The gang that attacked you? They weren't human, it was the AI. You remember how they all looked alike? How all of them 'froze' suddenly?"

She shook him off. "Well ... you did something to them with that device of yours. You–" She couldn't find the right word, so she finally said, "Hypnotized them."

"I told you, the mycelium signals are sending messages to the AI. Kind of like, 'I'm not here' notion. Because you were nearby, the signal reflected to you, too, and the AI assumed you got away somehow."

Taisa has had enough of this. She'd been stupid to come here. She hurried down the slope. "I'm done. If my father knew I was here–"

"Good thing you mentioned him. Let me ask you something. When was the last time you saw your father?"

"What does he have to do with any of this?"

"I'm trying to prove a point," he yelled after her. "Answer me, does he come visit?"

"That's none of your business."

"It's been years since you've last seen him, hasn't it?"

"He's busy. And he lives far away. He sends me a message every morning."

"Always at the same time?"

Taisa stopped short. How could Yanko possibly know this? She had to admit she found her father's preciseness odd, but never truly questioned it.

Yanko cut in front of her. "He looks the same, sounds the same … and never talks about anything else but the modified."

Her heart hammered. Sweat trickled down her spine as her life flashed before her eyes. Indeed, her father never asked her how she was or answered her calls. But for her, this was the norm. As was the life she'd been living all these years. "You're the one who's been filling people's minds with nonsense. The one who's responsible for the upcoming riots. Aren't you?"

"Is it so hard to understand that not everyone is as compliant as you are? Wake up, Taisa! ID scanning, facial recognition, fingerprints, retina scans, body mapping, brain mapping…" He took a deep breath. "And that food you're having? The substance that's making everyone sick? Dying? Why do you think your daily health checks are mandatory? It's because the AI sustains you. But because you're a low-level worker who has another few years to live, this thing sees you as a burden!"

She whimpered. It was all too much to grasp. Even if there was an AI who controlled them all, she couldn't stomach the idea her father was a part of it. "No. No, that can't be true."

Yanko took her hand in his, caressing it gently. "I know it's a lot to take in. The AI that runs your city has done a hell of a job hiding its identity and getting the humans who live there to hate and fear us. But soon, it won't need humans to grow. And it no longer needs you, which is why it sent a squad to terminate you."

She couldn't stomach this. She needed time to process all the information. Call her father. Beg him for an interactive face-to-face chat. Trembling, she lifted her gaze. "I want to go home."

His lips formed a line, and he shook his head. "Of course you do."

The trip back seemed like a lifetime. They rode in absolute silence, Yanko staring through the windshield and she at her trembling fingers. When they reached her tower, he flew off without a word. Distraught, she rushed to her condominium and called her father, but after many failed attempts and redirected calls, she switched off her comms for the day.

The night had never been that long or daunting before. For the first time since her childhood, she was questioning everything she knew. She remembered the crazy man on the Hyperloop train. What had he said to her again?

"Get out of here, luv. Run as far as you can. Even the walls have eyes, I tell ya."

Sleep-deprived, she headed to work the next day. The men and women she rode with in the Hyperloop train looked dead inside. And if she was being honest with herself, so did she.

Shaky, she got off the train and had barely gone a block when a familiar voice called out, "Isn't it a bit late for a girl like you to be out on her own?"

Taisa froze. It was the same gang that had attacked her three nights ago. There were at least ten of them this time. They were all identical. She didn't even bother checking her tracker. If Yanko was right, they weren't human.

They surrounded her, and everything became clear. Yanko was right. Her father was dead. These men were a part of the AI that controlled her city.

And they—it—wanted her dead.

They beat her with their Kiyoga Batons, stabbed her with their tungsten knives, shot her with their laser guns. The weapons appeared in their hands in the blink of an eye and disappeared just as quickly. They dragged her beaten-up body around, kicked her ribs, and stomped on her stomach. She didn't even have the strength to scream, let alone put up a fight. Her life force would soon abandon her.

The next second, they all froze. Horizontal and vertical lines stretched across their bodies, and gentle rustling mixed with the street sounds. Footsteps rang on the tarmac before someone picked her head off the ground and pulled her closer. The warmth of another body against hers comforted her. She gathered what little strength she had left and lifted her gaze.

It was Yanko. He drew out a syringe and whispered, "I'm sorry it had to be this way."

•   •   •

Taisa squinted. Rays of light danced around her, caressing her body. A soft breeze tickled her face, teased her skin under the white cloth that covered her.

A sudden frenzy took over. Her sharpened senses bombarded her with inputs. The smells. The colors. Light casting playful shadows. The steady movement of a woman's chest.

She tried propping herself to her elbows, but the pain in her stomach and ribs stopped her halfway up.

"Careful now," the woman said. "The DNA has set in nicely, but you'll still need some time to heal."

Taisa found this odd. She'd never been treated by a living, breathing person before, only the AutoDoc. "Where am I?"

"In our commune," the woman replied. "You were lucky Yanko got to you in time. You were…" The woman paused, as though choosing her words. "Well, it doesn't matter, does it now? You'll be back on your feet before you know it."

Taisa frowned, trying to remember what happened. Although the images in her mind were blurry, one was certain. The gang—the AI—had attacked her. It had wanted to kill her. As a matter of fact, she remembered being in so much pain, she wondered how it was possible she was still alive.

Then it hit her. "Wait a minute. You said the DNA has set in nicely." Taisa swallowed. Her heart was thumping louder than ever before. It was both satisfying and scary. "The alien DNA?" She was going to faint. "Yanko injected me with it, didn't he?"

The woman looked at her, her pupils dilating. "You would have died otherwise. And you're no good to us dead."

Yanko walked inside, carrying a big basket filled with fresh produce. Even from afar, the smells were distinct, real. Fulfilling. "You need to eat. Your body is still weak from all the synthetic poison the AI fed you with, but this will give you strength."

She stared at him, struggling to process everything that had happened. "You could've just injected me when I was here," she hissed. "Why didn't you?"

A tall silhouette appeared at the hut entrance. "Because we're not monsters."

The individual in front of her had alabaster-white skin with a bluish hue, and patches of fur around the joints. Judging by the size and the bulky build, it was a male. His ears were pointy, and he had eight fingers on each hand. His feet were wide with an elastic webbing between the toes. Just by looking at him, her emotions stirred, like a river that broke the dam, flooding her.

"Wait … when they said the aliens left a DNA strand…"

"They weren't exactly right. But they weren't wrong either. It was easier this way."

"And all those children, they are yours? Are women forced to be intimate with you? How is this any different from what the AI is doing?"

The alien took her hand, and visions of the future in which the planet was thriving ran through her mind. Her breathing steadied. A force inside her shifted. For the first time in her existence, she had a clear vision and an even clearer mission ahead of her.

The pheromones weren't seducing the humans or controlling them, but simply inhibiting their fears and helping them see beyond what they knew to be true. Some chose to be modified on their own free will and some–like her–had trouble letting go of the construct the AI had built for them and returned to the city. The modified prevented the killings, but not because they cared for human life. They needed more people on their side to take down the AI cities and prepare the planet for the alien colonization. It was the only way to save Earth.

The alien sat next to her and clasped her hand. "Treasure the Earth…"

"…and it shall give you treasures in return," Taisa finished the sentence, slightly saddened by the fate of humankind.

It was always about the planet and its resources.

For the AI, it was the people, since they enabled its growth. For the aliens, it was the Earth itself. And the humans? They were just pawns in the clash of titans.

B. K. NTOURIS is an alien whose ship has crashed on Earth when they were but a hatchling, currently living in the UAE because it's just hot enough. They are also an up-and-coming editor and the only extraterrestrial member of the CIEP. When not writing, they enjoy roasting in the sun or watching sci-fi movies and series to have a good laugh.

Twitter: @BKNtouris
Instagram: @b.k.ntouris
Website: bkntouris.wixsite.com

Shadow Masked

AMBER FORBES

THE RUBY FLEET captain's office gleamed. Banners hung on the wall, flanking the official holo-portrait of the queen, and there wasn't a speck of dust anywhere. But the captain was absent. Kara reclined in the guest chair, her face an outward mask of calm, despite the long wait.

The doors swished open. The tardy captain strode in, an ensign at her heels.

"Forgive the wait." Captain Jun slid into her seat and tugged the braided sleeves of her jacket down. "As you can understand, I had to confirm your credentials with HQ." She flicked a glance over Kara, her brown eyes darkening to near black. "A Council aide is a rare sight out here."

Kara inclined her head. "Of course. Ensuring the Empire's security is your main concern. Which is why I am here, in person."

"A Fleet officer could have come." Jun pinched her thin lips.

Kara flicked an imaginary speck of dust off her pants and glanced at the queen's portrait before pinning Jun with a hard stare. "You would question the decisions of Her Majesty's Councillors?"

The ensign stiffened, his near-silent gasp reaching Kara's hearing. Long used to not revealing her augmented senses, she kept her focus on the captain. Captain Jun cleared her throat, her hands clasping and unclasping.

"I thought not," Kara said. She snapped her flexi open, the thin tablet stiffening and holding its size. With a few taps, she accessed the intel that had brought her out to this small lunar city on the fringe of the Ruby Zone. Kara raised a brow at the ensign. "Does he have clearance?"

"Yes." Jun folded her hands. "Ensign Fener will take point on … the intel … you have brought us."

Kara eyed the sandy-haired ensign for a moment longer. He remained steady under her intent gaze, and she nodded. He'd do.

"There have been credible reports that an illegal cyber gang is operating out of this city. I am here to confirm the veracity of this information and to bring confirmation of its erasure back to the Council."

"Cybernetics in my city?" Jun frowned.

"There's evidence that this gang is running a cybernetics chop shop."

"Surely you're mistaken. No one would dare go against the teachings of the temple or Her Majesty's edict."

"This is no rumour," Kara said. "We can't become complacent and allow this to happen. We don't want to repeat history and have it bring us to the edge of extinction." It had been like an arms race to see who could live the longest, but the birth rate had fallen drastically low. It had taken generations to recover..

She knew all too well that some people didn't care about the laws; they'd do whatever they pleased. Even if they killed innocent citizens. She waved her hand, pushing away the thoughts. "Irregardless of the morality of it, the Council is concerned. With advances in technology, cybernetics could become a significant security threat. We're concerned that implants will be developed that can bypass Fleet security checks."

"No Imperial citizen would willingly make themselves an outcast," Jun spit out, but her voice wavered. "Surely they wouldn't risk prison time and the forcible removal of any implants they got." She pressed her fingertips to her brow.

"It appears that the promise of quick and easy power has lured them in and blinded them to the severe consequences." Out of their view, Kara clenched her hand, the nails digging into her palm. The pain grounded her, kept her in the present. How could anyone voluntarily subject themselves to becoming a freak?

Jun whipped her head around to Fener, strands of dark hair from her ponytail flying out. "Why didn't we know about this?"

"We've heard rumblings, but not this. You know how tight-lipped the Undercut gets, and I'd bet my last pay that's where they are." He shook his head.

"The Undercut?" Kara asked.

"It's the market in the old section of the original lunar base. The locals don't like us being here, and that lot are the worst of them."

The captain turned sharp eyes on Kara. "You should assist us in our investigation. After all, your face isn't known to the locals, like ours."

. . .

In sharp contrast to the quiet and orderly atmosphere in the Fleet office, the Undercut hummed with energy. Kara ambled along with the throng of people, all the while assessing the area. Holo-projections advertising everything from clothes to food jumped out from stalls and tiny stores crammed into the scavenged walls of the original lunar base. Credits changed hands and people yelled, each one louder than the next, all fighting to be heard over the cacophony. Kara used her aural implants to filter out the sounds, ready to pick up the minutest mention of cybernetics.

She suppressed the twitch of her lips and slid a glance at Fener, who had dressed in drab, worn clothes to blend in. "Slouch, or even a child could pick you out," Kara murmured to him. He was no Fleet Intel.

Fener's lips turned down and his shoulders tensed. He didn't appear to like her advice, but at least he didn't stick out as much now.

"This way," he snapped and pushed past a crowd of rowdy ship hands and deeper into the myriad of buildings and shops that made up the warren-like structure of the Undercut.

She followed behind, wishing that she didn't need the Fleet's assistance on this job, but if she hadn't notified them and they'd picked up on it, she could have ended up in a world of hurt. Not to mention that they could have blown the sting operation before she'd got it off the ground.

She eyed Fener. He wouldn't have been her first pick for a contact, and she didn't know if she could trust him to safely extract her if this mission went sideways.

He paused at a five-way intersection, head darting back and forth, before impatiently waving her down one of the garbage-strewn paths. Bedraggled awnings and discarded crates with faded ship logos cluttered the way. He stopped at a crick in the path and pointed at a small store with a broken sign flickering sporadically. The narrow alley looked innocuous, but her implants had already highlighted several well-hidden surveillance cameras ahead and she was keeping out of their field of view.

"That's the place," Fener said. "If your intel's right."

"You know this area well."

Fener shrugged a shoulder. "Altercations happen down here all the time. You're on your own from here. They'll tag me as Fleet the second I go any further." He tugged his hood lower and tipped his chin at the alley. "The cameras down there aren't ours. We'd blow your cover before we even started. Signal me if it gets dangerous."

Kara inclined her head in agreement and waited out of sight until Fener had disappeared before she entered the clothing store. A chime rang out in the back. The acrid scent of laundered clothes hung in the air. She squeezed through the racks of coveralls and other work gear jammed into the tiny space. Boots, goggles, breathing masks, and tear-resistant clothes all vied for attention.

A cramped counter was wedged into the back, a curtained entrance behind it. On the back wall, a board displayed various examples of embroidered ship and company logo patches, all neatly pinned up. A surveillance bot in the shape of a cat sat on the counter, digital eyes staring. Out from behind the curtain bustled a middle-aged man, face weathered and wrinkled.

"Welcome, welcome," his voice rasped. "What'd you be needing?"

Kara glanced around the store again, before meeting his smiling eyes. "I need some custom tailoring. A mutual friend—Ray—sent me." The code words she'd spent a week hunting down had better work.

With an eyebrow raised, he stared at her. "We do many custom jobs." He waved at the board of patches. "What kind are you after?"

"The full works."

"Got some ID?" He patted the security cat.

She pulled out the ident card she'd fabricated with the Ruby Fleet's assistance and handed it over. It should hold up to any scrutiny. Hopefully.

"Wait here." He disappeared into the back room with her card.

She let her eyes wander over the store and fidgeted. It's what a normal person would do. What would make someone so desperate to search out this gang?

She pressed her lips tight. The Council wanted this place gone and so did she. She wouldn't allow this cyber gang to prey on the dreams of the people that came here.

The cat drone stared at her the entire time.

The curtain swished open as the storekeeper returned.

"Here." He handed the card back. "Ray will see you now." He reached under the counter, and with a click, a section slid open. "This way."

Maintaining her composure, she followed the shopkeeper into the back room. They entered a small office with another door leading out. From the other side of it, she could hear the whine and clank of machines.

The man didn't hesitate and ushered her through that room to a large workroom.

Wary-eyed workers averted their gazes, but one stood at the wave of a hand and shuffled over to a machine sitting quiet against the back wall. With only gestures, the woman directed Kara to stand before it, facing a small aperture. She pressed buttons and the machine whirred; the aperture shifting rapidly, before spitting out the completed product. She plucked it up and handed it to Kara, then stood woodenly, much like a lifeless automaton.

The translucent silken material slid through Kara's fingers, the fibres imperceptible.

"Press it to your face and don't remove it until you leave the Undercut," the shopkeeper said while shooing her forward. "You'll have some anonymity and it'll throw off any facial recognition scans. Your own mamma wouldn't recognise you."

Kara did as instructed, holding the thin film to her face. The material tightened as it came into contact with her skin, adhering to her as her face tingled.

At the nod of the shopkeeper, the stone-faced woman led her down a narrow corridor that wound and twisted away from the store and deeper into the bowels of the Undercut. Steam hissed and metal bulkheads creaked. Bursts of raucous laughter filtered through air vents, underpinning the silence of her guide. Ensign Fener had better be tracking her movements, or this would be a waste. She couldn't afford to reveal herself.

The tunnel ended in a heavy sealed door. The woman punched in a code on the pad next to the door and cast one long look at Kara before disappearing back up the tunnel, leaving her alone in the dank warmth, waiting.

With a hiss, the door opened to reveal a masked and hooded person.

"Single-use credstick." They pointed at a slot in the wall.

Kara inserted her credit stick and it disappeared into the wall. It looked normal, but the transfer would set off a tracking worm. She'd infect and trace every section the credits were sent.

Past the entrance alcove, they directed her to stand next to a lithe, average-height man. The waiting room, for want of a better word, was surprisingly spotless. Neat and sterile. It appeared to be a well-run and profitable operation. Several other people, faces also distorted, milled about the room. No one's eyes met, and suppressed nerves filled the space.

Most of these people were ordinary citizens of the Empire, not criminals. Just those wanting to get a leg up with work or overcome insecurities. The ones who wanted something extra and lured in by the promises of the gang.

Yet they were risking everything for it.

As the time ticked past, the man beside her bounced on the balls of his feet, a slight hitch on his left side. He caught himself and pressed his hand against his thigh. He darted a look at the entrance, and their eyes met. The man let out a short laugh and rubbed the back of his neck.

"I can't believe I'm here," he whispered, the mask distorting his voice.

"Then maybe you should leave?" Perhaps she could stop one more person from being caught up in this whole operation.

He stilled. "I can't. No. I won't." He made a fist. "I'm going to get a life and do what I want," but he petered off, his voice filled with depression and hopelessness.

"Why do you need to come here for that?" Kara cocked her head.

He licked his lips, eyes darting around before he lowered his voice. "I wanted to be a professional dancer. I'm damned good at dancing." His shoulders dropped. "Was."

"What happened?"

"Dancing doesn't pay the bills, you know? I had to work. There was an accident … I lost my leg." Bitterness laced his words. He shrugged. "The vats regrew it, but the doctors and techs weren't careful enough. This is what I got. I'm just a factory worker, so why would it matter?"

He rubbed his palm against his worn pants. "But for me? I can't leap anymore. My leg won't land right." Beneath the face mask, she could see the ghost of a smile.

He would risk it all for his dream?

"You'd give up your humanity and risk life in prison to … dance?" Kara clenched her hands.

"You're pretty nosy," his voice went flat.

She'd messed up. She needed to get back into her role, and fast. Shrugging and rubbing the back of her neck, she replied, "I'm so sorry. The more nervous I get, the more I can't stop the questions. My friends are always telling me to shut up." She licked her lips.

"I'll stop bothering you," she said as she turned away.

"Wait." The man tipped his head back and sighed. "I get it. Coming here is pretty nerve-wracking."

"Yeah. I talked myself out of it so many times, until, well," Kara waved a hand at herself, "I made it here. I'm still terrified something bad is going to happen."

He hummed in agreement. "I felt the same, but my dream won out. If I can't dance, I have nothing to live for, anyway. So what'd it matter if the Fleet locked me up? Besides, they said it'd be super discreet. No one should find out."

His head drooped. "I know I'm risking a lot, but aren't you here for the same reason?" He waved his hand. "Oh, not to dance, though with your build and grace, you'd be well suited." He clicked his tongue. "But aren't you trying to escape the shitty cards life dealt you?"

Kara shook her head. "I have my reasons."

"Fit in? And you come here?"

"Next," a man dressed much the same as the person who had opened the main door gestured to the hopeful dancer.

He patted her shoulder. "I hope you find what you need."

She watched him disappear behind tightly sealed steel doors. She would have to destroy his dream to complete her mission.

Shortly afterwards, another hooded figure escorted her through the same doors and then into a deep space cargo container that had been retrofitted into a surgical consultation room. It wouldn't have gone amiss in an actual hospital if you ignored the ceiling of struts and bolts.

A beaming man dressed in medical scrubs stood up at her entrance and welcomed her into the room. The two armed guards at his side brought home that this was no ordinary consultation.

"Forgive this uncivilised process, but they'll need to check you before we proceed further." He placed a gown on the patient table and pointed to a shelf next to it. "Once they are done, change into this and leave your items there."

After they scanned her for weapons and—she assumed—spyware, they left her alone to change into the thin gown.

Flashes of memories assailed her. Her vision dimmed. Scenes of her own modifications, being strapped down, changed—turned into a monster. Shattered glass and blood littering the floor.

She snapped back to the present. Body tightly held, suppressing all sounds and movement. She pressed a hand to her chest and the sensation floated away, numbness seeping in.

Time she couldn't waste had slipped by. The gown flapped against her thighs as she bent over the medical terminal. With quick efficiency, she hacked into their medical records. This gang's security protocols had nothing on the military grade ones she was used to.

Her implants were far more illegal than any of the ones she saw in these records. They might be discreet, designed to be hidden from the Fleet and casual onlookers, but none were bio-cybernetic. None were like hers. At least she could breathe easy over one thing.

She shunted the information straight into her brain, recording it with her ocular implants. This wasn't just for the Ruby Fleet, but for her boss as well. The information zipped past as she dug deep. A familiar face leaped out at her, just as her augmented hearing, courtesy of both DNA manipulation and an implant, warned her of the criminals returning. She quickly grabbed the data before erasing her presence in the files.

The door slid open and they found her perched on the edge of the table.

The quasi-doctor pointed at Kara's clothes and one goon rifled through them.

"Can't be too cautious, you know?" The hack sat down on a swivel stool. "We're all in this together. The Fleet will be all over you if you aren't careful and we can't have anything come back to us, now can we?" He smiled pleasantly, but it didn't reach his cold eyes.

The enforcers stood by the door, faces obscured. She made herself glance at them and reminded herself to put on a nervous act. Sometimes, she forgot how. Knowing she could easily take them down, even if they restrained her, leached any fear she might feel from this situation. But she had to remember her cover identity. Anyone else would feel highly vulnerable. Especially if they were a petite female human, like herself. Except … she rubbed the rough fabric of the gown between her fingers. Unpleasant memories nipped at her. She bit her lip and swallowed, widening her eyes, hoping it would work.

"Ahh, sorry about those two," the doctor sighed. "I'm afraid they have to remain. We're risking much to help you. You understand?"

She nodded. Her act must have passed muster. They'd kept their guard down.

"Now, what can we do you for?" The hack held up a battered and scratched flexi.

"I … uh." She licked her lips.

She hated this. Hated being in a gown, in a medical room with impersonal eyes staring on. Hated how it reminded her of things she thought long suppressed. It sent her back to a time she wanted to forget, when she'd been stripped of her humanity and experimented on. Even though she'd escaped, she'd borne the burden of the illegal cybernetics forced on her. Unlike the people here, she hadn't had a choice.

Nor could hers be removed, not without causing her death. She was stuck.

The knowledge that she could break out at any time calmed her. Not that she could leave them as witnesses. If anyone saw her, the very Fleet she was helping would lock her away for life—if she was lucky. If she wasn't, they'd try to remove her augmentations and she'd die on the operating table.

She might be stronger than these gang members, but she had too much to lose by being careless.

"Come, come," said the hack. "Don't be shy. We're here to offer you the world. To give you what the Empire wants to deny you." He leant closer. "You can be the best you. Better than anyone else. And no one will know what you've done."

That wintry smile returned. "Keep in mind, we cannot give you any cybernetics that would be noticeable by others, especially by the Fleet. This is all for your safety, you understand. We wouldn't want you being thrown in prison. But we can perform miracles you wouldn't believe. You can be faster, stronger, have better hearing, better sight. You want to be more flexible, done. More youthful skin? Easy. A tattoo that doubles as a secret code? We've done it."

She clasped her hands. She already had most of those, and to a standard this gang would never attain. But she had to get all the data she could.

"You can?" She made her voice quiver.

"Your dream is our reality." He twirled the flexi and flourished his hand. "Don't let those archaic Imperial laws restrain you. They are only keeping you down and holding you back from your true potential."

He flashed a perfect smile that felt like slime oozing down her back. "Credits are the only limit." He paused and let out a forlorn sigh. "But what are mere credits to your happiness?"

The man was a born charmer and salesman. No wonder the gang had him as the first point of contact; he sucked the victims in, charming and dazzling, until it was too late for them to realise it was all an act.

How many people had these criminals deceived? They didn't care about her. The profit they were set to make from her would be astronomically high. Not to mention the future blackmail potential. That's how she'd discovered this operation in the first place.

She clenched her hand as she suppressed the urge to throttle the thugs right then.

Time to play along. She licked her lips and tucked her hair behind her ear. "I … I want to be a singer. Better than the stars."

"Ahh, you wish for fame?" The doctor grinned, probably because he saw blackmail credit signs zipping by.

"I know I could do it!"

He held his hand to his chin and cocked his head to the side. "Getting a perfect voice is no easy feat. It involves many aspects of your body, from the length and shape of your vocal cords, the shape of your mouth, and even how you use your diaphragm. Depending on what you wish to spend, we may need to modify your hearing for you to identify pitch. The connections you'll need. Well, we might be able to assist with that as well, for an additional price. Hmm, let me see."

He tapped away on the flexi, muttering to himself. "Yes, this is what I estimate it'll come to for all of that work and my superior skills." He rotated the flexi to show her, expanding the screen size with a flick of his wrist. "It'll be more than what's currently on the credstick you provided, I'm sad to say."

"I can pay the extra." She'd cut them if they ever tried to bring a scalpel near her body.

"Well then," he grinned and set the flexi to the side, "let's start the assessment. You do understand that I won't be giving you any implants this time? You'll have to return for the actual procedure once we have prepared the needed cyber implants. It's a delicate process."

She nodded and laid down at his instruction.

It made sense for the first time to be a consultation. They could then track her afterwards and make sure she didn't rat them out and could actually afford to pay. At least, that's what she'd use the time for if she ran this cyber-gang.

But she didn't have time to come back.

She had to get the solid evidence the Fleet needed just as soon as she finished this farce of a consultation. He wouldn't be here for much longer either, unless he was terrible at his job.

As the doctor assessed her, he stopped and stared. Hard eyes met hers. "You already have an implant. Who are you?"

And his time was up.

The enforcers surged forward as the doctor stared at her with hands clenched and nostrils flared.

"Restrain her!" he yelled. "Right now!"

She had to deal with them, and fast. A controlled burst of adrenaline surged through her as her training kicked in.

With one hand braced on the table, she kicked out, sending the hack crashing into the terminal.

The two thugs lunged for her, stun rods out. She flipped off the table and grabbed the stool as she sailed over it. One thug swung at her. The rod hummed with electricity as it whizzed past.

She caught it in the legs of the stool and wrenched it out of his grip. He stumbled past her. Lightning fast, she slammed the rod into the base of his skull. He fell and convulsed on the ground.

Cold air snaked against her exposed flesh as the gown settled against her thighs.

The other thug stared at her. His grip tightened on his stun rod, but he didn't move.

His mistake.

Kara lashed out at him, her foot catching him under the chin. His head snapped back with a crunch. Before his lifeless body hit the ground, she'd spun and tossed the gown off.

Yanking her clothes back on, she checked for her connection to Fener. Static came over the line. Her lips tightened. She turned and stared down at the quasi-doctor and the unconscious thug, her hands hanging limp. Killing didn't get easier, even though she'd known she'd need to take them down before she left this room.

She couldn't afford to leave loose ends.

At least they were already unconscious. They wouldn't feel their death. She knelt and with the flick of her wrist used her enhanced strength to snap their necks. Rifling through their pockets, she found a datafilm. She snagged the paper-thin digital storage device, as it would be very useful.

The door clicked shut behind her and she fried the electronics with the stun rod, sealing it shut. After a fast scan of the corridor to check for potential threats, she set off in the direction away from the waiting room.

Sticking to the shadows, she snuck unseen through the facility. Her augmented hearing warned her of incoming threats, which she avoided with swift reflexes and silent feet. She slipped inside a secured area, the hum of servers surrounding her. Jackpot.

Her fingers made no sound against the holo-screen as she hacked into the gang's systems. It didn't take her long to find what she needed. She even used the datafilm from the quasi-doctor to download the data as it bypassed their security protocols. As an extra precaution, she uploaded a time-delayed virus. This facility would be in chaos even if something happened to her. It never hurt to be cautious.

The information on the datafilm weighed upon her. It listed all the people that had received an implant. She could crush it. Let all these people go. She glanced at the corridor leading to the consultation rooms. They'd wanted these changes, paid for them. Made the choice to risk everything for them. The man she'd met, he just wanted to dance. He wasn't harming anyone. What gave her the right to take it away?

An ache built in her chest. She clutched her fist to her breastbone; the datafilm held firm. She could still shut this operation down without letting the Fleet know the names of all the victims. All it would take is a tiny amount of more pressure…

She squeezed her eyes shut. Those far more powerful than her had already made the decision that there would be no leniency for either the criminals or those caught in their web. She was in no position to fight for others. She released her breath, slipping the datafilm into a secure pocket and allowing a calm mask to sweep over her face again.

It was time to get out of here.

The heavy door to the main waiting room loomed before her. Soon, she'd be in the clear. Time to play it safe and walk out the front door like nothing had happened.

She tried her connection to the Fleet again, but it was still static. Not that she was surprised. The gang most likely had deployed blocking signals for just such a case.

The door opened easily and she stepped back into the bright and airy first room. A few other people were there, including the dancer she'd first met. He must have just left his consultation. She strode towards the entrance, but didn't even make it halfway across the room before it swished open.

A startlingly handsome man—his face perfectly symmetrical—entered, flanked by lithe and dangerous looking bodyguards.

Kara went on the alert, the datafilm burning in her pocket. She kept up her steady steps. She could go around them.

The man smirked as his cold eyes met her own. "You've been a rude guest, if an enterprising one."

She stopped and rapidly assessed the room for another escape option. "Me?" Could she buy time? She had to try.

He flicked a manicured hand at one of his bodyguards. They pulled out a flexi and a section of the wall came to life as a holo-screen lit up.

"You clearly underestimated me," the gang leader said.

A vid of her in the main concourse of the Undercut played on the screen. The leader pointed at Fener.

"You shouldn't have been so arrogant. You think I don't recognise him as a Fleet officer?" He laughed. "I know you're Fleet and undercover. You didn't seriously think that I'd let you escape, now did you?"

Gasps echoed in the room and the other people scattered, getting as far away from her as possible. The sour reek of fear permeated the room.

Kara tried the Fleet comm again, but it was dead. "Let me go. It's the best option for you." She kept her eyes pinned on the leader.

He raised a brow, the smirk back in place. "Oh, are you waiting for someone?" He stepped aside and, as he did, two gang members moved forward, shoving a bound man before them.

"Fener," Kara said. She reached out for him, but aborted her action as the gang members raised their weapons.

"Time for you both to die." The leader raised his hand.

"Wait," Kara snapped. "If I die, a virus will destroy this place. You'll lose everything."

"You expect me to believe that?" he sneered.

"She's a computer expert," Fener blurted out, the whites of his eyes showing. "That's why they sent her here."

"Check it, now," the leader snapped at a gang member, who quickly scurried from the room.

The man turned to Fener with a calculating look. He smirked. "On second thought, I have a better idea." He flicked his fingers at Fener. "Hand over the abort code, or I'll kill this officer."

Fener started, his mouth gaping. "You can't do that!" He struggled against the gang members holding him, his face twisting.

"I can do whatever I want. I hold all the cards." The leader remained impassive.

Fener blanched and sent her a pleading look. "Do it. Tell him the code. It's our only chance." His voice cracked.

Kara knew she could so easily resolve this by showing the leader her augmented body. He'd know she was no Fleet personnel then, but a criminal like him. Yet, she couldn't. The only difference between them was she'd decided to work for the Empire. But to remain useful, she had to prevent others from discovering her upgrades. Her jaw tightened. He'd realise she wasn't bluffing about the virus.

The hopeful clients pressed themselves back against the walls, some with eyes squeezed shut, others paralysed and staring.

The gang member from before dashed into the room and whispered to the leader. His face went dark as he turned on Kara.

"So, you weren't lying." He gestured and a gang member shoved Fener to his knees as another pointed an arbo-tech pistol at the back of his head.

"Hand it over, or he dies. This is your last chance."

"What are you waiting for?" Fener glared at her as he yelled. "Give them the code. He's going to kill me!"

Kara stared down at him before turning to the ringleader. "Go ahead, shoot him."

"What?" Fener jerked back as much as the tight hold on him would allow.

"You think I'm bluffing, little aide?" The leader shook his head. "You really shouldn't be where you're not wanted or needed. Sadly, it's too late for you, just like it is for this officer. I can't have anyone interfering with my business."

He held out his palm. "Now be a good aide and hand over that datafilm and the code to the virus. If you don't, I promise you I'll personally make you suffer a very painful and long death."

Kara stepped back.

"For Eternities' sake, just hand it to him!" Fener screamed. "You're a nobody. You'll never escape from him."

Kara arched her brow. If only he knew. Fener's presence was inconvenient: she couldn't use her abilities while he looked on.

"Ahh, Officer Fener, it appears she wants to see you tortured." The gang leader grabbed the officer's hair and yanked his head back, all while staring her down. "How long will you hold out seeing him slowly flayed alive?"

Kara smirked. "You would kill your own protection? Tsk, you must be desperate."

"What?" Fener's jaw went slack as the ringleader straightened. "What are you talking about?" Fener's eyes darted to the side.

"Fener, did you really think I was here just to eliminate this gang?" She shook her head, drawing out her words while everyone stood transfixed. "I knew from the start you were corrupt. You took bribe money and turned a blind eye. I just didn't think you'd make it this easy to catch you. How much did he pay you to sell me out?"

"I never did that," Fener stuttered, his face flushed. "There's no proof!"

Kara held the datafilm up between two fingers. "What do you think's on this? You're lucky you didn't get those strength implants yet. I can't imagine your medical colleagues in the Fleet would be the nicest if they had to extract implants from a crooked officer."

The ringleader backed up as his eyes flared. He pressed his finger against his ear. "Team two, report … I said, report!" He paled and pointed at Fener. "You're a fool. You led them straight here!"

He spun and dashed for the exit.

Only for a lithe form to rise before him, and with full grace, high-kick him across the throat, before landing with a wobble.

"You think I'm going to let you get away with this?" The amateur dancer pressed one booted foot on the ringleader's chest. "If I have to lose my dream, you can suffer the rest of your life for it."

Noise and commotion filled the room after that as Captain Jun and her team surged into the room. With quick efficiency, they subdued the rest of the cyberware criminals, as well as Fener. Amidst the noise and commotion, Kara shut off the virus she'd uploaded. The Fleet would want to scour the rest of the data for anything else suspicious, plus they'd need it for evidence.

Captain Jun took command of the room, swiftly barking out orders.

"Captain," Fener cried out as an officer cuffed him. "I've been framed. You have to believe me."

"Silence," Jun said to Fener. Her eyes blazed. "You think I didn't have my suspicions already? You fool, you brought this on yourself."

She turned her back on Fener and strode over to Kara. "Are you injured?"

Kara shook her head as she handed the datafilm over to Jun. "This is everything you need to prosecute them, as well as confirm Fener's involvement. Anything else you might need is on their main server."

"Thank you for responding to my request for your assistance. I'm sorry I had to be so cold at the start." Jun tipped her head toward the squawking Fener and the silent ringleader. "I'll deal with both of them. The Council has nothing to worry about."

"Your cooperation will be noted, Captain. I trust you'll ensure the safe removal and fair treatment of everyone that has undergone cybernetic enhancements?" Kara flicked her gaze to the aspiring dancer who was talking to a Fleet officer, hands gesturing and waving, his face animated.

The captain followed the direction of her eyes and her lip curled before she pressed them together. "If that is the Council's wish," Jun muttered. "I should throw the lot in prison to rot for becoming cyber freaks.

Kara clenched her hand. Too easily, the captain could have been giving her the same look. "They are victims preyed upon by this gang, and one of your own. There is no need to make them suffer more. Get them help and leave them be."

The captain stiffened before finally nodding. "That will depend on their level of involvement in this scheme, but I'll take your advice into consideration."

She barked out an order to her team before turning back to Kara. "If I didn't know better, I would have thought you were Fleet Intel. Are you sure I can't convince you to stay on here? We could use someone with your skills."

A caricature of a smile tugged at Kara's lips. Her skills. Her burden and curse. "I will be returning to the Council to provide my report. Take care, Captain Jun."

"Ahh well, it was worth a shot." Jun shook her head and strode over to the ringleader.

Kara observed the scene. The almost cyber freaks lined up with the gang that had exploited them. Fener was still cursing her and everyone else, while the ringleader stared blankly at the wall, ignoring all questions. None of it was her concern anymore. She'd completed her job. The security of this sector had been assured, once more.

Maybe one day she'd find the freedom to live as her true self, but this wasn't it. She slipped into the shadows along the wall and headed to the transport waiting to take her back to the capital and the next mission.

AMBER FORBES accidentally moved from Australia to the USA and became an actual alien. Her writing explores the concepts of society and humanity, but don't worry: they're also full of aliens, spaceships, and questionable choices. When not writing the Rhaslok Chronicles, starting with Shadow Within—more Kara for you—she can be found spoiling her four cats or playing the latest video games.

Website: amberforbes.com/join
Insta/Twitter: @amberaforbes
Amazon: Shadow Within

Street Wise

S. A. SACKINGER

ARIADNE MENDOSA LEFT her firm late for her appointment with her lawyer. The lawsuit her stepbrother had served her had to be dealt with. Her father had left her three million dollars. The rest of the estate went to his second wife. Stephen was claiming dibs on half Ariadne's cash for himself, saying it was meant for siblings.

Her stepbrother, Stephen, didn't need any of the money. He already made twice as much as her father had. So what possible reason did he have for the suit? Like it or not, she was going to have a lousy autumn.

She had just turned down Pacific Ave when she felt a tremendous pain in her back. She tried to look back to see what was there, but it was hard to make out the details. Then she was sliding to the sidewalk, and drowning in the dark.

· · ·

"Hello? Are you alright? Hello?"

Ariadne opened her eyes and looked around. She was sitting on a park bench somewhere near the ocean. People were crowded around her.

"She's coming to. Everybody stand back." A man of about thirty and wearing a hoodie had his arms spread out wide. Everyone moved back about half a step.

"What happened?" Ariadne asked.

"You got hit by something and fell down," a woman with a young teen boy eagerly volunteered.

"I didn't see anything hit you." The hoodie man said. "It looked like you passed out. There's nothing near here that could have fallen."

"But I saw…," the woman insisted.

"Well, I'm alright now," Ariadne concluded.

"We called 911." The boy with the woman looked excited by all of this.

"You shouldn't have," she responded, "I'm leaving now."

"But they'll be here any minute!"

"I'm fine. Goodbye," and she got up and started walking down the street. She didn't hear any siren yet, so she suspected she would be out of range by the time the ambulance arrived. She tried to think about what had happened to her, but her memory failed her. There was nothing there. She knew her name and nothing else. Aimlessly, she turned uphill. The incline was a steep one, and she started running out of breath after about four blocks. Ahead of her was an old woman pushing a grocery cart up the hill. With little air to speak, she just nodded at the old lady and continued on.

After about twelve blocks, Ariadne passed a park and saw a bench made of cement invitingly empty. She could go no further. Sitting on the park bench, she tried again to remember anything about her life before she had fainted. She kicked herself for having fled the ambulance. Surely something serious must have happened if she could remember so little. Looking through her coat pockets, she found a tissue and a restaurant stub, nothing more. She checked her skirt and blouse—no pockets.

"Hello? Uh … Hello?"

Whatever that was, it was coming from inside her brain. It wasn't from *her* mind, though. Crazy people heard voices. Maybe that's why she couldn't remember anything. She was crazy. Now she was glad she hadn't stayed for the ambulance. She would have been locked up! It was better being out and about and able to find out who she was. Someone must recognize her at some point. Something must stand out, discoverable, as she walked the streets.

She looked around. The park was full of different species of trees and a stream with ducks in it. It made the experience tranquil. She decided to stay for a while and collect her wits, such as they were.

· · ·

Ariadne woke up with a blinding headache, walking along an urban street. She stopped two feet from the intersection, and looked around her, eyes scrunched to slits to keep the sun from gouging out more of her brain. It was early morning. Only two other people were visible and they were opening up a storefront and sweeping the sidewalk.

My name is Ariadne. I live at ... no, the memory wasn't coming. *I live in the country of ...* again a blank. *I work at ...* no. Nothing. For all she knew she was a vagrant, one of the masses of homeless.

It occurred to her that her mother would have been appalled at that thought. With a pang she realized she thought of her mother in the past tense. Her mother had died a long time ago, she sensed by the texture of the heartache.

So it wasn't total amnesia, but it wasn't much to go on either.

"Ari! What are you doing sitting in the middle of the street? It's cold out here? You could catch your death!"

"You know me?" Hope welled up in her heart as she looked into the rheumy eyes of an old man in tattered clothes.

"Don't you remember, honey? We met last night. You were walking around half dazed. It's happened again, hasn't it?" The man held out his hand to help her up.

Confused, Ariadne took the man's hand and came to her feet.

"Hello? I reside in your head. I don't remember anything from the past. I know that I'm a symbiote. You must be my host."

"If we head over to the soup kitchen they'll be opening up breakfast in just a few minutes. If we're quiet and don't make no fuss, we'll get to stay in the warm until lunch is over."

Ariadne concentrated on the timbre of the man's voice; it was high but gentle and it held a little quaver, as if he were older than the sixty he looked. He wore ill-fitting clothes that had seen cleaner days. In contrast to her refined ensemble they were out of fashion and well worn, but his shoes looked new and fit him well. He linked arms with her and headed away from where the shopkeepers were opening for the day.

"My name is Jasper. I figure you don't remember that."

"Jasper. Yes, it happened again. I don't remember anything before twenty minutes ago. What's happening to me?" she wailed.

"Now, now, settle down, missy. You're gonna be alright. Here we are at the soup kitchen. Just see how much better you'll feel after a cuppa and some breakfast in your stomach." He led her down the ramp and into a huge auditorium, to the long line of people waiting for their food. "I'll get yer coffee."

The massive coffee urn was situated near where they came in and everyone served themselves the hot, strong drink. They used real cups. Some had chips or were handleless, and most of them had crazy sayings or logos on them. Jasper took the closest two and filled them both with the black brew. He toted them back to a table, old but well maintained and clean. Leaving one coffee as a placeholder, he took the other one to Ariadne.

Their place in line by this time had caught up to the servers. Now they could see why they got to the front so quickly. Today was oatmeal. The people who made the breakfast tried to make it edible by mixing in maple flavoring and sugar, but maple syrup was expensive so they bought the fake stuff. The end result was something that tasted vaguely sweet and smelled like imitation maple syrup and alcohol. Many of the people were passing by the oatmeal and just taking toast.

"Er … he-hello?"

Ariadne heard the sound in her head again. She looked around anyway to see if she was mistaken and she wasn't going schizophrenic. No one was looking at her. She continued to ignore the voice in her head and followed Jasper.

"I'm pretty sure I got this right. Hello?"

"OK, pretty lady, so tell me everything you remember. Anything at all." Jasper came back to the table with his coffee and slid onto the chair across from her.

"It's like you said earlier. I woke up walking along the street where you found me. Nothing from beforehand came through."

"Now, sweetie, plenty came through. You still know how to talk and walk. You know you like coffee and don't hate gruel … pardon me, oatmeal."

Ariadne laughed tentatively. "I'm better off than I thought, I guess."

"What's yur husband's name?"

"I don't…" She paused, then laughed. "I don't have one."

"Good!" Jasper nodded his head. "It's all still in there. We just need to work to get it out."

"Hello! Answer me, dammit!"

Ariadne, startled by the forceful voice in her head, said, "Hello. Who are you?"

Jasper looked at her concerned. "What's this? You know me. I'm Jasper."

But Ariadne was too busy listening to the answer from inside her head to pay attention to Jasper.

"It's about time I broke through. Listen, I'm a symbiont. I'm attached to your brain stem. What happened? Why am I here?"

"I don't know what happened." Ariadne said carefully.

"OK, we'll start there. Finish breakfast and we'll go back to the last place you remember."

"No need, Jasper, we were two steps away from it when you found me." Internally, Ariadne tried thinking at the symbiote instead of speaking outloud, *Did you hear that? I don't remember you either. You must remember something about how you got here! Think.*

"My name is Telvecki. I come from a different world. I can't remember the name of it! I'm guessing, but it seems when I contacted you we wiped each other's memories."

Stop! Wait. I need to get my bearings. Ariadne then switched to speech. "Jasper, can you help me learn my way around here?"

"Sure thing! Let's start by seeing if you have anything on you. Do you have any ID? A wallet maybe?"

She started patting her clothes down, looking for pockets. In her inside coat pocket she located a paper that said, "Inspected by 537" and in the coat's outside right pocket a pair of gloves. Other than that and the high quality of her dress, coat, and gloves, her clothes were bare of information.

"What about a purse? Do you remember a purse?" Jasper said. "Maybe we should go check the first place I found you. See if there's a purse found in that area."

"OK. I'm done with breakfast. We can go now." They finished off their coffee and put their trays away. The day had gained warmth and brightness while they were in the soup kitchen. As they left, Jasper turned a different way from what she remembered. She realized it was because he remembered her from yesterday. A different place she didn't remember being lost in.

"This is where I first saw you." It was a twenty minute walk from the kitchen. The area looked like it was part of a university. Large lawns surrounded brick and ivy buildings and well used walkways. Despite the liberal placement of signs, they found it hard to locate the administrative wing. Finally finding the right building, they entered to find a name board with office designations. Frustration got the better of them, so they knocked on doors until they found someone in. The middle-aged gentleman who answered the seventh door amicably gave directions to the real admin building. Then, finding out they were looking for the lost and found—which was next to the nurse's office of all places—he directed them again.

"We're looking for my purse," said Ariadne. "I don't suppose it showed up in your lost and found?"

"I'll go look. May I see your ID?" the woman at the counter said.

"I suppose it'd be in the purse, hun." Jasper said with a kind smile.

"Oh! Of course. What does it look like?"

"I'm afraid I don't remember which one I was using today." Ariadne tried looking apologetic.

The woman seemed startled by that, but without saying anything more she headed into the back.

"Will you ever speak with me?"

I don't know what to say. Ariadne thought her reply.

"Tell me how you feel about having a symbiote."

Right now?

"If not now, then when?"

A short time later, the woman came back, her hands empty. "I'm sorry, ma'am, but we don't have any purses back there, not a one."

"Well, thank you for trying," Jasper said, and they turned to go.

Ariadne was surprised at how let down she felt. Up until now, she hadn't been too worried about getting back to normal, but just a little thought impressed upon her just how cut off from the world she was. No ID meant no access to food, transportation, or lodging. All the basic necessities were tied to who you were. While money was looked upon by the general public as the thing that separated the successful from the great unwashed, proof of identity was just as important. It didn't help that she had no way to get an ID either.

It was approaching lunchtime so they broke off from expanding the search and headed back toward the center of town.

"You have been so kind to me, Jasper! How can I ever repay you?"

"Repay me? What for? I didn't have anything planned for today anyway. You saved me from getting all teary eyed over my own situation. But for the grace of god and all that..." Jasper looked surprised.

"Well, I guess I'll look for someone who I can help. How's that as payment?" Ariadne said.

"The more of us that can help, the less stress there will be and the less people there will be to kick us to the curb."

"Is this true?" Telvecki asked. *"Do your people enact violence upon homeless people?"*

Humans tend to act with violence at times, but 'kick us to the curb' is a figure of speech. It doesn't necessarily mean actual violence.

"What is violence that is not actual violence?"

Ariadne had to think about that for a minute. *Talking hate or instilling fear are two ways to perpetrate violence without actual violence.*

The soup kitchen was much fuller than it had been for breakfast. All the tables were packed and they had to wait until someone left before getting their food and sitting down. It turned out that a single seat came open when they got up to the service counter, so Jasper graciously gave it to Ariadne. As she set her tray down, she noticed that on one side there was a young man who spent his time passing his fingers back and forth in front of his face. The man on the other side of him was trying to get him to eat.

"Come on Greg. You need to eat something. Don't make me tie your hands down!" He said in frustration.

As soon as she sat down, the symbiote started talking. *"I've been checking your body over to see if there was anything troubling you. I found that your liver was struggling so I fixed it. You also need to eat better! The food you put into your stomach today had very little nutritional content."*

"I can't control what I eat!" Ariadne whispered, "not until I get off the streets, anyway."

"Oh. I'm sorry. I didn't know you were force fed."

"I'm not, but if all you get to eat is food that isn't good for you, you eat that."

"That's logical."

"What was that? What did you say?" the man next to her demanded. He was looking at Ariadne with a frown and his jaw jutting out. "There ain't nothin' wrong with the food. You can just leave here if you feel that way, prissy pants!"

"I wasn't talking to you. I'm sorry you overheard."

"Yeah, I bet you are! I eat here every day. It keeps me alive. If you can do better I suggest you get out of here." The man took another bite and looked over at her again. "I said git!"

Ariadne hadn't finished her lunch, but she thought better of staying. Quickly, she picked up her tray and took it to the washer. "Can you point me to your bathrooms?" she asked the washer as they accepted her tray and began scraping the food into a trash bin. The man mutely pointed to the left and she followed his direction.

She was startled to see the condition of the women's bathroom. All the toilets were mostly clogged up. The painted areas were marred with graffiti scratched into it. Something wet lay on the floor in three of the four stalls and wet paper towels and toilet paper had been stuffed in two of the sinks.

Ariadne sighed. Picking the cleanest toilet she could find, she used it, then left.

. . .

"We should join together: become one. Maybe then our memories will be restored."

Where are you? Are you really on my back?

"Not anymore. My spine now rests with yours and I have healed your back. Physically we are one now. Let our minds merge."

Why are you doing this? We've seen the evidence that we aren't compatible. Trying to merge may be the reason we have no memory of the last few days.

"That couldn't be. If I were incompatible with you, I would not have been able to merge with your spine. Physically, we are simpatico."

We both need to find out why we are losing memory first.

"We're losing memory because we're not fully integrated."

How do I know that you won't take over my mind?

"That is a guarantee I can't make. I do not know that my mind won't be subsumed by yours."

Ariadne thought about the merge. It wasn't so much the action she feared, it was that the symbiote may have already influenced her into it. If she went against her gut feeling, though, she could be going against her real wants. In the future she would have to reverse any decision she thought of, for fear it was merely the influence of the alien. Who knew when the alien would reverse his tactic? If she mind melded, she could see his thoughts and be sure of what his true feelings were. Even if that didn't happen, putting her trust in his plan sounded less crazy than the convolutions inherent in reverse psychology.

Then what do we do to finish the merge? She finally asked the symbiont.

"Think of a song you know. I will sing a harmony. Gradually we should be able to make the harmony and the song beautiful. Then we will sing in unison, then harmony, and continue in that manner until we switch without lag. Then we will be together."

Tentatively at first, then with more assurance, she mentally sang the old tune, *It's only a shanty in old shanty town…*

Ariadne sat on a bench in a small garden. The rustling of the flowers made a susurrus of harmony all on its own. Into the night she sat there, her eyes closed but not asleep, listening to the inner song. Gradually, she could feel the song become a part of her. Switching from harmony to descant to melody became more intuitive, less forced. Finally they brought the song to a stop.

"We remember so little! The ride through the atmosphere … the walk down Commerce Street … the contact and the days of wandering, no day remembered in full. Will it always be that way for us?" Ariadne/Telvecki asked.

We're remembering more and more as the day goes on. Give it a chance!

Ariadne/Telvecki stood up and headed for the wharf. This early in the day most of the people there were students from a local art college. They welcomed people from all walks of life to come watch the waves and get their picture drawn. Today was no different. A young woman came over to Ariadne/Telvecki and asked them to pose. They said yes.

Later that day they were climbing the hill to see about getting a sensible pair of shoes from a local church. Jasper had told them about the community closet. They hoped to find a better coat as well. On the way, they passed an old woman pushing a shopping cart uphill and failing miserably.

"May I help?" they asked the old woman.

"Why, aren't you sweet! If you push and I pull we could manage quite nicely. By the way, my name is Mrs. Lavinia Platt. I thought I had enough spunk to make it up the hill but I ran out of steam at Court D." Mrs. Platt looked to be in her seventies and with the shopping cart, she also carried an open umbrella. It wasn't raining. "You're new here."

"I suppose so," Ariadne/Telvecki said, "I've been here for about two days now."

"Well if there's anything I can help you with, let me know. Speaking of which, do you have an address?"

"Well, no," they responded.

"Then we must go over to Guadalupe House and get you set up with one."

"Is it a shelter?"

"No. It's run by the Catholics. You can shower there if you get to it at the right time, and sometimes they have dinner that you can come to. That's all they have. You got to be willing to let them pray over you, but they don't force you to pray with them like some of the other charity places do."

"Thank you, Mrs. Platt." Ariadne/Telvecki smiled at the woman and put their shoulder to the shopping cart.

. . .

The next day, Ariadne woke up at first not remembering anything except her first name and being connected with a symbiote. *Are you still there, Telvecki?*

"*I'm here. We've melded minds. I remember that. I remember there were thousands of us. Now there is you and me. We came from space. Do you remember?*"

Ariadne thought about it for a minute. *Yes. You healed me.*

"*I did. Where are we now?*"

I don't know. We don't remember this street or what happened yesterday except for with us. Ariadne/Telvecki looked around a bit more. They were standing in front of a dress shop, with a pile of clothes spread out by the door. The entrance was recessed, giving shelter of a sort. They gathered up the clothes and stepped out into the light. It was just barely morning. *Something about food. We know a place to go for breakfast. Well, I knew a place. We remember knowing. We don't remember the place.*

"*A soup kitchen,*" Ariadne/Telvecki responded. "*Somebody brought us to that place.*"

We need to write this stuff down! Ariadne/Telvecki checked the pockets of their new/second hand coat to see if the had any way to do that. They found a pencil in their coat pocket but no paper came to light. Looking around the area, they noticed paper taped to a phone pole. One side was a plea about a lost dog, but the other side was blank. Using the pole as a hard surface, they folded the paper and wrote, "Slept in the doorway of a clothing store at Pacific and 27th." Then she stuffed the paper and pencil in her coat pocket.

"Jasper!" they cried with sudden inspiration, "The name of the man who brought us to the breakfast place was Jasper."

"That's right! We remember now. It's nice to remember his name, but it doesn't help us to get there. We're hungry."

It'll come, Ariadne thought, *We remembered the man's name, we'll remember the place as easily as trying to recall something that happened yesterday. Well it did happen yesterday!* They started to laugh. *We* **remembered**. *That's the biggest thing.*

By noon they had begun remembering what the streets looked like near the soup kitchen, and had lucked upon one of those streets. They made it inside with time to spare and happily joined the lunch line. Turning away from the service with a loaded tray, they searched for Jasper. They found him seated at a table far from the food line. "Jasper!" Ariadne called out.

The man looked up, startled, then waved at them to come join him.

"Well, fancy meeting you here!" Jasper smiled. "Looks like you're starting to remember stuff."

"Nothing past yesterday," Ariadne/Telvecki said. "Just yesterday. I remember meeting Mrs. Platt and where the soup kitchen is, and of course you."

"Do you remember the university?"

"Yes, and the lack of a purse. Mrs. Platt took us … me to a charity store where they gave me a warmer coat and a pair of sneakers." The depressing part of that particular little journey was that no one there knew how to get a state ID without a birth certificate or passport.

"What about before yesterday? Still nothing?" Jasper peered earnestly into Ariadne/Telvecki's eyes.

"Nothing."

"Why don't we flag down a cop and talk to them."

The police department had its headquarters on F Street, just next to the courthouse. The architecture didn't match anything around it, making it look somewhat out of place. Once inside, the scenery improved. People strode through the wood paneled lobby with purpose, disappearing into the bowels of the station. With nothing to lose, they followed a woman to a window with a police officer behind it.

"How may I help you?" the officer asked when they got to the window.

"This here little lady has lost her memory."

"We can let you look at some photos. I take it, you've already gone to the emergency room at the hospital?"

"No, not yet," Ariadne/Telvecki answered. "We aren't in an emergency or anything."

"I'd think you would have an urgent need to find out what happened to you," the police officer leaned on the shelf in front of the window and gave Ariadne a pensive look. "Give it a try. Check with them first. Next!"

Having been dismissed, the two friends shuffled away from the window and headed out of the station.

"St. Joe's emergency room is just up the hill," Jasper said, rubbing his nose.

"I suppose I'm ready to go to the hospital." They said to Jasper.

"You sure you want to do this?" Jasper grabbed the last of his bread and stuck it in his pocket for later. "Hospitals give me the willies. All that sick around—it's sure to make you get something."

"Your hospitals make you sick?" Telvecki inquired.

Not usually. Germs and diseases like viruses are in higher concentration in hospitals. It stands to reason they can be passed from one person to another.

"Wouldn't it be safer if the hospital were segmented so that only those people who have viruses enter the area where viruses are being treated?"

Ariadne/Telvecki stopped walking and closed their eyes to pay better attention to what they were thinking. *Are you remembering your world from before?*

The alien symbiote laughed. *"You know, I think I am!"*

"Ariadne? Is something wrong?" Jasper tugged on her sleeve.

That got their attention and they opened their eyes.

"I was just remembering something." Ariadne/Telvecki patted Jasper on the arm. "We can get going again."

The hospital was a very short walk from the soup kitchen. Once there, Ariadne/Telvecki understood what Jasper meant about hospital waiting rooms. The room was large enough to hold seventy or eighty people and it was packed. A line formed at a window near the entrance and from there people got into a less formal line waiting for seats to clear. It took them an hour to make it through that gamut and to find a seat.

"Jasper, you have been wonderful to come see me through this, but I can't ask you to wait until they call me. As you said, it may take hours."

"There is some snifflers in here. You better watch out."

"I'll be fine." They patted Jasper's hand.

"Ok," he said uncertainly, "I'm gonna go then."

"I'll see you at the soup kitchen tomorrow."

"Tomorrow is Sunday. There is no kitchen on Sunday." Jasper peered around the room. "I'll come get you after you see the doctor. OK?"

"It may take half the night!" they exclaimed.

"Oh. That's right." Jasper chewed on his lip for a minute. "I'll get some bread at the pantry. We can share. Meet me at the kitchen doors tomorrow early. I have to be gone from the parking lot by the time church starts at eight a.m."

"I'll try. Take care, Jasper." Ariadne/Telvecki called after the man who had helped her so much. *I wonder what makes him tick? He was clearly uncomfortable in here.*

"We could help him become more comfortable." Telvecki said.

What? What do you mean?

"I can heal others just as I healed you. All you need to do is touch them."

Ariadne shuddered. *You would force their minds to change!*

"Of course. But only where their thoughts are troubled."

Would they be conscious of the alteration?

"No. Not unless you tell them." Telvecki sounded puzzled.

That's out of the question! Ariadne shuddered at the thought.

Six hours later, they were still waiting to be seen. It didn't look like they'd be seen any time soon, either. Security guards came in about once an hour and chased off those people who were trying to sleep in the chairs. They decided to cut their losses and leave.

They grabbed their coat and fled the hospital.

That night they slept in a vacant lot under a tree.

In the morning, Ariadne got up as the sun was coming up. She assumed that it was before eight o'clock so she headed over to the church parking lot. This was where a number of poverty level services were performed during the week, but on the weekend it was all parking for the church.

Ariadne/Telvecki saw Jasper waiting along the wall that was part of the soup kitchen. "Good morning, Jasper. I hope you've not been waiting too long."

"Just got here myself. So how did it go at the emergency room?"

"It looks like I'm on my own. The waiting got the better of me after about six hours. I think I want to try remembering on my own for a while. How can I work to get money when I have no idea what I can do?"

"You can always panhandle."

"What's that?"

"You go out on the street and ask people for money," Jasper explained with a knitted brow. "It's best to make up a story that will make them sympathetic toward you. Tell them you need the money for something practical, like a meal or a bus ticket for work."

"People really do that?"Ariadne/Telvecki asked.

"They sure do. But you gotta watch out. People can get really mad that you're doing this. I've heard of panhandlers being beat up, cut; they get cursed at all the time."

Ariadne frowned. "Why?"

"People think panhandlers are all drug addicts or scammers. It's true a lot of them are! Still, some aren't. They're people who have dropped out or been kicked out of the mainstream. It can be because they're druggies or because they're crazy. It can be because something happened, like they lost their home in a tornado or their job because of downsizing. Teenagers who get pregnant get tossed out of their parent's house, or kids who can't tolerate living with their parents run away. I know a guy who refuses to go inside a building! He's a vet who got caught in a building that was blown up."

"How did you end up on the street?"

"When I was seventeen I started going out with a sixteen year old. Her parents weren't happy about that so when I turned eighteen they pulled me up to the courts and got me on statutory rape. I went to prison for a year, and they put me on the registry…"

"What's the registry?"

"It's a list of all sex offenders; those who rape and murder as well as those who date a minor. When I apply for work or to rent a place, they do a background check. Up comes my name on the registry and out I go onto the streets. I haven't been able to find constant work my entire life. The longest I ever worked in one place was three years and that was because I lied about who I was."

Just then, a car pulled into the parking lot. Jasper pulled his hands from his pockets and pushed away from the building. "It's time to go. Church is coming. Let's go up to H Street to the coffee shop. I'll treat you to a cuppa."

"*So much sorrow on your planet!*" Telvecki sounded in awe of Earth. "*How can you stand it?*"

After the vociferous session in the parking lot, Jasper had gone silent. The hill on the way to H Street was steep and he needed to conserve breath.

We have no choice. There is suffering in any walk of life.

"*You remember this?*" Telvecki asked, testing again their union.

I don't really. I just feel it. Ariadne duplicated Telvecki's earlier awe.

"*What if we could help the people like Jasper helped us?*" The symbiote asked. "*Remember how I healed the harm I did to your back? We can do that to other people.*"

But most of the other people are here by circumstance. You heard Jasper.

Telvecki sighed. "*If they have something physically wrong, sure we can heal it.*" Telvecki was silent for a moment. "*What if we asked them what they would want?*"

• • •

The bower that surrounded them was meant to keep private the fumbling and groping of a lover's tryst. It did just as well to cut the wind that chilled in the predawn hour. It had been two months since they'd sat here the first time and melded with Telvecki. They were one now. They pulled the knit cap down over their eyes to shade them from the street lamp glare and drifted back to sleep.

The nightmare again woke Ariadne/Telvecki in the light of day. They stayed motionless in the hope that this time, it wouldn't melt away from awareness. It did, though, leaving them with the frustrating feeling that they were supposed to be doing something important and they were terribly late getting to it.

Sighing, they folded, then rolled their blankets tight and stuffed them into their knapsack. They had another hour before the soup kitchen would open for breakfast. With luck, they'd be able to wash their hair and brush their teeth before the women's room got too filthy to abide.

Shouldering their knapsack, Ariadne/Telvecki began the long trek up the hill. It would have been nice to sleep closer to the soup kitchen, but the cops patrolled diligently in that neighborhood.

On Wilkers Street, they met Mrs. Platt struggling to pull her shopping cart up the steep grade. Ariadne/Telvecki tossed their knapsack on top of the odds and ends in the cart and pushed it from behind. Mrs. Platt gave them a gap-toothed grin.

"Why, aren't you the handiest thing to have around!"

"How's your leg doing today, Mrs. Platt?"

"That's the funniest thing." The old woman tugged at her dress to try to reposition the bra underneath. "Ever since we had our talk the other day, it hasn't given me a lick of trouble." Mrs. Platt frowned for a moment. "I hope this won't affect my Social Security check. They won't take me off it 'cause of this, do ya think?"

Ariadne/Telvecki smiled. The woman was in her seventies. It was doubtful the checks she received were due to the leg. "I don't know, Mrs. Platt. I'm not too bright about that sort of thing."

"You're heading to the soup kitchen, aren't you, Ariadne?" It wasn't really a question. Mrs. Platt was well aware of the woman's routine. "Now you be careful there. Them men that comes into those places are up to no good."

"It is monitored, Mrs. Platt. They wouldn't try anything in there. They could get banned, you know."

"Oh, child, you are just too trusting. The people that run that place, they don't got a clue about what goes on in there." They'd reached the turnoff where Mrs. Platt went her own way. Touching her fingers to Ariadne/Telvecki's shoulder, she peered nearsightedly at their face. "How you got on the street is none of my business, but you ain't like the others, child. If those greasy men suck you up and spit you out, the world will be less by it."

"I will be careful. I promise you, Mrs. Platt."

"See that you do." The old woman frowned mightily, then headed off toward home.

. . .

When Ariadne/Telvecki reached the soup kitchen, there was already a respectable crowd milling around the door. Picking their way through the dried loogies and cigarette butts they leaned their back to the brick side of the building.

"What's up, momma?" The man was probably a courier for one of the local drug dealers, to judge from the clothes. The kitchen was easy pickings for them because the free hot meals attracted people who would rather spend money on drugs than on nourishment. Dealers stayed well away from this all too public area. Instead, they sent in users whose job it was to locate prospects and steer them toward the "drug store." Often they would have the shills take the money as well. That way, the transaction became unclear, harder to attest to. Police hated that. Ariadne/Telvecki just ignored him and soon he turned away.

A few minutes before seven, the double doors opened and the smell of hot coffee wafted out on the warm air. Ariadne/Telvecki filed in with the rest of those waiting and quickly went to the women's room. The doors had been taken off all the stalls again. Some of the women must have been using the bathroom as a place to get their fix. Taking off the doors was the administrative response. It didn't stop people from shooting up, it just made everyone feel humiliated.

They went quickly to the sinks and turned on the tap. The hot water didn't turn on: another humiliation that didn't work because the people using the sinks for washing–clothes and body–had so few choices. Using one of their mittens, they quickly soaped themself down and rinsed off. The cold water gave them chill bumps but if they washed fast enough, it wasn't too bad. Once done, they shrugged back into their coat and went to get morning breakfast.

The line wasn't long this morning. Perhaps it was the oatmeal and bread served up again as a "nutritious meal" that kept them away today. Tomorrow, they would eat first because it was scrambled eggs and bread day.

They said hello to the man who, two months ago, had refused to enter a building. He sat next to them on their left. On their right sat Greg. He was listening intently to a young man, his hands resting on the table. When they finished eating and bussed their dishes, they left eagerly into the bright morning, looking for others who needed their wishes granted.

S. A. SACKINGER is a retired computer geek with strong ties to both the right and left coast US. She has a self-published novel now out of print and several short stories published in CovWord magazine and the e-magazine, Signals; she also has entries in two anthologies: Into the Unknown and Beyond Human. For fun she reads sci fi books and plays D&D, or buries herself under her cats.

Augusta Block

A. RAVEN DEMORY

I

On the first day of my fifth year indoors, I woke up to the drone of a vacuum capsule whizzing through its tube en route to my pod. A slender column of mid-afternoon daylight stung my eyes from between drawn blackout curtains as I sat upright, but the first thing that came into focus was the stark-white blaze of a screen.

It glowed like a memory of the sun, casting my whole world in dawn—a horizon of crumpled sheets behind me, a metropolis of empty ramen cups at the far edge of the pod, and a platoon of ants on maneuvers on the desk at the foot of my bed. My employee awards hung above the hatch that led into the corridor, beside the vacuum tube that transported my food, my water, and whatever had just arrived in the receptacle beside me.

As my terminal booted up, my gaze fell on the capsule's contents: a cupcake. Blue icing. A flickering LED candle. Sprinkles.

A note was pinned to the capsule's inner wall.

"Happy five years, Cath!" I read aloud, still half-asleep. "Orinoco Multimedia, LLC (NYSE: NOCO) just wouldn't be the same without you. Your request for time off has been denied. Go Eagles!"

The terminal finished its boot cycle with a triumphant sting of music while the capsule rumbled back through the tube. I entered my password, then my access code, then my fingerprint, then a blood sample. A retinal scan unlocked my work profile, and I started my shift, basking in the terminal screen's light with dilated pupils.

The cupcake was stale.

Winston, my canine digital assistant, wagged his tail at the sight of me from the corner of the terminal window. He was a scruffy mutt of nondescript pedigree, with a personality that had adapted to me over the last two hundred sixty weeks. I smiled and pet him with my cursor.

A hundred messages appeared across a dozen chat windows, but I ignored them. They didn't pay me to read about middle management's golf outings or fellate the executives' egos during quarterlies. I didn't give half a damn about stock prices unless it was layoff season and even then I only tracked them from a distance. They sure as hell didn't pay me for my attitude.

They paid me to save Truth (capital T) itself from a rising tide of self-replicating lies, or at least that's how the recruiter framed it before I started negotiating my rate. Afterward, he just called it data entry.

I fed Winston with a scroll of the mouse wheel. A shower of heart emojis floated across the screen.

A photo album appeared in the terminal window, sourced from the Newsfeed. Thirty-six photos of an idyllic Parisian vacation cascaded across the screen, posted less than a minute ago by a woman named Gina Kovacs. She was in her early thirties with two toddlers–a boy and a girl–and a baby on the way. Black dye covered prematurely graying roots, and her fiance stood behind her, smiling in every photo as they traversed the Louvre, the Arc de Triomphe, and the Canal Saint-Martin with two unruly children in tow. They embraced on the corner of Beaumarchais and Pas-de-Mule under fading dusk. They enjoyed a window seat at Epicure, framed in floral drapes and three-stemmed candelabras. Notre Dame rose above them with twenty-eight statues in a row and eighty-four panels in its rosette. Everything checked out.

Behind her crooked smile was the subtle worry that something would go wrong. After seeing countless faces like hers, there was no mistaking it. Tugging at the edges of happiness were fears of money, of isolation, of impermanence. Nowhere was it more obvious than in the final picture–a family portrait overlooking the Eiffel Tower, taken by a bystander I could tell Gina deeply mistrusted.

This was the telltale sign. The Eiffel Tower only has three horizontal crossbeams on its second tier.

With a single keystroke, Gina's Parisian vacation was erased from existence. The account was disabled and dismantled before the next album loaded, and while I finished off the cupcake a server farm in Chicago scoured itself in search of derivative works and reposts.

I smiled, content. Winston emitted another heart.

Domingo Wong, my supervisor, appeared in a chat window as a stylized avatar, wearing an Eagles jersey and pantomiming typed dialog.

"Good save, Cath," the message read. "Ready for the big game next week?"

"A day in the life," I typed in response, tossing the cupcake wrapper into the pile with the ramen cups and empty soda bottles. I'd already processed five more accounts. Three real ones. Two glaring fakes, both generated by the same Cambodian content farm and posted to the same content feed. "I don't really follow football. Eagles make the cut?"

"You bet they did. Stay off 95 on Sunday if you don't like traffic. I've added a point to your store account for that catch of yours. It's cleared for any food or non-alcoholic beverages you'd like. That one made it through three passes before it reached you. No one else on the team could've caught that."

"No one else on the team has my eyes. Sometimes you just need human intuition."

The avatar mimicked Munch's *The Scream*. "You sure you aren't a cyber? Superhuman? You're an endless archive of random trivia with an eye for detail like I've never seen before. Anatomy, geography, astronomy. You've probably rooted out a whole internet's worth of bots and secured *millions* in assets."

I rolled my eyes. "I bet. Just got a head for it."

"Don't ever leave. I don't know what I'd do without you. This is your higher calling, you know."

I ignored that message's vaguely-threatening aura. It wasn't like I had anywhere to go anyway. It had been exactly five years since I'd last left the apartment and I'd begun to wonder if I still knew how to talk to people that weren't hiding behind cartoon avatars, or how my *higher calling* fit into Orinoco's bottom line. Exactly one thousand eight hundred twenty-six days had passed since I'd seen the sun, but the alternative was far less pleasant.

The thin line of skin that had been exposed to the gap in my curtains had already begun to blister. A few minutes in open daylight would be enough to peel the flesh from my bones and blind me. My pod was a prison, and my warden was solar urticaria, a condition with inscrutable origins and no cure.

Three accounts later, I replied: "If you think you need me now, just wait until the sixth-gen AIs release. In six months you'll need ten of me."

Domingo's avatar frowned. It stroked Winston lovingly. "This about the time off request?"

I hesitated. I would've been lying if I said it wasn't, but despite Dom's praises I knew that I was constantly one mistake away from collecting unemployment. The line down my cheek itched at the thought.

Fifty more accounts followed: three fitness influencers with incorrect anatomy, four news outlets with commentary on nonexistent crimes, a comedian performing to a faceless audience, a handful of documentaries about impossible Saharan wildlife, and countless vacations to imaginary places.

Flagged, deleted, banned, scrubbed. There was a time when spotting AI-generated content was easy, but the telltale details got smaller every day. They were better at posting than humans were— the false worlds they created seemed better than reality itself.

I fought the urge to scratch. "One of these days I'm going to have to see a doctor, Dom."

"Doctor?" Domingo's avatar donned a doctor's coat and stethoscope. "That puts me in a really tough position, Cath. I know you know what I mean. Why don't you use that extra point to get some healthier food? Maybe some vitamins? You've got to take care of yourself."

I stared into the webcam perched above the screen. I almost forgot he could see me. He had a twenty-four-seven livestream of my entire world, from the blackout curtains to the front hatch. He could hear the neighbors arguing before I could. He could detect my pulse increasing before I noticed it and send calming messages through the terminal.

Who was I to question him?

"I'll order some vitamin D or something," I typed, mindful of my wording. "Got to keep my edge, right? I'm beginning to wonder if there aren't any real people out there at all."

The avatar pointed a pair of finger guns at me, winking. "That's the right headspace, Cath. Stay in that headspace. There's a new program releasing soon and I want you to be ready for it."

"Ten-four, Dom. Sorry."

"When year-end reviews come around, I won't forget today."

This was a rare instance when I wished I didn't solely communicate by typing. Depending on the tone, what Domingo said there and what he meant could be vastly different things. My interpretation settled on the vaguely threatening one.

The avatar took a neutral pose in the corner of my screen and the next image appeared, bordered in red to denote that the automated system had already flagged it as a likely forgery. I took a sip from yesterday's crumpled-up protein shake as the photostream loaded with its credentials.

The account belonged to a man named Nick Flux, contained two photos, one video, and had just been created. Metadata pinned its location to the country's geographic centerpoint, a common tactic of people who preferred anonymity.

The first post was a photo of a man's hand, holding a brick with the imprint of a defunct brickyard.

AUGUSTA BLOCK, it read, all caps. It was rough and weathered, not unlike several thousand other bricks that served as locational clues. This one pinned Flux's posts to the East Coast. Georgia or South Carolina, maybe Florida, though I'd even seen a few here in Pennsylvania.

They were practically artifacts, once found in brick roads across the South but now in diaspora across the country for various repair projects—a detail I immediately noted.

The second photo made my blood turn to ice. It showed a young woman, hogtied to a chair, restrained in a dimly-lit room draped in white tarpaulins. Unkempt red hair was secured with a rubber band. Her nose was broken, and several scabbed-over cuts on her left temple suggested she had been restrained for several days. She wore loose-fitting pajamas with a sarcastic message on the chest—a generic brand from any number of department stores.

The facial recognition software couldn't place her, but everything else checked out.

Winston whimpered, no doubt reading my bloodless expression. I realized I had been frozen, eyes locked with this woman for at least a minute while my quota timer ticked onward. I couldn't bear to look any longer, but my fear of what would come next kept me there.

The third post was a video. The hand and its brick. The woman and her restraints. It appeared to me as a set of disjointed images, each more horrifying than the one that came before it. I looked away, dizzy and overcome, but the sound—the *sound*—was inescapable.

This was real. I had never been so sure of anything.

At last, the camera faltered, tipping backwards on an unsteady tripod. A blood-spattered popcorn ceiling came into view, then an arched window with a brickwork sill, snow clinging to the edges. The architecture, the row houses across the street caught in a half-glimpse, the smokestacks billowing on the horizon.

This happened here in Philadelphia.

II

"Thank you for dialing 911, America's premier emergency hotline since 1968. Please stand by while a representative processes your deposit."

I cursed under my breath while the emergency line played smooth jazz. I calmed Winston down with some treats.

"Insufficient funds," the operator droned. "Please verify your payment method."

The operator read back my card number and I cursed a second time, louder, wondering how many Orinoco smile points it took to make a dollar. I peered through the slit in the curtains, catching the brick building at the end of my street in a half-glimpse before the light burned my hand. Dazzled, I flagged the post and typed a message to Domingo.

"Dom, call someone. That post is real. That account killed someone. 17th and Wallace."

"You sure?" Dom's avatar appeared wearing sunglasses and a Hawaiian shirt, petting Winston. "Cath, you know criminal reports are a whole escalation process. Our team just handles verification. If you want me to escalate, I need you to be a thousand percent sure, OK?"

"Just look at it!" I lost my composure as another wave of panic smothered me. "It's real, Dom. Someone's dead and I can't afford the deposit on a 911 call."

Dom's avatar shrugged. "I'd need to escalate it to see your photo reel. Privacy policy. I'm sorry, Cath, but I'm in a really awkward position."

"Fucking escalate it, then!"

Dom typed for several minutes, then erased, then typed again. Thought bubbles drifted from his head. At length, a wall of text filled the chat box. "I know you want to go above and beyond here. I know that's how you operate, but this is past the bounds of your role. Facial scans didn't bring up anyone in our records, and three layers of verification flagged it as a likely forgery. If you want to investigate on your own time that's your prerogative, but I'm going to have to push this one through. I'll delete it from my end. Please watch your tone."

Just before the post and its account were deleted and scrubbed from the internet altogether, a fourth entry appeared. It resumed where the former posts had left off, from a phone fastened to a toppled tripod. A motionless hand, bloody and pallid, lay palm-up on a white tarp that covered a threadbare carpet strewn with bills that confirmed the address.

Motionless, then not.

The hand twitched. The fingers flexed. A strand of red hair moved at the edge. Then, as if dragged, they slid out of view. The video continued, thirty more minutes of an empty room.

I knew what I had to do. With my arm already red and blistering, I counted the seconds until dusk would fall.

III

The moment the sun disappeared, I crawled into my pod's half-height shower. Icy water stung my face, and the red-haired woman's scream was in the hiss of a faucet that wouldn't warm up.

Grey scum sloughed off me and down the drain.

I saw myself briefly in the mirror. The afternoon sunlight had left its mark—scabbed-over scar in a perfectly-straight, diagonal line across my face. I was hunched from countless hours at my workstation, and skin that had once been merely pale had taken on a sickly, greenish hue.

I dressed in a threadbare tracksuit I'd been using as pajamas and shoes that hadn't been put on in years. Winston cried as I prepared to leave, a flutter of broken hearts encircling him. I pet him with the terminal mouse, remembering, if only briefly, that he was only a computer-simulated facsimile of a dog—a program that constantly rewrote itself to appeal to my altruism.

"Sorry, boy," I reassured. "I've just got to go check on something. I'll be back before you know it."

It was the truth. When I left the pod, my terminal would power down and Winston's program would freeze. When I returned, he would power back on and shower me with as much affection as could be given from the corner of a screen. He would never age. He was fully sapient and likely smarter than me, and someone could argue that he was *better* than the real thing. His only limitation was that he was trapped. His composition prevented him from leaving that corner of his screen, the same way mine kept me indoors.

I had always thought the way he preyed on my sentiment and desire to nurture was deceptive and insidious. Now, I was reminded of how ancient wolves once domesticated themselves by becoming gentle and cute.

Were they that different? Had artificial intelligence begun to domesticate itself or had we become starving wolves, lurking in the forest just beyond the light of AI's campfire?

I realized then that maybe I had become too cynical. With a tinge of guilt and a pang of fear at the thought of the outside world, I transferred him to my phone. His tail wagged from the second screen.

I fed him another treat with my last available point and wrapped a blanket around my shoulders.

"There you go, boy. We'll make a good team, you and me."

IV

The door hissed open and the silence of my building gave way to the static drone of a dead city. Purple sky appeared in slots and cracks between buildings overhead and I emerged, one shoulder constantly pinned to the nearest wall. Late-winter chill hung in the air, with a dampness that soaked through my threadbare clothes. The only warmth I could find radiated from my phone, overheating with Winston's simulation. The blanket I had draped over my shoulders billowed as I crept, fighting to straighten my neck and stooping spine —an ache that only seemed to get worse.

No one was outside. I was thankful for this, partially because I had forgotten how to act around people, and partially because I knew my appearance would probably terrify them. Hunched and creeping, making my way around the block to the tram stop, with sickly pale skin and a cascade of overgrown and oily hair, I must've looked like a bloodthirsty vampire.

My head swam with images of the red-haired woman. My heart thumped with the steady rhythm of a brick, repeatedly crushing her skull. I tried to shake it out of me, but soon I gave up. It had broken me, but in a way I was glad. If it hadn't, I wouldn't be out here trying to save her.

I rounded a corner and nearly collided with a running child. He must've only been four, running from a mother who was chasing twenty paces behind him.

He stopped, dumbfounded. I watched as the surprise gave way to fear. He took a half-step backwards and I almost laughed. This kid hadn't existed the last time I walked down this street. His phone hung limply in his hand, blinking with morphing, undulating images of bespoke cartoon characters.

Winston barked. The kid's mother caught up, stared straight into my soul, and they passed without a word or another glance, a song with no melody playing as the next cartoon began.

I waited alone for the tram. As the sky began to drizzle, an empty tram screeched into view and stopped in front of me, plastered in advertisements for movies no one had made. The door opened and the driver locked eyes with me. I took an uneasy step inside and pressed my phone up to the scanner. It declined.

"Points or exact change," the driver said. "Read the sign."

Her words caught me off guard. I hadn't heard a human voice in longer than I could remember. There was a tinge of horror in the way she looked at me.

"Uh, uhhhh," I wasn't sure what I was trying to say, but that wasn't it. "Mmmh."

The tram clattered off and around the bend, into the tunnel by the cemetery.

"Act normal, dammit," I chastised myself under my breath. "Normal. You're just out for a walk. Out walking your dog like a normal goddamn person."

By the time I made it to the subway stop the rain had already drenched the blanket and my shoes were soaked through. I jumped the turnstile while the attendant looked on as the northbound train screeched onto the platform thirty feet beneath Broad Street. Each car was packed shoulder-to-shoulder with faces that looked like my own. The sight of the crowd made my heart race. The brick continued to strike. The red-haired woman's face lost distinction, blurring into shaggy clods of meat and loose skin.

The absurdity sank in.

I had spent the last five years living in the same city as these people. Were it not for my disease, we could have been conversing or commiserating. If we weren't all hermetically sealed in living coffins, we could have been friends. The red-haired woman—I could have recognized her face from somewhere. The cashier at the bodega, the writer at the cafe on the way to work, the teacher at the school halfway to the cafe in another life, she could have been anyone. Someone.

In this life, though, she was a ghost, plucked from oblivion for just long enough to cry out before being plunged back under. She was an object—a *commodity*, a product of an algorithm that, in part at least, refused to admit she existed. And I was still a part of that oblivion, unsure whether she was alive or dead.

Nick Flux cackled over it all. I let the train pass, then jumped down onto the tracks.

To the dismay of the attendant rising behind me, I escaped into the pitch-black maintenance shaft and ran with an ever-quickening pace into the abyss beneath the city. Gravel crunched beneath my shoes over the far-off scream of wheels on iron. Winston's screen glowed in my hand along with distant headlight beams, reflected off concrete pillars as far as I could see into the blackness.

Winston reassured me with the closest expression a dog can make to a smile. He had been the result of a decade-long study on employee morale, remote work and isolation. Everyone who worked at Orinoco had one because of their well-documented ability to retain employees and improve productivity. He had been something to care for, and given that I was taking him across town I began to realize just how effective it had been. He had kept my focus sharp while I rooted out the ghosts of a dead internet. His mere presence had interrupted numerous anxious spirals, breakdowns, and attempts on my own life. Now, he was helping me navigate the real world—a place so foreign to me that the mere thought of it made me panic.

Winston had a higher calling, and he rose to the occasion. With me, it was far messier.

Halfway down the Broad Street tunnel, I was struck by a question I had never thought to ask.

What use did Orinoco have for me? What use did a trillion-dollar multinational technology corporation have for a diseased shut-in with an eye for details? In an age where sitcoms were created with algorithms and played on livefeeds, where art was created by the consensus of machines, where human interaction was all but replaced by sycophant chatbots, why did it matter that Gina Kovacs had never actually seen Paris?

Why did it matter that studios had created celebrities that didn't exist?

Why did it matter that Nick Flux had kidnapped a woman and tortured her for the world to see?

V

Nick Flux's house loomed at the end of a three-hour walk, one of a hundred identical row houses lit in the smolder of the approaching dawn. I recognized every detail from the video that hadn't ceased its playback in my head—the subtle sag of the upper-story windows, the misaligned fifth slat of the blinds, the chipped blue paint on the sill. I approached it without caution, crossing the asphalt and stepping up over the cracked sidewalk to the front stoop. Yellow light flickered from a streetlamp, which seemed to grow a halo as the rain and fog descended. Aside from the white noise of the rain and the distant grind of a tram, everything was still and silent.

A brick was missing from the stoop. Bits of mortar clung to the socket where it had once lain, wreathing the words *AUGUSTA BLOCK* in grime.

I pried a second brick loose and carried it for self-defense, opening the front door and heading inside. I crept up the stairs, the faint sounds of a sitcom drifting through thin walls.

"Sure, Jake. I would love to go out to the store with you today."

"Great, Colleen. That makes me very happy. What would you like to buy at the store with me today?"

"Well, I would like some celery, some onions, some ground beef and a pumpkin to carve."

A laugh track swelled and a sense of loneliness like I had never felt in the last five years fell over me. Was it like this for everyone, or was I completely broken? Was everyone so numb, so desperate for engagement and so isolated from each other that the mere sound of an automated voice gave them solace?

While the knowledge that this terrifying feeling was universal would help ease my fears, I hoped that it wasn't. No one should feel the way I do. Whatever made me like this, if it made others feel the same, it should have never existed.

I arrived on the third floor at the door to Nick Flux's apartment and reached for the knob. The sitcom was coming from behind it, from a TV turned up too loud.

I looked at Winston. He sat down, head cocked to one side.

"I know, boy," I whispered. "I know."

The apartment was empty. There was no trace of the woman from the video. There was no chair. There were no restraints. There were no tarps, no brick. I frantically searched the cabinets—the shelves, the drawers, the closets, the fridge—and threw my hands up in a combination of disgust, horror and fear.

Where was she?

"Colleen, I seem to have gotten my head stuck in this pumpkin."

"Let me get my pocket knife out, Jake. I'll make a Jake-o'-lantern."

Winston paced on-screen as I made another pass. Behind the sofa, under the mattress, under the oven, behind the air vents. I checked and checked and checked. Nothing. No one. Old mail verified the address. The final video verified the window and the carpet. She had been here, but any trace of her or her fate had been completely erased.

Where was she? Could Dom have been right all along?

My mind swam with questions that had no answers. Then, I saw it.

A scuff mark. An inch-wide patch of tape residue by the windowsill where Flux had taped his plastic sheeting. It was a single clue—one that no one else would have noticed—but that single blot on the wall all but proved that I hadn't imagined it.

Thump-thump! The noise sent me ducking for the nearest hiding place. It rang out again, like someone had struck something with a sledgehammer, and as I hid behind an overturned table, I watched

Winston point toward the wall that separated Flux's apartment from his neighbor's.

A third time. *Thump-thump!* Something had struck the wall and begun to rustle, flopping dully behind it. The sound continued as a low rumble as I rose and approached it. Roaches scattered in the kitchen and I put my ear up to the wall. The blanket slid down my shoulders and fell to the floor.

Footsteps, but not walking. Speech, but not words. My mind struggled to resolve it, deep enough in the uncanny valley that no light reached. After listening for what felt like hours, a single, familiar sound emerged.

Nick Flux's rasping, cackling laughter.

I raised the brick, then tiptoed back out into the hallway. I could hear the sound, louder now above the sitcom's staccato bursts of synthetic applause. Thumping, then shuffling footsteps, then laughter. I listened again, raising the brick to protect myself against some unseen foe.

The woman's scream rang out and set me shivering. Almost reflexively, I tried to open the door to the next apartment. Locked. Frantic, I pushed at it, but it wouldn't budge. I kicked it and punched and screamed and cursed, smashing the knob with the brick until it gave way and snapped off its pin.

The building fell silent, leaving me to wonder whether the cacophony had been a hallucination. The ache in my neck returned and I tried in vain to straighten it before I peered inside.

Winston turned my flashlight on and I rewarded him with a pat on the head.

"Thanks, who's a good boy?" I tried and failed to lighten my own mood.

The door creaked open, revealing a pitch-black apartment and something rolling in the darkness beyond the hall. Readouts and machinery blinked from the walls. As the door swung, the shaft of light from the hallway widened. It shone inside and lit it and its occupants dimly. In an instant, the motion stopped. I recoiled.

Countless half-formed silhouettes sat, crouched in corners and lying splayed across the floors, furniture and counters in a tangle of almost-human forms. Some were naked, some clothed. Some were old and withered, others young and lithe. Eyeless and featureless faces, all had frozen, pointing toward me in the cold chiaroscuro of the hallway light. None of the figures even ventured to quiver or breathe, as if they were waiting for my own input to determine their response. One in particular, a blurred, twisted form with red hair, squirmed as if it was trying to mirror my own movement. A half-formed mouth spat in cackling rhythm.

I ran. Across the hallway, down the stairs, out the front door and onto the sidewalk, but I didn't stop there. Winston barked and snarled. There were thumps and alarms and squelches, but I couldn't place their sources. There were screams, but I couldn't tell whether they were my own.

A block passed, then another and another, until my heart felt like it was about to explode. Sunlight scalded my skin. I collapsed, panting and wheezing, and my phone slipped from my grasp. Glass crackled against concrete. My back arched in agony.

As I reached out for my phone, Winston whimpered from the splintered and flickering screen, then was gone.

A man appeared, standing above me. He was tall and well-groomed, with a cropped beard and a birthmark across his cheek. He wore an Eagles sweatshirt, and even in my delirium I could tell who it was. Even here and now, he resembled his avatar.

"Dom?" I murmured, the first fully formed word I'd said to another human being in five years. My skin flushed red.

"Cath," he began in a baritone that shook me. "I can't say I didn't warn you not to pursue this. I knew you were perceptive but I never expected you to be this persistent."

"Who are they?" I gasped, choking down tears that had begun to flow. "What are they?"

Dom responded sternly. "Remember what you said about the new 6th-gen AIs? It's so much worse than you know. That line between real and fake isn't getting thinner. It's *blurring*. I've added ten points to your account to cover bus fare back to your apartment. Take that day off, too. See a doctor. You look like hell."

"Is that it?" My voice grew louder as I became reacquainted with it. Blisters spread across my hands. "What are you using me for? What do you need me for? Everything's synthetic out here. None of it's real! What am I doing here? What's my goddamn higher calling?"

Dom's eyes grew cold and deep, as if saying anything at all was subterfuge against a corporate machine far beyond his control—as if it was his own miniscule act of rebellion. He held a brick that read *AUGUSTA BLOCK*.

"You train them," he said. "You make them real. You will never speak of this again."

A. RAVEN DEMORY is a Florida-based author who writes suspenseful cyberpunk fiction and cosmic horror. Her novel Keter Hardware is slated for publication late this year by Orchid's Lantern. During her free time, Raven enjoys autocross, gardening, and making music under the name Saint Serene.

Insta/Twitter: @saint_serene

Filling the Void

BRIANA BEDORE

Entry 1:

I used to pull on my habsuit and drift through the blown-out corridors of the station, out in the ruins beyond our bubble of temporary life support. Dr. Skaya scolded me every time she caught me doing it, and now it's forbidden. She says she can't imagine why I would want to go back to being a washed-up almost-corpse, as if my behavior is a self-destructive expression.

It's not. It's self-soothing. Like the way babies are calmed by the sound of running water, or being swaddled, anything that reminds them of being in the womb. I don't remember the accident that destroyed the station, or anything at all, really. Only the nothing-place of being a speck of debris in a wreckage that had nothing to do with me. I am homesick for it. Finding my memories might quell that pang, as Dr. Skaya says it will, but there couldn't possibly be enough of a life to drown it out. It's too big, too patient.

She gave me this journal—one of her spares—as a consolation prize. "You want to touch emptiness? Try the blank page." I feel exposed, not adrift. It's different.

She feeds me bits of information like I'm a starvation patient. First the feeding tube, then fattening morsels, then coaxing me to have more and more of an appetite on my own. We started with "The company records say your name is Vess Liddel," and that I've survived a horrific accident, then something about Vess's job as a research assistant, and onto trying to get me to remember my relationships or my taste in music. I don't even remember being called Vess.

When I told Dr. Skaya that, she asked, "Do you feel like someone else?"

I don't feel like anyone at all, but I think that would upset her, so I say, "Nothing really fits yet," and it makes her smile.

Dr. Skaya has a wonderful smile, but it isn't tender. It's proud, self-satisfied. All of her expressions are selfish; she makes them for herself and forgets that anyone is looking. Her hair is blonde (silver at the temples) and her complexion is waxy (especially pale around the eyes) as if her skin is sun-faded silk. Most of the time, she looks like she's trying to pick up a lost thought that is more important than the conversation you're trying to have with her.

Skaya usually has a little ceramic stick in her mouth or poised between her fingers. When she puts it between pursed lips and inhales, the end shimmers with starry blue light. I asked her what it was, and she said it was a medical device prescribed to people with stress problems. It signals the brain to release certain chemicals that offset cortisol. I asked her if it helped, and she said that she'd developed too much resistance to it. It's a compulsion now, a shadow of something that mattered.

She calls me "Vessouchka," a diminutive.

Every day I answer her questions and sit still under her instruments until she shifts to her real work and shoos me from her lab office warren. Now that I can't go drifting, it's hard to find distractions in the derelict station. I guess writing helps.

Sometimes I go through the cabins of the dead crew, looking for clues about myself or the accident, but it's boring at best and voyeuristic at worst. There aren't many cabins in the safe sector, mostly closets housing research equipment. They were studying the asteroid belt nearby, taking mining shuttles back and forth to find interesting rocks. Ores, or fossils, or something weirder. They didn't leave behind much more than meticulously sorted gravel.

And anyway, even if I found evidence of other people's relationships with this Vess person, would I recognize them? Maybe I'm hoping to find anything as familiar as the nothing-place, anything tangible, but I don't expect to. When I catch glimpses of my little feminine body in the glassy patched windows or the gossamer plastic sheets I think "What is that?" not even, "Oh, a stranger," or, "I don't like the way I look," but "What is THAT?"

Dr. Skaya says that everyone feels that way about themselves at one point or another, says that when her roots started to turn gray and she noticed that she sighed like her mother, she felt like she was wearing someone else's body. Said her husband was better about embracing change, but that we all get confused and disgusted by ourselves eventually.

I study my cropped, peachy hair and tiny, crooked nose like I'm studying Dr. Skaya's equipment. I struggle to read my own face as much as I struggle to read the fuzzy, marbled images of brain scans she puts on the projector, trying to read the dead people's memories in the slow-motion dance of neurons.

They make sense to Dr. Skaya.

Everything makes sense to Dr. Skaya.

She says I'm lucky the insurance company sent her here, that *she* found me. A clean-up crew wouldn't have noticed I was still alive. "What providence to be an amnesiac rescued by a memory scientist," and all that.

My memories are only a charitable pastime for her, of course. Dr. Elisavet Skaya is, I'm assured, one of the premier forensic memory scientists in the Intersystem Group. A "scalper." Corporations, governments, judicial systems, et cetera, hire her to sift through dead brains and extract testimonies from them. She was sent here to look for coherent perspectives of the accident. They're paying her to find someone to blame.

She has a hard time with my memories because I'm still alive, and we can't "pop the hood" and find where the problem is. Dr. Skaya worries that there's deeper damage, and frets that I'll have an aneurysm over lunch or something. I wear a crown of wires and nodes to bed so she can make scans of my subconscious activity while I sleep, and she says the notebook can be a tool to capture my conscious thoughts.

"Once they're on paper, words don't move while you're not looking," she says. "Memory is biased, mutable, but an honest journal is like bottling a moment in time. As magical as anything I do in the lab."

She promised she wouldn't read it (please don't), but thinks that if I write enough, maybe I'll open the door to myself by accident.

The only doors I know are airlocks, and all they do is hold the Nothing out.

Entry 2:

Writing writing writing loops of letters this chair is uncomfortable writing writing.

I get to watch her work today. I'm trying to be unobtrusive.

The lab was already set up by the time Dr. Skaya found me, and it's too cramped for two people. She repurposed the old research sector of the station for her own use, building a tangled nest of wires, screens, and projectors all cocooned by walls of plasticky tarpaulin that could (theoretically) keep the vacuum of space from pushing its way in. Most of the old furniture got pushed out of an airlock, and now it hovers outside the ruined station with the rest of the debris. When you look out a window, space looks like an untidy room.

There's a series of zippered doors that separate the different chambers: Dr. Skaya's work area, the "evidence morgue" (the old geological sample locker with the most nuanced climate control, bodies stored where rocks used to go, just as inert and fragile), and another room for the huge, humming servers (this is where all the brain scans and memory reels are stored, and is—I think—the real morgue).

Dr. Skaya has been showing me old pictures and songs again today. I can't stand how lonely these exercises make me feel. It feels like a lover asking me if I remember the significance of an obscure date, or the first thing we ate together, and admitting that I have no clue is like admitting some condemnable apathy. Dr. Skaya says, "It's nothing, Vessouschka," every time, and I know somehow she's consoling herself over another failure, not me.

I asked her to show me more of her real work to change the subject. "How do you know where to look for the right memory?"

She brushed me off and tried to get me to do some sort of word association, so I pressed her to show me the way the preserved brain is loaded into the projector.

She rubbed her face and said, "Vessouschka, you are such an empty cup, all you ever have are questions and grabbing hands."

That seemed kind of unfair, but she gave in. It's easy to get her talking. I'm all the company she has, if you don't count the pods full of bodies.

"Unless you have extremely specific parameters," she explained, "finding the right memory is like searching through the communal sewage system for a drop of water you drank a week ago. Most scalpers are looking for the mind's final memories, which makes it a little simpler. Skimming the first few off the top isn't so bad."

She tells me how reading memories isn't like plugging into a movie stored in the brain. At first, you get a single labyrinthian snapshot of data—some of it is encoded imagery from the occipital and lots of noise describing smells. Background chatter of physiological processes. Dr. Skaya is more interested in the chemical semaphore of emotional spikes: pain is like a red flare in a dark sky, easily mistaken for the embery smoke of anger.

It's all tangled with itself and every other memory that touches it, as delicate and interconnected as a knot of microscopic spider silk. If you dive too far into one memory, it might unspool into other memories that the experience triggered. The fear of death in the last moments turns into the fear of abandonment as a child: transmuted, diluted, and useless, and you have to start over.

Notes about the scanner:

1. Pull the brain from the patient's body, open it like a book.

2. Prop it open, splayed, on the tray like you're saving your page and you'll be back later. (It looks like a clam's dream of a butterfly.)

3. Place it onto the scanner's open drawer, then insert the nodes at these folds. (See sketch!)

4. Push in the scanner drawer. (Make sure it has enough fluid to populate the tank first.)

5. Lock the tank.

6. Tank automatically fills with the greenish amberish conduction liquid, and the nodes light up the brain until it shimmers with electric, involuntary thought.

The machine collects the data from the artificially-stimulated brain matter in unfathomably dense streams of code. It cascades over the displays so fast that I can't catch the individual symbols, it's just threads of unraveling light.

Dr. Skaya puts her hands on her hips and squints, reading and sifting, waiting for whatever it is she's looking for. Then, she'll catch something and punch in a complicated sequence that tells the machine what to isolate. It prints her selected information on a long, rubbery ribbon of re-printable film. She layers that with other tapes of film and feeds the whole stack into another machine (a blocky thing like a bloated microscope). Finally, she settles onto her creaking stool and leans into the brightly lit viewfinder.

Today, she patted the stool and let me have a turn. The padding on the viewfinder is worn thin, molded to Dr. Skaya's features, and the backlight is so bright that I didn't think my eyes would ever adjust. As I blinked back tears, the layered, magnified code showed up in a little window, and I could scroll left and right through the long tape by turning a wheel on the side of the machine. It's unintelligible: overlapping numbers, letters, dashes.

"You see, Vessouschka," Dr. Skaya said, leaning over me, "the fingerprints of life's last moments. This series of symbols describes the smell of iron in the air." She put her hand over mine to turn the wheel and more symbols rolled past. I could feel her breasts pressed against my shoulder. "Here, someone else's face close enough to bite your cheek, followed by an unconnected memory of an intimate moment." Her breath on my ear.

I untangled myself from her and the viewfinder, tripping and muttering something about how it's interesting but I don't understand it, then retreated to my corner and my notebook. She likes it when I use the notebook. She leaves me alone if I'm writing.

She laughed at me and reclaimed her stool, turning back to the light pouring out of the viewfinder. The skin around her eyes is bleached from it.

· · ·

Later, she had a whole memory knit together onto a data card and loaded the rendering into the projector. The images were a little uncanny, sometimes too stiff or too fluid. We watched through the eyes of someone walking out of the undamaged station cafeteria and into a lounge to light up a stresstick. At the right-hand corner of the screen, a dark circle flickered, like a burn mark.

I pointed at it, the shadow of my arm cutting through the picture. "What's that?"

Dr. Skaya waggled her stresstick and talked over the soundless memory.

"Those marks show up in renderings when the patient uses a stresstick," she said.

In the memory, alarm lights flashed and bits of space junk shredded through the room.

"There was a fad for a while," she continued, "where people would use them to tag memories for scalpers - the chemical spike makes them easier to find. But people overdo it."

The screen scrambled in a feverish mess of shrapnel and strobing lights, then went dark.

"Take me for instance." Dr. Skaya pulled the data card out of the projector, stresstick held in the corner of her mouth. "I use this every day. My brain would be an endless ashtray for some poor bastard to dig through. They'd never know what was important to me."

I think she does that on purpose. Everything she does is deliberate. Though by that same token, if everything seems deliberate, then maybe nothing is?

What *is* important to Dr. Skaya?

Entry 3:

I've started having dreams. I dream of the station, mostly. When it was whole.

(Dr. Skaya is very pleased, she says it's the most encouraging sign my mind is healing. She wants me to absorb every bit I can, but I don't want to fill the open parts of me with more noise. I don't want to fill myself with dark, scribbling thoughts the way I fill this notebook. I don't want to get used up like this.)

When the dreams started, I didn't recognize the station without the ragged holes in the walls and static of suspended junk. In the dreams, I perform different tasks or walk through the halls, looking at everything from different heights, looking through different pairs of eyes. Skaya says it's normal to have dreams where you're not always "you."

I don't recognize "me" in any of it. My sense of self slides through these mundane events, frictionless and slick and alien in the pristine station. It's like looking through dead people's cabins.

I've started to notice a through-line, though. There is a man I always see. Sometimes I just pass him in the hall, sometimes he stops by where I'm working. Once I ate a meal with him. He has dark brown skin and shiny black hair that falls in waves past his ears - sometimes it looks nice, and sometimes it looks like he needs a haircut. His eyes crinkle when he smiles.

I see other people repeat in my dreams, too. The security officer whose uniform has grown too tight, the intern with their glasses tied to their head, the maintenance worker who whistles. But only the man with dark hair—a geologist, I think—comes every night.

I asked Dr. Skaya: if I'm dreaming in the third person, why don't I see Vess's face every night? Dr. Skaya says that dreams and memories are imperfect that way. Maybe I have seen myself and I just don't recognize me. According to her expert opinion, my mind isn't good at the "I Am" function: the Ego aspect that decides what the Self is, and what it isn't.

I disagree, but I keep it to myself.

I am not ... I know I am not ... I am not notebook scribbles.

Entry 4:

I'm putting off sleep as long as I can, trying to match Dr. Skaya's odd hours.

She was up watching memory reels in the lab. I watched too, in secret, peeking around the corner.

The projector showed sepia smears of workers unloading hunks of rock from one of the station shuttles. Some of them were taking a break, standing off to one side using stressticks. The audio was watery, but I heard someone mention that he's been trying to quit the sticks now that he's not nearly so stressed.

Someone else said, "You eggheads. Man, how does this not stress you out? One mishap and we're just a can of kipper snacks."

"Life back home was harder, I guess."

Dr. Skaya didn't take notes.

Now, I can hear her talking to herself in her cabin.

. . .

Dreamed of a man with dark hands making dinner to eat alone, watching the clock.

Entry 5:

I'm pretending to write while Dr. Skaya works. I'm pretending to write while she looks over her shoulder, I'm pretending to think about my thoughts I'm pretending to write I'm pretending to remember pretending pretending pretending why does she care?

Is she pretending, too?

Entry 6:

I dreamed about Dr. Skaya.

I was sitting on the edge of a bed while she sat at a small vanity, her head in her hands. She was fresh from a shower, her sallow skin washed out against the white towel she wore, her gold/silver hair curling at the ends while it dried.

"E," I said, my voice frayed and soft as I could make it, "can you name a single day in the last year that mattered to us? One good memory?"

She looked back at me, wretched.

I continued. "So what does it matter if I take a year away on a new assignment? You won't even notice I'm gone."

"Of course I'll notice, Helgen," she seethed. "How am I supposed to cope without you?"

"What about my coping?"

"Coping?" She laughed. "Cope with what, mineral substrates in space dust?"

"Coping with *you*, E." I tried not to shout. My skin is dark, like the geologist's. I'm wearing an old pair of boxer shorts, soft from too many washes. "My wife's morbid-ass job is killing her and killing our marriage. That takes a toll on me, too, and I don't get to cope."

She was trembling, her thin mouth a hard line. "Why don't you ask for a divorce already? Get it over with."

"I don't want a divorce, E. I want to study rocks and sleep in a different bed and not hear about the memories of murder victims. I want you to find a way to cope that isn't dependent on me."

"How noble. Leaving me so I can get stronger, you *martyr*."

I sighed and picked up a little white stick from its charging station on the nightstand. I put it between my lips and inhaled, forcing myself to steady my breathing as my heart rate automatically slowed.

A burn mark flickered in the top right corner of my vision.

Dr. Skaya shrieked. "How dare you!" She picked up a perfume bottle and hurled it against the wall. The crystal flower exploded and the heady chemical mess went everywhere.

"Christ, E!"

"Are you marking this memory for me to find later, so I can relive the moment you left me? How heartless are you?"

"I use this because I'm *stressed,* can you imagine why I might be stressed?"

She slumped, trying to hold the towel over her breasts, and cried.

I took a pillow off the bed and left to sleep on the couch.

. . .

When I woke up in Vess's bunk in Vess's body, I yanked off the wiry cranial apparatus so hard it scraped my scalp.

Dr. Skaya—Elisavet, E—asked how I slept and I said, "Fine." I told her the apparatus gives me a headache and she said it's important to record my neural activity while I sleep and I'll have to deal with it. She looks at me with a murky expression somewhere between exhaustion and disdain, and I try not to think about her crying, naked but for a sagging towel.

These dreams are memories. But they're not mine.

Entry 7:

Today I checked all of the bodies in E's morgue. The room used to be full of mineral samples, and now it's stuffed full of portable, inflatable sarcophagi. Dozens of bright blue inflated tarpaulin body bags filled with a cocktail of corpse-saver. Little bubbles of the underworld. Spider eggs. Each one has a window so you can look at the face. Some of the windows are covered with tape and a label, masking the bodies that are too mangled to have recognizable features.

Found a few bodies I recognized from dreams. Couldn't identify a single sign of Helgen, the geologist, even in the most tattered remains.

E found me shining a torch into one of the windowed sacs. I thought she'd be mad.

"It's refreshing to see you taking an interest, Vessouschka," she said. "You used to be a research assistant, you know. Maybe you could be *my* research assistant? Learn some code, load brains into the–oh, don't make that face, Vess."

I pursed my lips and shrugged.

"Whatever. How about you join me on my trips out into the station? I'll look for bodies, and you can do your driftwood impersonation where I can keep an eye on you." E tried on a gentle smile to convince me it was an earnest offer.

I accepted anyway. Maybe I can find Helgen.

Entry 8:

Went out with E today to help her look for "evidence." Slipped away to look through crew cabins, but that sector housed maintenance staff, not researchers. No sign of him, and E won't let me get far.

Spent the rest of the day drawing a map in my notebook so I could cross off rooms.

he's real he's real he's real

Entry 9:

Went through the shuttle pilots' section of the station today, where the damage is especially bad. E clipped our suits together, then periodically clipped herself to handholds along the walls. I bobbed along next to her like a sullen balloon. I could see our section of the station through the gashes in the walls, across the puddle of space.

What if E put his body through the airlock?

What if one day I look out and see Helgen sitting at one of the spaced tables, eating dinner alone?

Entry 10:

I didn't put on the apparatus last night when I went to sleep. I dreamt of him anyway, hitting the stresstick hard before E came to bed on her birthday. I woke up wearing the device.

I tried to figure out how to reset the keycode on my cabin's door, but I can't customize it. All the furniture is built into the walls or bolted down, and I don't own anything to make a barricade.

I can't keep her out of my room. I can't keep her out of my head. ~~don't read this~~

Entry 11:

I wish you would tell me the truth. I can't hide anything from you, but you get to keep everything to yourself. Trying to keep me, too, locked up in my cabin. Wait until I fall asleep and then rummage around in my head. All you are is locks and walls and a little bubble of hateful air that I could pop with this stylus.

Maybe it could pop a habsuit. Or skin.

scribble scribble scribble scribble

God, people say in distress, *God.* I wish I knew how to swear, or what to swear by. Something to call out to that's bigger than Doctor Elisavet Skaya.

I'd swear by the Station. A body filled with bodies and infinity.

I don't want to talk to you anymore, E, I won't write for you to read and smile to yourself and pretend that you don't know the things I wrote down and the things I dreamed.

I write to the Station.

· · ·

I confronted E about sneaking into my room while I slept, and she said it was her duty to look after my recovery. I asked why I was with her, a scalper, instead of a real doctor, and she only laughed.

"Why isn't the research company trying to reunite Vess with her family?" I pressed, "Or pay reparations?"

E didn't even look up. "No one is coming for us until my investigation time allowance is up, my naive Vessouschka."

"Do they know I'm alive?"

"It doesn't matter." The stool squealed as she leaned away the viewfinder. "The station is too remote, no one's making a special trip for you." She looked at me carefully then, squinting her washed-out eyes. "You should be grateful that I care for you so well. Sharing my rations, my expertise. I don't have to be so selfless."

"You want *something* from me," I whispered, clutching at my courage, trying to raise my voice. "I used to think I was another piece of evidence, a clue to the mystery of the station, but are you even trying to find out what happened?"

"What happened?" E blinked at me with a desiccated, long-suffering look. "There isn't a grand mystery here, Vess," she hissed, "there never is. The answer is always the same: someone was stupid, careless, or petty, and then awful things happened."

She stood up and crossed the room, then grabbed my jaw with one hand like I was a bad dog.

"You want to know what killed everyone?" She asked, voice rising. "A shuttle pilot came in too hot, tried to stop, and all the unsecured gravel in his open cargo hold came loose and shredded through the station. Like buckshot ripping through aluminum foil." She shook me by the jaw. "So I need you to stop pretending like any of this matters and *wear the apparatus like I told you to.*"

And then E locked me in here. Told me that the only freedom I have is the freedom she gives me.

I can't fall asleep or she'll come in and put the apparatus on my head and give me dreams of him.

Help me, Station.

You must have had a way to call settled space when you were whole. There must be a way for Skaya to communicate to her employers.

What if she's not actually talking to herself at night? What if she has a hidden comms device?

Entry 12:

I got out.

I chewed up a few pieces of notebook paper to make a paste, and when E came to give me dinner (trying to make me apologize in exchange for food), I managed to put the wad of pulp into the door's lock, which kept it from sealing properly. When she settled into her own cabin and I heard the muffled sound of her rambling, I pulled on my habsuit and left.

I found a storage closet in the wrecked pilot's sector with only a few pinprick holes in the walls. There are even some old habsuit support tanks in here to resupply. I've tethered myself to one of the bolted-down supply racks so I can sleep out of sight of the door. I've figured out how to hide the notebook between my suit and the life support system on my back. She won't get it, even if she finds me.

I imagine her calling for me in the research sector while I'm far away, safely insulated by the soundless vacuum of space.

When she leaves her nest to look for me, I'll sneak back into her cabin. Call for help, maybe, or take rations and find a way to hold out until her pickup arrives. Or I die in this closet. It doesn't seem so bad.

Entry 13:

I can't trust that anyone will be able to look through my memories and understand what happened. I have to write it down, I have to know that the words and events will stay still, stay clear, no matter how long it takes someone to find us.

I was sleeping in the closet when E came looking for me. I felt the subtle scrape of her carabiner clip pulling along the railing of the wall outside, and the plodding rhythm of her bracing her hands. The vibrations woke me up, as if the station itself warned me. She opened the door and shone a torch inside, then moved on.

Once she was far enough away, I snuck to one of the blown-out hallways. I could see the research sector across the reach of empty space, and knew it was my best shot at getting back before she did. Checked that everything was secure. Wondered if I'd be able to figure out the propulsors on the suit. Lined up my trajectory. Made the leap.

I thought it would feel like falling. But instead everything *else* fell. The detritus outside the station fell around me like gentle rain as I hung suspended, and the station rushed forward to catch me. I hung on the hull by the magnets in my gloves and boots, relishing the thrill of those few seconds. It had been a gamble, a *choice* to touch the void. I felt at home that close to death. I thought I had courage enough for anything.

There was another breach in the hull close by, and I was careful to choose an entrance that wasn't too narrow for my suit. Being careful takes so much time, and I kept thinking of Dr. Skaya catching me. Dragging me back inside and prying me out of my habsuit. Even once I was back in the safe bubble of oxygen and grav field, I kept the suit on, visor open.

Her cabin was locked, so I found the heaviest thing I could lift (her creaky metal stool) and bashed at the mechanisms until the door gave way.

It was embarrassing how obvious it all became.

I knew E had repurposed one of the researcher's cabins for her own use, but I thought it was a choice of convenience. No one should have set foot in this place, let alone stayed here for months.

The hull of the far wall had been compromised in the accident. She'd patched the largest gash with tarpaulin and rolls' worth of repair tape, then made dozens of other improvised plugs. Part of a plastic folder, ration wrappers, random scraps pasted to the walls to create a kaleidoscopic cocoon. She was holding back death with nothing but refuse and obsession, because she had to stay in *this* cabin. Helgen's cabin.

His inflated coffin pod stood up against the wall, labeled clearly: *H Skaya*. I could see him through the pod's window suspended in corpse-saver, dark hair drifting over a half-pained, slack expression. The top of his empty skull peeled back like flower petals.

I looked for any sort of communication device in her things, upending bags and digging through footlockers. Some of it was hers, but much of what I went through had been his. I recognized clothing from his memories, found a used up stick of familiar-smelling deodorant that had rolled to the back of a drawer. I knew even as I searched that E had never been talking on any device when she rambled away every night. She'd been talking to her husband's body.

Then I found her journal. A notebook, twin to this one. It might be kindest to let Elisavet Skaya speak for herself:

Found H's body in his cabin. Cranial cavity undamaged.

I shouldn't have taken this job. I can't bear to write down "Cranial cavity undamaged" as if he was just another piece of evidence.

I'm above this. Death is an old, bitter adversary I haven't feared in many years. If memories can be reclaimed from the dead, then why not a mind, or a soul?

———————

H's body is too damaged to reclaim.
I won't mourn, I won't accept this.

———————

Found a suitable vessel. The body is alive enough, a vegetable, salvageable. I was hoping for a male body -- is it a genuine preference, or just what I was used to? If something goes wrong, I could probably overpower this smaller body anyway.

My report currently states that there were no survivors. I don't know how I'll explain things if the initiative succeeds and I have a living, breathing crew member I want to take home. I'll cross that bridge when we come to it. I won't talk myself out of this before I've begun.

~~Perhaps I can smuggle the vessel out in one of the morgue pods?~~

———————

Transplant successful, vessel's body is recovering. God, I'm so tired.

Oh death, where is thy sting?

———————

Most of my energy goes to babying this vessel, feeding, hydrating, moving it, yet I forgot to eat again. I sit up at night listening to its heartbeats, wondering when it'll wake up and say something I'll recognize as his words. I think about that moment when I want to give up.

I practice by talking to H's empty body, and I can almost hear him saying "I forgive you, E."

The vessel woke up today, but has yet to manifest proper consciousness. It sleeps mostly, and rarely reacts to stimuli. His brain must've been more damaged than I'd surmised.

The vessel is doing its best to perceive itself and its surroundings, everything is wonderland—mad and unrecognizable. At least it can walk and use the lav on its own. It retains a base foundation of memory and understanding, pulling from references of a planet and childhood it has not experienced itself. He's in there. I can coax him out.

Vessel has no discernible interests or attachments. It keeps trying to kill itself in the blasted out parts of the station, floating like a goldfish at the top of the bowl. The hell of an egoless mind at play.

I wonder if I can remind the brain where it came from—feed it enough images of him to make the vessel curious, prime the earth for an identity to root. If I can fabricate a reason for the vessel to be interested in Helgen, maybe his mind will manifest, blossom like a sneeze in a petri dish.

I have enough data from the dead who worked with him. It might whet the subconscious appetite.

Vess is sometimes flustered in my presence or caught off-guard by my actions, but I don't think its reactions denote attraction. I'd hoped that being more overt and making physical advances would reignite something in Helgen's mind, but it only pulls away from me.

I worry that I muddied the waters by introducing other minds' memories to the brain, even if they were all memories of him. It was reckless of me. I know now that I can only use memories that I pulled from his brain before inserting it in the vessel.

I wish I'd dug more before crossing that particular point of no return. I thought those memories would repopulate, reemerge on their own.

I wish I had better memories to feed it.

An epiphany: If I want him to exist in the way that I remember him, then shouldn't I use my own memories as its blueprint? My perceptions of him, my desires? Do I want the real Helgen back, or do I want *my* Helgen back?

Of course, pulling memories from living minds and uploading them into other living minds is technology that doesn't exist yet. I should have anticipated from the beginning that this would be a project of years, not weeks. Perhaps if I can teach Vess enough about scalping, it could help me with the procedure.

I need it to be willing to stay with me, to submit, until I can complete the project.

This fucking marionette of a body is trying to keep him from me. Continual, exhausting resistance. She stopped using the apparatus.

I wonder if I should scrap the entire resurrection project and discard the vessel. Take parts of him home and try again. The body was already reported dead, no one would care.

I'd try it if I was sure that his brain would survive.

———

Vess ran away, taking his brain with her. Helgen, are you leaving me again?

E returned while I was distracted by her journal.

The broken door stuttered open and she stood in the doorway holding her habsuit like a discarded skin. Surprise looked ugly on her, but it didn't last long.

"Easy now," she said, raising her free hand and stepping into the room. "You're probably in shock. You don't need to react right away."

She was afraid I'd hurt her, lash out, rage. I felt an unexpected sensation: a crushing feeling, deep in my chest. The pressure of benthic depths. All of it—the journal, Helgen's body, E's expectations of violence—it all just ... *crushed*.

Meanwhile, E came closer, one hand out like the journal was a loaded gun she needed to get away from a maniac. I handed it over. My lip quivered, my eyes hurt.

She held the journal behind her back, where I couldn't reach it, where it couldn't hurt us. "That's right, it's alright," she cooed. "You must have so many questions, but I'm with you now."

"I don't have any more questions, E."

"Oh, Helgen—" she rushed forward, dropping the journal and the habsuit so she could wrap her arms around me. "Helgen!" The joints and nodes of my suit dug into me under her death-grip embrace. Helgen's pod looked over us.

"I'm not your husband," I said, trying to back away. There wasn't anywhere to go, not with three of us crowded into the cabin.

"You are in the ways that matter," E insisted. "Don't be afraid my dear, I know you're in there."

"Helgen is dead," I pushed her off of me. "You can't fill me with memories like you're stuffing a scarecrow and expect to remake a person. There's no one here." I tapped the side of my habsuit helmet.

"I don't believe that," she said, regaining her balance. "You have unique desires, aspirations, enough of a sense of self to reject being Helgen. I may fail at the resurrection, but I'll succeed at something else. I've created a new individual, a new human consciousness."

"I'm not—"

"You don't have to be Helgen, you could be our *daughter*, born of both of us—"

"I'm not—"

She reached through my open visor to hold my face in her hands. "I shouldn't have been so narrow-minded, I'm sorry, you can be this new person. Together we'll rewrite everything science thought it knew about the mind, about death—"

I was pinned between her and the hull. "I'm not going with you."

"But you *are*, Vessouschka." Her features hardened into a proud smile. "How else are you going to get off this station? I am your only choice. I *made* you, you belong to me, who could you be except the identities I feed you?"

"I am not ... I am—" I tried to finish the sentence, gulping, as her nails dug into my cheeks. I always knew what I wasn't, but I couldn't find what I *was*. There was no Self that I could hold up like a shield between us, no way to make her see me. Unless I didn't have to be anyone, or anything.

I pulled the writing stylus from my pocket.

I am not. I am not. "I am Nothing."

Holding the stylus in my fist, I popped the membrane of the tape and tarpaulin behind me, letting the Nothing in through the patched hull.

The atmosphere vented, shrieking as it flew through the tiny hole. I stabbed it again, again, making a constellation of holes for the Nothing to come through.

Elisavet clung to me and I triggered my helmet visor shut. It snapped down on her hands and she pulled away, stumbling, as the escaping air pulled and pulled, like everything was trying to get away from her. Objects tore through the damaged membrane on their way out to space. We all slid towards the tear in the wall as it became a bigger and bigger door.

She was screaming something at me, at Helgen, but we couldn't hear her. The Nothing reached in and took E, dragging her out into the void. She fought the whole way.

I was ready for my turn when Helgen's pod slid along the wall, heading for the tear. The pod plugged the gap like a balloon in a windpipe. I waited for the seal to fail, for something else to break, but Helgen held the door closed against her.

· · ·

That's it. I don't know how long he'll hold the gap. I broke the hatch to the cabin, so I can't quarantine the breach. I know I won't be able to wait for the company to come to pick up Skaya and her data. The grav field is alright, but there's no more atmosphere, and I ... I don't have enough claim to life to plan a daring survival. I want The Body's family to have their daughter back. I want them to mourn for her properly. I don't want to be in the way.

I think that the morgues—the physical and the digital ones—will be alright until help comes. There's enough power to keep Skaya's lab running for a long while.

I've written everything I can think of, and I have E's journal, too. I'll keep the journals in the space between my support pack and the suit, so they'll be found with The Body. I doubt scalpers would be able to sift through all the minds and memories I'm carrying.

If they look in my mind for the truth, they'll find everyone else who died here. But if they read the journals, they'll find me: the empty space between them.

A body full of bodies and infinity.

BRIANA BEDORE is an American mutt who has been sighted skulking about the Wasatch Mountains. She writes science-fantasy and fantastical sci-fi—whatever the lovely middle of that Venn diagram likes to be called—and has stories published with Lower Decks Press. When coaxed into polite society, she also works as a costume designer and artist's model, but is happiest pointing at pretty things in nature going "Ah!".

Twitter: @bri_bedore

* 9 7 8 1 9 6 7 0 0 1 0 1 9 *